SHADOW OF DEATH

SHADOW OF DEATH

HEATHER GRAHAM

mira

mira™

ISBN-13: 978-0-7783-3349-4

Shadow of Death

Mira
22 Adelaide St. West, 41st Floor
Toronto, Ontario M5H 4E3, Canada
BookClubbish.com

Printed in U.S.A.

For Daniel Palmer, Lisa Gardner, Kathy Antrim, Gregg Hurwitz, Kathleen Miller and Karen McManus, and the wonderful little family we formed during our days in Sharjah. For Kim Howe and all that she does for so many. And very especially for the Sharjah International Book Fair team, Qurratulain Yahya, Abdul, Mohammed and all their wonderful people. Their graciousness created one of the most amazing experiences for us all. And to the UAE, an incredible country where diversity and kindness can be found throughout.

SHADOW

OF

DEATH

A Stygian Darkness

And when he had opened the third seal,
I heard the third beast say,
Come and see.
And I beheld
And lo, a black horse,
And he that sat on him had a pair
Of balances in his hand.
And I heard a voice in the midst of the four beasts say,
A measure of wheat for a penny,
And three measures of barley for a penny;
And see thou hurt not the oil and the wine.

PROLOGUE

Caves

Carey Allen paused, looked around, and breathed in deeply. She loved this area of Colorado just outside of the bustling city of Denver. The sky on a day like today was amazing. Blue just touched with delicate white puffs of clouds here and there. And the air! It was fresh, clean, delicious, and the scent of nature was wonderful.

Of course, she shouldn't have been where she was without permission and a guide, but she was an experienced hiker. She had climbed all manner of mountains, and she had received her diver's certificate at Lake Mead and gone on to cave dive! Hey, it was America. She was an adult, she knew what she was doing, and she had every right to be here.

She closed her eyes for a minute, listening to the sound of the nearby waterfall. Then she dove into the freshwater lake, shuddered slightly at the chill that seized her, then let it fall off. Surfacing, she looked back to the shore.

Don Blake was watching her with admiration, she hoped. She'd had a crush on the man for the longest time, and she'd enticed him out by telling him she knew the caves here and had explored them on her own before. He waved to her.

"Come on in! The water is great!" she told him.

"Freezing!" he countered.

"Wimp!"

He laughed. Don was anything but a wimp. He'd served two tours in the Middle East and was still in the reserve. Tall, not dark but red-headed, and very handsome. Working with him at Barrington Advertising, she'd fallen a bit in love the minute they had met—something, she hoped, she'd kept to herself. She had tried very hard to always be casual, fun, and flirty, not like a puppy with a wildly wagging tail.

But when they had talked about the caves, he'd shown a real interest in her.

"Wimp?" he returned and, as she knew he would, shed his hiking boots and socks, dropped his backpack and dove into the water.

Carey swam toward the waterfalls and the entry to the caves she knew she would find behind them. She hadn't slipped in here in months, but nature had created the phenomena of the falls and the caves over hundreds of thousands of years. They couldn't have changed much in a few months.

She crawled up the rocks that rose behind the falls and waited for Don. He arrived shortly, dripping as he joined her on the rocks. They'd both worn tank tops that would dry quickly, but the hiking pants would take longer. In the crisp air Carey had loved so much, it was cold.

"Follow me!" she said.

There was a winding path that led into a slew of caves,

some deeper than others. And, of course, as they progressed, it grew darker within.

She stopped, turning to Don and smiling. "Well, I guess this is as far as we go—"

He was frowning. "What's that light?" he asked.

She turned. He was right. There was a strange glow coming from deeper within the earth.

"I don't know," she said.

"Shall we?"

"Well, of course!"

They headed in the direction of the light. Nearing it, Carey suddenly felt the earth slipping beneath her feet. She'd hit an odd angle in the earth and it...

Led to nothing.

She fell and fell, landed hard, hurt everywhere, and wondered if she had broken bones.

She tried to move and cried out to Don.

"Careful! There's a slope and...nothing."

He didn't answer her. The dim light they had seen was pale here, barely alleviating the darkness. She turned, trying to see if her limbs would work and to assess her position.

That's when she saw him.

The dead man.

His face was skeletal. His eyes were open. No. He didn't have eyes. He just had eye sockets. But they seemed to be...

Staring. Staring into her eyes.

She screamed. She forgot her pain as she tried to inch away. And as she did, she saw the dead man wasn't alone. There were other bodies there and all of them...

Down to bone. Not all were completely decomposed, just...

Down to nothing but *mostly* bone. Flesh remained on some limbs. Decaying fabric clung to other forms. Some of them had eyes that were still partially there and remained open, just catching the glint of pale light that seeped into the deep hole.

The scent of death rose around her, so she used her hands to push back. As she did so, she touched something small and hard, dark and plastic. She barely registered she had touched something as she started to scream and scream as she cried out for Don.

There was no answer. Her cries grew hoarse. She managed to drag herself to her feet to seek a way out...

There was nothing but dirt; no holds, nothing. No way out of the deep hole in the earth into which she had fallen.

She looked at the thing in her hand and then she looked around at the starved and rotting corpses around her. There were no children, she thought thankfully, not that she could see. She was losing her mind; she could die here, too. She didn't know what had happened to Don. He wasn't answering her, so he must have also fallen...

Into a pile of dead.

No, no, no, no, he had to be okay. He had to be out there... going for help, she thought. And then she looked at the thing in her hand at last.

She held...

A horse. A tiny little black plastic horse.

Confused, breathing in death, she felt terror sweeping into her like something liquid and icy cold.

And she started to scream again.

1

The sun was just rising. Amy Larson emerged from the water, dripping, feeling the rays of brilliant heat fall on her. The day was beautiful, perfect and warm. It was wonderful. There were few places on earth she loved as much as she loved the Florida Keys and Key West. In all honesty, the best beaches could be found on the state's west coast but to her, the Keys were a little bit of heaven. Key Largo was an escape from the massive metropolises of Miami-Dade and Broward Counties. And moving southward, the smaller islands were a taste of a purer time. Marathon offered the incredible Dolphin Research Center, and on down to Key West one could look out for the tiny Key deer. Then at the tail end, Key West itself is the island of rich history, bizarre stories, music, and water sports.

It had been good to come here. Hunter had needed to be here after taking a bullet; even with a vest on, he'd needed a bit of convalescence. Yet, while trying to shake off the last two cases they'd worked along with the salt water, memories still plagued them of the murders in the Everglades that had begun the bizarre Four Horsemen case and those that had followed when she'd received the little red plastic horse in the mail.

Because it wasn't over. Someone wanted to play God, and they were using the Four Horsemen of the Apocalypse and Revelations to do it.

She smiled and slid down on a towel next to Hunter Forrest. He turned to her and ran a finger along her cheek. "This is the life," he said softly. "I almost feel guilty. Days in the sun, diving this afternoon, nights with the sunset and the music. I could do this forever."

"No, you couldn't," she said, amused. "You became an FBI agent because you were a child stuck in a horrible cult, and an FBI agent saved you and your parents. You need to be out there. You saw how your mom and dad got suckered into it. They saw people needed help, and those with a lot of money liked to keep it and weren't always generous. Some people—some rich people—are great. But what your mom saw made her want a better way, and she thought she had found it. You saw evil could masquerade in many forms." Her smile faded slightly. "You grew up and became an FBI agent because you're determined to slay the evil that man does to his fellow man."

"Sure. Right. Well, you know, second choice. Wrong era to be a knight in shining armor. And you've met my folks. They just wanted the best, and they were young and naive and looking for a better way. Anyway, we are what we are. But Clint Bullard is playing tonight. We'll have some dinner, listen to him sing and play…maybe one of us will join him on a country music hit. We won't stay too late, because we have a great room with those windows that open to the sunrise."

"Sounds good, especially since we only have a few days left before vacation and leave time are up," Amy said. She sat up pensively. It had been weeks since the showdown that had left Hunter injured, and his bones had healed. And while they worked for two separate agencies—he was FBI and she was Florida Department of Law Enforcement—she was now on loan to the FBI because of the Four Horsemen case. And although they'd taken down some of the players in the deadly enterprise afoot, they knew another shoe would drop.

Someone out there wanted the Apocalypse. Or they were in it for power or money or both and made use of the easily beguiled they could use in their quest. People who believed they would be the chosen when the world came to an end. And if murder was asked of someone, it was simply a means to an end.

"What are you thinking?" Hunter asked, studying her face.

She loved Hunter. Everything about him. Tall, dark, blue-eyed and fit not just because of his chosen vocation, but because he loved doing things. He loved the water, boats, and watching college and pro football games, along with basketball, baseball, and hockey. If he didn't know about something, that was okay, he was eager to find out.

And he cared about people.

"I can't help it. I mean, I have relaxed, I swear. But I was thinking of my old partner John Schultz and the first cases. I will miss him, but he will enjoy his retirement. I think back to the first case with the white horse, and finding the woman crucified in the Everglades. I think about putting away a bad guy, and then receiving the little red horse when we were vacationing before. And I think about the crazy lady we put away after that, and how she's still convinced she's a warrior and the lives she took don't matter because she'll be lifted up at the end. And I think—"

"Hold on," Hunter said quietly. He had reached for his phone; she hadn't heard it ring. He'd kept it on vibrate.

She watched his expression change as he listened. "All right. What time did you say? Thanks. Yep, we can do it."

When he hung up, she knew.

"The black horse?" she asked.

He nodded, still studying her face.

"We have a plane to catch," he said.

"Okay," she said slowly. "First out of Key West. And then where?"

"Denver. Via Miami. There has been a rash of disappearances, apparently."

"But why would that indicate anything to do with the Horsemen cases?"

"A little black plastic horse. This time, it was received by a colleague of mine, a guy I worked with years ago. Andy Mason, Assistant Field Director out there. He has no idea where it came from. It wasn't mailed to him—it was on his doorstep when he went home last night. The entire agency has been briefed on what did happen with the previous Horsemen cases and to be aware we've been warned it isn't over. Andy talked to the brass, and we're to join him and see if the horse and the missing people do align. Andy is a good guy and a good agent. He didn't miss the little horse, and he's the one with the theory the missing people may have something to do with the horse."

"No luck on getting our crazy incarcerated 'red horse' to talk, right?" Amy asked.

"She has an attorney who has advised her to keep her mouth shut. Poor attorney. Our 'red horse' is so proud of herself for being in her position, she doesn't seem to appreciate the fact she shouldn't be saying she orchestrated life and death. I think she really is a true believer."

"She wanted to go into politics. That's what I can't wrap my head around," Amy said lightly.

"And God help us all. She had it together until the end. Imagine if she had started in office in state government and moved on to *national* prominence."

"Terrifying. Anyway—"

"Hey, vacation was ending. And they have a nice place for us in a hotel on the outskirts of Denver. I mean, it won't be hot, and our days won't be filled with diving and our nights with music and heat—"

"Hey!" Amy teased. "Mr. G-man, it will be hot wherever you are."

"Thanks—I'll take it," Hunter said. "So, our plane out of here is in just three hours—"

He paused, stopping to look at his phone before answering it again. He sat silent for a moment before saying, "Um, sure, thanks."

He hung up, grinning.

"Never mind. Our plane is in two hours, direct to Denver."

"And we're going to get to the airport and through security and—"

"Private plane," he told her. "The brass is sending us off right. We won't even have to worry about lunch."

"Cool. Okay, so…"

They still had to hurry. They had to forego the tour of Fort Zachary Taylor they had planned for later. They had to make good time—it was a six-hour flight at best. With the time change, they'd get a few hours back, but now that they were going…

Amy wanted to move.

Within two hours, they were in the air. It was one nice

plane—Amy had to thank the powers that be who had provided for them.

Amy looked out the window. She really did love Key West.

Hunter was at her side. "I know. I'm sorry. Watching sun and sea and a bit of nirvana disappear into a tiny spec."

She turned to him. "I was thinking it was darned nice to be partnered with an FBI agent who draws this kind of attention from the bigwigs."

He smiled. "Depends on the case."

"Hunter, will this end?" she murmured. "There could be copycats out there. There were so many people involved, people who lost loved ones. This horse left on your Agent Mason's doorstep...maybe it's someone playing games. This is big and it could be endless—"

"Well, yes, I figure the Apocalypse can be big," he said, and she loved the way he spoke, half teasing, half respecting her words. "It will not be endless. And there will not be an apocalypse. Because these people aren't believers—not in any true religion."

He was right. "But what is the endgame?" she murmured.

"Now on that," he said, "as of now, well. Hmm. I don't know. But Denver is great."

"Yeah, it's a great city," she agreed.

And it was nice traveling on the private jet. But as they flew, she found herself bringing up the Book of Revelations and going through its various stanzas.

"'And he that sat on him held a pair of balances in his hand,'" she quoted aloud.

"And I heard a voice in the midst of the four beasts say, A measure of wheat for a penny, and three measures of barley for a penny; and see thee hurt not the oil and the wine,'" Hunter finished.

"And from what I'm reading, biblical scholars say it refers to hunger, to famine, and to disease," Amy said.

"Well, we didn't need a criminal mastermind for the disease part," Hunter said. "But it's also true there are many diseases that have been controlled—but can still be cast out on the public with purpose. But you'd need access to a lab and... hunger. Famine. And 'hurt not the oil and the wine'—from what I've read that refers to the wealthy. I don't know what we're dealing with here or even if the missing persons cases are part of this, but we'll land on the answers soon."

Amy nodded and looked out the window. She was taken by the scenery beneath her. They'd left behind the eternal blues and greens of the Everglades, the ocean, the flat land, and now traveled over miles of dusty colors, land that rolled and curved, and crossed hills and mountains in all kinds of colors. She smiled, loving the beauty of the country. She had always known she would be with the Florida Department of Law Enforcement, but she realized she loved the diversity of the ground itself, the expanse that was the country; she felt a passionate swell of determination.

They would find the black horse.

The captain's voice came over the speaker warning them to buckle in.

They did so. Amy watched as they came down to earth in the city of Denver.

Andy Mason was at the airport to meet them, sweeping up one of their bags, smiling and nodding as Hunter introduced Amy to him. He was a big man, maybe in his late forties, dark-haired, but with one streak of solid white heading back from his forehead as if the coloring was that of a backward skunk.

"Of course, we've all been on alert across the country. But I didn't come across a body—and God knows with some of the media that's gone out, some kid who knows what I do for a living might have thought it was funny to leave a plastic horse on my porch. But we've gotten calls lately from police stations between here and Boulder. People have been disappearing at an alarming rate. Now, those disappearing are adults, and adults are legally allowed to disappear if they choose. But from the people I have managed to get to interview, their loved ones don't sound like the kind to disappear. And just yesterday, we got a new one. So, if you're good with it, we'll leave your baggage in the trunk and I'll take you to speak with a woman who is insistent something had to have happened to her friend. I've checked you into the hotel already," he added, handing Hunter an envelope with hotel key cards.

"Thanks. And fine with us," Amy assured him.

"Amy likes to hit the ground running," Hunter told him and grinned at her as they both climbed into Andy's SUV.

She tried to smile in return. But while she'd honestly relaxed and enjoyed the time they'd had together just playing in Key West, the knowledge that nothing had really ended kept haunting her.

"The woman I interviewed about her report is Hayden Harper. She's midforties, and an advertising exec at the Barrington Agency," Andy Mason told them as he drove. "She reported her friend Carey Allen missing when she didn't show up for a lunch they had planned. She was told, of course, that someone wasn't considered missing just because they didn't show up for lunch. Hayden was persistent. When Carey didn't show up for work the next day, she hounded the police again. And with all that has gone on, the police informed us. I came out to see her, and she sounds legit and may give us real help. She doesn't live far from Red Rocks. Amy, have you ever been to a performance of any kind at Red Rocks?"

"I have not," Amy told him.

"An incredible place. A natural amphitheater. But there is so much incredible here. We're going to have to show her around the place, huh, Hunter?"

"I spent some time here four years ago, I think," Hunter said. "Yes, Andy, Colorado is amazing. The natural wonders are phenomenal."

"I mean, you're from Florida," Andy said.

"Hey!" Amy protested.

"I mean, it's just flat, right?" Andy said.

She laughed. "We have a few hills in the Ocala region. We also have the only continental reef in the country, alligators *and* crocodiles—"

"I'd head straight down for that," Andy teased.

"Freshwater springs, diving in sea and in freshwater, the Everglades—"

"Great place to hide bodies, I understand," Andy said.

"Where there's a will, there's way," Hunter said. "I've seen bodies hidden in just about every possible geographical location. Yes, Florida is a great state. Colorado is a great state—"

"She just has to see some of our beauty," Andy insisted.

"I'm sure I will," Amy said.

Andy was pulling into a driveway. The house they were visiting was two-story, built to resemble an old colonial. The yard was well maintained; and she knew it didn't matter what state they were in, the owner was making an upper-middle-class income.

"She's nice; you're going to like her," Andy said.

"Great," Amy murmured.

Hayden Harper *was* nice—and anxious. She opened her front door before they reached it and quickly asked them in. They had barely stepped across the threshold and already she was eagerly asking if they'd be more comfortable in the dining room or the parlor. Andy told her they were happy wherever.

She wanted to get them coffee, tea, or—though she wasn't sure if it was allowed—something stronger.

"Ms. Harper, we're fine, thank you so much," Amy told her. She wished she could alleviate some of the woman's anxiety, but she knew it could be terrifying to wonder what had happened to friends or loved ones. She thought the woman was usually composed and at ease. She was closer to fifty than forty, an attractive woman some might call "completely together" with her casual but perfect linen pantsuit, impeccable makeup, and beautifully coifed silver hair. "Please," Amy added, "if you'd like something, feel free. We're here to listen to you."

The woman nodded, then led them into her dining room and indicated the chairs. "I'm fine. Maybe I'll get coffee. Maybe I've had too much coffee."

Maybe she had, but Amy said gently, "You need to do what works for you right now."

The woman smiled. Maybe she had grasped for some of her executive training because she managed to calm down.

"I'm fine. Too much coffee. So. I'll tell you about Carey. She's one of the finest little artists I've ever met. She can do sketches at a meeting with a client that blow your mind. We became friends soon after she joined the agency. She's a health nut. A vegan. And she runs and hikes and you name it. The kid is in perfect shape. And that's what I've been trying to tell the cops. She was going hiking. She told me she was super excited. She had enticed a boy she'd had her eye on to come with her on an adventure. Here's the thing. We have caves and waterfalls you're only supposed to visit with licensed guides. And I'm pretty sure Carey intended to go *adventuring* where she shouldn't go," Hayden said. "I talked to her on Saturday just before she started out. She was supposed to meet me for lunch on Sunday. She didn't show, and I couldn't make the cops understand Carey didn't do things like that. If she couldn't make something, she'd call you. She's that kind of courteous. Then her phone started going straight to voice mail. It's Tuesday now, and I know something has happened, and something worse could happen if she isn't found soon!"

Hayden was passionate.

"Do you know who she was meeting? Or taking on her adventure?" Hunter asked.

Hayden shook her head. "She wouldn't tell me because she didn't want to jinx it."

"Is anyone else from your office missing?" Amy asked.

Hayden frowned. "Um, I don't think so. But that's hard to say because our account execs have to travel out of town to see their clients, so… I don't think so. But I don't know who is supposed to be here now and who isn't. Of course, I can do a roundup of our secretaries and get some schedules, if you think that will help." She frowned. "What makes you think the man she's interested in works at the agency, too?"

"We meet people at work," Andy said, glancing dryly at Amy and Hunter. "Sometimes, especially at the executive level, we spend all our time at work and, well, there you go."

Hayden nodded. "I will find out. But time is—"

"Where do you think she went?" Amy asked. "And we will start looking while you start trying to get us more information."

"You got a map?" Hayden asked.

"We all have phones with great GPS," Amy assured her.

"Of course." She looked at Amy skeptically for a minute. "Special Agent Mason said you were in from Florida."

"That's right. I'm the one from Florida, though," Amy said. "Hunter has worked all over," she added, hoping to assure the woman.

"And I'm here," Andy said. "Colorado born and bred."

"Of course. Okay, here," Hayden said. "This area has the most gorgeous caves and waterfalls, not far from the Arkansas River. Worst comes to worst, you'll see some spectacular scenery. But the area can be dangerous, too. There are areas people see with a guide from one of the companies, and areas the ranger service controls. But Carey has done just about every hike and walk—and swim—possible in the state. And if she were going to impress someone, I think she mentioned this little bit of land right here. The rangers' office police part of it, and part of it is policed by the county."

"We'll get hiking," Amy said, rising.

"You'll have a couple of hours of daylight left at best!" Hayden whined.

"We'll use those hours," Hunter said. "Andy, can you get us a ranger?"

"Of course," Andy said. He looked as if he were about to grin at Amy and realized Hayden Harper was far too anxious for any kind of levity. "This isn't flat land, you know. You up to it okay, Amy?"

"I think I'll be okay," she told him. "Thankfully, our things are still in the trunk."

"And you can change here and move quickly!" Hayden said.

"We can do that," Amy said.

They did, and fast. In minutes, they were both ready in khakis and hiking boots. They headed out with Andy who was—more or less—the same size as Hunter and had borrowed clothing from him so they could all drive out. He'd also talked to the park services, and they were set to meet with Ranger Sam Harrison at the site.

"Well," Andy said as they drove out, "I did want you to get to see the scenery."

"And it's beautiful," Amy assured him.

It was.

As they left the suburbs behind, the earth became dramatic with rises and falls, colors and spectacular flowers that grew despite the crisp dry air. Then before her, Amy saw the rise of cliffs with areas where water cascaded down, catching what remained of the sunlight.

"Beautiful," Amy whispered. "Outstanding."

"I told you," Andy said.

There was a park service car before them, and a ranger leaned against the driver's seat already waiting for them.

"How do you do? Ranger Sam Harrison," he called to them. He looked to be in his midthirties, wore his hat high on his head, and sported a mustache and neatly trimmed beard.

They introduced themselves in return and listened as he told them, "We do have wildlife talks out here—and on occasion, we bring people by boat under the falls and into the caves. I was behind the falls just yesterday, though, and didn't see a thing."

"Were you in the caves?"

"No, just in the boats." He grimaced. "We use some stolen jokes. Disney's *Jungle Cruise*. We show people the backside of water."

"Okay, I'm sure people love the tours. But how do you reach the caves?" Hunter asked him.

"Oh, we use the same small boats," Harrison said. "It's just a different tour. If you want to get over there and into the caves, I'll get some boats for tomorrow. The only other way is to swim—"

Amy glanced at Hunter and he nodded, knowing she meant to get there now. She was already removing her sweatshirt, determined she'd best keep her boots, even if heavy in water, for whatever flooring they might find in the caves. Her Glock was waterproof, though she was sorry to wet the nice new belt and holster she'd just purchased. But they would dry.

"Oh, she's going to swim," Harrison said, his face twisting with surprise and confusion.

"Time may be everything. We'll get there now," Hunter told him.

Amy smiled, then turned back to see him already doffing his sweatshirt, too, and heading toward the crystal water. It really was spectacular, the falls appearing to create bursts of crystal in the air as the water poured from them.

Cold water! Very, very cold water!

Maybe that was good. Amy moved quickly. Hunter reached the rocks behind the falls as she did, hopped up and reached for her hand. She took his and murmured, "We aren't going to have much light, but I do have my little penlight."

"And I've got mine. These lights are small but powerful. We're going to be okay. And tomorrow, if we need to keep searching, we *can* take boats."

"Hah, hah," Amy laughed dryly. "Sorry. I believed that—"

"We needed to move. Me, too. That was—refreshing."

"You mean freezing."

"I do," Hunter said. "But be careful. Caves here can lead to more caves."

"Okay, so… Hunter, she had to have come here. From everything we heard and learned, she's the super sports girl who would do something like this."

They were following an opening that led to the cave on the right. Then it split. Hunter indicated he'd take the left.

Amy kept going.

Beneath her feet, she felt as if the ground changed. It had been rocky and solid. Now slippery dirt seemed to be covering it, and the ground itself seemed to be headed on a downward slope. She moved more slowly, then—only wincing slightly at the concept of the mud—she went down like a snake to slither forward.

And she was glad. The earth would have given way beneath her feet.

Amy threw the slim but powerful light she held down into the hole.

She'd seen so much.

And still...

She'd seldom seen a sight quite so horrible.

"Hunter!" she called. "Hunter, careful, it's slick, it's almost a trap—maybe it is a trap. Come, quickly, please!"

As she called him, she realized she'd inched closer to see better; the slick mud was taking her down. She didn't fall. She just slid down to lie next to a body.

Her gag reflex went into motion, and she couldn't believe she hadn't been warned earlier by the smell of death. Running her light over the muddy hole in the middle of the cave, she could see bodies were in different stages of decomposition.

Some of the dead lay with their eyes, or what remained of them, open in horror.

Some no longer had eyes. Cavernous sockets seem to stare out at her.

Hunter was there, somewhere near her. "Hey!" she called. "We need a team, Hunter. I can't even count. I don't know how many people are here."

"Lord!" he exclaimed, and she could see he remained by the ledge, looking down at her. "Calling for help. I'll be right with you," he told her.

She was trying desperately not to breathe through her nose. She almost dropped her light; when she did so, she saw there was a woman near her. She didn't appear to be decomposed. Amy reached over to touch her.

She was cold. For a moment, Amy thought there was no hope since the woman's limbs were so cold.

Still, she sought a pulse at the woman's throat.

29

And it was…there. Faint, but there.

"Hunter! We have a living person!": she shouted. "I think it's Carey Allen!"

He was back with her in seconds, sliding down the strange embankment, rolling next to her, then making it to his feet and drawing her up to hers.

"She doesn't appear to be injured, just…"

"Finding herself here, it's amazing she didn't have a heart attack," Hunter said, looking around.

"This is…really crazy. How are all these people here? They don't appear to have been shot or stabbed, though it's hard to tell," Amy murmured. "The black horse," she added thoughtfully.

"Trapped—and starved. Hunger and famine," Hunter said.

"Starved. Oh, my God, you mean they were purposely trapped here and left to starve to death?"

He nodded. "You can tell," he said quietly.

"Okay…"

"Amy, look at that man. Look at his leg."

She did. Again, she fought her gag reflexes. The man's pant leg was frayed and mostly gone. So was his flesh.

He'd been gnawed.

"Rats," she murmured hopefully, looking at Hunter. "It's a cave, and if not rats, Colorado is known for its wildlife. Creatures chewing on these poor people."

"Desperation in human beings—not creatures," Hunter said quietly. "Down here, if a park ranger wasn't right above, you could scream forever; and no one would hear you to help."

"Then, you think…"

"Yeah, cannibalism. I believe we'll discover the creatures chewing on them were human. Human beings starving to death, losing their minds, and becoming both insane and desperate."

He hunkered down by Amy where she had knelt by the living woman, the young woman she believed to be Carey Allen. He frowned and reached for her hand to uncurl her fingers. And produced a child's little toy.

"The black horse didn't just arrive—he's been here!"

2

"Your FDLE agent, she's…uh, pretty amazing," Andy Mason said quietly to Hunter. He shook his head in confusion and watched as squads from forensics worked with the medical examiner's office and a host of police and federal agents to remove the bodies they'd discovered in the pit within the cave.

Amy had traveled with the EMTs to the hospital; she wanted to be there when Carey woke up.

If she woke up, of course. But the EMTs believed she would.

Andy turned to look at Hunter. "Or you're amazing, or you're both amazing. You've found… Well, hard to tell who they are—but I think you landed and in a few hours solved more missing cases than we have in *months*." He hesitated. "And you were both right on not waiting. That girl…another twenty-four hours and she might well have been dead from exposure. Your partner, though… Man, she was just determined. And if not for the two of you…"

"Sometimes, we're lucky," Hunter said. He smiled. Amy was amazing. She was a striking young woman who might have done just about anything with her life, but she had chosen law enforcement. And while her eyes were exceptionally beautiful—an emerald color with streaks of gold near the pupils—she had a way of looking at a suspect that made the suspect believe she was seeing the truth, whether the suspect was willing to share it or not. Yep. She was "all the right stuff." And more to him. She knew and understood his past.

"This is crazy. So crazy," Andy said. "You know I read all the reports on cult killings in the Everglades, and then the gang stuff so recently… I knew that damned black horse meant something. But Hunter, for me to have gotten that horse, someone has been following you. Physically or on paper more likely. They must know your past—at least as far as being a law enforcement agent goes. Know you worked with me, and that I would call on you and Amy."

"At this point, we can't be sure of anything. The problem is we can also be looking for anyone." Hunter inhaled deeply and shrugged. "Some people are believers. You come up with the right *messiah*, and you can convince some people that just about anything is true—no matter the facts. Then again, there are people out there who are the messiahs—who know telling their lie often enough will make it truth for their *flock*. They are out for themselves and no one else. They don't care who falls by the wayside on their way up, how many broken lives and dead bodies they leave behind—because they have an agenda. I believe the person or persons behind all of this is the latter. There's something to be gained here."

"Wait," Andy said, shaking his head. "How does a cult in Florida help any with all the other crazy stuff going on?"

"Power. Someone is trying to create a grid of pure power. To bring about anarchy and then seize the moment."

"Some of these bodies...they've been here," Andy said quietly. "Whoever is behind this has been luring the unwary here for some time."

"Or kidnapping them, tossing them bound into a trunk, and then throwing them into the pit. Rather bold, too. While the rangers don't take any kind of tours that deep into the caves, they come close enough. Whoever is behind this knows schedules."

"You're not suggesting that a ranger—"

"I am not. Anything is possible, of course. But it's easy enough to observe schedules. Whoever is behind this knows when not to dump a body."

"But we know Carey came here to enjoy the swim and the hike. You believe she was an accidental victim?"

Hunter shook his head. "Andy, I wish I had answers for you. She may have been accidental—and all of the victims, no matter how they got here, might have been random. The grisly death of human beings and an assault on the abilities of law enforcement might be the point here."

"Not that I haven't seen bad," Andy muttered, "very bad. But this..." He broke off. They both watched as the forensic and medical teams worked to extract bodies and any possible clues from the tricky ground.

There were three medical examiners working the scene itself. Two appeared to be in their later thirties or early forties while one was young and probably new to the job.

He'd looked a little green entering the pit, but he also seemed to know what he was doing. And no matter how green he might be, he intended to work the scene with all professionalism.

"Kyle Ingram," Andy murmured, indicating the young

ME. "He's only been with us about two years now. That's Mike Adler leading things up, and Joe Vargas who has been with the ME's office almost as long as Mike."

"Hey, he looks miserable but determined," Hunter said.

"Right. Courage isn't a lack of fear, it's doing the right thing even when you're afraid," Andy murmured, still distracted. "She was holding a black plastic horse, and one was sent to me. It's as if they want us to...catch them?" he asked Hunter. "I mean, that's kind of crazy. Wait. The whole thing is crazy. And horrible."

"There's always an endgame," Hunter murmured. He grimaced and turned to his friend. "Hopefully, we'll discover just what that is."

It was crazy. *Why would the little horses be so visible both in the pit and sent to Andy?*

In the pit...maybe it was part of someone's idealism on what they were doing. But to have a horse sent to Andy...

Was there someone out there who did want the killers caught?

One of the older medical examiners, a man of medium height and build with thinning gray hair—the man Andy had pointed out as Mike Adler—made his way toward them, shaking his head. "This isn't just murder," he said. "It's torture."

"Were the victims dead when they were deposited here— killed by other means?" Hunter asked. "Of course, we were lucky and found the one young woman alive. But on the others—assessing what I could without possibly destroying something forensics might find—I didn't see any gunshot wounds or anything that indicated the use of a knife or other weapon."

"No. No. No bullets, no knives—nothing that would have been quick and merciful. And that's what I mean—being left to starve in muck and darkness, knowing help will never come?" he said. "They died slowly. Some faster than others. We need to do autopsies on all the victims, but they've died from the elements—or because their hearts or lungs gave out—or they starved. Oh. I'm sorry," he said, looking at Hunter. "I'm Dr. Mike Adler, lead ME."

"Special Agent Hunter Forrest," Hunter told him.

"Main FBI," Adler acknowledged knowingly. "Well, let's hope you can help. Sorry, Andy! No offense, I just... Well, hell. This is bad."

"I am not offended. I want all-hands-on-deck," Andy assured him.

"Right," Adler said. "And we're going to take any help we can get, too. Anyway, we'll start with the autopsies in the morning. These bodies..." He paused, grimacing. "In time, we see almost everything, but this...so many. They are going to need a lot of work. Anyway... Special Agent Forrest, welcome and thank you for being here."

"Thank *you* for your work," Hunter returned, lifting a hand as Adler headed off to one of the boats that would bring him across to the morgue vehicles.

"We need to get identifications," Andy murmured. "I don't think we'll have much until tomorrow, if then. I'm going to head into the office and get started on going through our missing persons reports. Oh, I'll drop your suitcases at the hotel—and one of the police officers will get you to the hotel. I'll have your bags taken straight to the room; and in the morning, you can ask at the counter for the keys to your vehicle. Um, Amy will tell us immediately if she gets anything from Carey Allen?"

"Of course, she will," Hunter assured him.

"And you—"

"I want to go back through the caves."

"The forensic teams here are good," Andy assured him.

"I know that. I just need to look around a little more for myself."

"All right. Go for it," Andy told him.

Hunter lifted a hand again as Andy walked to the edge of the rocks and hopped into one of the little tour boats run by the rangers.

Hunter turned and headed back into the caves. One thing was bothering him. To reach the pit, they'd all used the boats or hopped in the water as he and Amy had done.

Of course, it was possible the victims had been rendered unconscious or unable to resist, but dragging them through the water and over the rocks wouldn't be an easy task.

Hunter believed there were more ways to the pit—ways that might lead out to a far easier access.

He meant to find it.

It was beyond gratifying to know the fact she and Hunter had moved so quickly had apparently saved a life. Carey Allen had been lucky. She had no broken bones; and other than dehydration and exposure, she had suffered no other ill effects.

Dr. Emil Firestone, in charge of Carey's case at the hospital, told Amy that Carey had two main factors which had worked in her favor—she was young and she was in excellent health.

"You take someone with pulmonary or cardiac issues and put them in a position like that, and well, I don't think that person would be so lucky. But we'll have to wait for ME reports to find out what happened to the others."

Amy winced. "Do you believe...some resorted to cannibalism?"

"I'm not a neurologist or psychiatrist but I believe in a pitch dark hole in a sea of mud for days on end, and if physical deprivations didn't kill first, a person's mind might well unhinge. I talked to Mike—sorry, Mike Adler, one of our medical examiners on the case—and his preliminary report suggests no one was attacked by another in the cave. There were eighteen people down there besides Miss Carey Allen. He believes several deaths were the result of heart attacks. Others were dehydration and starvation. The victims must be identified, of course. The caves themselves helped with strange levels of decomposition. However, it appears whatever small blessing it might be, there were no children brought there to die."

"Small blessing," Amy agreed. "May I speak with Carey? I promise, I'll keep it brief."

"Give it another fifteen minutes. I'd like her oxygen saturation to be a bit better. Are you all right with that?"

"I'm fine, of course—" Amy began.

But even as she spoke, a nurse in Amy's room came out to the hallway, shaking her head and looking a bit frantic.

"She's trying to get up! She keeps saying no one is looking for Don! I can't get her to calm down, she's insisting she needs to speak with the police," she said.

The doctor stared at Amy.

"May I? Perhaps I can calm her," Amy said.

Dr. Firestone nodded. "Yes, please," he said quietly.

Amy hurried into the hospital room.

Carey Allen was sitting up in bed. The monitors and IV attached to her were in precarious shape as she struggled against the attachments. Her skin was pale. Her light brown hair had been pulled back into a tail to keep it from her face. Her eyes were huge wet blue pools—she wasn't sobbing loudly, she was just dripping tears.

"Miss Allen, Miss Allen, please! I'm Agent Amy Larson and we need you to be calm to help us find whoever it is you're worried about. Please! We need you…your friend needs you… and you must take care of yourself first so you can help us."

Carey Allen stared at her blankly for a minute.

"I'm alive!" she whispered.

"And the doctors say you're going to be fine. But we need

you to be calm, and to get well, and that way, you can help us."

Carey blinked, winced, nodded, and started rambling.

"I'm… I'm grateful I'm alive. I think I'm so good—such an adventurer, an explorer. And competent—I am competent. I love hiking! Caves, waterfalls…and I was so stupid! I fell in and—oh, God! The bodies. I was in a sea of bodies, staring at me… They didn't have eyes. They couldn't have been staring. It looked as if they were staring, though. But… I'm here. And Don… They won't tell me about Don. But I don't think he was down there with me. I was awake… I screamed and screamed. I fought and I struggled and I tried to get out—and I couldn't get any kind of a hold on the mud and I knew I was dying. I'm alive. I'm grateful. I'm terrified, but mostly, I'm afraid for Don. Don't you see, if he's hurt… if he's…dead, it's all my fault!"

"First, nothing to do with this is your fault. It's the fault of whatever monstrous human being out there is doing this," Amy said. "But I do need your help. Who is Don? I need his last name. Was he hiking with you? I need your help so we can hopefully help Don together."

Tears streaked down the young woman's face.

"I—I've had a crush on him. He's—he's just a great guy. He's an advertising exec with my company. He's…phenomenal." She paused, wincing painfully again. "He likes adventure, but I should have never gone to the caves with him. But—"

"But no one out there would have expected what you found, Carey. You must quit beating yourself up."

"But if he's dead—"

"It is the fault of the person or persons murdering people. And Carey, please, we always have faith that someone might be alive. We search for them with that hope in mind. What is Don's full name?"

"Blake. He's Donald Blake. He's tall and handsome...his hair is reddish like yours, and he's thirty-three years old. I know that because Hailey Mumford in the Human Resources Department told me his age. I just... I mean, it's tough, you know. It's still hard for women to just walk up to a guy and say, hey, coffee, dinner, or drinks? Well, not all women, I guess. But I must be preprogrammed or something. I thought if he liked me, he'd ask me out, and he didn't."

"Well, what is the official word from your company? Are employees allowed to date?"

"Yeah. At least, there's no rule against it. So long as work goes on at work, Mr. Barrington is fine with it. Oh. Malcolm Barrington is the CEO—I guess that makes sense, since the company is called Barrington Advertising. It was started by Malcolm's grandfather—it's an old and respected agency and still privately owned. And Malcolm's okay—he's never a jerk to employees. Honesty. That's all he asks is honesty. He'll try to help employees with kids when the schools are off. He even has a room with video games for older kids, and he has blocks and a little gym for little ones. I'm sure that as far as bosses go, he's really cool. You just can't lie. You can be sick, you can have a sick mom in Omaha or something, but you can't lie."

"Sounds like a good enough guy. What is your position there?"

"I'm office. I'm Accounts and Negotiations. We have a brilliant Art Department, and six people on the sales team." She fell silent and her eyes started to water again. "You must find Don! Please, if something has happened to him..."

"It's still not your fault," Amy told her determinedly.

"But it is. He wouldn't have been there. And…he wasn't with me, you're sure? I mean, he wasn't…"

"Carey, he wasn't there."

"How can you be certain?"

"Because the people there, other than you, had been dead at least a week."

Carey leaned back and Amy told her, "Please. Try to rest. I know it won't be easy. Please believe me. I'm going back out there and we'll find Don." She wasn't going to tell Carey they would find Don—they'd hunt until they found him— dead or alive. "I'm going to call my partner who excels at cases like this, and we'll have every law enforcement agency in the country looking for him."

Carey looked at her and nodded. She finally seemed to have calmed down.

"You will let me know…right away if you find him? No matter how you find him."

"I promise," Amy told her. "For your part, please, do everything the doctors tell you. The best you can do for us— and for Don—is get well and strong as quickly as possible. I will check back in with you tomorrow morning, I promise, and every morning until we find him."

"You can do that?" Carey asked hopefully.

"I can and I will," Amy said. "And if you think of anyone else who might help me—"

"Mr. Barrington. He will know if Don was supposed to be somewhere, if he… Oh! Do you think Don would have thought I would have just left him there in the caves? No, he'd never think that, right? But…"

Her voice trailed. She was beginning to sound distressed again.

"No. No. He would've called me—he would've worried

when I didn't answer. If he was okay, he would never have just left me! Unless he thought I left him. Or..."

"Carey, get strong. I'm going to start finding out about Don right now, I promise," Amy assured her. "I'll do this—and you be strong. For me, okay?"

Carey nodded again. "I'm going to try. I swear."

"Good. I will get back with you, but I'm going to work on this," Amy told her.

She walked out of the hospital room. The young nurse was waiting just outside.

"Thank you!" she told Carey.

"What happened to her, I have a bad time imagining. It's so horrible," Amy said. "But hopefully, she'll be calmer for you now."

"She's hysterical about that young man. And it doesn't sound as if it's going to come out okay for him."

"Hard to say. We're going to start looking."

"In the dark?" the nurse asked.

Amy made a face. "There's going to be a lot of necessary research that can be done in the dark, no problem."

"I guess you don't work nine to five," the young woman said. "And, of course, neither do we! Shifts."

"Right. And nine to five? Not often, anyway," Amy said. "Thank you. Take good care of our girl."

"I will."

Amy waved to her, walked down the hall, and pulled her phone out to call Hunter. She frowned when he didn't answer. Hunter was excellent about answering the phone.

But he didn't answer when she dialed again.

She then tried calling Andy Mason.

"Hey, kid, where are you? How is Carey Allen doing?"

"She's given us something to work on. She didn't go to the caves alone. She went with a man she had a huge crush on—one she never saw or heard from after she fell into the pit. She's terrified he may be dead somewhere, and it's all her fault," Amy explained. "Andy, I've got another missing person at the moment. Hunter isn't answering his phone. Is he by any chance with you?"

"I'm at my office. I left Hunter at the caves. He was still watching what was going on. I got the feeling he felt we'd missed something, and he didn't know what it was himself. You could go on out there. It will be dark soon, but I know the forensic teams are still at it, and they have some lights rigged."

"All right. I'll get on finding Hunter. In the meantime, can you look for a man named Donald Blake who works for Barrington Advertising? As I said, he was with Carey at the caves. She's afraid he's dead in there somewhere, or hurt, or... Anyway, we need to find him."

"Will do. I'm on it," Andy promised. "Let me know as soon as you're with Hunter."

"Right," Amy promised. "Oh! I came in the ambulance—"

"Gotcha. Go down to the entrance. We have a couple of agents headed to the hospital to watch over Carey—just in case someone really wanted her dead and finds out she didn't obligingly die down there. Cassidy and Cromwell. I'll let them know one of them needs to stay, and one needs to drop you back off at the caves."

"Thank you," Amy said.

Ending the call, she continued on down, dialing Hunter once again.

Her call went straight to voice mail.

"Where are you?" she muttered to the phone.

Of course, it gave her no answer.

Reaching the front of the hospital, she had no difficulty discerning the vehicle that belonged to the men Andy had sent, Cassidy and Cromwell. One of them remained behind the wheel of a black SUV while the other stood by the side, waiting. He was in a simple black suit but to Amy the suit along with the vehicle shrieked FBI. She thought he was about forty, a solid man, just slightly graying, who appeared to be pure muscle.

"You're Special Agent Amy Larson, FDLE," the man said.

"I am. Special Agent Cassidy—or Cromwell?" she asked.

"Cromwell. Cassidy is behind the wheel, and he'll get you back to the caves. You'd best be advised, though, even with the lights our teams have up, it's getting dark. And the terrain in that area—caves, waterfalls, cliffs—can be dangerous in the dark at the best of times."

"I'll be careful," Amy promised.

He was studying her, she knew. She was about five-ten and made a point of keeping fit. Amy had heard that in later years the FBI had recruited more female agents, so she didn't think his concerned perusal had to do with her gender—but rather the fact she wasn't FBI at all. In fact, she was FDLE on loan from the state of Florida.

She smiled. "Trust me, there are connections here, and I know the connections. No, I haven't spent a lot of time climbing cliffs, but I swim like a son of a gun, and I am a crack shot."

Cromwell smiled. "Sorry. It's just... Wow. Hard to talk anymore without worrying that... I am not coming on to you, I swear it. I'm not trying to be out of line. You must be aware you're very attractive and...feminine and you're not from here, so..."

Amy laughed. "It's okay. And thank you. Please trust me. I'm pretty good at what I do."

He grinned and nodded. "Okay, then. I'm going on in to keep our girl company." He stuck his head back into the vehicle for a minute. "Hey, Cassidy! I'm going to need coffee in a bit so get back here after dropping off Special Agent Larson!" He grinned at Amy again, opening the passenger side door for her. "He's a newbie. Gotta give him a little grief."

Amy nodded and slid into the SUV. She glanced at Cassidy and said, "Hello, and thank you."

"No problem," Cassidy said, smiling. He was young, Amy thought, in his midtwenties to maybe thirty, tops. He continued with, "Cromwell will be sending me for coffee all night! Thinks it's his duty to make sure I understand the hierarchy. He's a good guy, though. I'm glad to be partnered with him. So." He frowned slightly, glancing at her before shifting the SUV into gear. "We're being briefed and brought up to speed on all this. Someone out there is trying to bring on the Apocalypse?"

"Step by step," Amy said. "And figuring out each play... Well, everything changes constantly."

"Right. We've been told there will be a meeting in the morning. You and Special Agent Forrest are to head up the investigation. Though...is this the investigation? Did Carey Allen stumble into that pit—and ruin the whole thing for whoever it is who thinks he's representing the black horse in the whole Revelations thing? I mean, is someone really a religious fanatic, or...just someone who likes to see people die, and thinks playing with passages in the Bible is a cool way to make that happen?"

"We don't know."

"I thought you'd been on two previous cases—"

"We were. But we don't have all the answers. We thought we were done once—then we received a little red horse. This time...a little black horse."

"I started doing some research. Have to admit, I didn't go to any kind of religious school and skipped Sunday school a lot! But scholars suggest the scales carried by the rider of the black horse indicate famine. So...is that why the victims in the pit were starved? Left to dehydrate and starve?"

"In someone's sick mind—or calculating mind—sure. Some people suggest it's the weighing of sins against decency and a man's—or woman's—good deeds. We don't know what we have going on yet. We don't know anything at all."

"But you've been asked back," Cassidy said. "Not just by the FBI. But by the killer or killers themselves."

She glanced at him, smiling. "You must know many a criminal has such an ego that he or she thinks it's fun to tease law enforcement."

"Yeah, you're right. So we need to be smarter! And take your time getting out—let me know if I can do anything else. I'm not in any hurry," Cassidy said.

"Gotta find my partner," Amy said. "But thank you."

They had arrived back at the entrance to the water and the caves. Lights had been strung up to illuminate the forensic vehicles and the area.

Stepping out of the SUV, Amy quickly saw the ranger Sam Harrison was still there. He leaned against his car, watching and waiting.

"Sam!" Amy said, hurrying over to him.

"Hey. How is Carey?"

"She's going to be all right. She was worried about a friend who came with her, and Andy Mason is finding out what he can. No one stumbled on more bodies, right?"

"No more bodies," Sam assured her. "Not—yet."

"Let's hope not ever," Amy murmured. "Have you seen Hunter?"

"Not since... Not for several hours, no. Have you called him?"

For a minute, Amy felt a chill of panic settle over her.

Why would Hunter just disappear? He wouldn't, not unless something had happened to him!

No! She couldn't think that way. Hunter was an excellent agent and incredibly competent.

Nothing had happened to him!

One of the women working forensics who had been walking by must have heard them. She stopped and said, "Special Agent Forrest was working the caves a while back. I talked to him from the pit. He was moving deeper in, saying something about simple physical logistics. I haven't seen him since."

"Thank you," Amy told her. "Okay. Well, Sam, should I swim or can you get a boat to take me over?"

"A boat—even I would freeze my butt off at this time of night!" Sam said. "But going over there right now might not be a great idea. They want everyone pulling out in the next thirty minutes. It will be full-on dark with only a sliver of a moon, and the temperature will drop like a brick."

"Yep, I get it. But I'm going over there," Amy said. "You going to help me or not?"

He looked at her, shook his head, and murmured, "You are one determined woman, Special Agent Larson. But—you bet. I'll grab a boat and we'll go on over together."

3

The caves went on, twisting and turning, deep into the cliffs rising above them and the freshwater lake and springs encircling the cliffs and running through them at various places.

It was easy enough to recognize the areas where rangers might bring guests on tours to display the natural wonders of the state.

It was also easy to recognize where it would be dangerous to bring groups of people, areas where the rock hung low and winding paths were narrow and small.

There were also areas where there were more deep trenches of mud created naturally by the flow of water and the irregular height of the caverns and natural "alleyways" throughout.

Hunter hadn't begun to imagine the scope of the area when he had begun his search. Nor could he tell if any of the other pits might contain human bodies.

He'd paused at one point to call Amy and find out if she had discovered anything helpful from Carey Allen, but the caves apparently repelled satellite communication. But there was another way out—he had convinced himself that was true—and logic supported his supposition. In a maze like this, there had to be another opening. Perhaps several. Somewhere else, at least, where the force of the water had to have worn away more of the rock.

He knew he'd been searching for a long time and was about to call it quits and head back out the way he had come when a turn he hadn't expected showed him a long opening that led back toward the mud pit where Carey Allen and the others had lain. It ran almost parallel to the route he had just taken.

But if he turned the other way...

It had grown dark. Police lights had filtered through enough to let him search with the aid of his trusty penlight. But now he frowned because he couldn't see the origin of the trail clearly. He hurried in that direction.

There was an opening, low to the ground. He hunched down to look through it and saw a narrow crevice led to another cavern—and that cavern had an entry at the other end. Snaking his way through, he hurried to the entry. It was broad and easily accessible but was covered by a rock protruding just feet from the entry. After sloshing his way through a foot of cold water to the rock, he discovered a swath of overgrown land was not more than five feet behind it. He heard the blaring sound of a truck's horn and knew a road couldn't be far beyond.

He stared at the night and felt his phone vibrating in his pocket. Glancing at it quickly, he saw Amy was calling him.

"Amy, I found it," he said.

"Oh, my God, Hunter, you had me scared to death! Why haven't you been answering?" Amy demanded. "Carey Allen is worried sick about a friend who was with her. Agents are trying to discover if he's all right or if... Oh, Hunter! You jerk. I was becoming just as scared!"

"Amy, you know me. You know that I'm careful—"

"And you took off alone. And you didn't answer—"

"The caves don't like cell phones. We're going to have to get walkie-talkies or something because we're going to have to dig deeper—literally—into what is going on here. Did Carey say anything helpful? Did she see anyone?"

"How are you on the phone now?" she demanded.

"I'm outside the caves again."

"I'm at the entrance now, and I don't see you anywhere!"

"Because I found another way out—and in. I'm heading back out. We're going to need to get some experts and more forensic workers out here. I passed at least three other areas where the land gives way to pits. These are a little lower and a little easier to see and avoid. But if there is someone in any of them... Well, we need more help to thoroughly search."

"Gotcha. But I'm still going to smash your head—with a pillow!" she said angrily.

Hunter smiled. "Okay, and I'm sorry. But you shouldn't panic so easily regarding me. You need to have faith in me."

"You don't want me to care so much that I worry?"

"I didn't mean—I'm sorry!"

"You're almost forgiven."

"Good. What about Carey Allen? Did she see anyone who—who was responsible? Did someone throw her in or—"

"No, she wasn't thrown in, but she was with a friend. A guy she had a crush on—Don Blake. Agents and police are searching for him right now. He's an ad exec with Barrington Advertising, the same company Carey works for. She's terrified something awful happened to him, and she's convinced it's her fault because she talked him into coming out with her for an adventure. You didn't come upon more bodies did you?"

"Not that I could see. But there are more mud pits. I'm heading back through the second entrance to see if someone smuggled the unwilling in this way. There are parts you'd have to have real control over someone to navigate, but it's more than possible. I'm going to lose you so I'm hanging up now. I'll see you in about ten minutes."

Hunter made his way along the second corridor within the caves, paralleling the track he had taken. At first, as he reached the area where he thought he should have found the pit, he came across rock. Then he realized that—as at the opening he'd discovered—the rock hid the narrow pathways one might take to stand across the pit from the access point that had been achieved by Carey and then by Amy and him—and then the crime scene people, forensics, and medical examiners.

He could see Amy talking with one of the forensic team as he made his way around the rock. He waved to her and warned, "Stay there, I'll make my way around the edge."

It could be precarious, he knew, but knowing made it possible to hug the cavern walls as he skirted the giant pit of muck and mud. He could picture what had been done, though he was certain the medical examiner's office would help him see more clearly. The killer—or killers—had rendered his victims pliable. Most likely they had been unconscious, either through drugs or a blow to the head. The victims had been dragged through and dumped. There was no footing to find to crawl out of this pit—this one was deep. And tours didn't come far enough in for anyone to hear a scream unless that scream had come at certain times.

Again, he thought whoever had done this knew the park's schedule and just when rangers would and would not be in the vicinity.

Did that mean Carey Allen *had* been an accidental victim?

Possibly. Maybe even probably. But impossible at this point to know for sure.

Amy held back as he approached her. Of course, by then several forensic team members had hurried over as well, anxious to hear his description of where he had been.

"This is Carson Meyer, director of the teams we have here tonight. He's gradually shifting teams," Amy said, "but—"

"But I will be here through until morning," the man Amy had been speaking with—CSI Carson Meyer—told him. "We've been at it for hours now and need fresh eyes and strength," he added dryly.

Meyer had been working it hard enough, Hunter noted. He was a man in his late thirties or early forties, straight, lean, and wiry with close-cropped dark hair and serious gray eyes. He was covered in mud. Hunter realized he was probably rough looking himself.

"There's a shaft I just came through that leads to another area like this, and the entry appears invisible from here because there's a rock just feet away that causes it all to blend into the cave walls until you're right on top of it. There would be no way to suspect it was there. It ends in much the same manner out on the other side, around the corner from where we've been parking. There is also a labyrinth of smaller caverns and a dozen twists and turns I followed from the entry over there." He paused and pointed to the path he had taken. "There are more pits. I didn't see more victims, but I didn't go into the pits. We need more light back there."

"And personnel," Meyer murmured. "But we'll get on it. We won't stop. I promise you."

Hunter nodded. "Thank you."

"No, man, thank you," Meyer said, studying Hunter. "We're not happy you found a bunch of dead people, but the list of missing persons around here had gotten long and...well, I'm in forensics. But our local cops are going to be grateful as hell."

"Not yet. We don't know what the hell has been going on yet," Hunter said.

"You just came in from South Florida today," Meyer said, nodding toward Amy who had obviously explained their appearance. "I'm on this—I promise you. Get some sleep. We'll still be here in the morning."

Amy was looking at him, nodding. "Right. Teams are looking for Donald Blake and teams will rip up this place. Let's get—" she said, and then paused. "Let's get to our hotel room and get some sleep."

"Right," Hunter agreed.

Meyer smiled suddenly. "Good luck getting into a respectable hotel! You look like a kid who's been rolling in the mud on a wet day at the playground."

Hunter nodded, grinning. "Yeah. But Andy Mason had us all set up. We're good."

"Good thing. Try not to scare any kids in the lobby. Oh, wait. I think it's three in the morning. Shouldn't be too many people awake at this hour."

"Right. Okay. Good night," Hunter said.

Amy echoed his words and turned to make her way to one of the little boats. A man quickly jumped on it, ready to take them back to the bank. There, a police officer was ready to drive them to the hotel Andy Mason had already checked them into.

It wasn't until they were alone in the hotel room that Amy turned and threw herself on Hunter to hug him tightly.

"I'm sorry, Hunter, but I was so scared. So damned scared when I couldn't reach you."

"And I'm sorry, but Amy—"

"Of course, I had just been with Carey, and she was so panicked about that place and her friend, her crush, Donald Blake. And really! What if it had been the other way around? What if you hadn't been able to reach me? Come on now!"

"And that's why they generally don't let couples work on the same team," Hunter said.

"Ah, but I'm not FBI. I'm FDLE on loan!" she reminded him. "Yes…anyway, go take a shower. You're a mess."

"You just hugged me. So now you are, too."

"Good thing we at least changed into hiking gear. Our clothing may need burning."

"So they may. Good reason to take it all off, huh?"

She grinned, dropped her bag and walked toward the bathroom. Even though there was a lock and a bolt on the door, she still carried her Glock with her into the bathroom. Hunter looked around their room quickly. Andy Mason had seen to it that their bags were delivered, and they sat on the racks provided for luggage. There were bottles of water on a small refrigerator, and the room also offered coffee and a coffeepot. Typical, perhaps—but he was grateful to his old coworker. Andy would have made sure they had immediate necessities like water.

And for the following morning—yeah, coffee.

He followed Amy into the bathroom, set his own Glock on a towel shelf and peeled off his clothing. He figured he was pretty ripe.

Amy was studiously scrubbing her hair when he stepped behind her. He edged around her and let the hot water sluice over him. He could see the dirt that pooled at his feet and before touching Amy, he grabbed one of the little bottles of liquid soap and poured the whole thing over himself, scrubbing furiously.

Amy laughed, easing a washcloth over his shoulders.

"Don't remove any flesh!"

"Look at the tub."

"Yeah, well, some of that was me!"

She was behind him, smoothing the washcloth down his back and then pushing him aside to rinse out her hair. She eased around him again, running her fingers provocatively down his lower abdomen whispering, "I'm squeaky clean and drying off. And…hmm. The bed is just a way more promising venue than this icky shower!"

She stepped out and he grinned. He'd never thought he could share such a bond with anyone. He loved her, and he was in love with her. And while the physical was damned amazing, it was something more. Something in their minds or souls perhaps.

"On my way in a split second," he promised. "Okay, maybe a minute."

He scrubbed and rinsed his own hair, rinsed again and again, and finally stepped out and grabbed a towel.

Still drying his hair, he took his Glock from the shelf and made his way to the bedroom, setting the handgun on the bedside table.

Amy was already in bed, curled beneath a sheet, damp hair stretched out on a towel on her pillow. She had turned the lights off and tuned soft music on the clock radio.

He curled up next to her and reached for her.

Then discovered she was sound asleep.

He smiled. That kind of thing could happen when you worked endless hours in a row. A couple grew comfortable.

He didn't think they had let go of an iota of the excitement they shared in being together. He found her extraordinarily beautiful. And sensual.

But it would take him some time to get to sleep.

And there was no way in hell he would wake her now.

Because they would have their private time together, time that allowed them to savor what was beautiful in life—after watching so much of what could be so horrendously ugly.

He eased down at her side and pulled her against him.

And eventually, sleep did come.

"This room has never been this busy…this fully occupied," Dr. Adler told Amy and Hunter as they stood with him at the doorway to a large room where a half-dozen medical examiners and their assistants were busy working at silver-toned gurneys throughout.

"Anything yet that might help us?" Hunter asked.

Adler nodded grimly. "I believe we do. At least, we're connecting bodies with names. Sad, but still better than not knowing. Wondering is crushing."

"Yes, it is," Amy agreed. "But—"

"So far," Adler said, "it does appear the victims starved to death, or in a few cases, perished due to heart attacks or heart failure. There were very few broken bones, considering the circumstances. This all leads me to believe they were lured or brought to the caves and forced down into the pit and left with the bodies of those who came before them to suffer the same fate."

"Is that why some resorted to cannibalism?" Amy asked.

Adler frowned. "No, that's one of the strange anomalies here, and we've only just begun our work. Normally, we wouldn't have started until morning but due to the circumstances, we called an all-hands-on-deck and began the minute we had the bodies back here and washed. No easy task, I assure you."

"I saw some of the corpses," Hunter said. "They were gnawed on by something; and I couldn't help but assume it was another human being since a creature couldn't have crawled out, either, and the bite marks were not those of rats."

"No, no, you were right. But we haven't found a fragment of an ounce of human flesh in any of the stomach contents of the victims thus far." He winced. "With those victims… the gnawing was done before death, before they arrived in the pit."

Amy winced inwardly.

"They weren't bitten because someone was starving to death?" she asked.

Adler shook his head.

"Thanks," Hunter said. He turned grimly to Amy. "We're dealing with a very strange puppet master again. Someone who has convinced others terrible things must be done in preparation for the coming Apocalypse."

"A religious fanatic?" Adler asked. "I've had a body or two drained of blood because of a so-called vampire cult, but biting is new for me."

"Oh, I doubt the head man—or woman—is a fanatic. I'm imagining someone with a goal in mind—but someone charismatic who can sway and manipulate others. And I'm hoping we will discover a link between victims."

"Lists of those we've identified with approximate dates for their deaths and causes are ready for you at the reception area," Adler said.

"We'll be teaming with local agents and the police and start immediately," Amy told him.

"I hope you catch this monster. Before you find another mud pit," Adler said.

"I'm hoping there isn't another one out there already," Hunter said.

He looked at Amy; they silently agreed they needed to go and get to work. There was little more they could discover at the morgue now. They knew Adler would keep them up to date on any discovery.

In the car, Amy drove and Hunter put a call through to Andy Mason and asked if any progress had been made in the search for Carey Allen's friend Donald Blake.

"All right, so," Andy told them over speakerphone, "Don Blake had the day off when he went hiking with Carey Allen. He was not reported missing at work because he was supposed to be heading out to Las Vegas for a sales meeting. He did not make the meeting. At this time, his whereabouts are unknown. His phone goes straight to voice mail, and police did a wellness check at his home. Nothing is out of order and his car is not in his driveway. There is nothing to suggest he met with any foul play at his residence, but neither is there anything that suggests he's all right."

"Okay, I know teams are tearing apart the caverns. If he's in there, they will find him," Amy said. "We've gotten lists of the identified victims. We're heading to your offices—we'll see what is known about them. According to our lists, the police are notifying the next of kin. It will be brutal news for people to take in, but we're going to have to start interviewing them."

"Andy, have your heard anything about strange cults in the area?" Hunter asked.

"Cults?" Andy asked.

"The medical examiners haven't found human remains in the stomach contents of any of the victims. They were bitten by human beings, but not by any of the people they were with while in the pit," Amy explained. "You'll be getting Adler's reports. He's getting them out to our offices and the police departments. Strange behavior like that suggests the victims might have been part of a ceremony, something with a leader who appears to be a messiah of sorts preparing his flock for the days to come."

"Wait. People bit the victims—not just in a fight, but as in biting to take a chunk out?" Andy asked. "And not because they were desperate in the pit, but desperate—"

"Right," Hunter said. "We'll be in soon to find out what we can about the various victims, and then we'll start interviewing family and friends."

"Good," Andy said. "I'm here, conference room three, and I'll have one of our amazing tech researchers in here with me. What she can find on social media is extensive and awesome. She has helped us out many a time."

"Great," Hunter said. "We're almost there."

They ended the call, and Amy saw Hunter staring straight ahead. He shook his head and glanced her way. "I—I should understand. My parents aren't stupid people. My mother was naive and caring, but where we were...the bad happened undercover. And when they knew the truth, they were ready to get out. And I guarantee you, my folks would not have gotten involved with anything that had to do with human sacrifice. But there are people out there..."

"Who will believe anything. If it's on the internet, and it agrees with what they think, they accept it—against any display of fact and logic. We know that," Amy said quietly. "And usually, there's someone out there who knows their every word is a lie, but if you repeat a lie often enough—"

"You make it a truth. Not the truth. But a truth as seen by many," Hunter said. "I think we need to concentrate hard on the victimology. I don't believe random people were chosen. If this is a cult at work—and you'd seldom get a group of people who wanted to take chunks out of other people—there would have to be an underlying reason, a belief, as in a reason brought to them by a charismatic cult leader."

He hesitated and grimaced. "Remember during the witch-craft trials, hanging a witch was a good thing. And torturing someone into admitting they were a witch wasn't a bad thing. People can believe they're doing something ordained, no matter how horrible it is, if they believe they are involved in a righteous cause."

"And now we know they were either crazy or happy to believe because of land deals or whatever else," Amy said.

"The point is, there were people who were true believers and they thought Satan was trying to infiltrate their lives," Hunter said. "Then," he said with a shrug, "it was probably the norm. But again—"

"People often believe what they choose or what works for them," Amy said. She let out a soft sigh. "I wish we had something on Donald Blake. I'm going to need to go by the hospital and see Carey Allen again. I promised I'd keep her in the loop on everything happening."

"You don't have anything good to tell her."

"Well, in this, I'm going to need to stick with the truth—*the* truth—and not *a* truth," Amy said. "But I said I'd keep her informed. And... I don't know. Maybe there is something else she'll think of at some point that might help. I think we need to find out if anything else was going on at their work. At Barrington Advertising."

"Of course. Let's meet with Andy. We'll stop at the hospital after, and maybe take a cruise by Barrington Advertising and see how cooperative folks there want to be. If he wasn't taken at the caves—and he is involved somehow—he might have slipped up with a friend at the company. Or maybe someone at the company is involved. Anyway, we'll get what we can at the offices and then move on."

"Perfect," Amy told him.

They reached the offices and were quickly led to the conference room where Andy Mason was waiting, a large screen already showing images projected from a computer being controlled by a young man in the room. Andy quickly rose and the young man rose as well, shaking hands as they were introduced. He was in his early twenties, wearing a suit and tie, but still looking boyish with a shaggy haircut and clean-shaven cheeks.

"Jay Hughes, agents," the young man said.

"Young and brilliant. The young and brilliant manage to do great things with tech," Andy said.

"I don't know about brilliant, but I try—and I work in an office. You guys in the field have my utmost admiration."

"Thank you," Hunter told him. "But the field work couldn't exist half the time without the leads you find, so we make a team."

"Sure. Great," Hughes said. "Anyway, I obviously need more time for deep digs into these people. But so far, we've identified five of our missing persons. We've got the most recent pictures they had taken before their deaths, have their work info, etcetera, more on some than on the others. If you're ready?"

"We are," Hunter assured him.

"Take a seat. It's like a movie with commentary," Andy said.

Amy grinned and took a seat opposite the screen and then Hunter did the same. The picture of a man with shaggy hair, a mustache and trimmed beard appeared on one side of the screen with a lineup of writing on the other.

Jay Hughes read aloud. "This is Gavin Peterson. Forty-six years old. He was a professor at the local community college, married, two children, but recently separated. His secretary is the one who reported him missing; but his wife, Loretta, lives in the area and works at the library. Both children, Ted and Candy, go to out-of-state colleges. Adler's report suggests he was one of the first to go into the pit—he disappeared almost six months ago."

Amy glanced at Hunter.

This—whatever this was—had begun some time ago.

Jay Hughes hit a button on the computer, showing the man's driver's license, social security card, and even a likeness of his insurance information.

"Has the family been notified?" Amy asked Andy.

He nodded grimly. "The detective on the missing persons report informed the estranged wife and the man's kids and his college."

"I think we need to see Loretta Peterson and find out why they were separated," Amy murmured.

Andy nodded. "I figured that was something you wanted to do yourself. As far as Jay has found so far, the man wasn't into groups of any kind, and he had a stellar work record."

"Okay, second victim identified—" Jay said and then paused and shot another image and info up on the screen "—is Rodney Marks. He's a contractor, no children, fifty-five, known to be a bit of a man about town. Liked to party—I was able to get onto one of his social media sites. No criminal record, a few parking tickets, and that's it. He wasn't reported missing until a woman complained of an odor coming from his house. Poor cat died trapped in there. His car was in his driveway, no sign of foul play—he was just gone. Medical examiners' office estimates he'd been in the pit approximately three months." Jay flicked another key on the computer. "Our third person is Estelle Benedict, forty-nine, rising in political circles. Again, she had no children and was not married. She was a bonds attorney and earned a place on the city council and was aspiring to go much further. She was reported missing by her partner. I don't know if this is relevant in this day and age, but partner is a woman. She didn't hide the fact she was gay, but she didn't put an emphasis on it, either. Her focal points in her political career had to do with insurance and medical attention for all and fair wages that allowed for even entry-stage workers to afford living quarters." He was quiet for a minute. "I would have liked her. Oh! Sorry, I know, that's neither here nor there—"

"Hey!" Amy said softly. "It's okay to admire the woman. She must have been great. What about her girlfriend?"

"Brenda Hayes, freelance art restorer. She must be good. Most of the major museums in the west have used her artistry at one time or another."

"We need to see her, too," Amy murmured.

Hunter nodded. "And Dr. Adler estimates she was killed approximately seven weeks ago," he said as he read the screen. "There seems to be a month between killings. Of course, there are many more bodies to go, but I'm curious if they don't coincide with religious holidays or others," Hunter said.

"I'll study that this afternoon," Jay said solemnly.

"And if this does have anything to do with a purist cult, her sexuality could be important. It could be why she is dead, why she was *chosen*," Hunter murmured. "Jay, have you found any dirt on the two men you showed us?"

"Not yet. I can dig."

"Well," Amy said, "we can finish out the day with a few trips. We can see Loretta Peterson and Brenda Hayes. Mr. and Mrs. Peterson were separated. If there was something, Loretta might be willing to tell us. And it sounds as if Brenda and Estelle were close—Brenda may know something about Estelle's activities."

"Right," Hunter said. "So, about our last two identified bodies—and do we have hard copies of this info?"

"Depending on what you call hard copy," Hughes said.

"Andy sent it all to your emails. And our last two are...? First, Xavier Alexander, musician, unmarried, scores of conquests, reported missing when he didn't show up for a gig. He's been dead three to four weeks. He was one of the victims...with bite marks. Thirty-one years old. Lived alone, but, again, a wellness check showed nothing out of order—and his car in the driveway. He was just gone. And last but not least this fellow, Arthur C. Graves, inherited millions, lived in a dozen mansions in a dozen places, and so his family doesn't even know when he went missing. He was sixty-six, left behind four children and ten grandchildren, and three estranged ex-wives. Uber-rich. Adler said he's been dead about a month."

Amy quickly checked her phone. As promised, all the information had been emailed to them. She pushed her chair back.

"Jay, you are great. Thank you so much," she said.

"Not that great! I'm going to find out more for you, of course."

She grinned. He was young, eager, and not aware of just how much of what he did helped to save people out on the streets.

"We're going to swing by to see Carey Allen and then slide on over to Barrington Advertising to get a lay of the land. Then we'll stop by and see Loretta Peterson. Maybe there's something she can give us. And we'll get to Brenda Hayes. Andy, if—"

"Jay and I will work on finding out who may know something about the others," Andy assured them. "We are working in tandem with the police, so we will have plenty of people out there."

"Thanks," Hunter said. "Shall we?"

"Ready!" Amy agreed.

They greeted others as they left the local headquarters and

returned to the parking garage. The hospital was their next stop. Hunter drove this time; Amy studied her phone.

"I believe they have something in common," she murmured, "but what? They're such a mixed group with a musician, a politician, gay, straight, superrich, just working the American dream…"

"Sins," Hunter said.

"What?" Amy asked.

Hunter took a deep breath, still watching the road as he spoke. "Sins. If this is the work of a cult—and logistics tell us there have to be several people involved with this—then, as we were saying, they might have been brainwashed into believing they were doing a good thing. Like cleansing sinners so they could meet their maker. Maybe dying in the pit was a way for them to reflect on the evils they had done."

"But taking out chunks of human flesh?" Amy asked softly.

"Okay, say some of this flock is trying to atone themselves. Maybe a bite of the sinner helps the biter expunge some of their own wrongs?"

"Wouldn't a bite of the pure and innocent be better for that?"

"One would think. But who knows what crazy mantra they might have been taught?"

Amy was silent. Hunter had been assigned to the case in the Everglades where they'd first been teamed together because of his knowledge regarding just what could happen when enough people began to believe in such a mantra.

"Maybe it's a way of…taking on some of the sin of another?" she suggested at last.

He glanced her way. "Could be. Anyway, here we are. Let's see if Carey has remembered anything else that might help us. Of course, we'll assure her several agencies are busy trying to find her friend, Don Blake."

Amy nodded. But as they stepped out of the car, Hunter paused. She saw he was answering his phone and she waited.

He listened, spoke briefly, and ended the call.

"They found one more body in the caves, deep in one of the pits," he told her.

"Oh, no. Is it Don Blake?" Amy asked.

He grimaced. "They don't know yet. So…do we see Carey now, or do we wait?"

4

Hunter had decided to let Amy determine their course of action.

She decided they should head to the advertising firm first. If she saw Carey now, she would feel compelled to tell Carey Allen another body had been found.

But they didn't know anything yet.

And it didn't make sense to upset Carey until they did. The woman had been through enough. Instead, Amy called the hospital room and spoke briefly with Carey, telling her they'd be up to see her in the afternoon and would tell her anything they might discover by then.

Barrington Advertising was in an impressive freestanding building just on the outskirts of Denver. The receptionist who greeted them, a perfectly coifed and dressed woman of perhaps forty-five, was icily polite and pleasant, but at first told them there was no possible way of seeing Mr. Barrington without an appointment.

Hunter produced his badge. Her attitude changed.

"Um, just a minute, please," she murmured, putting through a call. "Mr. Barrington will see you immediately, of course. He's so concerned! The penthouse elevator, right there, will take you straight to his office."

They thanked her.

The building was just five stories, but apparently the penthouse office covered the full fifth floor.

The elevator opened into an expansive foyer. Barrington's desk, a sleek modern piece of furniture with the man's computer built right into the framework, sat toward the rear of the entry space in front of floor-to-ceiling glass windows. Comfortable chairs sat before the desk while a few more were scattered around the room against the wall. At least ten people could sit in the room if a meeting called for so many.

Doors led to other rooms in both directions, probably to a bedroom or a room with a daybed, at least, for those times when the CEO and owner worked well into the night. According to Carey Allen, Barrington was a decent boss. If so, it was nice to see a decent man could create this kind of an enterprise.

Barrington was behind the desk studying his computer when the elevator pinged to announce its arrival on the floor. He immediately stood.

He appeared to be a man of about sixty, bald—if he did have hair it was cleanly shaven—with dark brown eyes, a solid chin, and cheekbones that helped give him the look of someone with great dignity.

He immediately stepped forward to offer them both a hand-shake.

"I spoke with Milly, and I understand you're Agents Forrest and Larson, correct?" he asked. "Malcolm Barrington. And I'm horrified Carey suffered and even more horrified for those who died in that terrible pit. Who would ever imagine? We are known for such natural beauty here, and the falls, rivers, and cliffs are so beautiful. I find it hard to accept the fact anyone would twist our nature into something so evil. I am rambling, sorry. I'm an advertising man, and sometimes the more one talks, the more ideas come out. But on this... I'm sorry. I'm happy to do anything. Anything," he said.

"Thank you, Mr. Barrington. You haven't heard from Don Blake yet, have you?" Hunter asked. "Do you have any way of contacting him or any of his contacts such as other friends, clients, or fellow employees?"

Barrington shook his head grimly. "Don was due out in Vegas because one of his accounts is a privately held casino hotel out there, The Bunny Hop. Mari Malaga is their head of promotion. When I spoke with her, she said she and Don had a *tentative* meeting set, but he didn't show up at her office, and she tried reaching him to no avail. None of us has been able to reach him—and I fear the worst, except that... no one has found him yet, right?" He winced. "His body?"

"No. Of course, we'll keep looking for him as a missing person," Amy said, glancing at Hunter.

He might have been found. He might be the corpse in the second pit.

They just didn't know yet. He agreed with Amy's assertion the man hadn't been found; they didn't know anything more about the body.

"I have asked his team to assemble everything he was working on. And he took his laptop with him everywhere, but he had a large desktop here. We would be happy to have you tear it to the ground if necessary. I just..." Barrington broke off. "Have you seen Carey?" he asked anxiously. "She is a lovely young woman and a hard worker. It breaks my heart to think of her suffering."

"We have seen her," Amy assured him. "She's doing well."

"I'm so grateful to hear that. I know Hayden was beside herself with worry. I insisted she take the day and spend it with Carey in the hospital." He sighed again. "We are a team here. I know some places of business can be competitive, but we compete against other companies. In here, we're a team, and it promotes friendships. Thirty-five employees and all of them are damned talented and good people. And Don... I can't... I just can't... I mean, God, I hope he's just off somewhere, except—"

"Except, it wouldn't be like him?" Hunter asked.

Barrington nodded grimly. "I admit, I am terribly worried."

"Of course," Amy murmured. "Well, what we need from you is the computer, of course. And lists of your employees— we will have to speak with them each individually. No one is a completely open book. Someone may know something more about his habits or quirks or—"

"Wait. I'm confused. From what I've understood," Barrington said, frowning, "Don Blake was with Carey Allen when she fell into the hole. If he'd been there—and been okay—he'd never have just left Carey in a hole."

"Unless he thought she took off on him," Hunter suggested.

"Why would he think that? I'm sure the man knew she had a crush on him because the rest of the office knew, certainly."

"Do you allow office romances?" Hunter asked.

"I don't disallow them, not if the work is done," Barrington said. "And I've already arranged for lists of my employees, the date they began here, and more to be sent to Special Agent Andy Mason."

"Of course. Thank you. Any disgruntled ex-employees?" Hunter asked.

Barrington shook his head. "No, I don't lose employees. I don't hire people who are not going to be good at their jobs. One of my accountants, Herb Green, left, but he had a great offer on Wall Street and he was anxious to move to New York. I've had a few people retire—with full benefits. There's no one who could be angry enough to want to hurt another employee. I know it sounds too good to be true, but that's the benefit of being a private company. And one that doesn't pit salespeople against salespeople."

"You're sure you know all your people that well?" Amy asked.

"Well, you want to speak with everyone. And you've met Hayden and Carey. Carey is traumatized, of course, but nothing to do with work. In fact, her work will be here whenever she is ready to return to it. Barrington Advertising is hopefully a ray of light in her misery."

"Thank you," Amy told him quietly. "We are moving on this afternoon, but perhaps we could return tomorrow and start speaking with your people?"

"There's a charming conference room just beyond that left door. Very comfortable. You are welcome to make use of it, and you can tell me how and when you would like people brought up," Barrington said.

"Thank you. We will see you then," Hunter said. "A private room will be appreciated."

Amy gave him one of her beautiful smiles. "Yes, thank you so much for your help, Mr. Barrington. We don't mean to waste anyone's time, but—"

"If it will help you find Don Blake, there is nothing I wouldn't do," Barrington said sincerely.

They smiled and thanked him before walking back to the elevator. On the ground floor, they thanked his receptionist.

She nodded and almost smiled but watched them with a worried frown as they left.

Hunter glanced at Amy. She smiled and nodded, and they turned back.

"Milly, right?" He asked.

"I'm, uh, yes. Milly—or Mildred—Garrison."

"Forgive me for bothering you first, but we're going to be here tomorrow speaking with everyone. Mr. Barrington has just given us the go-ahead. Do you know Don Blake well? Can you think of anything at all that might help us?" he asked.

Milly Garrison shook her head. "I'm... Well, I'm out here. I'm the face of the company when people arrive, but I don't spend time in the main offices, on the floor... I mean, everyone is great, but I can't say I know my fellow workers well. I know how upset and worried everyone is. Oh, I mean, I'm upset and worried, too—but I'm not someone Don Blake would have confided anything to. I know they say he went with Carey and I hope he's okay..."

"They *say* he went with Carey?" Amy asked.

"Oh, I mean, as far as I know, he did. It's just...well, Don was—is—very good-looking and he knows it. And he's... nice! I don't mean he's not nice. It's just Carey can be kind of shy, and she's the outdoor type. And from what I've seen, Don likes the ultrasophisticated more... I don't know. More elegant woman."

"I thought you didn't know him well," Amy said, frowning.

"I don't. But I'm the receptionist. I see people who come to meet people, and some of Don's clients are well... He does some clothing and makeup accounts. I've seen him with model types—and I wouldn't have hurt Carey for the world, but I personally didn't see Don Blake being interested in Carey. She is truly sweet and kind, and everything about her is warm and wonderful, and… I just never saw the two of them together. I mean, I knew she had the crush, but…he's a charmer. And I sure didn't see him wanting to settle down anytime soon."

"I see," Amy said, and smiled. "Thank you so much. We really appreciate your opinions and your candor. It could really help us find Don Blake. We'll see you tomorrow and thank you so much again."

"I—you're welcome, of course! We all want to help. I'm just not sure we can."

"Right. One big family," Hunter said, hoping his smile appeared as sincere as Amy's.

They left the building at last. Amy glanced at him.

"Well?"

"Kumbaya," Hunter murmured.

"You think something there is suspicious?" Amy asked him.

He shook his head. "I'm not sure what. But when something looks too good to be true, it is. Private company, one big family. I don't know. And we do know Don Blake *was* with Carey—and if they were so not right for one another, why was he with her?"

"So, you're suspicious of the company or Don Blake?" Amy asked him.

He shrugged. "I'm not sure on that one yet. And if we do find Don Blake's body—"

He felt his phone vibrating and quickly glanced at the caller ID. He glanced at Amy. "I think we're about to find out. It's Andy. Putting you on speaker, Andy," he told his friend and coworker.

"Hunter, our guy in the pit can't be Don Blake," Andy told him. "Same approximate height and weight, but not Don. No match on dental work. And another reason it couldn't have been Don—Adler estimates the body was deep in that pit for a week to ten days. And something was different—this guy was shoved deep into the pit. He didn't die the way the others did. He was stabbed straight through the heart."

"Stabbed?" Amy repeated.

"Stabbed with precision," Andy said. "They've dug through that place for hours and hours now. They haven't found the weapon. And thankfully, they only found the one body."

"All right, then, thanks. We're going to take a cruise by the hospital to see Carey, and then interview Loretta Peterson and Brenda Hayes. Just leaving Barrington Advertising now."

"Anything?" Andy asked hopefully.

"Not yet. We're coming back tomorrow. We'll keep in touch."

He ended the call and looked at Amy. "Well, now we can tell Carey that while we haven't found Don, we can still hope he's all right."

Amy smiled and said quietly, "I know we work the case, what's needed for the case, and we can't let emotion into it—"

"Can't say I really agree with that mantra. Sometimes, emotion is good," he told her. "Amy, it's okay for you to like Carey, and you don't want to cause more pain to a traumatized woman if you don't have to. Seriously. We've both been at this for a while now. We're doing all right. Okay, mostly. Even if you did fall asleep on me last night."

"Oh! Well, you could have woken me up."

"Too cruel. Not even I am that cruel," he teased. He grasped her hand as they continued walking to the car. "See, I know there will be more nights to come."

She laughed. "And days. You know, days when we're looking out at and playing in beautiful semitropical waters—and then plowing into dark, mucky pits."

"Well, sure. There is that."

She grinned. "Let's get to Carey! We still have a long afternoon ahead of us."

They'd reached the car. He realized he was still smiling. This case was intense—just as the two that had come before it. But there was something about this partnership that was amazing. They could both accept it. The work. Neither of them could do anything else. And while that would probably ruin many an outside relationship, for them it strengthened everything.

Amy knew where he came from. She understood the darkness that had haunted his childhood. She knew him, as few people ever would. She accepted everything about him.

His phone rang again as he geared up the car. It was his supervising director, Charles Garza, and Hunter quickly informed him they were playing it safe.

They'd find an agent sitting outside Carey's hospital room. Local police had watched over the floor when she'd first gone in. But as it appeared she was no longer in danger, the watch had been curtailed.

Andy Mason decided they needed to keep an eye on their one living victim.

"Maybe it's overcautious, but this thing is huge, and we need an ending," Charles Garza said.

"I don't think it's being overcautious at all," Hunter quickly informed him. "Amy and I are on our way there now. She is allowed visitors, and we understand the friend who reported her missing is with her now."

"I don't care who it is. We need to keep an eye on her."

"Agreed," Hunter said.

They ended the call. Amy was nodding; he hadn't put the phone on speaker mode, but she had apparently heard or understood what was being said.

"Not a bad idea at all," she murmured. "Though Hayden is with her—"

"And no one—no one—is above suspicion at this time," Hunter said.

Amy nodded. "Right. Agreed. But I wonder if there is anything else either she or Hayden might be able to tell us. According to Milly, Don Blake was…well, out of Carey's league. But he was eager to go with her when it was a physical adventure. Physical as in sporting, not as in…"

Hunter laughed. "Not as in sex."

"Right. So, maybe they know what kind of thing Don was into. If he thought Carey had just taken off on him, where might he have gone?"

"I don't know and, as to most of this…we don't really know for sure about much of anything yet. Maybe."

"There are probably more important things to get to, but—"

"We started early—we go to the hospital, and Loretta Peterson is next on the list and then Brenda Hayes."

"Unless we find out something new from Carey or Hayden."

Hunter nodded. "Eventually, it all has to be done."

"Uh-huh—but we could find Don Blake, right?"

Hunter shrugged. "If he chooses to be found."

"You think he's in on all this—whatever this is?"

Hunter was silent a minute. "The rider on the black horse carries scales. I can't help but think this has to do with weighing a person's sins."

"From the way Milly talked, Don Blake did a lot more sinning than Carey."

"There are so many sins…seven deadly ones. Lust, gluttony, greed, sloth, wrath, envy, and pride."

"Well, I guess Don Blake might fall into lust or pride or

maybe even greed. But where would Carey fall? If she didn't happen to be an accidental victim—and if this theory holds truth at all?"

"Carey, huh. Hmm. None. Unless her crush on Don could be seen as lust. And you're right—I may be way off base. Anyway, here we are. We check in with Carey and we move on."

"Gotcha!" Amy said.

At the hospital, they found a young officer—in uniform—seated before the door. He appeared to be barely out of college, a good-looking kid with a crop of light brown hair and bright green eyes. But he rose as they approached, giving them a nod and a slight frown while he waited for them to state their business there. They produced their credentials and the officer smiled. "Hey, you're the guys who cracked this thing. Thanks—our list of missing persons in the county was getting out of hand."

"We haven't actually cracked anything," Amy said. "I'm afraid we found your people, but not in the way we would have wished to have found them."

"Of course not, and I'm sorry. I'm Josh Bentley," the officer said. "I'm hoping to make detective one day, and I think it's amazing you got here in the afternoon and made a major discovery on this many cases in just a couple of hours. Sorry again—all city and county police around here are talking about you. In a good way! And we are all ready to help with whatever you need, on duty or off. Just say the word."

"Thank you. When we're all working together, that's always the best," Amy said politely. "We need local help, for sure."

"What's gone on here today—anything?" Hunter asked.

"I called it in when the woman visiting arrived. I was given the go-ahead to let her in, but I spent a large part of the first hour or so going in and out, just to check on Carey. But it seems these two are good friends. Hayden cried and Carey cried and they hugged and…now, they're just sitting together, watching television, talking."

"Thank you," Amy told him. "We're not going to be long."

"I will be here. I don't even take a break for the john until my replacement comes on," Bentley assured them.

"Okay, then. You can feel free to take a break for the next fifteen minutes. We won't leave until you're back," Hunter said.

"Really? Maybe I will get some coffee."

"Go right ahead," Amy told him.

He smiled, lifted a hand and started down the hall. Amy and Hunter entered Carey's room. Carey was sitting up in her hospital bed. Hayden was seated in a chair next to her, and the two of them were watching a sitcom together.

But Carey looked anxiously to the door as they entered, then brightened and smiled as they came to stand by the bed and greet both women.

"Thank you so much for coming," Carey said.

Her eyes were bright today; her coloring was good. She'd probably be released from the hospital soon.

"I told you I'd report every day," Amy said softly. She grimaced. "I wish I had good news. We're looking everywhere, and teams of police and FBI are searching phone records, credit cards, traffic cams—you name it. We will find Don."

"Not if…" Hayden began, but she saw the way Carey looked at her and she quickly added, "Not if he did just take off for some strange reason."

"You meant, not if he's in a mud pit in the back of the caves," Carey said.

"Okay," Hunter told her. "He's not in the mud pits in the caves. Forensic teams have gone through the entire web of a national erosion system there and Don has not been found."

"So, we remain hopeful," Amy said.

"Of course, of course," Carey murmured. "I just can't... I was finally out with him. And now...this. Do you think..."

"Carey, he would never have left you there on purpose," Amy said.

"But if he didn't—" Carey said.

"Maybe he's in hiding. Maybe he saw whoever was luring people into the caves or dragging them there from elsewhere and dumping them. And he's hiding. The thing is, Carey," Hunter said, "at this time, we just don't know."

"Right," Carey said. "And thank you. Thank you for coming, and for being honest with me."

"Hey, I've been here all day!" Hayden reminded her.

"And I am so grateful!" Carey said. "But! You were saying you wanted to go to the real coffee bar downstairs and get something," she told Hayden. "We joked about just how bad the coffee is—well, you know. Hospital food and all. Nutritious, but..."

"Not the best!" Hayden said, wrinkling her nose.

"Go get coffee," Amy told her. "We'll stay until you get back."

"Oh. Uh, you sure? I mean, I'm not sleeping here or anything. I'll leave when visitor hours are over, and I can wait until then," Hayden said.

"We're here—go," Amy said, giving the woman an encouraging smile.

"I—uh, okay! Can I get you anything?"

"Me. Just a good, normal coffee, black," Carey told her.

"We're fine, we grab things on the go all the time," Hunter said.

"Okay, then. Decent black coffee for Carey," Hayden said. "I will be right back."

She left the room, and Amy took Carey's hand. "Seriously, how are you doing?" she asked gently.

"I'm okay. I think they're going to let me go tomorrow. They're just watching and counting electrolyte levels or something today. Physically, I'm… My numbers are a little bit up, but fine."

"That's great. But you will see a therapist, right?" Hunter asked.

"Everyone says I should," Carey said with a sigh. "So, I guess I should. Mr. Barrington highly recommends it. And he's the boss, so…"

"Hey, is he really as great a boss as he appears to be?" Amy asked.

"Sure. He owns the company and he treats us all great. We go through all kinds of interviews before we're hired. He wants loyalty, but he gives it in return. The same with respect. My job is great. I love it."

"That's nice. Super," Amy murmured. "So. How did you wind up getting Don to go with you to the caves? We heard he…"

"That he's a player," Hunter said flatly.

Carey grinned. "I found out he's an outdoors man. Oh! If you open that side drawer, I did a really—really—bad map. It has some of the hiking trails we talked about—and some of the more adventurous climbs. I'm a hiker, not a climber, but we talked about intimate places people go with picnic lunches, where camping is nice and allowed, and… I talked him into the caves." She frowned. "I was bored, playing around, but take that picture. I don't know how or why he would have wandered off, but I kept thinking about places we'd talked about and maybe…" She shook her head, looking sad and worried again.

"Carey, like we told you before, any little thing may help.

We'll take your drawing, and it just might help us. At the least, we'll check out the places you have marked," Hunter said, opening the little bedside cabinet drawer and seeing the drawing Carey had created.

She wasn't that bad. The drawing was crude, yes, but surprisingly clear as it marked out water, land, cliffs, valleys, camping sites, and ranger stations.

"This is great, thank you," Amy said, looking over Hunter's shoulder.

"Well, I'll be sending you on a beautiful trip, anyway," Carey said dryly. She shook her head. "I should just be grateful, and believe me, I am! I am so grateful to be alive, and I could never thank you enough. But I can't help but be so worried!"

"And that's understandable," Amy said. "But we won't stop. We will do everything in our power to find him, I promise you."

"Thank you," Carey whispered.

The door to her room opened; Hayden was back. Hunter looked at Amy and inclined his head. She nodded.

"Coffee for my sister from another mister!" Hayden announced.

"Perfect. We'll get back to work," Hunter said.

"And we will talk to you tomorrow," Amy assured her.

"We've been watching reruns of *The Golden Girls*," Hayden said. "So sad, they're all gone now, but that Betty White, she was so amazing! And it's still so fun to watch."

"Great show," Amy agreed. "So, we're gone!"

She waved and walked out the door. Hunter followed her. She had paused to speak to Officer Bentley who had made good use of his break and also held a cup of coffee.

"Call on me for anything, day or night, on duty or off!" Bentley said.

They thanked him and headed out. Hunter had folded Carey's drawing and stuffed it in his jacket pocket; he withdrew it and handed it to Amy.

"Who knows?" he asked.

"I'm all into hiking and the wilderness," she said. "But are we—"

"Oh, we are. I'm truly curious to see what Loretta Peterson has to say about her ex."

Amy glanced at her watch. "Well, still fairly early. We'll have light left if we don't spend too long with her—"

"And then Brenda Hayes."

"Right."

"Amy, come on, you know this won't be solved overnight; but every step we take will bring us closer."

"And of course..."

"Of course?"

"He probably is dead."

"Or in on it."

"Well, next up is Loretta Peterson," Amy said. She shook her head. "Barrington seems to think Don Blake is a good guy. Milly seems to think he's a player."

"And he could be both. It doesn't sound like he was committed to anyone, and there is no law against being charming and dating a lot of women."

He could see Amy was grinning.

"A charming player who could be part of a serial killer ring. Sounds great!"

"Well, it's all speculative now."

She shook her head. "I can't help but think that getting out and seeing some of these places Carey has drawn may be helpful. I mean, if he is in on it and hiding out for the moment, we could find him. That is possible. Especially if we bring in rangers and police who know the area."

"And we will do that. Right now… There's the turn. And watch for the house number… There. It's time to speak with Loretta Peterson."

The home was an attractive suburban ranch-style dwelling with a well-manicured lawn and fresh paint. There was a semicircle drive with a navy SUV parked in front.

Hunter pulled behind and they got out of the car.

"What are you thinking?" Hunter asked Amy as she surveyed the place.

"I was hoping his kids aren't here," she said. "I know we're supposed to be professional and speak what's necessary, but finding out your dad died in a pit…"

"It's never easy. Even exes have feelings," Hunter said.

But before they even reached the door, it was flung open. A slim attractive woman—as neatly put together as her house and yard—stepped out onto the porch.

"If you want to know if I know anything about what my ex-husband was doing, I don't," she said flatly. "And if you want to know if I'm sorry he's dead—I'm damned sorry I'm not! Oh, I didn't kill him, I swear it. I just can't be too sorry the cheating bastard is dead!"

5

The woman wasn't a murderer, Amy thought as she sat at Loretta's kitchen table a few minutes later. Hunter had indicated they should agree to coffee, and at this point of the day, coffee seemed like a good idea.

It was obvious the woman was truly bitter regarding her ex-husband. That she wasn't really glad he was dead was also obvious. She was torn. He'd done horrible things to her; but he was her children's father, and she hurt for their offspring.

"What was the problem, exactly?" Amy asked her gently.

Hands flat on the table, Loretta let out a long sigh, staring at nothing. "I guess I hate myself as much," she murmured. "He was a cheater throughout our marriage, but I was too blind to see it—or I didn't want to see it. But he stayed with me. Maybe for the kids, or maybe he was already working on long-range planning. You see, I'm an only child. My parents were extremely wealthy—and when they died, well, that made me a wealthy woman. He slipped up and left his cell phone on the bed just after answering a text, so there was no passcode necessary to see what he was doing. I didn't start out trying to pry, but the first line was *I can't wait to see you naked again. Soon, every night of our lives!* And so, I looked at the rest of the texts and found out he'd been waiting—waiting like a vulture—for my parents to die so he could sink his hands into their money! It was everything I could do not to betray myself to him, but I got out of the house, ran to the bank, and tied up all the money in trust for my children. He didn't know. He thought he was still sitting on a pile of money, and he filed for divorce. Oh, ironically even sending me a text to tell me what he was doing! I texted back he could never come back to the house. I had his things packed up and ready to go, found a lawyer, and countersued. Of course, he wanted to come back to the house—God knows what he had where. So I arranged for a friend to be here when he came. I haven't seen or heard from him except through our attorneys in months now. Eight months to be exact. And I shouldn't wish anyone was dead. I'm religious enough to think God might smite me for that—but he hurt me so, so badly. And I hate myself for being stupid, or so needy I tried to be blind, convincing myself we'd been together for years and years."

She stopped talking, winced, and looked at Amy and then Hunter.

Amy set her hand on Loretta's where it lay on the table. "Loretta, don't be so hard on yourself. It's a good quality to see the best in others. And none of us ever wants to believe someone is seeing someone else. We are human, and you are human."

"I try," she murmured. "I just wish… I don't know. I believe the children saw him a few months ago. I was better with them—I swear. I think it's the worst thing in the world for one parent to degrade another in front of the children—because no matter what the problem, that person being denigrated is still a parent. Am I making sense?"

"Perfect sense. And again, Loretta, that's a truly fine way to make the best life for your kids."

"Loretta, we will find out who did this and hopefully bring closure to your children and to you. Do you know who he was sending the texts to?" Hunter asked.

"I do. Jasmine Drew. I don't know her well—I was told by a mutual friend he met her at a strip club, so I am assuming she's far sexier than I am."

"Do you know where she worked?"

"Fanny's Fancy Females," Loretta said. She let out a long sigh again. "I wanted him to find out he'd stayed with me all those years for nothing. I wanted him to realize when we were done with all the attorneys, he'd be dead broke. I didn't want him to be dead! I wanted him to hurt in something like the way he'd hurt me—not by dying slowly in misery in a mud pit!"

"Your children have been informed?" Amy asked softly.

She nodded. "They've known he's been missing, of course. They're hurting, but when they didn't hear from him…they knew something was very wrong. They're brokenhearted, but I'd convinced them into going back to school and now… well, they'll be home, and I'll make funeral arrangements with them and help them find out when the medical examiner will release the body."

"Of course." Hunter handed her a card. "Please, we will need to speak with them, and if you think of anything, any little detail that might be helpful, let us know."

"Right," Loretta said. She smiled bitterly. "I will call you and let you know when Ted and Candy get here. And I know they will be eager to help in any way. But you might do better talking to Jasmine Drew."

"Oh, we will talk to her," Hunter assured her.

"What about work?" Amy said.

"He had friends at the college, of course. We attended teas and things like that through the years. He was in the History Department. I don't know if they can help you, but a number of people in his department knew him fairly well. I wouldn't know who to say exactly, but if you just speak with the dean, I'm sure he can tell you more."

"We will follow up with everything," Amy assured her.

Loretta managed something of a smile. "Thank you," she told Amy. "You made me feel...a little better about myself."

"Good. Because his death is certainly not your fault. We can never hate ourselves for feeling pain when we've been betrayed. I'm hoping the very best for you and your children."

"Thank you," Loretta whispered.

"And thank you for the coffee," Hunter said.

The woman managed a real smile. "I do brew a great cup of coffee!"

"That you do," Amy agreed. She and Hunter rose. Loretta saw them through the house to the front door and waved.

"Am I driving?" Hunter asked.

"You are. Something about that name..."

Amy had her cell phone out and pulled up her email. She looked at one of the lists Andy Mason had provided for them, and then quickly looked over at Hunter.

"We're not going to find Jasmine Drew—not at Fanny's Fancy Females, anyway."

"Oh?"

"I believe she's on this list. Not as Jasmine, but as Jennifer. Jennifer Drew. And she was reported missing by her boss— Thomas Mallery of Fanny's Fancy Females. She has been noted as missing… She's down as having been gone at about the same time as Gavin Peterson."

"Two sinners," Hunter said, glancing briefly at Amy. "Two sinners—guilty of lust."

Brenda Hayes greeted them at the door to the row townhouse she had shared with Estelle Benedict. She was composed, but her face was drawn and weary, as if she had spent a great deal of time crying in the last hours. In her midthirties, she had straight shoulder-length dark hair and, in contrast, bright green eyes. She had evidently been having an "at-home" day, but even so, the velour sweats she was wearing somehow appeared almost tailored on her.

"Please, come in. I—I'm sorry, forgive me, I'm still trying to accept…to believe. And yet I knew in my heart Estelle was gone. We… Well, she was the love of my life," she said flatly, eyeing them, as if waiting for judgment.

"I am so, so sorry!" Amy said. "I wish so badly there was something I could say that would comfort you—but she is gone, and the best that we can offer anyone is our determination to see her killers face justice."

Brenda nodded. She was going to cry again.

"I'm sorry!" she whispered.

"No, no, it's all right," Hunter assured her, giving her a gentle pat on the shoulder. "It's all right."

After a minute, Brenda composed herself. She swept out an arm, indicating they should come in.

The parlor of the little townhouse was charming with a comfortable sectional sofa taking up the front corner of the room, a mantel filled with pictures to the left, and an amazingly large television screen facing the seating.

"A beautiful home," Amy murmured.

"Thank you! It was… Now…it's just empty," Brenda whispered. "We bought that mammoth television screen during COVID. We both worked a lot from home. Oh, that's how we met. I don't know what you know, but I'm a bonds attorney, too. Well, I wasn't going into politics—I personally hate politics. *Politician* might be synonymous with *liar*. Except for Estelle! She was so good. We all know there are issues involving color, race, religion—and sexual identification. Estelle never denied her preference, but it wasn't something she harped on. Oh, she'd speak up. She was an absolute believer that all men and women are created absolutely equal. But in that vein, she was focused on American medical benefits, social security, and immigration. And usually..." she said, pausing to wince, "even Estelle's so-called political enemies admired and respected her. It's hard to hate someone who refuses to hate in return, who searches and finds an answer to every question, who..." She paused, shaking her head again.

"You reported her missing, right?" Hunter asked quietly.

"I did. It took me a while to get the police to write a report. She had gone into her office. I knew the minute she didn't come home after work that something was wrong, horribly wrong. But she's an adult, and I'm not blaming the police, but they had to wait so long to file a report. Then others from her office began calling them and pretty soon, we all knew she was missing. The detective on her case believed—and still believes, if I'm not mistaken—that a political rival killer her or had her killed or had something to do with her disappearance."

"But you don't believe that?" Amy asked quietly.

"I told you. Estelle had a way about her. We'd be an amazing country if every person up in Congress was like her. She *listened* to others. She never resorted to name-calling. She could come up with a compromise on any issue."

"I would have loved to have known her!" Amy said, rising

and walking over to the mantel. Estelle had been blond with dark eyes, almost in perfect contrast to Brenda Hayes. The mantel held numerous pictures of the two of them together, on a beach, at Red Rocks, and at what appeared to be a food bank where they were dishing out plates of food side by side.

"It couldn't have been a political enemy, right?" Brenda asked. "They—they found her in a pit with other bodies...lots of other bodies. What would that have to do with politics?"

"We don't think—" Amy began.

"We are just beginning our investigation," Hunter interrupted quietly. "But please rest assured this is a number one case. Police and agents from the local and federal levels are on this. We will investigate every possible angle."

Brenda looked at Amy and said, "It's my fault. Our fault. For being...what we are."

"We don't know that to be true at all," Amy said. She took a deep breath, looking at Hunter before continuing. "Only ignorant people hurt others for reasons having to do with a person's personal choices, or with their color or ethnicity or any other reason."

"And those people do exist? Why? Why do they care what others do in their own homes?" she whispered. "We never forced anything on anyone else! We even... Oh, we barely touched each other anywhere that was public, because people do judge and they can be hateful."

"Brenda, I..."

"We know that," Hunter said. "But remember, we are investigating every possible angle. Do you have family? Is there anyone who can be with you and help you get through this?"

She nodded, smiling with wet eyes. "My brother is coming. He loved Estelle, too. He would volunteer anytime she needed him. She would have... She would have changed the world. She was so full of both love and reason and..."

Hunter handed her a business card. "Both our numbers are on that. If you can think of anything helpful, please let us know. Or if you just need us, please call."

"You two are...good," Brenda said, trying to offer a smile. "Thank you. And I—I will be all right, and if I can think of anything that might help..."

"Did she receive any threats?" Amy asked her.

"Not that I know about. I'm telling you, not even rivals or so-called enemies hated her—she was that good," Brenda said. "Why? Why would anyone do anything like this? To Estelle—to anyone!"

"We will do our best to find out," Amy murmured.

Brenda nodded again and walked with them to the door. When they stepped out, they thanked her. She thanked them again.

As they drove away, Hunter slowed the car and looked back. Amy turned to do the same.

Another car had driven up to the townhouse. A man got out. The door to the house opened and Brenda Hayes rushed out and hugged the man.

"Her brother. I'm glad he got here," Hunter murmured.

"I am, too. Brenda is devastated. And it's so tragic. Estelle sounds as if she was an incredible person and would have done wonderful things in the future."

"I agree."

"You're not going to say Estelle sounds so good that we should worry?"

"I'm not always cynical," Hunter said. "There was something about Brenda's words that rang true. She didn't gush. She never searched for words. Of course, as much as she impressed me, I could be wrong. I just doubt it in this case. Also, Estelle was a victim. And I sure as hell don't see Brenda as someone who would be mixed up in whatever this is. Then again, though this is just about the longest damn day ever, we've only just begun. So. Now we should—"

"Head out and start searching the areas Carey drew up for us. Call Andy, get the reports to him on what little we've discovered and find out what he might have found out—or if anyone else working on this has reported in."

He arched a brow to her and looked at his watch.

"So far we've been to the morgue, to Barrington Advertising, to see the loved ones of two victims, and now—"

"You know you're ready to keep going," she said. "I know you. You're trying to be reasonable, but you want to keep going as much as I do."

"Yeah, well, yeah. I guess we can eat one meal a day. If we stop for food, we'll lose a ton of daylight."

"Loretta Peterson really did brew great coffee. I drank a lot of it. I'm fine. But we can do drive-through burgers."

"Drive-through burgers it is. I'll find something quickly. Once we head out to some of these areas Carey put down for us, there's not much food to be found."

"We're heading almost an hour out of the city—and to the best of my knowledge, some areas close at dusk."

Hunter glanced her way quickly, his expression dry.

"I don't think Don Blake cares about the rules if he is hiding there. And there's so much wilderness, all the forested area is not under any kind of park control," Hunter said. "Study the map. And once we hit the area, give me an idea of the closest road to complete nothing. There are still some old shacks around. If Blake is alive and hiding, that might be just what he'd see as a perfect place. And call Andy, please. Tell him what we're doing. We'll see if we can get some help, though most likely others would want to start first thing in the morning."

"I will call Andy. I don't know why, Hunter, but I feel it's incredibly important we move as quickly as possible on this. And whatever we cover with the daylight we have left, we won't have to cover tomorrow."

"Wow. Good point," Hunter murmured dryly. "Call Andy. And after that—"

"I'm bringing up a map on Google," Amy quickly assured him.

"I have been here before," Hunter murmured.

"What?"

"I have been in this exact area before. I can't believe I didn't realize—or remember—that until now."

"You were here when you worked with Andy before?"

He nodded. "We prowled the area where we're headed looking for a kidnap victim."

"And?"

"We were lucky. We found him."

"You still want a map? Or you have an idea."

"A few. There's an old cabin up one of the trails, and it leads to a wide, level area—a plateau. There's an old tower there, too. I believe hunters once used it. And the land isn't part of any federal program."

"Is the cabin on any map?"

"Maybe not. Okay, google old cabins in this area. I'm pretty sure ownership is outlawed now, but the structures were never torn down. They were just left to decay and fall to ruin."

"Okay..."

She called Andy first; he would send reinforcements immediately—even if they'd only have an hour or so of light left by the time they got there.

Hunter found a fast-food drive-through, and they ate while he drove. He was surprisingly good at it, Amy thought, somewhat amused at his agility to down a burger and keep his eyes on the road and his hands on the wheel.

But then again, neither of them ever had normal working hours.

Hunter knew the place better than he had remembered. He found the highest point on a dirt road where he could park the car, and then he showed Amy a trail she would have never found on her own because the forest here was heavy.

"Spruces," he told her. "All kinds. Thick and heavy and hiding many a secret, I imagine."

They climbed together with Hunter in the lead. He glanced back at her.

"How are you doing, flatlander?"

"Younger than you," she reminded him, even if it was only by a few years. "You having trouble old man? Thirties—I think we're supposed to be fit and prime for a while yet!"

"I have never argued that. You are absolutely prime," he teased.

But a minute later, he held up. Glancing at his watch and looking to the sky, he shook his head. "The cabin is that way. The tower and the plateau are that way."

"So, we split up. You go right, I'll go left."

"Amy, call for backup if—"

"If I see anything at all, you will know," she promised. "And I may be the better shot between the two of us."

"You may be good, but—"

"But?"

"I really am a crack shot."

"That doesn't mean I'm not."

He laughed. "Okay, okay. I know how capable you are. But call—"

"And you do the same!"

"Of course."

Amy looked at the sky. The night was coming quickly.

"Maybe I am crazy," she murmured.

"You are, but that's okay. You're crazy in a good way. You're following your instincts. And we're all a little crazy. But hopefully in a good way."

"I like that reasoning," she told him.

He grabbed her and pulled her close, kissed her briefly, then let her go. She smiled as she watched him turn toward the left.

And she turned to the right.

What he had said about the trees was true; they were plentiful with heavy branches. She walked along, searching the ground and the branches, trying to see if anything offered her the suggestion someone had been by recently. And even searching for signs as she was and despite the coming darkness, she knew why people loved Colorado so much—it was beautiful here.

The air was fresh and clear, the scent of the spruces was mild and pleasant. The light breeze that moved around her helped create an aura of peace and nature's majesty.

The few remnants of daylight that had been left were drifting away, but to Amy's surprise, it didn't grow extremely dark. And she realized it was because a full moon was rising even as the sun was falling, and it cast a strange glow down upon the ground. Shadows remained; the darkness of the trees remained. But she could see ahead of her, and she could see the tower Hunter had talked about or the remains of what had been a tower.

She was almost there where she paused, dead still for a minute, listening.

Then she knew that she was right; she was hearing voices.

Hikers? Out this late while the night was coming on? Teenagers seeking absolute privacy? A drug deal? Or...

She moved carefully forward, realizing she was almost at the plateau, a place where the trees stopped growing because it was solid rock.

And there were people there. At first, she couldn't see how many. They talked among themselves but she couldn't make out the words.

She moved closer and closer against a giant spruce, letting the great arms of the tree shelter her from sight.

They looked like…

An odd assortment of normal people. Dressed for a climb. She saw an older woman clearly in the moonlight, and then she saw a young couple with a child—a boy—about ten years old.

Amy stepped back and pulled out her cell, calling Hunter and whispering to him what she was seeing. He was coming. He was on his way, but they were in opposite directions. She needed to keep hidden and observe until she had backup.

There were more people coming now, just dark shapes in the moonlight. They seemed to rise from a sloping trail on the other side of the plateau.

She watched as the figures gathered around a flattened rock that seemed to be just about in the center of the area. Worn by weather, the rock itself seemed to glisten in the moonlight.

A man stepped forward and lifted his hands; the others bowed in reverence.

Apparently, he was their leader, their priest, their shaman, their messiah. When he had received that honor due him, he began speaking. "We are gathered here—and you are the blessed ones, the ones with ears to hear the message, with hearts to understand. Hallelujah!"

"Hallelujah!" his flock responded.

So far, the group appeared…

Just like any group going to church or a temple.

Appearances could be deceiving.

And while this group looked different, she had seen such an event before, and it had been terrifying and horrible…no matter how "nor-

mal" these people, or even the leader, appeared to be. No, the leader wasn't wearing a dark-hooded cloak or vestments of any kind but rather a white jacket that appeared more like something a doctor might wear.

She tried to count the people flocking around him. They were all in different forms of dress as well—mostly jeans or khakis and sweaters or jackets. They were both sexes and appeared to be many ages, from the older woman to the young boy.

She glanced around from the cover of her giant spruce tree, but she couldn't see Hunter. He was on his way, and she knew he would move swiftly. She didn't want to call him again; she was afraid any noise she made might draw attention to her. But her cell phone camera was silent, so she began to take pictures but then stopped to watch what was coming next. A group of men were carrying a plank carefully up the steep slope that led to the mountain plateau.

And there was a woman on the plank.

She wasn't moving. She was covered in a white shirt. The moonlight caught her hair; it was blond and long and drifting around the plank.

Amy strained to hear the words of the leader who had raised his hands and was speaking to his "flock."

"Sometimes, it must be blood that is fed to the earth. Sometimes, the sin is great. Life on this earth means nothing for the great beauty of the true life to come which lies ahead, yet it is open only to those who are cleansed. Some need to reflect on their sins as life slowly seeps away. And yet there are those who may perhaps earn their way to Nirvana by giving their life's blood to the earth. For the earth is that which must care for us, the caretakers of others. And in serving the true Power, we must care for ourselves, while granting that those who might not know or see the truth, absolution is within their death. This I say verily."

"And so, we hear, verily!" the crowd called out.

The man moved his white coat aside and drew from it a massive knife. It gleamed under the glow of the full moon that had risen as the group had gathered there. "I cleanse thee of thy sins with blood so that your soul may rise to the Heavens!"

There was no choice. The woman on the plank was about to die.

Amy drew her weapon and she fired. And while she hadn't wanted to kill the man, an unbidden thought came to her mind.

I cleanse you of your sins, you murdering bastard!

6

Hunter heard the first shot when he was still about a hundred yards from what he believed to be Amy's position.

Seconds later, he heard a barrage of gunfire.

But he had moved swiftly, and he was relieved to see Amy was fine. She had taken up a perfect position, protected by the heavy trunks and branches of a few giant spruces in an area of scattered, high rocks that edged the flatness of the plateau.

As he reached her, the gunfire stopped as abruptly as it had started.

Amy turned to Hunter quickly.

"I fired the first shot. They were going to kill her," Amy told him.

"Who?"

"The woman… Look on that plank on the big rock there. I need to get to her. They left her…thank God. But they shot back in seconds while they were running away. They've scattered now. They took off, some into the trees that way…" She paused and pointed across the plateau. "And some down the trail that leads to the other side…or somewhere. But they're gone. Hunter, I think she's alive. Drugged or something, but alive, we've got to get to her—"

He nodded, understanding her urgency, but he had been an agent long enough to know someone could still be waiting for a chance to get a shot that might mean something.

"Slow down, move out slowly. You get to her, I'll cover you!"

He was watchful, moving ahead of her and toward the trees and trail to the left. The right edge of the plateau was clearly visible in the moonlight, and there was no place there to shield a shooter.

But moving carefully, shielding Amy as she reached the woman, he met with no resistance. Whoever had been there—the shooters—had fled. Still watchful and wary, he headed back toward Amy just as he felt his phone vibrating.

It was Andy, calling from headquarters to assure them an FBI SWAT team was heading up to meet them. Hunter quickly informed Andy of what had occurred, and Andy in turn warned the team to take it slow until their backup arrived.

"These guys know the terrain, Hunter. I know you do, too, but…remember, they're good at what they do."

A sharp, piercing scream sounded—almost louder than gunfire in the strange moonlit night. He saw the young woman on the plank was now conscious, and Amy was trying to calm her and assure her she'd be all right. He was torn between searching for the scattered shooters, watching over the young woman, and making sure Amy wasn't put in jeopardy while doing her duty to protect the would-be victim.

But he didn't have to remain torn; he saw the team Andy

had sent out had arrived. Five men and a woman in SWAT gear had arrived with weapons drawn as they moved carefully toward the plateau. The group knew the terrain and was probably extremely well trained.

Hunter lifted a hand in greeting. One of the men moved toward him, quickly introducing himself as Ben Crandon, head of the team.

"I arrived as the gunfire ended," Hunter informed him. "Special Agent Larson was watching a rite that was taking place when the girl on the plank was brought out. Special Agent Larson fired when the leader was going to plunge a knife into the girl's heart. Several of the *flock* had to be armed—her shot brought out a barrage of gunfire and then the group fled."

Amy was still standing by the plank, her arms around the young woman whose shrieking had turned to a torrent of sobbing.

Amy looked at him a little helplessly.

"She was about to be stabbed through the heart," Amy explained and turned to the woman. "It's all right. You're safe now. We're law enforcement. Please, you're all right! I'm Amy, this is my partner, Hunter, and these others are with the FBI. You're safe. I promise I won't leave you."

"Thank you, thank you..." the girl murmured. "I'm Magda, um, Magda Kenward. "I'm... Oh, my God! I heard them when I was taken...hit with whatever that shot was. They were going to...cut out my heart and drink my blood. Oh, my God, oh, my God, oh..."

"Magda, you're all right now. We're here." She looked back at the others. "I had to fire at their leader. And I know I hit him center of the chest, but..." She shook her head, looking at Hunter completely perplexed. "He's gone. His body is gone."

"You're sure you hit him?" one of the team asked her doubtfully.

"Amy is a crack shot," Hunter informed him.

"I hit him. Dead center in the chest. I couldn't shout out a warning, and I couldn't fire a warning shot—he was seconds away from killing this poor girl."

"If he's dead...where is he?" Crandon was frowning, not wanting to doubt Amy, but there was no body on the plateau.

"They must have grabbed his body!" one of Crandon's people said. "Look—there's blood all over the rock there."

"So, the leader was shot and is most likely dead, but they couldn't let his body be found. Carrying that weight, it's not easy to navigate this terrain. They can't all have disappeared. Some might have made it to the road, but if others slid back into the foliage," Hunter said, "we've got to get moving and find anyone we can."

Crandon nodded, quickly giving orders to his team, but Hunter stopped him, telling him, "I want to stay on this here. I need one of your team as protection detail. We need to get this young woman down and to a hospital, and Special Agent Larson needs to stay with her at this point."

"Right. Driscoll! Take the first car—get this woman to the hospital with Special Agent Larson."

"On it!" the man named Driscoll said and turned to Amy.

Amy glanced at Hunter, giving him a wince and a nod. Yes, she wanted to stay with the young woman.

"Come on, come on, we're going to get you to safety," Amy said gently. "Magda, we're going to get you to a hospital. And this is Special Agent—"

"Toby. Toby Driscoll," the man said.

"Thank you," the young woman murmured. "I can't stop shaking. I..."

She looked as if she were going to fall. Amy caught her and the girl leaned on her.

Driscoll looked at Amy, arching a brow to make his words as much a question as they were a statement. "I'll take point?"

"And two of us will take the offshoots of the straight trail down," Crandon said, nodding to Hunter. "The rest of you, fan out, down the trail, back into the brush! Special Agent Forrest?"

"Into the brush," Hunter said.

They all moved. The victim's safety had, of course, been the first order of business. Now they needed to move.

Amy supported Magda Kenward. Driscoll was in front of her. The man was wearing a bulletproof vest. Hunter noted Driscoll took up the position of scout and protector in good form.

As they walked away, Amy suddenly turned back.

"Hunter!"

"Yeah?"

"There was one kid, maybe more, in the group! I saw a boy of about ten."

He nodded to her. "Gotcha!" he said quietly, turning to look at Crandon and the others.

They all nodded. It was good to know. They wouldn't be surprised by a child in the line of fire, and they wouldn't want to risk the life of a child—especially if a parent used that child as a shield. Being forewarned was being forearmed.

Even if the parents had armed the child.

Amy nodded and headed away with Driscoll and the young woman who had been intended as a sacrifice. Hunter nodded to Crandon who spoke to his team. "We move! Stay on earphones and mics and—Agent Forrest! Set up with us, I've got an extra set—"

"That's great. Thank you. Communication may be the key here," Hunter said, gratefully accepting the tiny mic and earphones that could keep him in contact with the others.

Then he nodded to Crandon and started down the trail that led down the cliffs to the opposite side.

They had returned gunfire, but ineffectually. Hunter believed some members of the "flock" were armed, but not necessarily well trained.

Someone out there was, however. Someone had thought to take the body of their leader. Someone who had an agenda.

He moved carefully, staying within the trees. And while he was sure Amy had hit and killed a man, he thought there had to be someone else in charge of the "flock" since they had been savvy enough to pick up the body and see it wasn't left at the scene.

The moon was amazing tonight, casting down a light that was generous yet soft, allowing for both illumination and shadow. The spruce trees that so richly carpeted the hills and cliffs in the area seemed to glow with a soft emerald sheen.

Colorado was truly beautiful. It offered crystal waters, rushing brooks, the richness of the trees, the sweet scent of the earth. It was pristine here; by day, it was a hiker's paradise.

And yet now...

He heard a shuffle in the trees ahead and held himself dead still as he listened.

The shuffle came again.

And then whispering. Muffled.

Then words he heard clearly.

"I'm scared!"

Hunter judged the whisperers had to be close—very close—for him to hear them. He heard the slightest rustling, a sound that could have been a bobcat or even an owl moving in the night.

Except now, it wasn't. The sound came from just a few feet to his left, deep in the cover of the spruce. Very carefully, he moved in that direction. He didn't want to startle whoever was there and cause them to shoot wildly.

And he kept hearing an echo of the words he'd understood—*I'm scared.*

Adults could be scared, too, but Amy had said there were kids in the group. He was almost certain there was a kid in the spruce ahead of him.

He heard shots from across the distance of the cliff—and so did the little group hiding in the spruce.

"They're here! Cops, someone—they're here! We've got to move!" someone said harshly.

And the group was suddenly in the dirt path that led to the valley level below, two men, one woman, and a boy.

The kid was ten to twelve years old, tall and lean, with a thatch of dark hair falling over his forehead. The woman looked to be in her late twenties or early thirties, the man at her side a little older, and the other man a little older still, perhaps in his midthirties. The first two adults were probably the kid's parents.

He held a gun and while he was startled to see Hunter, he was evidently the trained man in that group because he grabbed the kid, forcing the boy in front of him as a shield and taking aim at Hunter with his weapon.

"I'll kill the kid," he said, staring at Hunter.

And he would. There were times when Hunter would have tried conversation, when he might have believed he could have solved the situation without violence.

The woman screamed, lunging to save the boy, screaming, "No!"

The man's gun went off. The woman went down. The man took aim again as the kid's father screamed and started forward as well.

Hunter fired, and the man holding the kid went down in

a split second, Hunter's shot having caught him dead center in the forehead.

He holstered his Glock as he rushed forward, falling to his knees next the father and the kid, trying to ascertain the extent of the woman's wounds. The kid was down next to her sobbing, murmuring words that sounded like, "It was wrong, wrong, wrong, we're paying! No, Mom, no, Mom. oh, please, God, forgive us!"

"Peggy, Peggy, Peggy!" the man sobbed, trying to draw the woman into his arms.

"May be a through and through, he caught her in the shoulder. Use the jacket—get pressure on the shot. I'm calling for help," Hunter said, ripping off his jacket, wadding it and pressing it against the woman's shoulder and grabbing the man's hand to keep it down on the wound.

He used his tiny mic, letting the team leader know a suspect was down and a woman was wounded. They needed EMTs as quickly as possible.

He wondered again just how quickly help could come.

"You armed?" he demanded of the man.

The man shook his head strenuously. "No, no, I—I am not a killer, I swear it!"

The boy heard his father speaking. His eyes were glazed. He was staring at nothing, looking as if he felt ill. He spoke quietly, with pain and confusion.

"But we were there… We were watching! Father Mateus was going to… Oh, God, he was going to stab that girl and drink her blood and share her flesh—"

The man Hunter presumed to be the boy's father spoke again, his words passionate and tear-filled.

"That girl was a sinner, boy. She was a sinner! What we were doing would save her eternal soul," the father cried. "But not my Peggy, my Peggy never sinned, never… Oh, God!"

Hunter wanted to take the man by the shoulders and shake him hard. It hurt far more than he had imagined to hear the horrible credo that was being spoon-fed to the boy.

Somehow, he refrained from hitting the man squarely in the jaw. But he couldn't resist saying, "Curious. I have read the Bible cover to cover—especially the New Testament. None of us is without sin—and murder is, beyond a doubt, considered to be a sin."

The man looked at him and again, seemed more confused than anything else.

"You don't understand! It's coming—the Apocalypse is coming, and we were just trying to save that poor girl's soul!"

Hunter stared back at him, frowning. His words had been frightening enough.

That he believed them was even worse.

"Well, give unto Caesar that which is Caesar's, right? Caesar considers murder to be a sin—obey tax laws and others— and I'm afraid you're under arrest for attempted murder."

"No, no, no, I have to stay with Peggy, she's wounded—"

"Yeah, yeah, and without sin," Hunter murmured. "They will get her to a hospital."

He heard movement in the brush and turned; it was Crandon. Hunter was impressed to see he and one of his men had a canvas sheet between them and were quick to assess the situation. They pushed the husband aside to carefully transfer the woman to their pallet.

Crandon looked at the man who had shot her. "Dead?"

Hunter nodded.

"We have two more teams on the way and another ambulance down the cliff," Crandon told him. "They'll collect this guy," he said, nodding toward the dead man.

"I have to go with Peggy!" the man said.

"Sorry, you have to go straight to jail," Crandon told him

and shrugged. He paused and looked at the boy. "We'll call children's services—" he began.

"I'll take care of that," Hunter said. "I'll get him down and to headquarters. If you can deal with the rest?"

Crandon nodded grimly. "We've collected another small group. Info on all forthcoming."

Even as he spoke, another set of the SWAT group arrived at their point by the spruces.

"No!" the man shrieked as the woman was taken by a pair of the men.

"Hey, you can watch her down the trail!" Crandon said, as he slid cuffs on the man and pushed him forward.

"My mom!" the boy whispered.

Hunter stooped down before him. "I believe your mom is going to be fine. Honestly, I don't lie. I saw where she was hit, and I don't believe any vital organs were struck. You understand what I'm saying, right? They will take your mom to the hospital."

The boy nodded. "Am I going to jail, too?" he asked. "I'm sorry. I'm so, so sorry. I didn't... They just said we were going to go and see a woman cleaned of her sins. And then... I heard people talking before Mateus started to speak and they said... Oh, God, he was going to cut her heart out! We were going to drink blood and... Oh, God, oh... Are we all sinners? Could something so horrible save someone's soul?"

He set his hands gently on the boy's arms. "Son, I don't believe doing something so cruel would ever be anything God would think of as good in any religion."

"But—but—my dad isn't a bad man!" the boy said.

"We can be talked into doing bad things sometimes, even when we aren't bad men," Hunter said. "I'm Hunter. What's your name?"

"Brian. Brian Johnston," the boy told him. He lowered his

head and great tears rolled down his cheeks. Hunter stood and drew the boy to him.

"Brian Johnston, your heart is in the right place—and I'm going to see to it that you're all right, okay? Come on. Let's get down the trail. And when it's possible, I will make sure you know your mom is okay, and maybe even see her," Hunter said.

"Um, okay. Um…thank you."

"Sure."

Hunter led the way, heading down the trail. He found himself checking frequently on the boy. Brian. The kid reminded him…

Of himself.

His parents had been fooled into a cult. But there had been a difference. They had known murder was wrong—no matter what anyone had to say. And when the body of a woman who had been questioning their leader was discovered, his folks had known it was time to find help and get the hell out.

He called in when he reached the bottom of the cliffs with Brian, nodding to the numerous officers who were now escorting handcuffed members of Mateus's "flock" to police cars.

Crandon was down there, speaking to his men, ready to drive out himself.

Hunter called out to him.

"Crandon, thank you—thank you to all your teams!"

"You've done us the service!" Crandon called back to him.

They both nodded and waved. Hunter found his car and told Brian to come with him.

"Should I be under arrest, too?" Brian asked him.

"How old are you?" Hunter asked him.

"Eleven. Twelve in six months."

"You're not under arrest."

"They do arrest kids, right?"

"They do. But you are a kid, you were taken along by your folks, and you didn't want to be there. We'll find the right place for you. Hop in. We can talk on the way into headquarters."

"Okay."

As they drove, the kid still looked broken. He had soft brown hair that fell over his forehead and big brown eyes to match. He was still shaken, and without Hunter having to encourage him, he said, "They... I don't know. I had friends at school. And I saw them...and went to school...like a normal kid...up until just a few months ago. Then my dad and mom started talking all night, all the time, and my mom would cry, and my dad said it was happening, we had to be prepared. The world is going to explode. Maybe not all at once, but there will be fires and meteors will crash down and more horrible things will happen and the survivors will wander in agony, dying from radiation and whatever else. Only the good, those trying to follow God's commandments for the coming Apocalypse, would be spared. But for them, everything would be great. We would be eternal, living in the clouds...seeing nothing but beauty and knowing nothing but love."

He shifted in his seat to stare at Hunter. "They believe that!" he whispered. "My parents... I know they believe they were trying to save others!"

Brainwashing was an amazing thing, Hunter thought.

"'Those who can make you believe absurdities can make you commit atrocities,'" Hunter murmured.

"What?"

"A saying by Voltaire, a famous French historian, writer, and philosopher," Hunter told him. He looked over at Brian. "He was born François-Marie Arouet in 1694, but preferred his nom de plume, Voltaire. I spent a lot of time reading about him, once I heard that quote. The guy was way ahead of his time, believing in separation of church and state, and... Well, anyway, look him up some time. I think you would like reading about him, too. You are only eleven, and you knew what was happening was wrong. Because no one convinced you that something absurd was real. Brian, no one living has the answers to God. There are many religions—and the major religions of the world share one thing in common. They teach us to be good to our fellow man. They teach kindness and decency. When someone tries to tell you God wants you to commit murder, it's time to take a long look at the person and know you're being told something that is absurd."

Brian nodded miserably. "Will they be okay?" he asked anxiously. "My folks. They really aren't bad people. They did believe what was...absurd. They believe in our souls, in immortality—and that by doing what they were doing, they would make the girl go to Heaven."

"I *think* they will be okay," Hunter said, glancing over at Brian. "Especially if...well, if they help us understand who else is involved in...murdering people." He hesitated and then said, "Brian, I was a kid like you once. And my parents were good people. They wanted people to be good to other people, and they thought they found the right way. But when it got bad. They saw they were being played."

"Being played," Brian repeated.

"Here's the thing, Brian. I don't think Mateus believed anything he was trying to get others to believe. He knew what he was saying was a lie—but he has something he wants for himself and getting other people to believe and to listen to him was a way of getting what he wanted."

"What did he want?"

"That's what we have to figure out," Hunter told him.

Brian nodded. Hunter realized the boy was quietly crying. "What will happen to me?" he asked.

"Do you have close relatives who…someone close who would like to take care of you for a while?"

"Aunt Violet…maybe. I haven't seen her in…months. She… she told my mom she couldn't see her as long as she was… listening to crazy stuff about the Apocalypse."

"Where is she? What does she do?"

"She's in Denver. She's a professor at the college. She and my mom were close…and she was the best aunt to me until… until we just kind of stopped seeing her. She used to take me to museums and parks and bookstores and…all kinds of game places and arcades."

"We'll call her. I can't make promises or guarantees, Brian, except for this—I will watch out for whatever is going to happen. I promise you I will be there if you call me."

Brian was looking at him, his face tearstained.

"Is my mom going to die?"

"Brian, I swear to you, I don't think so. But we'll check in at the hospital as soon as she's gotten there and the doctors have had a chance to see her."

The kid tried to smile. "I am going to read up on that Voltage guy."

Hunter grinned at him. "Voltaire. Yeah. I saw a young reader book about him once at one of the bookstores. I'll find it for you."

"Really?"

"You bet."

Hunter thought dryly that a "young reader" book would be best, one that would teach more about the man's philosophy than his personal life since he'd had a married lover for years and years. Yeah. Young reader book—that was best.

They were nearing headquarters, and Hunter put a quick call through to Andy Mason so he could get the ball rolling with children's services and maybe find Brian's Aunt Violet.

Being with the boy, he hadn't yet called Amy at the hospital, and he was anxious to hear about the welfare of the girl who had nearly died up on the high cliff.

He was careful *not* to put the phone on speaker.

"I know one of the kindest people in children's services," Andy told him. "I will talk to her when we hang up. Crandon has given me a brief preliminary report. Your boy's parents are Peggy and Bret Johnston. They belonged to a Unitarian church just outside Denver until recently. She's a homemaker, he's a banker."

Hunter glanced quickly at Brian.

"And have we heard…"

"Nothing on the mother yet, I'm afraid. The ambulance has barely reached the hospital. Same hospital where the victim was taken by the way. I'm having agents posted there."

"Good call. Thanks."

"Be there in ten."

He ended the call. Brian watched him, still anxious. He wiped his face with his sleeve. "My mom got shot trying to save me."

"Your mom loves you," Hunter said.

"But it's my fault."

"Don't you ever say that and don't you think it," Hunter said firmly. "Brian, someone awful is out there causing a lot of really bad things. If you had been shot…your mom wouldn't have wanted to live. But you're okay, and I really believe she will be, too."

Brian nodded. "If she is all right…will I be able to live with her again? And my dad?"

"I believe they will face charges. And if they help investigators…well, they may not do much time, or… Brian, I don't know. The attorneys will sort it all out."

Hunter wondered about that himself. Today, they had been

part of a crowd that intended to watch a man stab a woman to death, dig out her heart, and share her blood and flesh like a group of vampiric cannibals. But if they cooperated and helped agents and police find out what was behind it all, there was a chance.

If they could realize just how badly they'd been brainwashed.

"What if there is an apocalypse?" Brian asked.

"An apocalypse can be many things to many people. We've always had things we fear—war, death, famine, plague. You name it—humanity has faced it. But here's the thing, Brian, it doesn't matter. It isn't our right to decide someone isn't living up to our moral code. It isn't our right to take the life of another, to torture and kill them because we believe something bad is coming. Okay, think about this—do you believe in witches?"

"Like flying on brooms and cackling and stuff?" Brian asked.

"Witches—who can cast curses on cows."

"I don't have a cow."

"You know what I mean."

"Only on Halloween," Brian said, and he almost smiled.

"Okay, so, go back a little over three hundred years ago in Salem, Massachusetts. They hanged people for being witches. But they never had any proof against them—they just *believed* there were such things as witches. You know about that, right?"

"Sure. We studied it in school."

"Well, they didn't just hang witches in the Massachusetts Bay Colony. They hanged Quakers—for worshipping a little bit differently. Thankfully, it all stopped and we entered what we call our Age of Enlightenment. Several of our Founding Fathers, born Puritans, became part of that Age of Enlightenment and wanted to make sure no one ever had a fight, or got a little scared, or even wanted someone else's land and claimed they were a witch. That's why we have a separation of church and state and—"

"The inalienable right to life, liberty, and the pursuit of happiness!"

"Yep, that's it," Hunter said.

Brian smiled just as they pulled into headquarters. Then he looked at the building apprehensively.

"It's going to be okay," Hunter told him.

The boy nodded and opened his car door. He stood tall and straightened his jacket. He looked back at Hunter.

"I'm going to help in any way I can. And I'm going to make my mom and dad help. I mean, if my mom…"

"We're going to go on faith right now," Hunter said. "As far as your mom and dad, we'll work on them and do the very best we can."

They started walking toward the entry when Brian suddenly stopped and turned to Hunter.

"What is it?"

"I—I heard people talking. Your people. And they were talking about Mateus. They were saying he had been shot—"

"Yes, he was shot."

"But…" Brian paused, wincing. "They couldn't find him. His—his body."

"Not yet. We will."

"I just realized… I think I know where they may have put Mateus!"

7

"We're still doing tests," Dr. Linda Barton told Amy. Barton was a no-nonsense woman. Her hair was neatly clipped short, hugging her face, and if she was wearing makeup, it was minimal. She was an attractive woman with a dignified manner, probably close to fifty and not at all the kind to shrink from age, but rather a woman who would always accept it with determination and growth.

"Blood tests?" Amy asked. "She is going to be all right?"

She hadn't gotten much out of the young woman on the way to the hospital as she sat by her side in the ambulance, holding her hand and trying to keep her calm. Magda had sworn again and again she wasn't evil; why had people thought she was evil? Yes, she was a stripper. But the club was legitimate. They did not sell the girls! Dancing was getting her through college.

Dr. Barton nodded. "Blood tests, urine tests. Right now, I believe a drug was slipped into her drink. We hear date-rape drugs a lot, but technically a date-rape drug is anything that makes a person more pliable and unable to defend themselves against sexual assault. Alcohol can be considered such a potion, and we all know that human behavior under the influence of too much alcohol can change. But I believe this woman was hit with either Rohypnol, a tranquilizer, and/or GHB, gamma-hydroxybutyric acid—also known by its street name of *easy lay*—just before she left the club where she works." She paused and shrugged. "I know the place where Magda dances. I picked my husband up there after a bachelor party for another of our physicians here. He said it was fun and totally aboveboard, and that's the general perception. Yes, girls dance to excite and please men—but the place is owned by a couple, and the wife is an ex-stripper who made her way through to a law degree by stripping and married a customer. They wanted a legit club. Anyway, whoever did this must have been at the club. Magda is doing well now. I'm more worried about her physical response to the mental pressure she's suffering now, rather than what was in her drink and what was done to her. I understand her would-be murderer was shot just seconds before the knife fell. Anyway, she wants to talk with you again—she seems to need you. And I believe she will be fine physically and sure as hell won't forget this. But with the help of some good therapy, she can get by it. Whatever the combo of drugs, we'll flush them out of her tonight. Of course, I know it's important you speak with her further, and… I've heard more about her vitals than what happened, but I watch and read the news. I've been hearing about the horrible events occurring, and you need to get out there and catch the monsters doing all these awful things." She hesitated briefly again and then rushed on with, "Mike Adler—Doctor

Adler, the medical examiner—is a friend. And he's told me about some of the victims discovered in the pits. I have to say, I am so grateful this girl has come to me—and not Mike."

"We're grateful, too," Amy said.

"You saved her. You shot and killed a man. You're a heroine."

"Dr. Barton, I'm sorry, I shot a man before he could kill someone else, but I'm never happy about taking a human life."

"Of course not. I'm sorry. I didn't mean to infer… I'm not a bloodthirsty person, quite the opposite, of course, but Magda has been doing a lot of murmuring…ranting, really. They intended to kill her and cut out her heart and eat her flesh?"

"That's what we're hearing," Amy said. "Agents are out there scouring the area now for the rest of the group. We'll get to the bottom of it."

She was confident and determined. And she believed her own words. She knew they would get to the bottom of it because neither she nor Hunter nor many others would stop until they did.

She just didn't know how long it would take. Or how many more might die before they stopped the "horsemen" from running rampant against them.

"May I see her now?" Amy asked.

"Yes—" Dr. Barton began, breaking off and frowning as she heard her name over the hospital's PA system. "Yes, yes, of course, and thank you. I've been told an officer will be arriving soon to keep watch. I have an emergency downstairs—"

"Go, go! I'll be here until I know Magda is safe," Amy assured her. She watched the doctor rush down the hallway and then Amy turned to the single-bed room near the nurse's station where Magda had been brought after triage in the ER.

Magda was leaning back, fingers working the bedsheets, eyes fixed on the ceiling above. She saw Amy and sat up, still a little unsteady but quickly realizing she could push a button on the bed control and raise the bed to a sitting position.

"Special Agent Larson! You're here. Thank you," she said.

"No, thank you," Amy told her. "You need to be resting. According to Dr. Barton, you're going to be just fine, but you need to get your system cleaned out—"

"I am *so* careful!" Magda said, shaking her head. "I mean, I know what happens in bars. In any bar—and no matter how good our security is or how great our bartenders can be— bad things can still happen. And we all have drinks during the night! Honestly—mostly water in bottles we bring ourselves. But it's okay to be friendly. Honestly, management never makes us have sex. Even lap dances are strictly monitored. But Lydia—the owner—warns us all the time we're adults, and we have to be responsible. But when people are being *normal,* we want to be friendly and talkative. Believe it or not, what many people need is someone who talks. We do sit with them, have a drink, and laugh and—mainly—listen. I was fine. Everything was fine. It was just a usual night."

"But the doctor believes you were drugged. And it would have had to have been near to the time when you were leaving your job," Amy said.

Magda winced, closed her eyes, and shook her head. "I was at the bar, I had a soda. But Vinnie was the bartender...he's a great guy. He would never do something like drug a girl and he wouldn't stand for it from anyone else."

"If he saw it done," Amy said. "Did you go anywhere after you got your drink?"

"I—no. I don't think so. Oh..."

"Oh?"

"I walked away from the stage to call Allison. She was going to try to get off early, and if she did, we were going to share a ride home. But she decided she was working another couple of hours because another girl called in sick, so… I finished my soda, thanked Vinnie, and left," Magda said, wincing again as she saw in her own mind where her innocent mistake had been made. "But Vinnie watches out for us!" she said.

"I'm sure he does, but he isn't infallible, none of us are," Amy told her. "But there are cameras in the club, right?"

"Everywhere!" Magda assured her. "Oh, my God, I still can't believe what they intended to do, what they would have done… They were going to cut my heart out! I'm a stripper given drugs—and they didn't even want sex. They wanted to kill me and drink my blood. Oh, my God, it's the most horrible thing imaginable. Why? Who would be so sick?" She leaned her head back, talking again with barely a breath. "The same people… I've seen it on the news. The monsters who wanted people to starve to death and die in the mud in pits, and what has happened to this world? So, so sick! They kept saying they were saving me—saving me! By cutting my heart out! How could anyone believe such a thing?"

"I don't know," Amy told her softly. "But I've heard if you're told a lie often enough, that lie becomes not *the* truth, but a truth you can come to believe. However, it doesn't matter, Amy. What was done to you was horrible, what was done to others was horrible, and we will get to the truth. That's why I need you to tell me everything, everything you remember. Small details can mean something, Magda. We will get the security tapes from the club, but do you remember anyone paying particular attention to you? Can you go through the time from when you finished work until you were snatched up and tell me everything, every little thing you remember?"

"I… Yeah. Sure, yes, of course, I will do anything I can to help you."

"Okay. Was there anyone there that night paying you special attention?"

Magda managed a soft laugh. "Special Agent Larson, I get lots of special attention when I'm on a pole."

"There would be a difference in this—someone who wasn't trying to hit on you, per se, but rather watching you—when you weren't on a pole."

Magda frowned, leaning back, thinking. She shook her head. "Not that I noticed."

"Okay, so then you dressed in the dressing room. Was anyone—"

"Only the dancers are allowed in the dressing rooms so, no."

"Okay, then you went to the bar and Vinnie poured you a soda."

"I had a few sips and I played a game on my cell phone. Then I stepped away to call Allison, but she had been calling me at the same time. Anyway...there was a game on the television over the bar." Magda shrugged with a wry grimace. "Guys were shouting at the television screen. I wanted to make sure I could hear her."

"Were any of the men at the bar trying to make conversation with you? Were they near you?"

"They were near me. Men gave me compliments, said hello, offered to buy me drinks, but honestly, they all seemed far more interested in the football game than anything else. After I talked to Allison, I went back to the bar for my drink, then I headed out to the street right away. I was suddenly so tired I could barely stand it. I was afraid I was getting something because I had no energy at all. I just wanted to get to my car—and get home. I was just a block down—heading to the cheaper garage where I keep my car—when there was suddenly someone behind me and... I couldn't fight. I couldn't even scream. He picked me up and threw me in the back of a van. I don't remember anything after that...anything until I heard people talking. And I thought I was dreaming because I couldn't open my eyes but they were talking about my sins, saving my soul, some whacked out stuff about a black horse and scales of justice, and how they would consume my heart, my blood, my flesh—and my sins."

"Magda, think hard. Was the man who plucked you off the street ever in the club?" Amy asked her.

Magda shook her head and almost smiled. "I didn't see much of his face. Every criminal out there must know you have to have a mask and a hoodie. I don't know. I don't remember what I saw of him. I don't remember anything at all."

"Not true. Was he white, black, Asian, Native American, Hispanic? Did he speak at all? Did he have an accent? Or maybe a scent?"

Magda frowned. "Okay. I just saw his eyes. He had green eyes. Strange green eyes."

"Was he the same man as the priest who was going to kill you?"

"I don't...know. The priest—or whatever—was a guy they called Mateus. And no, he had blue eyes. I never heard him speak, so I don't know if he had an accent. I think he was white. Oh!"

"Oh?"

"I do remember something!" she said excitedly.

"And what is that?"

"He smelled like that new stuff—there's an up-and-coming designer who has a sports clothing line out—an aftershave, lotion, and men's cologne. I know the scent because Vinnie got a bottle from his girlfriend and it's really nice stuff. Yes! He smelled just like Vinnie. Oh!" She stopped speaking, staring at Amy again. "But he wasn't Vinnie—not to worry. I mean, there is no way, and I didn't mean to imply that. Vinnie has dark brown eyes and he's a cool looking guy with a really mixed ethnicity—his skin is dark and his eyes are brown and it would have been almost impossible for him to have left the bar, gotten a hoodie and a van, and... Vinnie is the best guy in the world."

"Okay, thank you. We will talk to Vinnie, of course—bearing in mind he's the best guy in the world. He might have seen something you didn't," Amy explained quickly. "And you knowing that scent might prove to be important, so thank you for that, too." Amy hesitated. "Is there anything else, anything at all that you can remember?"

Magda was thoughtful but then shook her head. She looked at Amy. "Thank you! Thank you so much for saving my life!"

"Thank you so much for being so strong and making it!" Amy told her, placing one of her cards on the bedside table. "If you think of anything—if you need anything, anything at all—call me. And don't be afraid to get some rest. We're going to have a guard outside your room."

"Thank you," Magda whispered again.

"You just get well."

"I will. And...well, thank you for...for thinking my life was worth saving. I mean, to some people, maybe I would be a horrible person. A stripper. But let me tell you. I work with people who tip in restaurants, who are kind, who give to others... Strippers aren't evil, no matter what those crazy people think!"

"Magda, please, don't worry. None of us think badly of you. We just want to catch the people who are doing this."

Amy smiled and managed to leave at last, but she hesitated in the hall, not seeing an officer or agent to watch over the room. Then her phone rang and she answered it quickly. Andy Mason was on the line.

"Amy, everything moving along all right with the young woman?"

"Hi, Andy, she's going to be all right other than the trauma. We need to get to the club where she was working and have agents get their hands on the security tapes. She went to the bar for a soda before she headed out, and that soda was apparently spiked when she walked away from the bar for a minute to take a phone call. Also, she helped as far as whoever picked her up was white and had green eyes. She recognized his scent—a new designer scent—because the bartender uses it, but the bartender was not the guy who snatched her off the street."

"Still might have been involved."

"Hell, Andy, half the country could be involved in this. I haven't spoken to Hunter yet. How did it go on the cliffs?"

"Well, you and Hunter both fired your weapons today in fatal confrontations. You can speak with the shrink one session after the other, though, of course, both were good shootings, shootings that saved the lives of the innocent. But while you're at the hospital, a woman was shot trying to protect her kid when he was threatened. We've—"

"Hunter shot a woman who was trying to protect her child?" Amy interrupted incredulously.

"No, Hunter shot the man who shot the woman. My point is the woman—Peggy Johnston—is at the hospital where you are now. From what I understand, she's a total basket case. Apparently, the entire group there was a cult convinced that the Apocalypse is coming—and that the only way to save sinners is to drink their blood or eat their flesh to help take the sins from them. The black horse's rider carries the scales, and those who help cleanse others of their sins will be blessed in Heaven. Anyway, we've got the father under arrest, and Hunter is coming in with the boy. A friend of mine from children's services is on the way. A good woman. This is a kid who is going to need help."

"I can imagine," Amy murmured softly.

"Before you leave—"

"Right. There is supposed to be an agent here watching over Magda."

"Odin Thompson. On his way. He just texted he's reached the hospital, and he'll be tagged later by second shift. Amy, don't worry. She won't be left unprotected. But once Odin arrives, I want you to check with the doctor and find out how the woman who was shot on the cliffs is doing. It would be nice to tell the kid that even if his mother is a totally delusional nutcase, she's alive and healing."

"What will happen with these people, Andy? Can this be real? Can people really believe this?"

"Do all of them believe it? I'm thinking not. For some, it's a plan, part of an agenda we're not seeing yet. But we've seen it time and again. People *can* be convinced to believe just about anything."

"You're right," Amy murmured. "I'll see the doctor. I believe I already know her."

As she spoke, she saw a tall squarely muscled man in a dark blue suit coming her way.

"Does Odin appear as powerful as a Sherman tank?" she asked Andy softly.

On the other end of the line, Andy laughed.

"Yeah. That's Odin."

"He's here—I'm off to find the doctor."

"Excellent. One of Crandon's men headed after the ambulance with Brian's mom, and he'll stay there until a second shift arrives. I just want you to talk to whoever is treating her, find out just how serious her condition is."

"Got it. I'm on my way. Sherman tank is approaching me!" she told him.

Andy laughed and ended the call. Amy quickly stepped toward Odin and offered him her hand.

"Amy Larson?" the man asked.

She smiled and nodded. "Odin."

In turn, he smiled and nodded. Then his expression grew grim. "Don't worry. I'll see to it that no one unauthorized comes anywhere near her. This case..." He broke off, shaking his head. "People who are so brainwashed—who think they have the right to judge others—anyway, sorry! I will seriously be guarding this young woman with my life."

Amy smiled. "I get you!" she assured him. "Thank you."

She hurried to the nurse's station and discovered Peggy Johnston was just being transferred from the ER up to a room. Dr. Barton was still with her.

Amy hurried to the appropriate room, then waited by the door for a minute. The doctor was giving instructions to the nurse. She turned and saw Amy and gave her a grim smile. Excusing herself to the nurse, she walked out to speak with Amy.

"I thought she was going to need surgery, but it was a through and through. No vital organs damaged. The bullet didn't even damage her bones, though she'll be wearing a cast for a while. But barring the unexpected serious infection, she will be fine."

"Thank you," Amy said. "Is she sedated?"

Dr. Barton shook her head. "You may have ten minutes if you wish."

Amy hadn't expected to be able to speak with the woman, but she wasn't going to miss the opportunity. She thanked Dr. Barton and approached the bed.

She wondered what she would find—defiance? The desperate determination the cult on the cliff had been right in wanting to punish the wicked—and thus save their immortal souls?

But the woman's face was damp with tears as Amy approached the bed. She looked at Amy with wide eyes, unsure of who she was, and yet in such a state it might not have mattered.

"He—he—was going to shoot Brian! My son, my innocent son," she said incredulously. "And that man...on the cliff. He stopped him. I don't—I can't—how can it be truthful we need to drink the blood of sinners to save their lives— but then turn around and try to take the life of an innocent child? Brian is...a kid. Not sinless. But that's ridiculous, really. None of us is...sinless. But we didn't all dance mostly naked to seduce others, we didn't lie or cheat, and we weren't supposed to be witnessing a murder. We were supposed to be saving souls because... Well, I mean, I believe it is coming, the Apocalypse is coming. I mean...the pandemic, people so hateful... It's easy to see the end must be near, but now I don't even know about that! Brother Martin was going to shoot Brian—he did shoot me!"

The woman was in her late twenties or early thirties with long brown hair now a tangle beneath her head. She wore no makeup but had a well-proportioned face and enormous dark eyes, glistening with tears now as she looked at Amy— frowning suddenly as if determining who she might be.

"It's all right," Amy said quietly, setting a hand gently on the woman's lower arm. "My name is Amy Larson. I'm working with the FBI. And I want to first assure you, your son, Brian, is fine."

"And Bret? My husband?" she asked.

"He's fine." Amy hesitated. "Mrs. Johnston, I'm sorry to say this because I don't think you believe what you were doing was horrendously wrong, but your husband is under arrest as you will be when you leave the hospital."

"Under arrest?" she repeated blankly. "But—"

"Accessory to attempted murder," Amy said quietly.

"I thought we were saving her soul!" Peggy whispered. "But they were going to shoot Brian! He is good, and how do you shoot someone good? I mean, I understood many authorities may not have read the Bible. They might not have understood... Oh, God." She started to sob softly. "That the innocent would always be spared was a lie, so all the rest was a lie. We were going to watch Mateus kill that woman, and we were going to drink her blood, but if the one thing was a horrible lie, then..."

"We will get it all sorted out," Amy said. "But don't worry about Brian—"

"Call my sister. Please, call my sister, Violet. She loves Brian and he loves her. And I think she hates me now, but she won't hate Brian because..."

Peggy Johnston broke off and stared at Amy as if she'd suddenly been hit in the face with bucket of ice water.

"Because I was an idiot!" she said firmly. "Tell Violet... please, please, tell her how sorry I am! Beg that she watch over Brian. Whatever comes my way, I might deserve. But..." She paused again, closed her eyes, and sighed. "They told us we needed to bring Brian. They said he needed to learn now, because the end was coming quickly, and he had to know we were all responsible for others. We were our brothers' keepers. He didn't have much time to become a strong soul, because the end was near, and we had to be ready to rise to the greatness of Heaven. The fourth horseman would ride, and when he did, we all needed to be prepared. I think... I think it was just that the last few years... Well, it was easy to believe the end was coming with so much violence and hatred all around us!" She suddenly clutched Amy's arm. "You will call Violet, please?"

"Yes, yes, of course," Amy assured her. "Mrs. Johnston—"

"Peggy, please."

"Peggy, how and where did you meet Mateus and the man who shot you, Brother Martin? How did you become part of their cult?"

"Cult? No, no, they're just a nondenominational group. Oh. I am an idiot. They were…are, no, he's dead. Mateus is dead. I saw him shot before he could lower the knife. Dead center in the chest. Mateus found us at a church fair. He played games with Brian…you know, knocking bottles off shelves and the like. Then we went to lunch, and we found out he was an ordained minister, and he seemed so good and so sure. We met others. They all admired him so much. We started attending his church…"

"Peggy, where is his church?" Amy asked.

"Oh, well, right there. Right on the cliffs. That's where we always met. It was beautiful. We were surrounded by God's beautiful creation, nature. And Mateus reminded us a church was wherever we met in His name. I mean, that's true, right? But then…he pointed out all the signs. He told us we needed to prepare and… We were such idiots, but when I look back, it started out as…"

"Peggy, I believe you mean you thought you had joined with something good where it was important for you to be kind to your fellow man. You would be bringing Brian into a fold where he could grow, knowing that being a decent human being was the greatest thing asked of us," Amy said gently. "But let me make sure I'm understanding this. You were at a fair put on by your regular church, and he found you there?"

She nodded. "And he befriended us. And when we met

others... Well, they all spoke about how wonderful he had been when meeting them, and how he seemed to be an example of the love he was teaching us to show others."

"What about Brother Martin—the man who shot you?" Amy asked.

She shook her head. "He assisted Mateus sometimes. He would hold open a book and light candles. We used the rock where...where he intended to cleanse that young woman of her sins...as an altar. We would sing sometimes, and it was beautiful. Then he told us we must grow serious—and if we truly loved our fellow man, we would have to do painful things. We would have to absorb some of their sin so they could rise with us."

"Do you know anything more about Mateus and Martin? Last names?" Amy asked hopefully. Of course, if Hunter had shot Martin to stop him from killing someone else, they would have his body. That meant dental impressions and fingerprints, and they might find out about his identity and his associates from that.

Amy hoped they'd eventually find the body of the "minister" Mateus. It would help to get a jump-start on the men.

But Peggy shook her head, frowning. "When we met...he just went by Mateus. We never called him Father Mateus, but Martin was introduced to us as Brother Martin. We just... I don't know. I guess it sounds stupid. Oh, my God, now everything about this sounds stupid. We were stupid. Horribly stupid. I hope Bret sees it. I never thought...in a thousand years, I never thought anyone would hurt my son! When I saw he would have killed Brian, it was as if something in my mind exploded, and... I never believed he would shoot me for that matter. But he did it to escape! Martin wanted others to sacrifice, but he just wanted to escape! How could I have been so blind?" she asked a little desperately.

"We all want something better—we all want to believe," Amy murmured.

"I never saw the hypocrisy," Peggy murmured. "I will help you now, in any way. I mean, I don't know much, but they talked about the fact they had *saved* others. Bret and I hadn't been with the assembly that long. Others might know more about anything that went on before. I know how stupid I sound now, and it may be hard to believe this, but it was the most loving group of people. Polite, kind, courteous... We would go to the cliff and sing, listen to scripture... Oh, God. I guess scripture can be interpreted in many ways." She tried to sit up, but the pain was too much and she fell back, saying, "Please believe me. We were there. We fell for the words told to us. We believed the young woman had begged for help—"

"What?"

"We were told she had come to Mateus, knowing the Apocalypse was coming, and she knew how grossly she had sinned and begged him to save her soul."

"By being stabbed through the heart?"

Peggy shook her head. "I—I didn't know what he was going to do, but...even if I had realized then what he was doing, I would have believed in his love for his fellow man. I didn't see... I honestly didn't see anything until Martin threatened to shoot Brian. And I am humiliated to say this, but if I would have known then—realized then—how horrible it all was, I think I would have been afraid to protest—even before Martin and others showed they were armed."

Amy produced a card. "Fear can be powerful," Amy told her. "And I don't know exactly what charges will be filed, but I'm sure the DA will acknowledge the fact you're trying to cooperate. And I will call your sister. If you can give me her contact information, I will make sure we reach her."

"Thank you, thank you!"

Peggy accepted Amy's card and the pen and notepad Amy handed her. She jotted down her sister's name and phone number and handed the little pad back to Amy.

"Thank you," she said again.

The doctor was standing in the doorway. Amy knew she needed to leave so the patient could rest.

"I'll check up on you and keep you informed," Amy told her. She glanced toward the doorway and smiled. "Your doctor told me you should make a full recovery."

"I'm grateful," she said softly.

Amy smiled and left the room. She thanked the doctor again and looked for the agent sent to keep guard over the woman.

As Andy Mason had promised, a man was in a chair by the door. They acknowledged one another, and Amy headed on out while dialing Hunter as she did so.

He answered her immediately—just saying her name.

"Amy."

"Are you at headquarters? Andy told me you were with Brian."

"No, we're not at headquarters. Yes, I am with Brian."

And that was why he was speaking so carefully.

"I just saw Peggy Johnston," Amy said. "You can tell Brian his mother is going to make a full recovery. She'll just need a little time."

"Thank God," Hunter murmured. She heard him talking to the boy. "This is my friend, Amy. She's at the hospital. She saw your mom. She's going to be fine when she's had a bit of a chance to recover."

Amy heard a soft sob, and Hunter was quiet for a minute. She winced and worried about the connection he must have been feeling with Brian Johnston.

She knew when he was a child Hunter had come upon the

body of a woman who had questioned the head of a cult. He had to feel Brian's pain.

"Hunter? I'm going to head back in now. I have a little information. Apparently, that cliff was their *church*. Peggy didn't know anything about Mateus or Martin—other than when they had met, they had both seemed to offer nothing but love and kindness toward others."

"Heard that story before," Hunter murmured. "Anyway, agents have corralled several of the participants in today's almost-sacrifice. We'll get something from someone."

"Right. So—why aren't you back at the office?"

"Because Brian is helping me explore the area."

"I see." She didn't really see at all.

"Brian is helping me. He thinks he may know where they might have hidden Mateus. The, uh, man you shot who was going to kill the girl."

"Oh," she said. She still didn't really see. How might the boy know? Of course, she knew she had killed the man.

And his body had disappeared.

"We're looking for his body," he said very quietly. "We'll head straight back when we leave here," Hunter told her.

"Right. Of course. All right, I'm going in now, so I'll be there."

He didn't reply. Amy thought she had lost the connection. She frowned, and said, "Hunter?"

He was still there. When he spoke, his voice was taut and his words were hard.

"Amy, I'll call you back. I think we might have found a body. In fact, I'm afraid we might have found several bodies."

8

How the hell long had these killers been at it? Was there one leader jerking around the rest, or were several people handling the puppet strings of mind manipulation to kill, then disposing of some bodies in mud pits and others here—deep in a crevice of the cliffs where it was going to be a master engineering feat for medical examiners to begin to evaluate the dead?

Hunter drew Brian away from the crevice in the cliff as quickly as he could. He looked at the boy's face and saw he appeared to be in shock.

"Were you here before, Brian?" he asked.

Brian shook his head, pointing back toward the path. "My dad pointed over here…saying it was where God would recover those who had been helped. And I figured that…if God would find souls there, then…"

He turned away, falling to his knees on the ground, his

hands on his face. He was sobbing. "I swear, they're not bad! My parents aren't bad people. They...they're...not bad!"

They weren't necessarily bad people. Hunter knew far too many truly decent human beings who had fallen into cults, into a manner of mind control. First, a leader just needed to seek out the disenfranchised, those feeling a little lost by casual cruelty found in society. Friendship, love, and kindness were all offered. Equality was a given. Then bit by bit, it became obvious the love was offered with greater fervor to those who worked the hardest, who shouted the leader's name the loudest, who obeyed without question. For those who dared to disagree...

Jonestown. One example of what could happen.

And here...this. Not the death of cult members, per se. Unless they chose to leave or disobey, Hunter imagined. Or maybe, in the end, all were intended to die in a strange pact before the "End of Days" fell upon them. Convincing others to murder on such a scale as a way to save the souls of sinners was beyond heinous.

He set his arm around Brian. The Voltaire quote kept ceaselessly running through his mind.

"Those who can make you believe absurdities can make you commit atrocities."

And atrocities were certainly being committed.

"Brian," he said, hunkering down by the boy. "No kid should ever have to see something like this, and I am so sorry. I believe you and your parents were swept into something that...well...that was cruel and evil at the utmost, but they didn't know that." In truth, he had no idea just what Brian's parents had thought or known. But the boy had suffered enough traumas for one day.

He'd hung up on Amy, but not before telling her to reach Andy Mason and warn him they were going to need a small army to begin to remove the bodies pressed down into the deep crevice in the rocks. He thought Mateus, whoever he might really be, had to be the last broken and twisted form stuffed down the opening. But below him were another five or six individuals. He'd wanted to get Brian away, but in the bit of time he'd had to glance downward, he'd gathered they were in various stages of decomposition. The crevice, like the mud pits, had been a disposal ground for some time.

"Brian, come on, let's get back to the trail. We'll meet up with a few of my coworkers, and then I'll get you back to headquarters."

Brian nodded, allowing Hunter to help him to his feet and lead him back to the trail. By the time he did so, he saw another group of agents had been sent out and were hurrying up to meet him. He pointed out the crevice and warned they were probably going to need a fair amount of equipment to begin to extract the dead. The team leader nodded and assured him they were going to make the assessment. The medical examiners and personnel were on the way, and they could handle the situation from there.

Grateful, Hunter got Brian down from the cliffs and to his car. The boy hadn't spoken again.

Hunter knew he probably was too close to the situation, but then again who could understand what this kid was feeling better than him?

Brian had stopped sobbing and sat in the passenger's seat staring straight ahead.

"You're going to be all right," Hunter told him quietly.

Brian didn't look his way. He winced. "My folks..." He broke off and turned to Hunter. "Will I get to see them again?"

"I'm sure you'll get to see them again. I'm not a lawyer, Brian. I'm not sure what happens now. I believe there will be charges. The good news is your mom is going to be okay, and I believe they are good people swept up into something bad. But you saw that right away, Brian. You were wise for your years. I know you're going to be strong—you're going to help them. And in the end, it's going to be okay."

"You sound so sure."

"I am sure."

"How?" the boy whispered.

"Because I've been where you are," Hunter said. "Almost exactly where you are. And I'm okay. Trust in us, please. The head man out here—Andy Mason—will see to it you're taken care of, and we'll hope your Aunt Violet will help out."

"She probably hates us all with good reason."

"You'd be surprised how forgiving people can be."

In truth, he had no idea. He could only hope Brian's Aunt Violet was a forgiving soul, and hoped she did love the boy. Otherwise…

Foster parents often got a bad rap. But if Andy Mason said he knew a good woman with children's services, then whatever happened, Brian would be okay.

He turned to Brian. "Hey, it was horrible, I'm sorry you saw what we saw. But you were a tremendous help today. We will be able to trace people, to put a stop to a lot of horrible things because of you."

Brian looked at him hopefully.

Hunter tousled his hair.

"I don't know how everything will work out yet, Brian. But you're a pretty amazing kid. And you're going to be all right."

They were almost at the local headquarters.

When Hunter had parked, Brian looked worriedly at the building.

"It's okay. I promise," Hunter said. And he believed his

promise. Andy Mason ran a tight ship, and he was a man good for his word.

He set his hand on Brian's shoulder and led the way in. Andy himself was there to greet them as soon as they entered along with a woman who was perhaps in her midthirties with a quick, friendly smile, bright green eyes, *and* a professional demeanor.

"Brian, right?" she said, greeting the boy. "We've already located and spoken with your Aunt Violet, and she's going to be here pretty soon. And Assistant Director in charge here, Andy Mason, has already arranged you'll get to see your mom tonight. Oh, I'm sorry! I'm Belinda Montgomery, and I'm here just for you, to help you with anything you need." She flashed Hunter a quick smile, assuring him she was the real thing and was telling the truth.

"You found Aunt Violet," he said. "Great. And she—"

"She's on her way here," Andy said. "Belinda has a pack of computer games and other things to occupy Brian while we work out some kinks. You'll be able to speak with Violet when she arrives. She's anxious to meet you—the agent who saved her sister and nephew."

"Well, that's nice. I'm just sorry we'll meet due to her sister being shot," Hunter said. "I'll be glad to speak with her. Amy is here, right?" he asked.

Andy nodded. "Conference room three," he said, looking at Hunter with a slight indication of his head toward Brian.

He didn't want the kid to know his father was in there being grilled, as many suspects and/or witnesses referred to an interrogation.

"Brian—"

"I'll be fine—Ms. Montgomery seems very nice," Brian said.

"Well, thank you!" Belinda Montgomery said. "You don't

know me yet, but I promise I'll try to live up to that opinion!"
She smiled and ushered Brian off. She told him she'd set up
a game system in one of the conference rooms, and she was
ready to beat the pants off him in something called *Wicked
Wanda Wars*. He grinned and assured her he'd beat her instead.

"I'm thinking the kid has had enough already," Andy said.

"Thanks," Hunter murmured. "I'll join Amy, if I may."

"Sure. I know how you must feel, though. Don't leap across
the table to throttle the father, huh?"

"I will be the height of professionalism," Hunter said.

"I don't know about that. Just don't throttle our witness
in there."

A witness who had brought a child to a murder scene.

But no. It might take some effort, but he'd been at this
game a while. He wasn't going to throttle anyone.

He entered the room, and found Amy and Bret Johnston
were in there alone seated across from one another. Bret Johnston was not in handcuffs. He was under arrest and would be
held in a federal facility until he was arraigned and faced trial
for accessory to attempted murder. But Hunter was certain
the man hadn't had to be told his cooperation was something
a judge would take into consideration.

They also had to worry as well about his safety, and the
safety of his wife and child, and that of the others who were
scooped up from the cliffs.

They'd learned cult leaders could be vindictive. And with
this group, the priest or shaman or whatever name he used,
Mateus had already convinced his flock murder was a holy
thing if they were taking on the sins of those being murdered.

That would come later.

He pulled out a chair and took the seat next to Amy and
stared at Bret Johnston.

Johnston looked at him nervously, looked back at Amy,

and swallowed hard. "I am telling Special Agent Larson everything that I know!" he swore.

Amy looked at Hunter. "Problem is, he doesn't know much."

"We thought... All right, all right, so it started with Brian," Johnston said.

He was not going to leap across the table and throttle the man. He had promised.

"Brian?" he repeated, and he knew the sound of his voice was like a cannon. "Don't even try to blame participation in a heinous murder on an eleven-year-old boy!" he said. His words were tense as he leaned forward. "That is one great kid, and you..."

He sat back. Apparently, Johnston hadn't asked for an attorney. He didn't want to be the straw that broke the camel's back and have Johnston suddenly deciding not to talk.

"No, no, no!" Johnston said quickly, glancing at Amy. "At school. Some of the kids were being jerks to him. Bullying is a big problem these days, and Brian... Well, he could just let anything slough off his shoulders, but I was worried. We were at a festival and we met Mateus. He was great! There was one of those water-shooting booths—and as we watched, we saw Mateus lose on purpose, letting Brian win. He talked to us after, and we wound up talking about kids, and how cruel they could be. He mentioned our church was great and casually said he was a minister himself at his own nondenominational church. He said his flock was amazing. The kids were homeschooled, and all learned to be good to one another because they had so many activities. And we met people, and they did have all sorts of fun activities. Mateus knew how to be around kids of all ages. We took Brian out of public school and started up ourselves. Mateus was fantastic in the way he taught the kids about the cliffs, about God's beauty in nature, and how kindness was the greatest thing asked of us. Then…" He paused, wincing. "We'd all been through so much—the whole world, I guess, with disease ravaging the planet. When he told us there were signs, there had been signs already, and the black horse of the Apocalypse came to him each night…we believed."

"Were you involved with any of the murders at the pits by the river?" Amy asked quietly. "Trying to save sinners?"

Hunter didn't think an Oscar-winning actor could have pulled off Bret Johnston's look of stunned confusion.

"What? Oh! Right, yes, I mean no! No, no, no! I heard about it on the news, but… Oh, God, no! This was the first that we saw anyone about to be hurt—hurt, yeah, sorry, brutally murdered—but we really did believe she needed to be saved. It wasn't just what she did for a living… I mean, she didn't have to. Her father is richer than Midas, but she wanted to put herself through school, and that was a sin of pride. Mateus said she defiled her heart, mind, and body. But with the End of Days so close and coming on, she had realized her ways. She had come to him." He shook his head. "He made us believe!" he whispered.

"How many members were in his church?" Hunter asked.

"Forty? Forty-five. I never counted."

"Then, were they all on the cliffs today?" Amy asked.

"I—I'm not sure. I know that…" Johnston began before his voice lagged and his face knit into a frown.

"Yes?" Amy prodded.

"I know Mateus always told us he answered to a *higher authority*. I thought he meant God. But sometimes he'd be on his phone and… I think maybe he was talking to his *higher authority*. I mean, I really don't think God needs a cell phone if he chooses to communicate," Johnston added dryly and bitterly. He stared across the table at Hunter suddenly. "Brian! Brian is all right, isn't he? What's going to happen to him?"

"He's with a great social worker right now, and I believe he'll be allowed to go home with your wife's sister, Violet," Hunter said.

Johnston's face twisted into a knot of agony. "Violet—she'll take care of him?" he whispered hopefully.

"I guess Violet is really the forgiving kind," Hunter told him.

"She'll never speak to me again," he whispered. "But if she helps Brian, that will be okay! I'll just be thankful from whatever distance she requires!"

"What happened between you and your sister-in-law?" Hunter asked him.

Johnston took a breath and looked down as he spoke. "We had a falling out over the church. I asked her to join. She was incredulous, appalled we had decided to homeschool Brian. Vi believed that Brian grew strong at school, that he was remarkable and he did have friends—and all kids get punked now and then. But Brian knew how to handle it. She said we had turned into sheep, following some stupid *cult*. I said it was just a church and then I flew off the handle. I told her Brian was my son and I had the right to make choices. Then Peggy blew up at her for blowing up back at me and...she left. And we haven't spoken since."

"Do *you* know anything more about Mateus?" Amy asked him. "Surname? Where he's from, where he lives?"

"No. We saw him at functions or at his church. And it seemed so right! Church in the open—in the beauty of God's nature. And when we came into it, everyone was so nice— we were all looking for the same thing, for others who said please and thank you and good day, and meant it!"

"But you knew what was going to happen?" Hunter asked him.

Johnston winced and nodded. "There was a meeting at a bowling alley. It went on while the kids were playing. Mateus told us about this poor girl who had come to him, begging for help. And how he had prayed after, and then had a vision. In his vision, the rider on the black horse had come to him, telling him *the end* was very soon. And if he was going to help her, he had to be serious. He had to do what was painful, to have the faith and strength to do what was necessary." He paused for a minute. "I was to help him when we carried out our duty to God and bring her to be left at a fissure in the cliffs."

"And you knew where that was?" Hunter asked.

He nodded. "Mateus pointed it out to me from the trail."

"We need a list of names of everyone in your—church," Hunter told him.

"Of course. But..."

"But what?" Hunter demanded.

"We, uh, only ever used given names. I swear, though, I'll make a list. I can do approximate ages, who went with who... and you have others, right? Mateus and Brother Martin are dead, I know—but Martin wasn't the only acolyte. There were also Brother Josiah and Brother Gabriel."

Hunter glanced at Amy who was gazing at him. The *Brothers'* names were probably not real.

"They—they took Mateus," Johnston murmured. "One of them. I suppose they had to hide his body so they could go back and give it all the rites they believe...yeah, I would have...believed he deserved for being such a devoted servant of God." He looked from one of them to the other and said softly, "I don't blame you if you don't believe any of this. Until what happened... I believed with my whole heart. If Mateus said we had to kill that girl to save her, then I would have followed. And I know maybe you can't believe anyone could make such a turnaround, but…my wife and kid are *good*. The best. Kind, generous, you name it. And he would have killed Brian, and he did shoot my wife!"

Hunter believed him. He'd seen it before. Sometimes, people stayed brainwashed forever. Sometimes, they saw a truth, and it was as if a light had been turned on in their heads.

"I believe you," he said, rising. "Brian is a great kid. Before your association with Mateus, you and your wife were probably great parents."

"What happens now?" Johnston asked bleakly.

Amy stood. "Are you hungry?" she asked him.

"Um—I guess?" Johnston said the words as a confused question.

"You'll be charged and taken to a facility, but we may have a few more questions in a bit," Amy said. "Meantime, I can get you something to eat. Are you hungry?"

"Sure. Food. Thank you. I don't know if I can eat. I should try," Johnston said.

Hunter left the room with Amy right behind him. In the hallway, he heard Brian laughing as Belinda Montgomery stepped into the hallway from the room where she'd been with him.

She smiled. "That is a great kid."

"He's laughing. You must be great at what you do," Hunter said.

"You must be pretty great, too. The kid is okay…okay with being here. Okay with me, and though I still say he's going to need a therapist, you kept him…sane."

Amy glanced at Hunter as he smiled grimly.

"I know a bit about what the kid is going through. But you—"

Belinda laughed. "Hey. My ancestry is Irish, Asian, Jewish, and African American. My folks died early in a car accident, and my grandparents were all too old to raise a kid. I bounced around a few homes in my day, and I guess I learned to watch and learn, and I wound up with some wonderful people, too. I guess I just want to pay it back. I was ready to take him home with me, but it seems he does have an aunt who loves him. Of course, I need to spend time with her and the boy and make sure before I do the paperwork to get started on putting him in her custody."

"Of course," Amy murmured. "Any kid would be lucky for time with you. Brian is laughing, honestly laughing. In all this...well, it's pretty miraculous."

"Because he's a good kid," Belinda said. "Anyway, I'm going out to the front for a soda and a candy bar!" She hesitated a minute. "How is the father?" she asked.

Hunter glanced at Amy. "We think he's truly repentant, and he'll help us in any way he can—but we don't think he's lying when he claims he doesn't know much. Still, I don't want him seeing Brian yet."

"No. There needs to be some distance from this," Belinda agreed. "Well, I promised a candy bar and I don't like to break my promises—"

She broke off. Andy Mason was coming down the hall for them. "Aunt Vi—Violet Austin—is in conference room two," he said. "I've asked that she speak with the two of you and then Belinda. That work for you three?" he asked.

Hunter glanced at Belinda. "Hey, I'm on the hunt for a candy bar. Take your time. I plan to take mine and make sure Brian is going to be okay."

"Andy, we don't want to have Bret Johnston taken to a detention center yet. Can someone see to it he gets something to eat?" Amy asked. "After we meet with Violet—"

"We'll just see if we can get anything else," Hunter finished.

"I will make sure he gets food," Andy promised. "And we'll keep Johnston as long as you say." He looked at them all and inhaled deeply, shaking his head. "I've heard from the teams still out on the cliffs. It will be tomorrow before we hear anything on what might be discovered with the preliminaries at the morgue. They will, however, start on autopsies as soon as they are able to extricate the corpses. I'm assuming you'll attend?" he asked, looking from Hunter to Amy. "Oh, and last…you both fired your weapons resulting in death today. Mandatory session with our shrink. He's a good guy. You won't mind. Sometime tomorrow."

"Will do," Hunter promised. He looked at Amy, arching a brow.

"Time to meet Aunt Violet?"

"Time to meet Aunt Violet," she agreed.

They headed toward the conference room where Andy had Violet waiting for them. As they neared the door, Hunter saw Amy had paused and frowned as she glanced at her phone.

"It's the hospital, I think, the number…" she said, frowning as she answered. "Larson."

He held still, watching her as she listened.

"I'm sure it's all right and she'll be back—"

Amy broke off because the other person was speaking excitedly.

"Okay, okay. Right now, Carey, it's best if you get yourself calmed down." She glanced over at Hunter and spoke again. "All right. Hayden left your room and said she'd be back, but she hasn't come back. How long has it been?"

Amy listened again.

"Did she say where she was going? Carey, did she say she'd be back in five minutes, or was she going to go home, or—" Amy paused to listen. "All right. We'll get someone out to her place, and we'll see what we can find out. But if she said she was going home to feed the cat, she may have gotten tied up with something else. You can't upset yourself so much—"

Hunter couldn't make out the words being said, but he could hear the hysteria in the voice coming through Amy's phone.

It was Carey Allen, their first surviving victim, the young woman from the pit.

"Carey, Carey, please. I promise you. I'm at the local head-quarters now, and I can speak with the acting director here and get someone out to check on her. Please, calm down, try to rest, and we'll do everything possible to find her."

Amy finally managed to end the call, looking distressed. "I guess you got most of that," she told Hunter. "Apparently, Hayden has been spending time with Carey. But she has a life and work and a cat. She left the hospital a couple of hours ago, saying she'd be back. But she didn't come back, and Carey can't reach her on her phone."

"If it's just a couple of hours—"

"Wait, wait, wait! I know. She's an adult. If she wanted to, there is nothing illegal about an adult choosing to disappear. Normally, a person wouldn't be considered missing so soon. But Hunter, this isn't *normally.*"

"All right. We'll talk to Andy. He can have some folks get hospital security footage and check that she did leave and got safely to her car. And he can send someone out to her house for a wellness check."

"This is all so crazy!" Amy said.

"Go in and start talking to Violet. I'll find Andy and get the ball rolling to find out where Hayden got to, okay?"

"You're not being dismissive, are you?"

"No. I'm just trying to be rational and competent," he said, smiling slightly.

She smiled in return and headed on into the room where Violet waited.

He hurried down the hall, searching for Andy. His assistant indicated he had gone into his office.

Hunter continued on.

Rational and competent.

Right.

On top of everything else that day, he had a damned bad feeling.

Carey's worry was probably justified.

Whoever the rider of the black horse might be, Hunter was afraid that, yes, he'd somehow managed to take Hayden Harper.

And they needed to find her quickly. While she was still alive.

9

Amy knew the local agents and police were competent, and they would do whatever was necessary to check on the welfare of Hayden Harper. But Hayden Harper was an adult, and just because she'd promised to return to see a friend and hadn't—and even though she wasn't answering her cell phone—there was no reason to suspect something had happened to her. Adults lost their phones, ran out of battery, and got caught up in something else all the time.

Except the circumstances here were different. Hayden had been the one to report Carey missing.

They worked for the same advertising agency. Amy and Hunter had been to the agency. So if someone from Barrington Advertising was involved, Hayden might well appear to be an appetizing victim, especially if she could just be swept off the street.

But they had come from the cliffs where a man they knew as Mateus had nearly sliced out a young woman's heart. There had been bodies found in a crevice of the cliffs. Brother Martin had been shot and killed. And it could be the two of them had been the force between all the murders.

Amy wished she believed it.

But now a traumatized boy was in need. And they were lucky. Andy Mason's friend in children's services, Belinda Montgomery, seemed to be as nice as Andy had promised. More importantly perhaps, she was competent, aware of personalities and the needs of children coming from devastating conditions. She didn't patronize; she knew how to relate. Still, Violet Austin was the boy's aunt and was close to him. Amy was grateful the powers that be seemed to believe it was all right for him to be cared for by his aunt.

And although she was worried about Hayden, right now she needed to feel comfortable with the boy being cared for by his aunt Violet. She knew Hunter needed that assurance even more than she did. Violet wasn't sitting in any of the chairs; she was pacing up and down the length of table, obviously nervous and upset.

She looked to be in her late twenties, a pretty, young woman with wavy dark hair, beautiful eyes so deep of a blue they were almost a true violet, and a slim, fit figure. She hadn't had a chance to do much research on the woman, but she taught junior high school, was unmarried, hadn't so much as a parking ticket, and was two years Peggy's junior. Social media had pictures that went back to Brian's parents' wedding, and Violet was there as Peggy's maid of honor.

Violet stopped pacing as Amy walked into the conference room.

She didn't introduce herself; she stared at Amy worriedly as if they were part of a system that might take Brian away from her, possibly deeming her guilty by association with an accessory to attempted murder.

"Hi," Amy said, smiling and offering her hand. "I'm Amy Larson." She had barely introduced herself before she saw Hunter had completed his task and was entering the room. She quickly added, "And this is Special Agent Hunter Forrest. I'm sure this has all been shocking and traumatic for you—"

"I should have known!" Violet said. "I—I was appalled when they told me they were taking Brian out of school. They were all but sequestering him with people who were part of the Mateus family. My sister and brother-in-law claimed Mateus was incredible, that he was truly chosen by God. He knew everything about angels and demons and the Book of Revelations. And we should have all seen *the End* was coming! So many horrible happenings around the world. I thought it was all crazy, and I started just trying to warn them they needed to keep their world open, to see other people. Then they tried to get me to join in. Oh, everyone was so nice when you joined with them until it got competitive, until… I don't know. They believed. They truly believed all they were told. Mateus quoted from Revelations all the time. Oh, not at first…and I think the thing is he could have a truly magnetic personality. I met him a few times with them. I tried to remind Peggy about the horror of Jonestown, and how Charles Manson had created a *family*. And…she was just saddened *by me*! They kept telling me the End of Days was coming. She wanted to be among those taken by the Rapture and… I was impatient. I was angry. I told her she had a new family, and I was sorry, but I couldn't be a part of it. But I never stopped loving her! She is my only sister. Our parents are gone. And Brian is my nephew. I love him. And I am so sorry. I'm just… My God, I was so afraid of something like this! But even being afraid, I never imagined my sister might believe *murdering someone* was right!"

"It's all right," Hunter assured her. "We understand. Trust me. Even seasoned law enforcement has been shaken up. Please, though, would you sit for a minute? We'd like to talk to you, and then a lovely woman from social services is going to speak with you—"

"Will they let Brian come with me?" Violet asked in a whisper.

"I believe so. It's usually best when a child is placed in a familiar home with someone who loves them," Hunter said.

"Please, sit. Can we get you anything? Coffee, tea, water, a soda?" Amy asked her.

"I'd love coffee!" She winced. "It's so late...but I'd love coffee. I've already called in that I need a personal day tomorrow. I think..."

"That's great. Brian will need you tomorrow," Hunter told her.

"And maybe you can take him to see your sister."

"My sister is crazy!" Violet said.

"No, not anymore. Once she saw *Brother* Martin was ready to shoot her child, she was done with the whole thing," Amy told her.

"Really?" Violet asked. "Wait, what? They threatened Brian? I just knew Peggy had been shot, I didn't know—"

"She jumped in front of her child," Hunter said. "And I think we can believe her. Something like that might be compared to a light bulb going on."

"I believe she sees the truth," Amy said quietly.

"I'll get coffee," Hunter murmured. "I think I need some, too. It's... Wow. We are a few hours into tomorrow, which makes it today. I'll be right back."

He glanced at Amy. She knew he had needed to meet Violet. She could also see he believed the woman and could trust she cared deeply for Brian.

But he wanted to know if she had any other insights.

152

He'd be back quickly with coffee, and she meant to let him take the lead on delving into Violet's mind and into what she might not know that she knew. So while he was gone, she asked casually about their parents and growing up.

Growing up had been fine. Their parents had raised them in a nondenominational church, one that, in her mind, taught the right things. Their folks had just been normal. Working, raising their children, looking forward to vacations, just normal.

Hunter came back in with a tray filled with coffee cups, a small pot, a little cream pitcher and packets of sugar and sweetener.

"It is late. You made me realize how late. Or early," he added, grimacing.

He was good. He made Violet smile. They passed coffee around and then Hunter leaned back and said, "Violet, when your sister first became involved with this group and you saw Mateus and whoever else, did you get the sense Mateus was leading it all?"

"Oh, yes, definitely. They all believed he was a prophet. He had a great smile, a great way of telling a story and of playing with kids. At a fair, he would go to a ball toss, do well himself, and then teach the kids to do it themselves. It was easy to see how people liked him and fell for him at first. I think I still thought it was just a little weird they were involved in this new church in the wilderness. But then my sister stopped seeing her card group, my brother-in-law stopped playing poker. All so they could just be with this new church. Then they pulled Brian out of school—and for me, that was it. They had gone off the deep end."

"What about Brother Martin?" Hunter asked.

"I saw him a few times at the beginning. He did whatever Mateus said." She hesitated, shaking her head. "Peggy started quoting the Bible to me. End of Days! They had to be among the chosen, and they had to help whomever else they could. I said it was one thing to stockpile groceries and even build a bunker if you were afraid of war or natural disasters in the days to come, but I never imagined they could believe killing someone could save them!"

"And you never saw Mateus seem to listen to anyone else?"

"No. Except..." Violet began, stopping suddenly and frowning.

"What?" Amy prodded gently.

"Okay, and this was strange! I even said something to Peggy about it. Mateus was on the phone with someone and after, he said they needed to add in an extra meeting. There was a great deal going on, didn't we see it in the world? God had spoken to him. And when he was gone, I said to my sister, *what? God calls him on his cell phone*? And she said she really shouldn't be seeing me, anyway. I was a nonbeliever. I didn't recognize a great prophet when I was given the opportunity to know one."

Hunter leaned forward, his arms on the table. "Violet, thank you. And this is important. It was after the phone call Mateus made the announcement another meeting was needed?"

Violet nodded.

"Thank you," Hunter told her, reaching into his pocket for a card and nodding to Amy so she could produce one, too.

"I thought that, well, I know Mateus was killed. I had thought that meant it would be all over. But you don't think it's over, do you?" Violet asked worriedly. "Whoever talked to him that day is really the head of this—or the true great prophet, or an archangel, or God himself?" she whispered.

"Violet, we really don't know," Hunter told her. "But—"

"You know, I was already afraid for me. Peggy was so brainwashed and into that guy, I was afraid she'd say something about me. That when their *Armageddon* arrived, I'd be high on the list of enemies to be fought, but..."

She looked downward and winced.

Then she looked at the two of them, squaring her shoulders. "I dated a cop for a while. We're still good friends. He used to take me to the shooting range. I can shoot. And I do have a darned good alarm on my house with a darned good alarm company. I will *not* let anything happen to Brian."

"I'm glad your house is protected, but please—"

"Oh! I didn't mean I was going to go around shooting people. I just meant if someone did break into my house, I wouldn't be a wilting flower."

"We'll also see to it officers and agents are watching over the two of you," Hunter promised. "And if you don't mind, I'll give you a call now and then, too."

"Not at all—I'd be grateful. And I'm also grateful for any protection that's offered to me," she assured them.

Hunter stood, glancing at Amy. "I'm going to find Belinda and Brian," he said. He looked back at Violet. "This woman is wonderful. I think she's made him feel a little better already. But I believe you and your sister and her family were close and loving before all this, so I'm sure being with you is going to mean a lot to Brian."

"Thank you!" Violet said softly.

Hunter didn't have to find Belinda. A soft rap at the door sounded, and he quickly opened it; Belinda was there with Brian.

"Brian!" Violet whispered.

The boy ran to her sobbing. She engulfed him in her arms, and he hugged her tightly in return.

It was touching to witness. The boy truly loved his aunt Violet.

"We'll leave you all," Amy murmured, glancing at Hunter,

who smiled and led the way out. But when they were in the hall, she asked him, "Did you speak with Andy about Hayden?"

"I did. An agent is at the security center at the hospital going over the security tapes, and another agent is on his way to her home. And we have another stop to make—"

"Right. We're going to see Mr. Johnston—"

"Another stop. Conference room eight," he told her.

"Who are we speaking with?"

"Well, according to Andy in nonprofessional terms, a total wacko. Most of those picked up were terrified. They had heard they needed to *eat* the sins of others to save them, but they hadn't been part of murder before. They hadn't believed or realized until they were there that Mateus really intended to murder a girl, cut her heart out, drink her blood, and so on. I think they must have been told what the Johnstons had been told."

"And they're all murdering liars?" Amy asked, wincing.

"No. What happens is this—there will always be someone who realizes no matter what they're being fed, there's something seriously wrong with murder. Several dangerous cults through the years have been broken up because a member managed to get out, and get to the authorities, and tell them about *sacrifices*, torture, and murder. But they were all careful. They knew they might be the next sacrifice if they didn't make it to the authorities with their information. I think many of those who were there were simply terrified they might be deemed sinners and would be sacrificed or, perhaps in this case, *purified* themselves if they didn't obey their prophet. But this fellow—his name is Riley Franklin—told the arresting agents they were damned, because they had condemned the girl to the fires of Hell for eternity by saving her life in this world. He didn't know who had fired the shot, but we would all burn forever for having killed the greatest warrior, God's own prophet, who would face Armageddon. I don't know if it will lead us anywhere, but… "

"Maybe he knows the power behind the cell phone call," Amy said. "Do we know anything about his background?"

"Andy said it was what we might expect. His father abandoned the family when Riley was four. Mother was an addict. He was shifted from foster home to foster home after his mother died of an overdose. He might have made it. He grew up, married a girl he'd fallen in love with when they were just twenty, and then she was shot at the jewelry store where she was working. Nothing in his life was going right, so… Well, he was easy prey. He just took a job about six months ago at a Denver gas station. I'm thinking he might have followed Mateus here from wherever, or someone might have suggested he could find a true spiritual path here with Mateus. Anyway, let's find out."

He opened the door to the room where Riley Franklin waited. Riley was sitting at a conference table and stared at his thumbs as he twirled them. Amy thought he was young, early twenties, a thin man with unruly dark hair and a narrow face.

He looked up at them. "Again," he said.

"We need to—"

"You need to speak with me. Yeah, right," Riley said, not looking at either of them.

"All right," Hunter said. "I'm Special Agent Forrest and this—"

"I don't care who you are," Riley said. He finally looked up, staring at them. "You will burn for eternity. There was a chance for some of us. Mateus was trying to save others. You have condemned yourselves and so many others. Those innocents who never knew Mateus and might have risen in the Rapture. You have condemned them, too. And talk all you want. I don't have to talk to you."

"You are entitled to an attorney," Amy said.

"Yeah, yeah, I got all that already. I don't need an attorney. You can do anything you want with me. I don't have to answer to anyone on earth. I will be judged on a different plane, just as you will be judged and damned. You people murdered Mateus, the greatest."

"Really? Who told you Mateus was such a great warrior and prophet? Mateus himself, I take it," Hunter said.

"You didn't know him."

"I'm sure you've heard about false prophets?" Amy said dryly.

Riley Franklin had claimed he wasn't going to talk.

Despite that, he suddenly flew into a rage of words. "False prophet? Mateus was more than a prophet! Don't you understand? He was more than a prophet! He was the Archangel Michael brought back as flesh and blood to lead true believers until the time came. He was required to become the leader of his flock, as he is the leader of the other angels! Are you crazy? Or are you blind? Haven't you seen all these things the Great Book has warned about? 'This know also, that in the last days perilous times shall come. For men shall be lovers of their own selves, covetous, boasters, proud, blasphemers, disobedient to parents, unthankful, unholy, without natural affection, trucebreakers, false accusers, incontinent, fierce, despisers of those that are good, traitors, heady, highminded, lovers of pleasures more than lovers of God. Having a form of godliness, but denying the power thereof.' That is you! Are you so blind! You ignored the power, the power of a man, an angel, like Mateus!"

Amy looked over at Hunter as Riley finished his quote

and ran out of steam. "I seem to remember something about 'thou shalt not kill.'"

Riley exploded again. "She was a sinner! We were trying to save her soul. She was a sinner, a horrible sinner, making other people sin. She talked to Mateus. She told him she wanted to save her soul!"

Hunter frowned as he looked at Amy. "I never saw it written anywhere that the commandment read thou shalt not kill unless you think the person is a sinner."

"No, you're right. I never read that, either. But I also heard there was a prophet greater than Mateus. Even greater than an angel in the flesh on earth. Someone else out there who was saying who was and who wasn't a sinner, who needed saving and who didn't. Because Mateus was trying to save people, too, out at the cliffs, right? Letting them hunger, taking bits of their flesh, believing he could consume their sins and let them die now to save their souls."

"Well, of course, Mateus helped others! But..."

"But?" Amy said softly.

Riley shook his head. "*We* were his people."

"Did you help Mateus bring people to the pits in the cliffs? I know you know what I'm talking about. It's been all over the news," Hunter said.

"No. But I knew Mateus was called, and when he was called, he did what he needed to do to save the souls of others. Oh, don't you see! It's coming! How can you be so blind?"

"Who called Mateus? Who called on him to help?" Amy asked.

Riley stared at her, truly confused. "God," he said softly. "God, of course!"

"And God called him on a cell phone?"

"God could speak to him through the sun, through the clouds, through the wind—and, of course, I imagine, when he so chose, God could use a cell phone!" Riley declared passionately.

Amy glanced at Hunter. She thought they both knew the man had given them what they needed—assurance that while Mateus had been an *angel and prophet* to his group, he was not the master puppeteer.

"Interesting," Hunter murmured, glancing Amy's way, and rising. "Well, good luck with your time left on earth here," he said.

"You're leaving? What about me? I've been sitting here forever. When do you let me go? I need to go to work tomorrow. Today. I need sleep. I need to mourn! I need to say my prayers for Mateus. I need time—"

"Oh, I believe you're going to have time," Hunter told him.

"When do I get out of here? I'm sick of being in this room—"

"Oh, well, don't worry. You're not going to be in this room long. The next room is going to have bars around it. So... Well, here's the good news. You'll have lots of time to say prayers for Mateus," Hunter said.

Riley began to spew out obscenities and promises they were going to burn forever.

Amy smiled at him, shrugged, and followed Hunter out.

Andy was standing in the hall.

"Go home," he told them.

"Home?" Hunter said.

"Sorry, go to your hotel! That's an order. Not just from me, from your boss, Hunter, from Garza. And since Amy is on loan to him, he doesn't want her worn to a frazzle. This isn't going to go away. There are still several people you might want to talk to—"

"Not to worry, we're both exhausted," Hunter told him. "But I want to check on Bret Johnston. And what about Hayden Harper?"

"Did you find her?" Amy asked anxiously.

"No, she wasn't at her house," Andy said. "She did leave the hospital and get into her car and drive out of the parking lot. But—"

"What? She was going to stop off at the grocery store at one in the morning?" Amy asked. She winced. She hadn't meant to speak that way to Andy.

"I know you're worried," Andy said. "But you have to let it go for tonight. Have faith in my people. We're pulling traffic cams. We'll find something. Amy, I promise you, we are doing everything humanly possible."

"I know," Amy said quietly. "But has anyone gone in to see Carey? To let her know we really are searching for Hayden?"

"Yes, Amy, you know I have several people at the hospital. And she's been assured we won't stop."

"And we really won't stop, right?" Hunter asked.

"You know my word is good," Andy said.

"I do," Hunter agreed.

"And I am ready to keel over," Amy murmured.

"I just want to see Johnston and if Violet and Brian haven't left yet—" Hunter began.

"Now there's a place where we've had a win," Andy said. "Brian, Violet, and Belinda talked a while, and...with Violet's and Belinda's blessing, Brian is saying goodbye to his father."

"Oh!" Amy said, as she walked down the hall, then stopped.

"Room three!" Andy said.

She smiled, and Hunter was beside her, anxious as they pushed open the door.

Bret Johnston was seated and Brian was at his side. His father's arm was around him as he spoke. Belinda stood near the door and Violet was in a chair across from Bret.

Hearing them enter, Bret quickly looked their way. "This is true goodness," he said softly. "Violet is going to watch Brian as long as we need her to do so." He looked over at Violet. "I can't believe how close we came to losing her."

Violet glanced their way and shrugged. "They weren't losing me. They were throwing me away."

"Oh, God, Violet—" Bret began.

"Hey, it's all right. I'm going to be happy if you and Peggy have snapped out of it," Violet said. "The kid is my nephew and Peggy is my sister, and well, you're okay when you're not all crazy in the head." She smiled at Amy and Hunter and winked. "I do believe we're going to be all right."

"I think we will do prison time," Bret Johnston said quietly. "And that's as it should be, Brian. You were the smartest of us. Thank God we have you!"

"We'll leave you all, then," Hunter said. "You have our cards—if any one of you need us for anything, call us."

"And seriously," Belinda said, "we're *all* here, if and when you need us or just to make sure you're doing okay!"

Amy looked at Belinda and smiled. Whatever happened anywhere else, Belinda would make Brian a priority in her work and life.

"Good night, then," Hunter said.

They waved to the group, let the door close, and headed toward the reception area where there was a fair amount of commotion going on.

Agents were taking Riley Franklin out to bring him to his new room "with bars" until he was arraigned.

Amy didn't think a judge would allow him out before his trial, but it was possible a judge would deem him a fine candidate for a mental facility.

"Burn! Burn, burn!" Riley screamed. "You're all going to burn in the inferno of Hell forever and ever and ever! That's eternity!"

None of the agents paid him the least attention.

And when he was gone, Amy and Hunter looked at one another and shook their heads.

"We're out of here," Hunter said, as he took her hand and led her out.

"So different from what I leaned growing up," Amy murmured.

Hunter smiled. "Ah, remember what can be learned from wise ones among us, right? There's nothing wrong with the majority of religions in the world—it's what men can do with religion that can be bad."

"And you still have faith," she murmured.

"I do," he said, squeezing her hand. "I'm just more on the 'we're not supposed to kill' page than some others."

"But we both killed people today."

"To save others. And even knowing that, it bothers us both we had to take lives. That's why we have appointments with the shrink tomorrow before we can go on. That was what... just as it was turning dark? Oh, wait, I keep forgetting that it is tomorrow. We need sleep. And while many things may bother us, remember we both do this for what good we can do."

They hadn't quite reached the car, and she turned and almost tripped them both by hugging him.

"I...uh, what? That was nice, but—"

"Brian. Seeing him, I know that had to hurt you."

"I do feel badly about the whole thing. I just keep trying to wrap my mind around the fact his folks were going to just watch a murder."

"I think they really believed they could save a sinner."

"That's what's so terrifying—what people can believe." He shook his head. "There are even massive cults online these days. Luckily, most of the time they get only a little crazy, but history shows us some very bad things happen as well. But I feel good. Brian is an exceptionally smart and intuitive kid. He knew what they were doing was wrong. But he also loves his parents."

"Will they do time?" Amy asked. "Anyone brought in was arrested as an accessory to attempted murder."

"That's up to a judge and the courts. Anyway...sleep! Car is here, let's get in it."

They drove to the hotel and waved to the night clerk as they headed to the elevator. In the room, Amy realized she could barely stand the physical state of herself; she had to shower.

"I'm exhausted, but I don't think I could sleep with me after crawling around the cliffs in the woods and hiding in the dirt and... I mean, if you're too tired, you don't have to shower. I can stand you, just not myself. I am tired. None of that is coming out right! Just...um...whatever!"

Amy dropped her bag and started stripping as she headed to the shower.

She was grateful the hotel had good hot water and really decent water pressure.

She heard the door open and felt movement of the shower curtain as Hunter stepped behind her. She was so tired, and yet...

She closed her eyes, blissful, as she felt his hands move along her back and then her rib cage and her buttocks. She turned into his arms, reaching for the soap, sliding it over his body, feeling the ripple of movement and the growth of another body part.

Smiling, she kissed him as the hot water poured over them.

A few minutes later, they were thoroughly soaped and steaming from the fall of the water. But Amy pulled away, laughing. "I think we're too big for this little shower and for anything wild and exotic as the music of the rushing water plays!"

"Not only that, I'd feel real badly if I had to call Andy and tell him we weren't working at all tomorrow—later today—because we slipped and fell—together somehow—and have broken limbs!"

Laughing, Amy stepped out and grabbed a towel, tossed one to Hunter as he came out after her. But he used his towel on her which made her use her towel on him, and they managed to laugh and push one another out, almost tripping over one another, before falling onto the bed.

"Now see? We did fall," Hunter teased.

"There is so much to be said for beds," Amy replied.

Laughter turned into passionate kisses. She'd been so, so tired.

And yet for the moment, feeling his lips, the tip of his tongue, the caress of his fingers moving over her flesh...

She was blissfully awake and aware; they both grew more and more urgent, teasing, caressing, coming together at last...

And bursting into that moment of sheer sensation before lying cradled in one another's arms, curling together, something that made the act of making love even more beautiful.

He whispered, "I love you."

She smiled, and went into *Star Wars* mode, saying, "I know."

He laughed, and she whispered she loved him, too.

In minutes, she closed her eyes and slept. There was nothing so secure or comfortable or even more life-affirming, even after a rough day, than simply sleeping in his arms.

10

"Please!" Carey said. "They're still missing, and with everything that's discovered about whatever monstrous thing is going on, I'm more and more scared! No one has seen or heard from Don yet, and now Hayden has gone missing, too!"

Carey was being released from the hospital that day. Hunter and Amy were there. They were introducing her to a few of the agents who would be on duty watching over her home.

That was a two-pronged necessity. On one hand, whoever had failed to kill her at the pit might try again. They knew the dead "messiah" Mateus had helped lure people to the caves or dumped them there once they'd been kidnapped, but they also knew he had received orders from someone via his phone. She needed protection, and those watching out for her just might discover the identity of anyone sent to finish the job.

Amy answered her with the best assurance she could manage.

"Carey, we are aware. We've informed every officer and agent out there that Hayden and Don are missing and possibly in danger."

Carey was dismissive. "Possibly in danger? Amy! You know something terrible has happened. A woman like Hayden doesn't just leave, say she's coming back, and never show up. And Don! He was with me. I fell in a pit. And he hasn't been seen since." She paused, frowning. "They haven't identified any of the bodies found at the pits as Don, have they?" she asked worriedly.

"No, and they have identified most of the victims," Hunter said, glancing at Amy. "Carey, believe me, please. We are doing everything humanly possible. The federal government and local law enforcement have this case as an absolute priority."

Carey closed her eyes and leaned back. She was dressed and ready to go home, but she had been sitting on the bed, waiting for her discharge papers.

"I know. I know, and I'm so sorry," Carey said. "I just… I'm so lucky! I'm alive. And I am so afraid my friends might not be."

"We won't give up, Carey. Again, that we promise," Hunter told her.

A nurse stepped into the room along with the agent assigned to get Carey home and take first watch. Hunter and Amy excused themselves and stepped out into the hall.

"One down," Hunter murmured.

"Victim or cult member first?" Amy asked him.

"Closest," he said smiling.

"Peggy Johnston is just a few doors down," Amy told him.

"Okay, so Peggy first. Ironic, isn't it?"

Amy glanced at him.

"Peggy Johnston, about to take part in a murder to save

the soul of the victim, and Magda Kenward, the victim who didn't know others thought her soul needed saving," Hunter said. "Both are on the same floor of the same hospital. Of course, with agents and police watching over everything. Does Magda Kenward know one of the cult members who was about to cut her heart out is just down the hall?"

"Peggy is no danger to Magda now," Amy said, frowning.

"No, I don't think she is," Hunter said. "Trust me. I understand more about the Johnston family than most people."

"Of course," Amy murmured.

He shook his head. "And still after all I lived through, after all I've seen—we've seen now—it is hard to understand the human mind. Cults seem to offer the warmth, the friendship, the kindness, the belonging that people need. And there have been so many cases when people have gotten away, but many haven't—because they came to realize if they didn't go with the leader, they were in danger of being sacrifices or simply murdered as a warning to the rest of the members."

"I think it really was like a light switch with Peggy," Amy said. "I guess instinct kicked in or the simple depth of a mother's love for her child."

"They'll still need a lot of therapy," Hunter said.

"Right. So…"

Hunter and Amy nodded to the second agent in the hallway and stepped into Peggy's room. While she would be placed under arrest for arraignment when she was released from the hospital, she had not been chained to her bed.

She was reclined but with the bed set up halfway between flat and raised. Her eyes were closed.

An IV was still attached to her arm.

She heard them and opened her eyes. She saw Amy and started to smile, saw Hunter behind her and sighed softly. "It's you!" she said. "I… Thank you. You saved me. And Brian. I may not be worth it, but Brian is, and…"

"It's all right. It's over," Hunter said.

"It's not over. I have so much to apologize for!" she said. "It just…it just started out so good! Kids were never to bully kids. There were activities families did together. I never… How was I so sucked in?" Tears stung her eyes. "Violet has forgiven us! That's a miracle, that's true goodness! She'll take wonderful care of Brian no matter what happens to me…and Bret. Whatever happens to us, we deserve. And I will accept it. But I am so grateful Brian is with Violet."

"Peggy, we can't tell you what attorneys and judges will do—and you and Bret may face some time, but thankfully, Magda didn't die. And with real remorse, maybe sentencing won't be harsh. Some believe we're all the enemy, and anyone responsible for the loss of Mateus will burn into eternity," Hunter said. "Some of your group just might wind up in mental facilities for the criminally insane. There could even be community service and probation—but don't quote me on that because, again, Amy and I are not attorneys or judges."

"We were just checking on you. How are you feeling?" Amy asked.

"They're keeping me out of pain," Peggy said. "I will be all right. I lost a lot of blood. They're giving it back to me, bit by bit, and monitoring me. I don't think I'll be in here too long. And I'm so grateful. Again, I thank the two of you. They're letting Violet bring Brian to see me! I want to see him so badly. I just pray he can forgive me!"

"He will forgive you," Hunter said with certainty. "He loves you. And he knows you would have died for him. And trust me, that means a lot to a kid."

"I just hope one day we can be a family again," Peggy said.

"You're still a family right now," Amy told her.

"Peggy, I have a question for you," Hunter said. "Violet mentioned she had met Mateus. And after a phone call, he said there had to be another meeting. Do you know who he was talking to or do you know... Was there someone he took orders from?"

"Orders," she murmured thoughtfully. "Now that you mention it...yes. We were at a fair. Mateus was being great with several of the kids there. Then he excused himself and answered his phone. When he came back, he was talking about a meeting that needed to take place. I think he said we needed to perform a rite. So maybe someone did tell him the young woman needed to be taken and her sins needed to be *absorbed* by others."

"You have no idea who he might have been speaking to?" Hunter asked.

Peggy's face knit into a mask of regret. "I'm so sorry. No."

"But when you think about it, you agree he seemed to be taking orders from someone?"

"Looking back now, I'd say it was obvious," she said quietly.

"All right, well, you take care," Amy said. "And we're glad you'll get to see Brian."

"He is truly everything," she whispered, then smiled and waved as they left the room.

Their last stop was with Magda Kenward.

She was sitting up in bed, watching a movie on the television set on the opposite wall.

She greeted them with a quick smile.

"Thank you!" she said. "Thank you! Amy, you did come to check on me!"

Hunter hadn't met her yet—not when she'd been conscious. Amy introduced him, and she thanked him, too.

"One more night. If I've responded well to everything to clean out my system, I get to go home tomorrow," she said.

"That's great," Amy told her. "Glad to hear it! By any chance—"

"Do I remember anything else?" Magda asked. She shook her head. "I'm so sorry."

"Agents are working to get a photo book together of the cult members they've brought in," Hunter told her. "Maybe you'll recognize one of them as someone who was hanging around the club."

"I will be more than happy to help in any way!" she assured them, and then frowned. She was looking toward the door, and Hunter quickly turned to do the same. There was a man standing there.

A man they knew from their visit to the Barrington Advertising Agency.

It was Malcolm Barrington.

The man was dressed for work in a handsome suit.

"Excuse me," he told them.

"Do you need one of us?" Hunter asked. "Have you heard from Hayden or Don?"

"No, I'm afraid I haven't—and trust me, this isn't like either of them. With all that's gone on and hit the news lately, we're all deeply concerned, all their coworkers, families, and friends. Hayden and Don are loved and valued. I came to check in on Carey and see how she was doing. I was delighted to see she'll be going on home. And since I was here, I asked one of the agents if he thought it was all right if I introduced myself and checked in with Miss Kenward. I wanted to assure her if she wanted a...different job at any time, we'd be happy to find a place for her at Barrington Advertising."

"That's so nice of you!" Magda said. "Thank you. I—I don't know what I'm going to do. I'm just paying my way through college—"

"And I will be happy to work with you on that," Barrington told her.

"Wow. I—I'm going to take a few days," Magda said. "And then—"

"The offer remains open," he said. "I'm sorry. I didn't mean to intrude. I was just here seeing Carey, and thought... well, you might want something different. Anyway, I'll get out of your hair—and know again, you're welcome at Barrington anytime."

He smiled a little awkwardly and turned away. Hunter nodded at Amy and went after Malcolm and stopped him in the hallway.

"I'm sorry—I am a man who knows protocol. I should have asked permission from you before going to that young woman's room," Barrington said.

"It's all right. Offering her a job was a nice thing," Hunter told him.

Barrington nodded, looking away. "I heard, too, that one of the members of that wretched cult was in here, wounded. I found myself wishing that... Well, I want to be the person who can forgive, but I think of these young ladies who came so close to death and...well. Anyway. I have not heard from Don or Hayden. Your people haven't found anything?"

"No, sir, I'm afraid not. Don was never in Vegas—we know that much."

"But you broke up the cult on the cliffs—"

"We think there's more to it than what we've seen," Hunter told him. "You're top brass at your company. It was nice of you to come in here."

"We are a private company and it is my company," Barrington said. "Naturally, I'm going to care about each and every one of my employees."

"Of course."

"And you are working to solve this thing all the way, right?" Barrington asked.

"At the local, state, and federal levels, yes," Hunter told him.

"Thank you. Well, as you said, I am the big cheese. I better get myself to the office. Thank you, and you take care."

"You, too," Hunter told him.

He headed back to Magda's room where Magda and Amy were both smiling.

"I think he wanted to offer me a *decent* lifestyle," Magda said. She shook her head. "I don't do anything evil. I don't even do lap dances, but the girls who work with me who do aren't doing anything horrible, either. The club has all kinds of rules. But I guess sex is just evil to some people. I have a boyfriend who knows what I do, and he comes in sometimes. Most customers know who he is. And he thinks...my dad has money. He's offered to pay for me. But I want to make my own way—and I swear to you, I don't do anything illegal or even morally wrong! All right, to some people maybe showing lots of the body is wrong? Whatever! I think I'm going to go home for a while. To my folks' place in LA. I'll be far from all this."

"That's not a bad idea. But let the agents here look out for you for the next few days, until you're really on your feet and..."

Magda looked at him and shook her head. "I am grateful. I can't tell you how grateful. But it seems like this... I don't know. It may go on a very long time. And back in LA, my dad's house—well, my folks' house, but my dad is the dude who made all the money. Don't get me wrong, my mom is great, just not a tech mogul. The house is safe. It has an incredible alarm system. And we have two giant Doberman dogs that patrol. And Dad is a crack shot. I can't live the whole rest of my life in fear," Magda said. "I need to feel something a little bit normal."

"That's admirable. I'm glad you can go to your dad's house—or your parents' home—and it's a well-guarded place. But let the agents here get you home, watch until you're up to par, and see you get there safely," Hunter said.

She smiled. "I will. I owe you two—and I promise."

Amy smiled and told her, "That's nice. You don't owe us— you owe you. Go forth and live a great life. Well, okay, you take care. We'll still check up!"

They said their goodbyes to her and left. They spoke briefly with the agents in the hall and headed on out of the hospital.

"Wow!" Amy murmured, looking around. "It's dark again!"

"Yeah, that happens when you shift your hours around."

They had slept in that morning. Then, before heading to the hospital, they'd gone into headquarters to have their sessions with the psychiatrist.

"And I'm hungry," Amy said.

"Me, too."

"And frustrated."

"Me, too. I mean, as far as the case goes."

He glanced her way with a grin. She punched him lightly in the arm before walking around to get into the car. "Okay, then, somewhere for dinner, and then we figure out where to go from here? There are more men and women who were brought in from the cliffs. I'm thinking we could talk to more of them. And I know the ME's office has been working to identify the dead so we can get a better grip on victimology. They'll find out who Mateus was and where he came from, and there could be some leads in his background."

"Right," he murmured and started the car.

Amy looked at him with a frown as they pulled out. "What are you thinking?"

He shrugged. "Okay, at a recent conference of psychiatrists, they had a number of speeches on ways to help *un*-brainwash people. Those speeches indicated there really is no proven data on how to help, and a lot more needs to be done. Sometimes, you get a leader who is just a magnet—so charismatic people flock around them. And then they discover they can make people do things. Often, they do have an ideology. Many are truly believers. Some come to believe they are messiahs or angels or someone above all others. My personal opinion of Jim Jones is he was a horrible human being. His mass suicide wasn't for a good reason—it was just because he knew he was going to go down. And if so, well hell, he'd make them all go out in a blaze of cyanide. Just my opinion. You have the Heaven's Gate situation where they all seemed to believe they were going to a higher level. And there have been smaller cults in which someone was truly religious. The groups started off in constant Bible study, then the leader decided he was special. And if you were against him, you were evil and then worthy of death. If you made a move against the core, you deserved punishment—death. And if you weren't one of the family, you were a sinner and deserved death. But—"

"But?"

"You also have people who learn how to manipulate others with promises and amazing speeches—with nothing but their own gain in mind."

"And," Amy said, "another quote here from John Edward Acton in 1887. 'Absolute power corrupts absolutely.' These guys get a taste of power, and it's pure euphoria."

"Okay, so in my opinion, an experienced one in many ways, whoever is behind this whole thing doesn't have an iota of holiness in his agenda and doesn't even delude himself into believing he does. There's an *endgame* in his plan, far more so than the concept of *End of Days*. I'm even starting to wonder if Magda Kenward was taken because she was a stripper and she worked crazy hours that allowed for a quiet street, or because there might have been the sheer power of killing the daughter of a prominent man in a brutal and bizarre fashion."

"It's all about money?" Amy asked.

"I don't know if it's money or power. Or both," Hunter said. He glanced at the clock on the dashboard and said, "All right. Dinner already."

"Or lunch, since we had breakfast at about twelve," Amy said. "And then we could—"

"Amy, we started off with the shrink. We've talked with Carey, Magda, and Peggy. Last night, we interviewed the one wacko who is convinced he's still going to be swept up in the Rapture while the rest of us will burn forever. As we said earlier, these guys have forgotten all about 'thou shalt not kill.' Some are convinced it's really the thing God would want them to do. I'm going to say we're at a dead end until we get more information on Mateus and the others who have been found in the pits and in the crevice up on the cliffs. We won't stop. I promised Carey and I mean it. But I'm thinking dinner, a normal bedtime, and an energetic start in the morning."

She nodded. "Did they find whatever cell phone Mateus was using?"

"Not that I know of—not yet. It wasn't on his body."

"Then whichever of his followers moved the body knew enough to make sure he wasn't found with his phone. That suggests to me one of the people brought in knows something about whoever Mateus spoke to on the phone."

"Or one of the people who didn't get swept up," Hunter reminded her.

"Think we should search the cliff area again ourselves?" she asked.

"We could. Or we could start going through the people who were caught."

"Both," she said decisively.

He grinned. "All right. Call Andy. See if there's anything new."

Amy put the call through on speaker.

"Andy, anything else happen we should know about?" Amy asked.

"Unfortunately, no," Andy said. "We're working on backgrounds of the victims now, but nothing is really standing out. We've been getting video in from every traffic cam in the state just about and have nothing yet on Hayden Harper or Don Blake. Trust me, we have everyone working on it."

"We spoke with Magda Kenward again," Amy said. "And if we get a photo roster—"

"Of the people taken on the cliffs, yes. We're working on it—we'll get an agent out to see her later this evening.

"Now, we've been working on your theory, Hunter. We're looking into the pasts of the victims identified. So far, no murderers or armed robbers, but we found a few with divorces, possible marital affairs, and an accusation of fraud. Things I suppose one could see as sins. Oh, a boss who seemed to fire a lot of employees. So, Hunter, you think this is real?"

"No," Hunter said flatly. "But I think this master killer—to keep his flocks here and there and all over—knows he has to accrue true believers, a real family believing in love and togetherness. His followers obey every command because they are so rooted in the belief, or so terrified they may be seen as sinners themselves if they don't completely follow the master."

"Yet, with this group, Mateus was the Messiah."

"Right. But someone was pulling his strings. He was taking orders on a cell phone. We need to find that phone."

"We'll get groups out again combing the cliffs at first light," Andy promised. "All right, so—"

"We're going to dinner," Amy told him. "And then—"

"Early to bed, early to rise," Hunter finished, grinning at her quickly.

"Folders on everyone we have will be ready for you in the a.m.," Andy promised. "And we'll be ready to see if Miss Kenward can identify any of the men or women we've brought in."

"Thanks," Hunter said briefly.

"Thank you," Andy said and ended the call.

"So," Hunter said. "What's your culinary inclination for the evening?"

"Food," Amy said briefly.

"That really narrows it down."

She laughed. "Room service. We'll take a real evening off!"

"All right. Now that definitely sounds like a plan to me."

In their room, Amy checked the menu and decided, "Grouper meunière! Sounds like a winner."

"Go for two."

"You don't have to—"

"Nope. Works for me."

Amy put through their order, then reclined back on her pillow. He checked his messages, then looked over bits of information Andy had sent him on the victims discovered in the pits.

Some remained unidentified.

The same was with the victims found in the cliffs. In a few cases, the bodies were no more than bones that had become disarticulated and fallen into the dirt below.

Even with the best experts and equipment, teams were

having trouble extricating everything that had fallen between rocks—including body parts.

He read the notices aloud to Amy.

"This is so monstrous, Hunter. I just wonder…"

"What?"

"Will we get to the bottom of it?"

"We will," he told her as he stretched out beside her. "So, what did you think of Barrington's visit today?"

Amy shrugged. "He supposedly is a good and caring boss."

"Don Blake. Victim or puppeteer?"

"Haven't a clue. But he is one or the other, I do believe."

"I find it interesting Don has been missing since Carey went into the pit, and now Hayden is among the missing, too. A security camera has her leaving the hospital, but they can't find her car on a traffic cam anywhere. Same with Don Blake. He just seemed to disappear. No one can trace his movements through a camera anywhere."

"You think Barrington might be involved?" Amy asked him. "Or!" she said, sitting up. "I know. You think Don and Hayden have both disappeared on purpose?"

"Not necessarily," Hunter said. "These people know how to brainwash others into a cult. And there is a master puppeteer. The master would have to be bright enough, I would imagine, to know you need to make a car as well as a person disappear. That way, they're missing. You find a car, and you can be pretty sure there *was* foul play of some kind."

Amy shook her head, leaning back down. "We need an answer somewhere. A solid lead that could bring us closer to the headman. Or woman."

A knock on their door alerted them that room service had arrived.

And the food was more than what he had come to know as

"hotel-decent." It was good. And when they'd finished eating, Hunter determined they were done for the day.

He pushed the food cart out into the hallway, and then made a dramatic reentry to the room, leaped across the last few feet to the bed, and drew Amy into his arms.

She laughed and told him he reminded her of a high school kid.

He thanked her for the compliment, and laughter continued between wet kisses and caresses and their clothing going flying in various directions.

It was a good night. They could talk about the case.

And they could let it go for a few precious minutes. Planting kisses down the length of her thigh, he murmured, "I am so in love with your body."

She angled her body around to press kisses on his back, murmuring, "Just my body?"

"Well, you know, your mind is okay."

She gave him a swat, twisted around, crawled atop him and warned, "Careful! I can be a dangerous woman!"

"Thank God for that," he told her, taking the lead, sweeping her beneath him and kissing her lips before saying, "I am madly in love with your brilliant mind and the beauty in your soul, even as you work in this monster minefield we've both found to be necessary. Madly, madly in love with... Oh, screw the poetry. I'm in love with your eyes when you look at me like that..."

"Lovely but really, all talk!"

"I'll show you all talk!"

Later, they lay together, just comfortable, touching, dozing, and ready to really get a good night's sleep.

Then Amy stirred, and he knew she'd heard her cell phone vibrating on the bedside table beside her.

She sat up frowning and Hunter did the same. He glanced at the clock.

It was midnight.

"Carey? Yes, yes, no, it's fine. I told you to call at any time at all. But…"

She listened as Carey spoke. All Hunter could hear was the hysteria in the young woman's voice.

"We'll be right there."

Amy threw the covers off and looked at Hunter.

He was already getting out of bed, waiting for her to explain.

"She's gotten a text from Hayden."

"And what does it say?"

"Carey, help! They've got me!"

11

There was a fine line they had to maintain with work. Caring for those who were victims and keeping the distance needed to carry out their investigation with cool heads and complete professionalism.

Amy knew how distraught Carey was feeling, and she had to put a check on her own sympathy.

She spoke with Carey, assured her there were things law enforcement could do. And there were things they could not do.

By the time they arrived at the offices, an agent had collected Carey's phone and provided her with another. The tech team had already done everything necessary to track the location of Hayden's cell phone when she had sent the text to Carey.

And it was startling to say the least.

Andy had beaten them in. He headed over when Hunter called him to tell him about the text from Hayden.

Andy was good, just as his people were good. No matter what the hour, they could get things moving.

"I'm not sure what the heck this means, but it seems Hayden—or someone with Hayden's phone—texted from the middle of the Everglades. The Florida Everglades," Andy said.

Amy looked at Hunter.

"All right, so this is all relating back to the beginning," he said.

It was beyond surprising, but maybe, it wasn't.

"Or it's possible someone has her phone, and it's a hoax," Andy suggested. "I mean... I know you two started this in Florida. Hunter, you were in the north of the state before joining Amy in the Everglades. But the killings now have been here—and at a high rate. Do you really think Hayden has been taken to Florida? There is a sound possibility that whoever has her knows about the two of you and sent or had someone bring the phone to Florida. Apparently tracing the phone took a bit of time, because the phone is in an area of the great old River of Grass where getting any kind of a signal is a task."

"It is possible it's a ruse, of course," Amy said. "But it is also possible it all relates, and that our real puppeteer is in Florida. We know someone was communicating with Mateus by cell phone."

"The man's followers claim he can talk to God via a cell phone," Hunter said dryly. "I mean, why not, right?"

Andy shook his head. "I don't want to see you two having to hop around on airplanes for nothing, especially since... Hayden may already be dead. But the decision of what you two do really belongs to your boss, Garza. You're on loan out here with us, just as Amy is on loan from the FDLE. But between the pits and the cliffs, we have a ton of dead here," he added quietly. Then he reminded them, "Carey should have been dead. You two happened upon her before starvation and the elements could take her. Magda Kenward should be dead. You managed to stop a man from stabbing a knife through her heart. You've been important here—the work here has just begun. I know I'm big on reminding all my agents and all those working here for any amount of time that we rely on each other. It's a conceit to think others can't handle a situation. But at this office, your insight has saved lives."

"Thanks, Andy. We're all happy, and you know that and feel that, when things work out for the victim or victims. But I'm thinking Garza will need to be kept in the loop. Anyway. Did we find out anything more about Mateus?" Hunter asked.

"We hit the national databases, and we have information on Mateus. There's nothing criminal in his record. He was born Leonard Filmore in Los Angeles, California, and grew up in Orange County. Only child, parents deceased. You'll love this—he was a karaoke host through his early twenties, and then disappeared off the face of the earth. That's what we've gotten so far. We also identified Brother Martin. He was born Martin Black in Houston, Texas. He does have a record. Assault, bar fight, so it appears. The other bar customer apparently hit a sore spot with Martin by suggesting he'd been thrown out of his house at eighteen for being worthless. That's from the notes the detective wrote on the case. Martin was charged in the matter, but when it came to court, he was released for *time served*. After his release, he disappeared."

"The family has been notified of his death?" Amy asked.

Andy nodded, looking over at Hunter. "I guess he was a poster child for the kind of person who needed to obey any order, no matter how heinous, from a charismatic leader. An agent from our LA office went out to his parents' home. Father practically slammed the door on the man, telling him Martin had been dead to them for years."

Amy watched Hunter nod thoughtfully.

"You're right, Andy," he said. "It's people looking for acceptance, for a *family*, who are easily broached. Especially when what appears to be higher ideals and true purpose are introduced. Then, of course, there's one more thing."

"Fear," Amy murmured.

"Yes. Fear. Once you're in, you come to realize that not obeying the will of the leader may be deadly. There was a case in Rulo, Nebraska, that was truly terrifying. The cult arose out of a sect; and after years certain members were so terrified, they obeyed truly horrific punishments that included sex with animals. And one member's child was severely punished for *bad thoughts*, until he wound up with his head bashed in by the leader—and still his father, who dug his grave, was too terrified to do anything. With good reason because he wound up dead, too. Fear can make people do the unimaginable. But first, you must be seduced into membership. Martin, having been so rejected by his family, would have been looking for what he received from Mateus—or what he perceived he received—respect, care, and belonging. Now for Mateus...hmm. Karaoke hosts tend to be outgoing, people persons. But somewhere along the line, he met someone who convinced him there was more."

"Maybe he went through a night of really, really bad singers," Andy said dryly. "We're having a tough time tracing anything on him since he seemed to have disappeared from his known world quite some time ago. His social security hasn't been touched, no taxes, no credit cards... He went by Mateus, and that was it. Others must have been supporting him. And after questioning all those brought in, no one has any idea regarding an actual address for him. But they did *tithe* to the church, and the church was a cliff, so we can assume their *tithing* was to support Mateus," Andy told them.

"Someone knows something, but a man like Mateus, using people as he did, might have kept it close. So close that maybe only Martin knew where and how to find him if he was needed," Hunter said.

"And Martin is dead," Amy murmured.

"And we believe he *helped* with the deaths that occurred at the pits—he didn't orchestrate them. So who did?" Hunter asked. He frowned and looked at Amy. She knew what he was going to say when he spoke again, "Is there anything even slightly flaky about Barrington Advertising?"

"Pardon?" Andy said.

"Malcolm Barrington showed up at the hospital. He said he was there to see Carey. But then he stopped in on Magda Kenward as well," Hunter said.

"Offering her a job," Amy murmured.

"Well, that was a nice thing, wasn't it?"

"If he was just being a good and decent nice guy, yes," Hunter said.

Andy was studying him. "Ah, but you think Barrington might have thought of Magda as a sinner for being a stripper?"

"Well, not just that—her family has money. She just didn't want to use it; she wanted to make it all on her own. And I did a little reading," Amy said, "on the web, various sites, and through social media. According to everything I can find out there, the club where Magda Kenward works is possibly one of the most transparent—sorry, no pun intended—and legitimate out there, meaning no sex sales on the side. But Barrington possibly believes any form of stripping is sinful."

"I don't know," Andy said. "Okay, Barrington heard what had happened, and he maybe just hoped he could help the woman."

"And maybe he could care less, and he just wants to keep an eye on her in case something else about her kidnapping comes up in her memory," Hunter said. "Or she's vulnerable if he decides she does need to disappear again and have all those sins of hers taken on by others. Most likely, he may just want her dead to protect his own ass. Yes, I'm speculating. But Carey was a victim, and Don Blake has gone missing. And they both worked for Barrington."

Andy shook his head. "Okay, I understand. We become jaded quickly in this business, and I'm not saying you're wrong. I'm just saying we need to keep our minds—and our options—open. We're still dealing with the attorneys on charging the group we picked up on the cliffs. Some are suddenly remorseful, horrified, and swearing they didn't know they'd come to witness a murder and to drink blood. Others are saying we're the crazy ones, Armageddon is coming, and we're condemning souls to Hell to burn for eternity. That group...none worked for Barrington Advertising. In fact, not a person we picked up seemed to have anything in common with the others—except for Mateus, who brought them together, who taught them about the depths of love they could experience while paving the way for angels of God to return and fight at their sides."

"Hayden is in Florida," Hunter said with certainty.

As he spoke, Andy's assistant came down the hallway, anxious to speak with them. "Report from tech, sir," the young agent said. "Another text came through."

"And it said?" Andy asked.

"*Help.* Just the one word."

Hunter shook his head. "Okay, someone else has the phone, and I'm assuming they want us to think Hayden is in Florida. Whether she's there or not, I don't know. But there is no way she texted hours ago and then just texted again now. Whoever is sending the texts is not Hayden."

"You agree?" Andy asked Amy.

"I do. First, when she was taken, they would have searched her for her cell phone right away. I believe Hunter is right. I don't think Hayden is sending the messages. I agree. They'd never let her keep her phone."

"So, Hayden is still somewhere in Colorado?" Andy asked.

"I think something is going to happen here," Hunter said. "The texts are a lure. It may be important to head there soon, but today...something is going to happen here. I'm afraid something might be planned against one of the survivors."

Amy's phone was ringing. She glanced down at it. Carey was calling her again.

"Carey, we're working—"

"No, no, Amy, I'm scared!" Carey said.

"Carey, there's an agent watching the house—"

"I can see the car. I can't see the agent! There's no one in the car, Amy. I'm scared!"

"All right, stay on the phone. You have the doors locked and—"

"Yes, yes, and the windows are locked, but... Amy, I'm scared."

"All right, we'll get out there right away. And not to worry, they'll reach your agent from headquarters and we'll find out what is going on. Please don't panic, Carey. It would truly be foolish for anyone to come after you, but we won't take any chances. Stay inside, keep everything locked and keep talking to me."

She was looking at Andy as she spoke. He nodded and then he started moving down the hall. "Come with me now. I'm bringing up Gleason's body cam—he was watching Carey's house. Gleason is a good man, he'd never just leave."

They followed him quickly. He walked over to the video computer and punched keys, but instead of the dashboard all they saw was static.

Gleason wasn't in his vehicle. Andy ran the tape back to see the preceding minutes.

Back to where Gleason sat in his unmarked car. They saw the officer turn his body to reveal that he was approached by a figure in a jacket, scarf, and hat. They couldn't see anything of the man's face; he knew there was on a camera.

He kept his head down.

They could see Gleason was appropriately cautious, but when told anxiously there was something strange on the back of his car, he groaned and exited the vehicle. They could see him follow the stranger and walk around the car, and then...

The figure had stepped out of the body cam's line of vision. Moments later, the feed cut to static.

Andy's assistant had followed him in. Andy turned to him, saying, "Get the forces on it. I want any piece of security footage anyone has from that neighborhood. Closest unit to Carey's place immediately—"

"Right," Hunter interrupted. "But have them observe and surround the place."

"And let us get there," Amy said.

"They can burst in and—"

"If this is a cult lackey, he'll let himself be killed, taking Carey with him. If the police or agents burst in, she's dead. We can be there in ten minutes—give us a chance," Hunter said.

"Go," Andy said. "But keep me informed, every step of the way."

Hunter nodded at Amy and they started out quickly.

"Do you think someone will be that willing to die?" she asked.

"Whoever was sent there? Yes."

"How do people ever get so crazy?" she whispered.

He smiled. "Normal people fall prey to all kinds of propaganda all the time. Needy people are seeking something to believe in. Mind control is one of the most frightening aspects of this job that we ever face. But you know that by now."

"So, we have to figure out how to use it in reverse," Amy murmured.

He glanced at her, grimaced, and nodded. "Talking. Finding the right points. And it's something I'm betting you're better at. We're all a bit jaded, but you find empathy for everyone."

"Not everyone," she assured him. "If I knew who was doing this...um. No, I don't think empathy would kick in!"

They were in the car when both their phones vibrated; it was a call from an Officer Zwick of the local police. He had checked out Gleason's car. It was empty and there was no sign of anyone near it. A door-to-door search was ongoing. He and his partner and one more team were assigned to the house, and they were holding position, and would not force entry to the house that had been under bureau surveillance.

"We're on our way," Amy said. Hunter was driving but she could glance at the gages on his GPS. "ETA eight minutes," she said.

"We aren't hearing anything from the house," Zwick said, "but as ordered, holding pat."

"Thank you," Hunter said. He ended the call and glanced at Amy. "There has to be something on video somewhere. That neighborhood is a family-oriented, middle-income area—but I'm willing to bet there are home cameras."

"The problem is those cameras usually pick up the front of a house and don't extend to the street," Amy said.

"Officer Zwick said Special Agent Gleason had disappeared completely. And now we think whoever made him disappear is after Carey and possibly in her house already. So, what did he do with Gleason? Could a camera have caught that?"

They both heard a buzzing again; their phones were vibrating. They glanced at each other.

The caller was Andy Mason.

"We got something from the third house down," Andy told them. "The fellow who owns it is a cameraman for a local news station. The police hadn't even reached him—he called it in. He has his front and back doors covered and both side lawns. The screens are in his laundry room. Doesn't make a lot of sense to me—but he was helping his wife with the laundry. He'd seen there was a car watching over Carey's place the last few days. But he caught the figure in the scarf, hat, and jacket getting Gleason out of the car. He took him by surprise and hit him with a stun gun just as a white van came down the street. Gleason is no lightweight but after the stun gun, he was deadweight—and he was slid right into the van. The van took off. The plates were so muddied they couldn't be read. We've got an APB out on the vehicle with a description of the make and model."

"And the man who tased him?" Hunter asked.

"Disappeared off his camera's range—going in the direction of Carey's place. So far, the police have no sign of him. Or any vehicle in which he might have arrived," Andy said.

"Maybe the van dropped him off and circled around, which left him time to take Gleason," Amy said.

"Sounds logical," Andy said.

"ETA, four minutes," Hunter said.

"All right. I'll leave you to manage. Do you have a plan?"

Amy glanced at Hunter. "I think we do," she said.

"And?"

"I'm going to knock on the door, call out, pretend I'm a friend who is going to get to her one way or another," Amy said.

"And Hunter—"

"I will be right behind her," Hunter said, glancing at Amy. "Backup."

"All right. Keep me posted. I don't need two dead agents. Play it—"

"Safe," Amy said. "You bet. But we are going to try to keep Carey alive."

"Safely," Andy said.

"Safely," Amy assured him.

"Who am I kidding?" they could hear Andy murmuring as he ended the call.

His words allowed Hunter and Amy to share a quick smile. "Might have mentioned that plan to me," Hunter said.

"You said we need to talk—get some reverse messages going. Call on something in him or her—we don't really know which yet—that causes them to pause and question their assignment. Right?"

"Right. But I didn't really suggest you just ring the doorbell."

She grinned at him. "We're supposed to start off non-threatening, logic suggests. I'm a hell of a lot less threatening than you!"

"Only in a physical sense," Hunter assured her. "Seriously, you can be downright terrifying."

She looked forward. They had reached their destination. Hunter didn't bother to find a distant location; he parked on the street in front of the house. As they got out of the car, Amy saw an officer at the side of the house step out from cover to identify himself and his position and motion to them that his partner was just across the way.

His service weapon was pointed down, but in both hands, and ready. Amy assumed the man was Zwick and it seemed he knew his business.

But even for a patrolman, the world could be a minefield. Officers learned quickly.

"Good man," Hunter noted. "In position, and I'm willing to bet he got there with his fellows without being seen. All right. We know our closest backup. But let's hope we don't need it."

"Agreed. Okay, you need to be the backed-up backup now," Amy told him.

He nodded, but she wasn't sure he looked happy. "I am really well trained. And besides, I've had your guidance."

"If only my guidance could keep people alive," Hunter said. "You're good. I know it. Go for it."

"Ah, but guidance does keep people alive," Amy murmured, pushing him back lightly. Then she rang the doorbell. There was no answer. She rang it again, and again, and again. Then she banged on the door.

"Carey! Carey, open this door! I know you're there! Oh, my God, are you okay? I'm going to call the police! I'm going to break the door down! I've got to see you!" she cried.

As she expected, the door opened. Carey was not standing there.

No one was.

She didn't wait, she pressed it inward. But she didn't step in.

"Carey! I'm going to call the police!"

An arm slipped out from the side of the doorframe, reached for her, grabbed her by the elbow, and pulled her inside.

It was the man captured on Gleason's camera. He was wearing a baseball cap pulled low over his forehead, a jacket, and a scarf that was still pulled high around his neck. He had light brown hair and eyes, and was old enough to maybe have graduated high school.

He held her with his right hand; his left hand was gripped around a stun gun.

"Hey!" Amy protested. "I'm not here to hurt Carey, I swear. I just want to see her. You must be George. She told me she was dating a new guy."

"George?" he said, and then he shook his head. "Right. I'm George. Carey isn't here right now. She ran to the store. But you need to come in. You can wait."

He held her elbow. And the stun gun was close. Too close.

She smiled as she drew her own weapon, breaking from him and aiming her Glock at him. "No, George, you're going to show me where Carey is. Right now. And she'd best be okay."

"No!" he screamed the word like a child. Then a look of panic came over him. "Shoot me, shoot me, shoot me, do it!" he shrieked.

By then, Hunter had stepped in behind her and then past her, grabbed the man by the arm and wrenched the stun gun from him. The man started to fight, but he was no match for Hunter. He was whimpering as Hunter cuffed him. Then he started shrieking again.

"Kill me, kill me, kill me! I have failed in my mission. Kill me!"

Amy hoped that meant Carey was still alive.

"Where's Carey?" she asked him.

She glanced at Hunter who gave her a nod and stepped closer to the man. There were tears in his eyes.

"I failed. I...failed. I... "

"I'll get the cops in. We'll find her," Hunter said as he stepped outside to wave to the officers and then walked back into the house to look toward the back and the kitchen.

The man fell to his knees, sobbing. "Kill me, kill me!"

Four police officers filed into the house. Amy waved them forward and said, "Please, find Carey."

"On it," one said, and they walked on by.

Carey looked at the young man, broken, silent now, but with tears streaming down his face.

"I'm not going to kill you," Amy said, kneeling to look into his eyes.

He looked at her, his expression both sad and slightly wild as he rushed to explain, "I was supposed to save her soul! I was supposed to...and now I'll have to die, but now I've sinned. I've failed to carry out my command, and..."

He broke off and then he looked at Amy with desperation in his eyes. "Don't you understand? If you take my life, it will be so much better."

"No. You've been fooled. You've been lied to," Amy told him as she shook her head and touched his face gently. "Murder is wrong. Taking the lives of others is wrong."

"But their sins could be cleansed."

"No. Believe me, please. The true commandment is 'thou shalt not kill.' And none of us is to judge others. None of us is without sin. I don't want to kill you, and there is no reason for you to die. How old are you? Twenty? Twenty-one?"

He frowned. "Twenty," he told her.

"You have your whole life ahead of you. A beautiful life. Please believe me, you've been listening to the wrong people. And Carey is alive, right? Because you couldn't kill her. When it came down to it and you looked at another life—at a young woman, terrified and crying and desperate—you couldn't do it. Because in your heart, you know. Murder is wrong, and it is not something that God—in any religion—asks us to do. Cold-blooded murder is wrong. 'Thou shalt not kill,'" she repeated.

He started sobbing again.

He didn't need to answer her about Carey. Hunter walked back into the room. "Cops are calling an ambulance—I reached Andy already. Carey needs a hospital—he hit her with the stun gun—but she's going to be okay." He hunkered down by Carey and the young man. "You didn't kill her because you're a good man at heart. You were supposed to and you did zap her, but you couldn't slice her throat or her heart. And you sure as hell couldn't drink any blood."

"No, he couldn't," Amy agreed. "Because somewhere down deep inside, he knew he wouldn't be cleansing her of her sins. He knew one of the main commandments was not to kill. We need to help him."

The young man shook his head, looking from one of them to the other. "No, no, you don't understand. I am marked. They will know I have the Devil's mark. They will hunt and hunt and...they will do so much...worse."

"Worse—like cut out your heart to drink your blood? And, hmm, you were one of them who failed, and they would make it the most heinous torture in the world to save *you*, of course," Hunter said.

The man stared at him, confused.

"But that's not going to happen," Hunter said flatly. "Because we're not going to let them get anywhere near you."

"You can't stop them—" the man began.

"Oh, yes. We can," Hunter assured him. "And we will."

"We're going to need your help. But we will keep you safe. You don't need to die. You're just a kid, really. Believe me, please. Look at me and trust in me. We will help you."

He nodded and hung his head down.

"What happened to the agent in the car?" Amy asked softly.

He shook his head. "I don't know. But I didn't kill him. I just hit him with the stun gun. Then they took him in the van."

"Who are they and where is the van going?" Hunter asked.

"They? Oh, Larry took him. He's one of the true archangel's trusted lieutenants. You see, Michael the Archangel is going to lead the battle when Armageddon comes."

Amy glanced at Hunter. Mateus had supposedly been the archangel—or one of several archangels?

"I believe the archangel is dead," Amy said quietly.

He shook his head. "No, the spirit of the greatest warrior angel, Michael, can enter different men. He can be several great leaders, great warriors, at the same time. We honor and we obey, because it was a kindness to take on the sins—"

"What's *your* name?" Amy asked.

"Ian," he said. "Ian. Ian McCormick."

"Ian, just here, just now, today, you're seeing you were led far astray. Please, think. You couldn't kill. This was a test, I believe."

"They'll see," Ian said miserably. "They'll see that I failed. They will say I am marked. I am marked by the Devil, and I wasn't good enough to deserve the Rapture. I wasn't good enough to take on the sins of another."

"But you know in your heart no one can take on the sins of another," Amy said firmly.

"I just—I just couldn't kill. I failed."

"No, Ian, you didn't fail. You triumphed. Because no man can take on the sins of another. You followed God's great commandment—you didn't kill."

"Really?" he asked miserably.

"You know—deep in your heart, soul, and mind, that I am right."

Sirens sounded. An ambulance arrived.

Carey was being taken back to the hospital. Hunter glanced at Amy and then rose to walk over to speak with one of the officers.

But he didn't get the chance.

Along with the ambulance and the EMTs, Andy Mason

himself had arrived. "I'll be driving back with you and this man. I have Crandon heading into the hospital with Carey. We won't leave her alone for a second. I think we all need to talk," he said.

Ian was crying again. "You can't save me," he whispered.

"The hell I can't!" Andy said. "We're taking you to a very safe place. And we'll need to talk, but you'll be surrounded by people who will make sure nothing happens to you while you help us straighten this all out, okay?"

"I deserve to die!" Ian said.

"No. No, you don't," Hunter said. "You couldn't do it. You couldn't kill. In my mind, that very much means you deserve to live. But let's get moving. We do need to talk and it's getting late. You need to get some sleep and so do we. All right?"

Ian looked at him and nodded slowly. Hunter clutched his shoulders and helped him to his feet.

Andy Mason took him by the arm and started for the car. Hunter called back a thank-you to the cops and the paramedics, looked at Amy, and pulled her up from where she knelt.

"You know what?" he asked quietly.

"What?"

"You are damned good with weapons and self-defense, but that...well, that was really good. I think you just saved a man's mind."

She grinned at him. "Well, you know I had help. From the best."

He laughed.

"I'll take that," he told her. "Come on. Let's get in, see if he knows anything more than he's already told us, and maybe get out of the office before the cocks crow again."

She nodded, grimacing, and then asked, "Hunter, what will happen to these people, though? Will they all go to prison?"

"Some will. It will depend on what crimes they're charged

with. Some will come out of this okay, and I'm afraid others will not. We've seen it happen throughout history. Propaganda has always been a powerful tool. The human mind can be the most powerful weapon known to man because it's the human mind that controls all else. Just like the human body, the human psyche is, in the great scheme of things, fragile. Amy, we do our part. Then, we trust in the laws of our country and in the humanity of it as well. Anyway... Hey. Let's get into the office so we can get the hell out of it at some point. The human mind also needs sleep. And you know, the body needs bits of the good and the beautiful to stay in good shape."

"And being together is a bit of the beautiful," Amy murmured softly.

"You nailed it," he assured her.

They headed for the car.

As they did so, Amy couldn't suppress a yawn. And she lowered her head, smiling to herself. Hunter was right.

She thought he was one of the strongest men she had ever met. And she believed in her own strength. But even so, they, like all other human beings, were fragile.

12

Hunter sat with Amy in a conference room at headquarters facing Ian McCormick. He appeared to be a truly broken and miserable man swimming in a sea of uncertainty.

Amy's words had touched him.

But he was now terrified.

"Ian, you know you're safe now," he told him. They'd gotten him a soda. He hadn't wanted food; he'd said he couldn't eat.

"I will never be safe!" Ian said quietly. "They're out there. They're out there everywhere and you never know..."

"Ian, please tell us what you mean. Who are *they*?"

"The saviors," Ian said. "I met them at the graveyard after my mom died. And they were...they were wonderful. They told me I should be grateful because my mother had been loved and chosen, and she was sitting in the sweetest seat of

Heaven, and she had sent them to me. I didn't understand at first, but then I did. They showed me all the passages, and we went over all the things that had happened recently. And it is coming to pass—Armageddon is on the way. The great battle would come, and only those who saw and believed could be among the warriors—but those who were deeply in trouble… they needed help. They needed their sins to be taken on by those of us who would be left to fight the battle."

Hunter's temptation was to blurt out, *And you believed all this crap?*

But he'd seen it before. Ian had apparently cared deeply for his mother. At the moment when he had been in the most pain, feeling horribly lost, they had given him friendship and comfort, and then they had drawn him in.

"Who came to you in the graveyard, Ian?" Amy asked quietly.

"A man named Mateus and he was with a woman. She was called Mother Mary."

"Mateus had a ceremony on the cliffs recently," Hunter said. "Were you there?"

He shook his head. "I was told I must watch the young woman at the house, Carey. She was crafty and canny, but she could be saved."

"Then you don't need to be afraid of Mateus anymore," Amy said. "Mateus is dead."

He nodded. "I know. I was told. By the new archangel."

"Who is the new archangel?" Hunter asked.

"He calls himself Gabriel. He was driving the van."

"Ian, you always knew murder was wrong. I believe you know and understand killing someone doesn't take away any of the sins others might have perceived they committed," Hunter told him, his tone quiet, soft, and sincere. He shrugged and gave the young man a grimace. "The world has always been a mess, so nothing happening really indicates anything for the future. But life is precious. Life is precious to all of us."

"I know, I know!" Ian said miserably, his eyes closed, his fists against his cheeks.

"It's all right," Amy said softly. "But these *archangels* are preying on people like you. People in pain, people who have been hurt. And what they're doing isn't for you. If there is a Heaven, your mom is there, I'm sure, because she raised a man who couldn't kill when he knew it was wrong. But these people will keep killing if we can't stop them. To do that, we're going to need your help."

He nodded. "I—I understand."

"We're going to send you to a sketch artist," Hunter said, "and the artist will ask you about the woman at the cemetery and the man in the van—the man who took Special Agent Gleason. Will you help?"

"I will help," Ian said. "I will help."

Amy reached across the table and touched his hand. "You're going to be okay—"

"If I leave here, if I go to jail, they will get to me," he said.

"You're not going to leave here, not now. And when you do, you'll go to a safe house, and you will be—safe," Amy promised. "They'll see to it that you're okay. We need to go now. We need to get some sleep and you need to get some sleep. That will help you remember more people or events, more information that might help us."

"We can and will help you," Hunter said. "And will depend on you to help us, so thank you. Someone will be in to set you up with a sketch artist and see that you're set for the night."

Amy rose to follow him out. But Hunter stopped and turned around. "Wait. We'll be here a bit longer. Amy?"

She stared at him blankly.

He smiled. "When we met, you were sketching away. Maybe you can—"

"Oh! Hunter, I'm okay, but the artists here are so much better. They're trained, they're professional sketch artists and portraits have never been my forte—"

"We don't need a drawing to hang in the National Gallery. We just need a sketch. We've gotten so focused on different aspects of these cases that... Hey, come on, Amy, please. Ian wants to help. He can meet with a dedicated artist later. For us, now...just an idea."

Amy nodded and sat down. She didn't look at him as if he was supposed to supply the pencil and paper. She always carried a sketchbook and he knew it.

"Ian?"

"Um, sure."

Hunter watched as Amy began with a basic face, letting Ian tell her how to shade it in to get an idea of the way the woman who had once approached him looked. Narrower cheeks, a bit younger, not a kid, not old...eyes, hair...

Hunter stepped in as Amy was fixing the brows on her creation. He frowned, feeling a strange, heated, and angry sensation sweep through him. He set his hand on the table and looked at Amy.

"Remarkable," he said.

She looked back at her drawing and then at him, winced and nodded slowly.

"Ian, thank you," Hunter said. "We'll still have an artist coming in, but...trust me, you've helped already. Amy, let's get some sleep. I believe we'll be traveling tomorrow."

"I—I'm glad if I helped," Ian said.

Hunter and Amy smiled and nodded and stepped from the room at last.

They'd found Mateus, previously Leonard Filmore, and he was dead.

Now, Hunter believed they knew who Mother Mary just might be, too.

"You saw what I saw?" Hunter asked Amy.

"I mean, I'm not a great artist, I—"

"Amy, the drawing sure as hell looks like Hayden Harper."

Amy nodded miserably. Andy Mason emerged from his office and headed their way.

"Ian just talked and Amy did a sketch. Her sketch resembles a supposed victim—Hayden Harper," Hunter said."

"But my sketches aren't... Well, I'm not a professional sketch artist."

"Professional or no, she's good," Hunter told Andy. "But let's make Amy feel better. Do we have any sketch artists on now?"

"We do," Andy said. "I'll get one in there. And don't worry. We'll keep Ian in holding here for the night and worry about what to do in the morning." He hesitated and shrugged. "Between every law enforcement agency, we are running thin on protecting this many people. We've got to get a handle on whatever the hell is going on."

"I swear, Andy—" Hunter began.

"No, no, I know you and Amy are about run dry, too. I didn't mean that. Go. I'll get done here what I can—"

"We'll be back in early. We'll see what the next drawing looks like. Ian may have just given us something we need, and the fight might be moving south again."

Andy nodded grimly. "Sleep," Andy said, and grimaced. "We've all been in this game, and we all learn being zombies doesn't help anyone. Decisions in the morning."

"You need some sleep, too," Amy told him.

"Not to worry—I get to sleep," Andy assured her.

At last, Hunter escorted Amy out of the building. She fell asleep in the car. Hunter didn't wake her. She was still sleeping when they reached the hotel's parking lot.

He smiled as he watched her. Life was strange. In the most god-awful circumstances, they had come together. He had found the woman he loved, a life partner, in the middle of pure horror.

An intended Armageddon.

That made him wonder about the endgame, but he couldn't dwell on it then. He exited and walked around, wondering if he could lift Amy out of the car and just carry her up to the room.

But her eyes opened as he reached in for her and her brows arched in a questioning shape.

"I was going to try and let you stay asleep," he told her. "You know, carry you romantically through the lobby, onto the elevator and into the room."

She laughed. "Hunter, the carrying thing over a threshold is after a wedding."

"Still—"

"And they might have thought you knocked me out or something and called the police. I really can't do any more paperwork tonight!"

He grinned and took her hand. She crawled out of the car and slid into his arms for a quick kiss before he closed and locked the door.

"Long day," she murmured.

"And exhausting."

"Um," she murmured.

The lobby was quiet when they walked through. Not even the night clerk was at the desk.

"See, I could have pulled it off," Hunter said.

"Sure. Maybe." Amy laughed "Okay. You're right, but it's

been a long, long exhausting day," Amy said. Yet when they were in the room, she shrugged and turned to him. "At least I had a nap," she reminded him, grinning.

"And I may not need a nap," he replied, pulling her into his arms.

They laughed together, fell on the bed, wound up tangled in the sheets and their clothing, laughed more, and then became passionately embroiled.

When he slept, Hunter slept well and deeply, somehow aware in his dreams he held her, knowing it was unlikely he'd have ever found anyone like her in all the years of his life if they hadn't come together even under these deadly circumstances.

Even sleep was good. Maybe amazing.

Except then he woke with a jump from the strident ringing of their phones—almost simultaneously.

"Mickey," Amy murmured, glancing at her caller I.D. and referring to Mickey Hampton, her supervising director at the Florida Department of Law Enforcement.

His call was from Assistant Director Charles Garza—his supervisor from the home office.

"There's been another development," Garza said.

"Has there been another call or text to someone from Hayden Harper's phone?" Hunter asked. "We're beginning to question whether Hayden Harper is a victim—or part of this."

"The Denver office's artist no doubt did a sketch similar to Amy's," Garza said. "Andy Mason sent a copy. But this has nothing to do with Hayden Harper directly. No, something different. Touching close to home," Garza added, his tone hard. "I've already spoken with Andy Mason. He'll keep his people working on the protection details, but you're going to be heading out."

"Now? Why? And where are we heading?"

Hunter was pretty sure he already knew where they were going, but it seemed like there was a new "why."

"It all has to do with Special Agent Gleason," Garza told him.

"Gleason? The agent who had been guarding Carey and was taken away in a van? Did they find his body?"

"Parts of it, Hunter," Garza said. "Last night, a family was driving along the turnpike and pulled into a rest stop. They like to travel by night so the kids can sleep. But their eight-year-old was awake and wanted to go to the restroom. As her mom was taking her, she suddenly stopped by one of the trash cans and started screaming. The mother looked—thought her daughter was seeing a theatrical prop or something similar at first and picked it up to show the kid. But it wasn't a prop. It was a hand, Hunter, a human hand. Of course, the mother freaked and they called local police. They ran the fingerprints. And as a federal agent, Gleason's were on file."

"So, they kidnapped him, got him down to Florida, and…
"

"We can only assume he's dead," Garza said. "Maybe even hope he's dead and that he died fast." He hesitated just a beat. "They found the hand. Then, there was an accident on Route 27 just on the north side of the Miami-Dade/Broward County line. Idiot passing—common enough. But he crashed into a tree—and a human foot fell down on his windshield." Garza was quiet. "I met Gleason briefly, years ago after he graduated from Quantico. Andy Mason told me he was a fine agent. Wife and two kids. I want you and Amy to get down there and find out who the hell did this. Damn it, Hunter, this is beyond sick, and we have to get this stopped now, whatever it takes."

"I agree," Hunter murmured. Garza was right. But he had

to wonder if he and Amy were targeted in this—if the puppet master had a plan for them to return to Florida.

Then again, there was no publicity on any of this. Would the puppet master even know who they were?

Then again, if they discovered the key player here, the last of the horsemen might still raise his head…ready when all else failed.

"Andy Mason has a jet ready for you," Garza continued. "Amy's place, I understand, is on the outskirts of Orlando, but we're having you stay farther to the south, in Broward County." He took a breath. "That's in the general area where the body parts have been found thus far."

"That's fine. Amy knows the territory, and we'll pick up working with police and FDLE agents she knows down there, as well as people in forensics. I am beginning to suspect the final play will be down there with those still hanging around who didn't wind up in prison after the incidents with the last 'horseman,'" Hunter said. "All right—we'll head to the airport. Please see we're sent everything we need to know, briefed on locations—"

"Hunter, please," Garza interrupted.

"Right. Yes, of course. You're already doing that," Hunter said.

"Loop me in on anything, no matter how minute."

"Yes, sir."

"How the hell does someone make someone else kill another person, much less chop that person up into little pieces?" Garza murmured aloud. "You've been working this all your adult life, Hunter."

"And I know the tricks played, I know the vulnerabilities played upon, and I still wonder sometimes myself."

"Get going," Garza said quietly. "We need this ended."

Neither of them said goodbye; they ended the call.

Amy was just ending her call as well.

"One body part was found in Miami-Dade and one was found in Broward County—the hand on the turnpike and then the accident that occurred on Route 27," she said. "And I take it your conversation was with Garza."

"Yep. Back to Route 27," Hunter murmured. "We have a jet waiting."

Amy shrugged. "At least they give us good transportation."

"There you go," he said. "And here we go."

"Right," she murmured. "Good thing we both know how to live out of suitcases!"

"Yep."

They were good at it. In ten minutes, they were out of the hotel; in another twenty, they were at the airport.

It was just past noon when they landed. The flight from Colorado took a little less than four hours. Garza had already arranged for them to pick up a car at the airport, and Amy had set up a meeting at the site where the foot had been found off Route 27.

She leaned back with her eyes closed for a moment and murmured, "I hope…"

"Yeah?"

"I hope…if Gleason is dead, which logic suggests we assume, that he was dead before they began taking him apart," Amy murmured.

Hunter was silent for a minute. "Let's hope," he murmured. He glanced at her quickly. "Amy, you know we need to find justice for him—and the others."

"Yes. I know. We've both been at this."

"And…"

"There is a small possibility he's alive."

"Then why do such things?" she asked. "Such horrible things to a fellow human being?"

"That's been a question through the thousands of years

throughout human history," he said. "Dictators have bombed hospitals, invaders slay indiscriminately, men and women shoot, slash, beat, and poison one another. We see too much of it. But remember this. Human beings are capable of incredible kindness, too. We've seen what people, strangers, will do for others—take them in during times of war or upheaval. Support hospitals, children, the sick and the disabled. Hey, come on, it's kind of a joke, but with some people it starts early—and there's a reason Boy Scouts help old ladies across the street."

She smiled at last, glancing at him. "Old ladies, huh? What about old men?"

He laughed and let out a sigh. "Sorry—old *people*. I did not mean to be sexist."

She laughed. "I know you didn't. I couldn't help myself."

They were heading down State Road 7 or 441 and he noted the immense rise of the Seminole Hard Rock Hotel as they drove along. It was a spectacular sight, visible from a distance.

"That place is impressive—quite an image on the skyline," he said.

"It is. I don't think you've seen it when the sun falls yet," Amy said. "All the colors that light up in the night sky with their light show! I love to watch it. I think they've done an amazing job with the Guitar Hotel!"

He glanced her way, grinning. "You're a casino hound? All this time. I didn't know!"

She shrugged. "I'm not a hound, but I do love that hotel." She hesitated and then continued with a shrug. "You know I'm friends with one of our forensics guys down here, Aidan Cypress. Aidan has a cousin who's in management at the hotel and we've gone to have dinner with him a few times. And okay, I've played a few slots, but it's like any other entertainment—you only spend so much, then that's it. But the pools there!" She laughed. "I play enough to get some great reduced rates during the week, and now and then, a comp. I love the pools! Hunter, they're so pretty and so nice. I love the slide and whirlpools at the *old* pool and the falls and the restaurants and the *beach* area at the new one...and you can get an amazing ice coffee at the hotel!" She shrugged. "Restaurants are great. The music is always good. Makes me happy. And most importantly, I love the culture of our Seminole tribe." She grinned at him. "They are the *unconquered*. They are the only tribe that never surrendered. The story goes that they are now descendants of the original two to three hundred Native Americans who fled into the Everglades during the Indian removal wars. Can you imagine? You've been out in the Everglades. Beautiful, and—even without major criminals on the loose—deadly. But they did more than survive. They held pat. And then, they stayed strong and moved into the future. They were the first Native Americans to purchase a major international corporation with Hard Rock! But there's so much more than the casinos to the people. Growing up, I loved to come down here and go to powwows and the musical events that were going on. They are putting huge money into education. Aidan is brilliant, one of the best experts in his field imaginable, but you've worked with him so you know that. The Seminole are tribal—and citizens of the city, state, and country. They are like all Americans. They can grow to be what they want to be, and they're still so darned special the way that I see it. And..."

"And?"

"I think it's cool something has worked out well for people. And their several casinos have been great for the tribe. Like I said, I love the Hard Rock Cafe there, too. It has the nicest staff, and...what's not to like about good music? Great concerts, too."

"Good music is great," he agreed. "I wouldn't mind a good concert after all this! And, hm. I do love a good pool, lying in the sun... Yes, it all sounds wonderful!"

"I'm taking you there," she told him. "I mean, in the future. When this is..."

"Over? Here's hoping." he said.

"Speaking of Aidan—" Amy began.

"We're about to meet with him," Hunter finished.

She nodded.

"And Special Agents Ryan Anders and Sean Masters," he murmured. "They were assigned point until we could get here."

The two were young agents—young proven agents. They'd already worked closely with Ryan and, through him, Sean Masters.

Ryan was capable of following someone and never being caught. He could change his appearance with the speed of a chameleon, making it extremely hard for anyone to note him as being on their tail.

Sean was equally talented, from what they had seen thus far.

"We're meeting them where the foot came down," Amy murmured.

"Yep. The foot isn't there—it's with the ME's office, of course."

"Of course."

Amy shook her head. They were off the main highway, heading west. Civilization had expanded through the years, with communities pressing farther and farther west from the heavily populated areas on Florida's east coast. There were problems with that, of course—you didn't encroach on nature without nature retaliating. In the western regions, there were many more complaints about alligators in swimming pools than there were in the long-established urban areas close to the coast. Then again, she'd once seen a good-sized gator calmly crossing I-95 once just at the Miami-Dade/Broward line.

They traveled west on 595, then on to 27. In another five minutes, they saw Aidan's forensic vehicle on the side of the road along with an unmarked car—Ryan's.

Hunter parked and they exited the car. At first, they didn't see any of the others, but the foliage to the side of the road was thick. If they'd walked any distance into it, they could easily be invisible.

"Hey," Amy said, pointing. "There's the tree."

The car that had hit the huge banyan on the side of the road had obviously been speeding. There was a huge indent in its trunk. The trees were pretty remarkable, though, with a root system that kept them going and going. Hunter thought this tree had to be a hundred years or so old, and while injured, it would survive.

Still some major damage had been done.

Then again, if you were haphazardly disposing of body parts, the tree was a good choice with branches of all sizes stretching in dozens of directions.

"Guys!"

Looking to the western side of the road, Hunter saw Aidan's face through the thick undergrowth. "There was a blood trail heading out this way. Took forever to find the little drops, and we didn't get them the day of the accident. But these guys were willing to search with me, so…"

"On our way!" Amy called.

"There's what's left of a really old path by the tree. It will get you out of some of the high grasses and bush!" Aidan called.

Hunter and Amy looked at each other and shrugged. They'd known where they were going, and they hadn't dressed in suits. Amy was far too experienced to wear a skirt.

They'd opted for jeans and boots and light hooded jackets.

The path wasn't much. It might have been there since the Seminole Wars of the early 1800s or been roughed out by sugar merchants of later years. But it was something of a path; as Aidan had said, it made maneuvering through the brush easier.

They saw the yellow markers Aidan had left. Hunter found he was nodding to himself. Aidan was damned good at his job.

He didn't think he would have ever seen the tiny droplets Aidan had discovered or realized they formed a trail.

They caught up with Aidan. He was a striking man, about thirty, his Native American heritage evident in his straight, ink-dark hair, eyes and strong cheekbones. Amy gave him a hug. He and Hunter shook hands.

"Well, here we are again," Aidan murmured. "We had whole crews out here after the accident, but I don't know. I kept feeling we missed something. We did. Something that may not give us anything, but...tiny, tiny blood drops. And I can't help but believe they might lead somewhere. Especially because—well, here we are again."

"Someone seems to have something on this place," Hunter agreed.

"Yeah, and I keep thinking it has to be someone deeply familiar with this area." Aidan shrugged. "Trust me, I don't discount anything, but the things being done... There is one sick puppy at the head of all this. A hand by the garbage on the pike—and a foot in that tree back there. In truth, it's as if someone wants you here."

"So, it seems, and maybe we're playing into it," Hunter acknowledged.

"But then again, whether we like games or not, seems like we have to play it," Amy said. "Where are Ryan and Sean?"

"Just a little farther in," Aidan said. "We're going over this area bit by bit... Hey," he added, grinning. "Strange, huh? I'm thirty-four and feeling like the old man here with those two. Thankfully, Hunter, you've arrived!"

Hunter grimaced. "Yeah, I may have you by a few months. And Amy's still a baby, not quite there!"

"It just goes to prove, those two are what? Twenty-five? But I'd happily work with them at any point. Open minds and a willing work ethic. Anyway, let me point out the grids we're working."

Aidan pointed out his markers and some of the tape he'd stretched out. He then directed their focus over to where Ryan and Sean were going over every inch of ground and shrugged. "Okay, so the agents are doing forensic work. But the plan was just to meet you here and let you get a grip of the latest discovery, but then I found I had to go over it all again, and I found a blood drop."

"Gotcha," Hunter said.

"I'll take the northeast," Amy said, "if that's okay. And you may go west, young man."

Hunter rolled his eyes, shaking his head. "Fine."

They headed into their "grids."

Hunter marveled again at Aidan's ability to see the most minute clue. In the deep brush, discovery meant looking at every leaf, every inch of earth.

He'd barely begun before they all heard Amy let out a fierce shout.

"Oh, God!"

He and Aidan turned quickly. She was standing at the center of her grid, shaking her head.

"Amy, what is it?" Hunter swiftly turned in her direction. "More blood?" he asked.

She shook her head. "More body," she said, her tone deep and pained.

13

"We've had a task force on this since we learned Hayden Harper's phone was used to send a text from the area," Mickey Hampton said. "And then, of course, our lab identified the fingerprints on the hand found off the highway as Special Agent Gleason. And now..."

Mickey let his sentence trail. *Now,* more had been found of Special Agent Gleason.

Amy's supervisor had arrived at the local FDLE office. He was a large man, tall and broad-shouldered, and could be imposing when he chose. As a supervisor, he was excellent, listening to his people and, as the saying went, he was a man who could play well with others. They'd realized early on that what they were battling had a long-term agenda; he was ready for the FDLE to work with the FBI and to have Amy, his state employee, on "loan" to the FBI for as long as it took.

"Here's what I don't understand," Amy said, looking at Hunter in the conference room where they were meeting. Special Agents Ryan Anders and Sean Masters were there—along with Aidan Cypress. "In Colorado, the puppet master or masters behind *this* 'horseman' have been playing on the religious angle. You hurt—kill—people because you're trying to help them atone for their sins and get to Heaven. That's the game played. But this...taking a federal agent, killing him, and slicing him to pieces to be discovered bit by bit... It doesn't make any sense."

"Whatever the game in Colorado, there's still been an arm of the enterprise down here. It's hard to see the endgame," Hunter said. "But I believe, too, this can be twisted to agree with the horseman angle. I'm not sure how, but out there somewhere, someone has something of a headquarters or at the least—a station of sorts—a place to kill or dismember a victim."

"More than possible," Aidan said. He grimaced. "There was a reason the Seminole people who escaped into the Everglades during the last of the Seminole Wars survived—never surrendering and never becoming part of the Trail of Tears and never signing a peace treaty. Going after them was too deadly and not worth the effort required of the army. Few people realized the extent of the land that is the Everglades in the south-central portion of the state. Now, you have tribal lands governed by the Seminole Tribe in accordance with American laws and the Department of the Interior—and you have privately owned land and state-owned land. I don't believe this station or headquarters is on tribal land. We have our own police force and it's a good one. Not that our other local police forces aren't excellent—but police tend to be busy where there are people. We have abandoned sugar mills out there along with century-old abandoned homesteads, park land, all kinds of land. And yet, so much is the same. Land that contains moccasins, coral snakes, black bears, alligators, even crocodiles in areas, the endangered panther—still a possible threat when encountered. Not to mention the fact we're now overcrowded with pythons and other snakes people decided to humanely dispose of in the Everglades. Whoever this is knows the Everglades and what they're doing out there. But I know the Everglades—and others working out there know them, too. Which puts us back to the beginning. You can hide all kinds of things in our River of Grass."

"Seems like the way to find out where they are is to be taken by them," Amy murmured.

"As in Special Agent Gleason?" Mickey asked dryly. "Kidnapped from Colorado."

"I think we'll see more happen here," Amy said, looking at Hunter again. "We were brought down here, I believe lured by Hayden's phone and…" She hesitated and then shrugged; it was what it was, and they dealt with the bad. "…and Gleason's body parts. But I think we were brought down for another performance—this by the third horseman. Somebody just happening out there in an airboat or on one of the trails is going to be taken. Maybe we'll find more body parts. Maybe we'll discover that they're planning another display—such as the woman killed and strung up when the first 'horseman' made his appearance."

"I say we get out there as something other than what we are," Ryan Anders said, looking around almost as if wondering if he needed to raise his hand to speak.

Amy smiled at him. He was young, but he was good. He was going places. One day, she thought, in years to come, he might take Mickey's place. He was great in the field. He could tail a suspect as few others could do, changing his appearance with ease. Today, he was just himself, nice blue suit, brown hair neatly combed, his eyes their natural amber color rather than covered by contacts in a different shade.

Hunter turned to him. "I'm afraid you might be right, Ryan. There is someone out there just waiting for a tourist or even a local fisherman or bird-watcher to sweep up and... well, use, somehow. I believe Gleason is dead, but I don't think they killed Gleason in accordance with any of their cult tactics. This was all done as a lure. It's doubtful whoever is behind all this even believes in God in any fashion."

"We can be fishermen," Sean Masters offered. "Or bird-watchers. No, fishermen, I think." He grimaced. "Hey, my grandfather talked about all the lodges they used to have out there—shacks where he and his cronies would hang out when they wanted to escape. Sometimes they were supposedly hunting alligators in season, but mostly, he said they sat around at night and shot up beer cans."

Amy laughed. "Yep, I had family with a *hunter* in it, too." She turned to Hunter and then to Mickey. "Then there's the Lost City and the area surrounding it. But that's been—"

"Lost City?" Hunter asked.

She nodded. "Supposedly, Confederate soldiers hid there during the Civil War but were discovered and killed by either local tribesmen or Union officers. Then, Al Capone supposedly had a still out there, and it's been investigated by the Department of the Interior, archeologists, and others. Haunted, of course, or filled with skunk apes. But the Everglades is filled with hammocks and ponds, dry land and wet, for miles and miles and miles. Yes, this person—or persons—could be running a major operation somewhere, just like Al Capone."

"So, that's it. How do we get the manpower to cover that kind of distance?" Sean murmured.

"We don't," Hunter said. "We concentrate on one area. North of Alligator Alley and west of Route 27."

"You mean…where we found the body displayed by the first horseman?" Amy asked.

Hunter nodded, turning to Mickey. "I'm willing to bet that whatever we're looking for can be found in that area."

Mickey rose, saying, "All right. We concentrate on that area. I'll video with the heads of the local police—and we'll bring the Highway Patrol in on it, too, so they know what's going on. Of course, I'll connect with all our FDLE people in areas near or touching, warn them what to be on the lookout for. Of course, I'll head to the tribal offices in Hollywood so the Seminole council is warned. Ryan, Sean, I like your idea. Don't go in as law enforcement."

"Airboats," Aidan said.

They all looked at him and waited.

Aidan shrugged. "The best way through the Everglades is via airboat, in my opinion, at least. My friend—our friend—Jimmy Osceola—owns an airboat, as do many members of my tribe, and other entrepreneurs. But I can talk to Jimmy. We can get a few airboats going by day, staffed by some who really know the territory and carrying a special kind of tourist."

"I'll approve it," Mickey said after a minute. He nodded toward Aidan. "I'll get people out from the Orlando office to go over the area again. All we've managed to come up with is a hand and a foot…"

"Sir, in defense of all those working out there, it's not a lack of effort or expertise. Looking for anything out there is like looking for—" Aidan began.

"A needle in a haystack?" Ryan suggested.

"A needle in a stack of needles," Aidan said. "But I do believe it will be important to search the area over again. And again."

"That will be done," Mickey promised. "And I understand. I'm not suggesting there was dereliction of duty on anyone's part. All right, Aidan, we will enlist Jimmy Osceola. If he's willing—he's civilian and he already found bad things on a tour not long ago with the 'red horse.' But if he's willing, his tour is a known one. We'll get at least another two to four airboats out there with agents while we'll also have agents with the forensic crews—which is near where the body was found with the first 'white horse'—and where Hunter has suggested we should be looking. I like your idea of just looking like tourists, Aidan. But if, as you two seem to think, Hayden Harper is involved in this, she's met both of you. Which would take you out of that segment of the play."

"Mickey, please—" Amy began, but she didn't have to say more.

"Not necessarily!" Ryan said. He smiled. "I can make them unidentifiable from a distance—even up close, really. Especially to someone who has seen them, spoken once or twice, but doesn't really know them."

Amy had seen Ryan change his own appearance so as not to be noted—and she had barely recognized him. She smiled.

Mickey shrugged. "Let's see on that. But—"

"Hey, some people were cops before they came to FDLE. Some went to college in business, and some in criminology. I happened to have been a fine arts major before turning to criminology. I was a great Cyrano de Bergerac, did my own nose. And I am damned good with costuming and makeup if I do say so myself."

"A little ego," Sean said lightly, "but he's telling the truth."

"Let's see what you can do. But I want every agent out there on high alert—in or out of costume. These murders are...heinous to the nth degree," Mickey said. "No one is unarmed but be careful lest being armed means someone using your own weapon against you. None of you is a fool, so I'm just talking to make it all fresh in your minds. Let's get on this.

221

Ryan, let's see what you can do. I'll have someone here get Special Agent Gleason's left hand up to the lab in Orlando. I'll see to it that FDLE, local police, and feds are aware of everything we believe might be going on. We've had an APB out on Hayden Harper—I'll add a warning to it."

"And on Don Blake. Hayden Harper was the one who suggested to Carey Allen she take Don Blake with her on one of her adventures—as in she steered them to the caves where Carey went into the muck and Don mysteriously disappeared," Hunter said. He leaned forward. "I don't think we should put Amy and me together as tourists on a boat—being apart, we might pull something off. Together, I think we might be spotted—or if we were able to encounter someone, they could be watching."

"I get what you're saying," Aidan told him. "I'll pair up with Amy."

Mickey frowned. "Aidan, you're not a trained agent—"

"Mickey, please, you have the power to maneuver whatever paperwork is needed to allow me to do this. Please. They're turning my ancestral lands into a nightmare alley. I'm begging you. I can pull this off. Oh, yes, I've completed all the firearms training necessarily. I can hit a crocodile straight in the eye—not that I would, endangered species as they are—but I could."

He was half smiling and half deadly serious. Mickey looked at him a long while before nodding at long last.

"I want to see what Ryan comes up with for Amy. Then we'll make the final plan."

Mickey left the room. Amy found that Hunter, Ryan, and Sean were all looking at her.

"You sure *you* want to do this?" Ryan asked her.

She turned to Aidan. "Are you sure you want to do this?"

He shrugged and smiled at her. "I don't think even Ryan

with all of his magical prowess can make me look like a white man—"

"Hey, man, you've got green eyes!" Ryan said. "There was a white man in there somewhere."

Aidan laughed softly. "Yeah, I like to think I'm the best of what America can be—a cool mix of many things. But let's face it—"

"It's not going to matter what you look like. They don't know you," Ryan reminded him. "Amy is the one we need to change up."

"True," Hunter murmured, studying Amy.

She was surprised he'd opted out of being with her, though his reasoning was sound. Apart, they might pull off being average tourists, bird-watchers, hikers, or nature lovers. She knew she feared for him as he feared for her—the main reason teams weren't usually composed of those who were couples.

He smiled at her suddenly, knowing exactly what she was thinking.

"Oh, don't kid yourself," he told her. "I'll be around. I'll be close."

"Okay," she said slowly. "So... I'm assuming we begin this in the morning. Ryan, I'll get some hair dye. Blond or brunette?"

"Dark, really dark!" Ryan said. "And you don't need to get anything. I keep a good stash of stuff to change with, though I usually just opt for a different style of clothing or cap. Can you wear contacts? Have you ever worn them before?"

"I can wear contacts," Amy assured him.

"How's your Spanish?" he asked her.

"Not bad—or too bad, anyway," Amy told him. "Hey, this is Florida! Half my friends are Hispanic or half-Hispanic—Patrick Garcia, José McKinnon. Of course, I have an American accent, but a lot of my friends have Hispanic parents but were born in the States themselves and have American accents when they speak Spanish, too." She leaned back, grinning. "This might be fun."

Hunter groaned.

"You won't need to head out to pick anything up, either," Ryan said. "I have everything we're going to need in my two-by-two office!"

Ryan wasn't lying. He had black hair dye, and she applied it in the bathroom. Hunter winced when he saw her, and winced again when Ryan gave her a short swing bob cut. He had "costume" contacts in many colors and she opted for an amber color.

Aidan had left them to contact friends and family members and secure airboats, while also making sure he warned them all as well. Mickey would contact the council, but Aidan would make sure the threat was known to be extremely serious.

By the time her hair was dried and Ryan had applied more makeup to her face than she'd worn in her life, she didn't recognize herself.

Hunter pursed his lips, shook his head, and shrugged.

"Kid," he told Ryan, "the theater missed out."

"Thanks," Ryan told him. "I like to think I can use everything life gave me in the best way possible. And I guess all of us who go into law enforcement are here for the same reason."

"Catch the bad guys?" Sean asked.

"Protect the innocent," Ryan said. "You know what I mean. I know you do." He looked at Hunter and indicated Sean. "This guy's dad invented a technical thing for airplane engines and made enough to feed the planet. Sean doesn't have to work a day. He does this because he wants to. And I know you guys—it's the same."

Aidan had come into the conference room. He looked at Amy, shaking his head. "Wow!"

"Thank you," Ryan said.

"You're a beautiful redhead, but we know the redhead," Aidan said lightly. "This brunette…wow. She's regal and…hot!"

"Hey," Hunter protested teasingly.

"Not to worry. Yuck. She's like my sister," Aidan assured them. "Okay, so, I was talking to a few of my cousins—" he began.

"How many cousins do you have?" Ryan asked.

Aidan grinned. "A lot. My name is Aidan Cypress, but I'm a member of the Bear Clan. We are a matrilineal society, which means I am Bear Clan through my mom, as are many of my cousins—close and distant," he told them. "We're set with Jimmy Osceola and my cousins Billie and Linc. But I talked to my dad, too."

"He's super," Amy murmured. She'd met Aidan's father several times through the years and he was one of the nicest and wisest people she had ever known. Retired now, he'd been with the Seminole police.

"And he had a suggestion. Amy, you know Florida and our history—including that of the Everglades—as few others do. He said you should appear to be a guide. We can do up a small group of agents—as tourists—and you can take them off one of the paths that leads from Route 27 toward the water—where the body was found in the 'white horse' case—and where Special Agent Gleason's foot and hand were recently found."

"And I could be in that group," Hunter said.

"And so could we," Sean agreed.

"Or," Hunter murmured, "we could be groups arriving in

separate airboats. We'd have watchers on the boats, and the group around you."

"I'm game for whatever you think will work," Amy said.

"And you might have become a brunette for nothing. We could do all this, and the crazy puppet master might kill someone again in Colorado," Hunter said.

"But we might be right," Amy said.

"We might be," he agreed. He rose from where they were sitting in the conference room. "All right. It's been a long today. Tomorrow will be longer—but with mosquitos. Anyone for dinner and an early night right after?"

"Sure. And I know a great place. The Field," Aidan said.

"An Irish pub," Sean told Hunter.

"I do love it!" Amy said.

"And, hey, everyone is Irish on St. Patrick's Day," Aidan said, grinning.

"It's not St. Patrick's Day," Amy reminded him.

"So? We'll pretend."

They agreed, checked out with Mickey, and headed to dinner.

As they sat at a table, enjoying the good food and live Irish music, Amy glanced over at Hunter. He smiled back at her.

Maybe the intensity of their work made times like this all the sweeter. They went with their waitress's suggestions and ordered the corned beef and cabbage one and all.

"This place is great," Hunter assured Aidan. "Food, music—and company."

"It's a favorite." He laughed. "One of my clan cousins is a host over at the hotel and casino, walking distance from here. Sometimes we have a great lunch there, and sometimes he comes over here and meets me to get some Irish on." He laughed. "Another all-American creation! He's Irish, Cuban, and Seminole. To be a tribal Seminole, you have to have at least a quarter of our blood in you."

"What a perfect Floridian, as well as American," Hunter said, lifting his glass to Aidan.

The band came on to play a version of "Danny Boy" made famous by the band Black 47. They were good, and everyone at the table enjoyed them along with the rest of those eating inside and outside the restaurant. But when the song ended, it was time to go. And the easy conversation they'd enjoyed while eating ended. They were somber as they said good-night.

But when they reached the hotel room, Hunter quickly drew Amy into his arms. "Please tell me you're not too, too tired. I mean, wow. So, I admit I'm much fonder of the woman I know, but, hmm. This is like being absolutely enflamed and inspired by two women in one."

Amy laughed and ran her fingers down his cheek.

"Wait!" she protested. "Does that mean you're really looking for a brunette?"

He shook his head, his expression serious as he looked down at her. "No. It means I'd be madly in love with you as a redhead, a blonde, or a brunette! But—"

"Tomorrow I think I'll be Scarlet Broussard, a brilliant historian and tour guide by day, a wicked party girl by night! So if you want, I can start being wicked party girl tonight!"

"Oh, I want. I want," he assured her.

They made use of the time they had. Enjoying a long, steaming shower. Laughing as they nearly tripped after one of their embraces as they headed to the bed. Pausing to look at one another and know what it meant to be together, then laughing and teasing again. What started as soft caresses on one another's flesh led to deeper and deeper intimacy, meshing together with the sensual urgency that seemed sweeter because of the comfort they shared more and more with the passing of time.

They dozed. She woke when he teased he wasn't going to be with a brunette all that often, and they made love again.

They slept deeply at last.

And then the morning came.

It was good to see Jimmy Osceola again, Amy thought, even if she had trouble forgetting about his possible involvement in another case.

Or the same case, since whoever was behind it all seemed determined to follow through with *four* horsemen. But Jimmy quickly assured her that he wanted whatever was going on to be stopped.

From everything she knew about him, and through Aidan, she knew he was a good man. Instinct wasn't evidence, but she was going to go with it for now.

"Some of this is our land, and some of this is park land," Jimmy told her gravely. She knew he had to be sixty, but he was built tall and solidly without an ounce of fat and his face retained a startling youth. He was a strong but kind man, she knew, and he loved what he did. "So, I want whatever is going on stopped. And if it wasn't close to home and personal, I'd still want it stopped because it's so cruel and horrible."

"You're a good man, Jimmy," Amy told him quietly. "Either that," she added lightly, "or a glutton for punishment."

He laughed at that. "You ready for this?"

"They'll tease me to death later, but sure, I'm ready!"

Of course, it was impossible to give any kind of lecture while they were riding in the airboat alongside the embankment—the sound of the motor cut out any such possibility. But sitting in the boat, Amy saw Mickey did have others out in the vicinity.

Other airboats were out there—ahead of them and behind them. Eventually, Jimmy cut the motor and brought the air-boat to an embankment, and showed them all how best to alight without sinking into the mucky land close to the water.

"So, here we are, deep in the Florida Everglades. The eco-system covers much of the southern Florida peninsula and is one of the most unique systems in the world and thus in the continental United States," Amy said. "But Florida! It was first inhabited by human beings about fourteen thousand years ago. But our tribes today are not those who originally lived here. As Europeans discovered and encroached upon the land, many original inhabitants died out or were absorbed by those who came this way after. As we all know, European settlers were not all kind to native populations. Ponce de León arrived in Florida in the year 1513 and gave the land its name—La Pas-cua Florida. It was Easter season, the festival of flowers to the Spanish, and the rich landscape apparently influenced Ponce de León. The land remained under Spanish rule from the six-teenth to the nineteenth century except for a brief time—1763 to 1783—when the British flag flew high over her. The land went back to the Spanish until 1821 when it became a terri-tory of the United States. Pirates had been raging along the coast, but the Americans brought in Admiral David Porter from the Keys who fought them hard and long. But something was happening that was not so great when we look back. Na-tive Americans were being forced from their homes to walk the Trail of Tears, which caused many Native Americans to flee, a number of them to the Everglades. Once, there were the Ais, the Calusa, the Apalachee, the Jeaga, the Mayaimi, the Potano, the Tequesta, the Timucua, the Tocobaga, and the Mikasuki. Seminole history really began with groups of Creek migrating south from Georgia and Alabama and possi-bly absorbing other tribes who had been here before. The first

Seminole War began in 1816, soon after the Battle of New Orleans and while the area was still officially under Spain. Some called it Andrew Jackson's War. The Second Seminole War began in 1835 and ended in 1842. There would be yet another, the Third Seminole War, which began in 1855. European Americans were determined to move the tribes out to reservations in Oklahoma, and up until 1858, they managed to move many Native Americans, starved and weary, to that state. But bands of Seminole refused to go, refused to sign a treaty. And who would blame them, since treaties had been broken time and again! Those who remained were truly the undefeated."

Amy walked as she talked, aware her little band of agents, along with Aidan Cypress as her "escort," were by all accounts giving her their undivided attention.

They were, of course, looking.

Looking all the while. Searching the poor trails and the surrounding foliage.

"During the Second Seminole War, Osceola—a tribal leader born William Powell in Alabama and whose mother was Muskogee and great-grandfather the Scotsman William McQueen—was taken by the United States Army under a flag of truce," Amy said, shaking her head. "He was tricked during the Second Seminole War, held first at Fort Marion in St. Augustine and then at Fort Moultrie in South Carolina, where he died. No, he was not executed—he died of malaria. But after his death, strange things happened. His doctor—who had become a friend—decided to remove his head from the coffin before he was buried. Rumor had it that the good doctor placed the head on the bedposts of his children if they misbehaved. He left the great Osceola's head and other relics to his son-in-law who reportedly *did not* make use of the head as a punishment but kept it in his office—which burned.

Of course, there are ghost stories about the proud Osceola prowling various areas, seeking his head."

"I guess some people have always been on the grotesque side," Aidan murmured.

"I guess so," Amy agreed. "There is so much more to this history, of course. There were amazing leaders among the Seminole, but as in all wars, there was blood and death on both sides. Remaining are the Mikasuki, with their lands south of us. Now, you may be Mikasuki and a Seminole, but if you're Seminole, you may not be Mikasuki. It's complicated. Upper and Lower Creeks, two different language groups, but when the Native Americans fled south to Florida, they all fell under the heading Seminoles. The Seminole were finally recognized as a tribe in 1957 and the Mikasuki as a separate tribe in 1962. I loved hearing about them being "The Undefeated" when I was growing up and attended every event they offered. Oh! And my friend Mickey Osceola was in a great rock band! Anyway. Heading south and across the Tamiami Trail, you can visit a Mikasuki—or Miccosukee—village and learn more about Florida's Native American culture, and how a fierce people survived so much for so very long."

Hunter came up near her, pretending to study a tree. "Keep talking," he murmured.

"Well! This is a spectacular eco area!" she said. "And there were other terrible problems. There was a time when feathers and plumage were all the rage in women's hats. Now you might have noticed some of the amazing birds around here. Spectacular great blue herons, storks, kites, egrets, ibises, vultures, and even bald eagles find homes here. In the late 1800s and early 1900s, it was estimated that forty thousand birds were killed for hats! But enterprising women came together for many of those years and finally, in 1918, the Migratory Bird Treaty Act was put into place, and many birds were saved from extinction by it. Now, flamingos are not native, but they have done well, and they are beautiful creatures. Our problem these days is one you might have heard about—an estimated three-hundred thousand nonindigenous constrictors, boas, and pythons have now made the area their home as well. This has endangered deer and other native mammals along with many small pets in various areas. They have been trying for years to cease the escalation of the creatures and in weird ways upon occasion. Like, we have the Florida Python Challenge—hundreds of hunters vying for the longest and biggest python caught and killed. A little crazy because we've now built on land that is etched out of the Everglades and I have friends in those areas who are more afraid of eager hunters than they are of the snakes—not everyone can actually shoot with accurate aim."

"Snakes! Big ones!" Ryan said, trying to keep up the show.

"We have our native species as well, many dangerous, including the coral snake, the eastern diamondback rattler, the pygmy rattler, and the moccasin. The Everglades is the only area in the world that is home to both the crocodile and the alligator. And mosquitoes! As you might have noticed, we seem to breed them big and hungry and—"

Her words were cut off. A terrified scream sounded from within the brush just behind Amy.

And then, a shot was fired from somewhere deep in the foliage.

Amy drew her weapon and started to run toward the brush; the scream had originated from there. But Hunter caught her and whispered, "No! Stay, you're not an agent, remember."

Aidan caught hold of her, drawing her back, and saying quietly, "He's right, Amy. Let Hunter, Sean, and Ryan take this! You look like a tour guide, be a tour guide, just hold here with me, looking scared!"

She slid the gun behind her back and leaned against Aidan. "I can't sit still if they come this way," she told him.

"Well, hell, no. I'm *not* seeing it as a good day to die!" Aidan said dryly. "So, we wait."

They waited. And waited.

And the morning remained still; the only sounds heard were the whispering breeze, a ripple from the nearby water, and the occasional cry of a bird.

14

Hunter raced through the brush, stopping when he nearly tripped over a body on the ground in a small clearing.

"Help! Help me, help, please, they... Someone took Sandra!"

Hunter dropped down by the man who lay on the ground, clutching his midsection. He looked to be in his midtwenties, with sandy-blond hair, clean-shaven cheeks, and desperate brown eyes. Blood was seeping from a wound in his abdomen, and Hunter quickly ripped up a piece of his shirt and set it under the young man's hands, saying, "Hold this tight! Keep pressure on it."

He had his phone out next, calling in for an ambulance.

"Help is coming—"

"They took Sandy! My girl. She screamed and I tried to stop them. They shot me and I guess they thought I was dead.

I may be dead. I may be dying. Oh, God, I'm so scared, but…
I love Sandy. You have to find them, you have to find her—"

Sean Masters burst into the small clearing.

"Oh, God!" the man screamed.

"Ambulance on the way," Hunter said. "Sean, hold here, please. Help him keep pressure on this. And you, sir, I need your help. How many? You said *they*. They took Sandy."

The young man on the ground winced with pain. "Two, both with guns." His hand shook as he lifted it to point. "That way… They took her that way."

Sean nodded to him and Hunter took off, heading in the direction the young man had pointed. *They* had a lead on him, but they were also dragging a terrified and unwilling young woman with them. He had to be able to catch them.

He turned onto a wider path that was bordered by a stream running through two hardwood hammocks. Halfway along it, he leaped over a frightened moccasin in his path. In the water, two bull alligators suddenly began a thrashing fight, reminding him that the dangers along the way here were not always human.

But it was these very dangers that suddenly caused him to find his prey.

He heard a shriek of pain.

"It bit me! It bit me! The damned thing bit me!" a male voice cried.

"Shut up, shut up!" another replied. "Don't be a baby!"

"I could die!"

"We were waiting in ambush, now—screw you! I'm gone!"

"No, no!" a woman cried. "Let me go, let me go—"

"You shut up or I'll shoot you!" the second voice said harshly.

They were right ahead of Hunter, behind a tangled group of cypress and mango trees close to the water. Hunter moved

235

carefully to the left, using the trees for cover. He eased around a cypress and saw one man was struggling with a pretty redhead, slapping her hard against the cheek and causing her to fall to her knees. The girl was young and very pretty. The man was in his late thirties, leanly muscled and fit but strangely dressed in sweatpants and sandals—not a good choice for the terrain.

Hunter had his Glock aimed at the man as he came around the tree, but the man saw him and dived into a mass of foliage and trees, leaving Hunter to follow—or to help the hysterical woman and would-be abductor as he screamed in agony.

He had no idea what had happened to the man on the ground, but it had to be his first priority to keep him alive—and hope he could help with information.

And the young woman...

She'd done nothing wrong.

For now, he had to let the other man go.

He reached the young woman, drawing her to her feet. Tears and grime bathed her face, and she cried, "They shot him! They shot Regan, they shot him!" she cried. "They killed him. Something bit that one. I hope it kills him. Oh, my God, we were just hiking and they jumped out and...they said they needed my heart!"

"You're safe," Hunter said. "And Regan is alive and—"

He broke off. They could hear the arrival of the emergency helicopter as the pilot sought a safe landing.

"Rescue is almost here for him now," Hunter said gently. "Let me get this fellow—" he began, indicating the man who had screamed about being bitten.

"He tried to kill Regan and he wanted my heart!" she said indignantly. "Please, get me to Regan, please, please!"

"Can't just leave him," Hunter said. He walked over to the man who lay on the ground, writhing. He was flat on his back, staring up at the sky, shaking and convulsing. Hunter reached down for the man, kicking the Beretta he'd been carrying as far from his reach as possible.

Except this guy wasn't reaching for anything. Now he was screaming in pain, screaming he was going to die.

"You're not going to die—medical attention is near," Hunter said. "Get up. Let me get you up! You said it bit you. What bit you?"

"Two of them!"

"Two of what?"

"Snakes, little snakes, but...damn! Hurts, hurts, so small, but... "

If he was right and two snakes had bitten him, it was damned unusual. Little. That meant coral snakes. Maybe he'd disturbed a nest? The creatures were born fully venomous.

He had to move before the EMTs left with their gunshot victim. Hunter didn't ask; he hiked the man up and over his shoulder and turned back to the girl, Sandy.

"Follow me!" he commanded. He wanted to give her more sympathy but he couldn't right then.

He hurried back in the direction from which he had come, an easy accomplishment now because there were many voices coming from the area as someone called for a stretcher. When Hunter burst through to where he had left the group, three young EMTs paused mid-action in packing Regan onto a stretcher.

"He says he was snake-bitten. Two small snakes," Hunter said quickly. "I'm assuming coral snakes."

"Ah, hell, two?" one of the EMTs said. "You know they're second only to the black mamba when it comes to toxin in the venom!"

"Yeah, but they don't deliver so well. Move! Two of them now, we've got to get to the hospital," another EMT said.

A third EMT was on the phone, conveying information about the patients he'd be bringing in.

Sandy had caught up with them. Screaming and crying, she rushed to Regan on the stretcher. "I can go with him, right? I can go with him—"

"Usually, yes," an EMT said. He looked at Hunter for help.

"It's too crowded. It's air rescue and the space in the chopper isn't intended for two patients but they'll have to take them both. We'll get to a car and get right to the hospital," he told her.

"But you—"

Sean, hunkered down by the stretcher, quickly said, "Lady, he's FBI. And the reason you and your boyfriend might live. Trust me—we'll get you to the hospital."

The EMTs quickly supplied a second stretcher. In minutes, they were gone. Hunter turned to the young woman he knew as Sandy, ready to explain they needed to get back to the water and the airboat and then on to the hospital. But as he spoke, his phone rang. It was Mickey. There would be an ATV there for them in a matter of minutes if it hadn't arrived yet. He quickly briefed Mickey on the situation. Hunter's supervisor would meet him at the hospital.

From far down a poor rock and dirt road that stretched to the east of them, he heard the honking of a horn.

The car had, indeed, arrived.

"All right," he said to Sean. "I'm going for Amy and Aidan. Sean, where's Ryan?"

"He kept going—you told me to stay here."

"All right," Hunter said. "Have the driver hold on. I'll ping their numbers on the phone's locator system if I can't reach them, and it shouldn't take long—"

"No, oh, my God, no, please!" Sandy cried. "I have to get there. Regan was shot for me, trying to defend me, and they were taunting him, saying they only wanted me for my heart, that I was a sinner and they were going to save my soul and...please!"

"Sandy, there are others out there—"

"Hunter," Sean said. "I'll go with her. She's not going to give us anything. You have one of them here, headed to the hospital. Let the emergency department do its magic. You won't be able to speak with him right away anyway."

"Go," Hunter said.

Sean nodded and Hunter watched as he left, taking Sandra by the elbow and heading out to the road.

When they were gone, he turned and headed back to the place in the clearing near the water where he had left Aidan and Amy. Ryan Anders might have headed back their way.

No one was there.

He decided not to shout their names but looked back into the dense brush where he had been before. Pulling his phone from his pocket, he hesitated. If they were tracking someone, he didn't want to alert that someone with a ringtone. Pinging wouldn't make any noise.

And he knew they were professional. They wouldn't have ringtones on their phones right now; they would be on vibrate.

Hell, it was a phone. He'd just make calls for now. He tried Amy's phone first.

To his relief, she answered almost immediately and he quickly brought her up to speed. He told her about the woman who had been taken, the man who had been shot and the kidnapper who had suffered from a snakebite.

"I'm back with Jimmy at the airboat," Amy told him. "Aidan insists I keep up my non-law enforcement identity, so... He saw you had one of the men who snatched the young woman, but not the other. Ryan called him to say he was tracking someone. As Aidan suggested, I'm useless here. I'm just being a terrified tour guide. I'm wondering, though, if I'm so terrified, how anyone will believe I'm back out here?"

"Hopefully, they won't have any idea you know anything about this," Hunter said. "I'll call Aidan and find out where they are."

"Do that. Should Jimmy and I go back for the car?" she asked. "Wait. Aidan is calling me. You're on hold."

The line went silent, but only for a second. "Hunter, Aidan found Ryan. They were heading back when they found a— found parts of a dead man."

"Parts?"

"Looks like whoever he was, he tried to cut across some water that might have been the turf of a large male alligator. They—they found a torso and legs." She hesitated. "Fresh."

"Great," Hunter murmured. "Right. You and Jimmy head for the car. I'll meet up with Ryan and Aidan, and we'll get a medical examiner and a forensic team out here. I'll leave them to deal here—I want to get into town and to the hospital where we have one victim and one would-be kidnapper. Call me when you're on the road as close as you can get to your lecture spot."

"Copy that," she murmured. "Use your family locator on your phone!" she suggested.

Hell, yeah. He was thankful for modern phones; they were all connected, so he pinged Aidan's phone to head to his location. It took him a while to reach Aidan and Ryan; he had to crawl through the massive root system of a banyan on one of the little "islands" that rose perhaps a foot above sea level. He had to move across a shallow stream of about a foot of water, making him glad he'd opted for tall boots today.

Then he saw Ryan and Aidan just by the side of the water by the torn remains of a man.

Joining them, he hunkered down, looking at the remains. It was the man he had seen before, he knew—the partner of the snake-bitten kidnapper, the one who had fled.

The sandals the man had been wearing had been lost and bare feet now stuck out from the man's legs, still covered in the sweatpants. It did look as if he'd been clearly snapped in two—something as unusual as a man being bitten by two snakes at the same time.

"I've never seen anything like this," Aidan murmured as Hunter joined them. "Alligator...when they take human prey or large prey, they twist in the water and drag their victim down. They drown them to get them to quit fighting. This..."

"Yeah, well, how many times have you heard about a man being bitten twice at the same time by coral snakes?" Hunter asked him.

Aidan frowned. "Okay, never. You sure it was coral snakes?"

"No. I'm just sure that whatever got him, he's in bad shape. I knew an ambulance was coming for the boy who had been shot, and I figured his best chance was getting to a hospital as quickly as possible."

"Seems nature did what we couldn't," Ryan murmured. "Stop them."

"No. This is still unusual," Aidan said. He looked at Hunter. "I'm not so sure it was nature."

"You think he was cut in half?" Hunter asked.

"No...look where the uh...guts are falling out, look at the jagged way the body is torn apart. I don't think we have an alligator—or even an American croc out here big enough just to open his mouth and snap a man into two pieces so cleanly. They, uh, like Aidan said, they drown victims, and then they tear them apart." He sighed. "Whole arms and legs have been found in the bellies of the creatures, but I still say this is not impossible, but certainly unusual. I wish we had the other half of the body. There's something not right here. I don't know. Something just doesn't seem right."

"When an ME investigates, he or she might discover more than we'd see or recognize," Ryan reminded him. "I mean, sorry, Aidan, I know you're about the best forensic guy in the biz, but an ME can be really good, too, right?"

Aidan almost smiled at that. "No medical degree here, Ryan. You're right. Hunter, you look as if you know this guy."

"I saw him before," Hunter said.

"Um, he doesn't have a face," Ryan commented with confusion."

"Look at the pants. How many people would wear pants like that into the Everglades?"

"Good point," Ryan commented.

"I've called it in," Aidan said. "We'll have an ME, his or her assistant, and a forensic team out here soon enough. We'll drive back with one of them, though I know I want to hang out here for awhile," Aidan told him.

"All right. Jimmy took Amy back for the car. I'm expecting her to park nearer to the road. So, Ryan, are you staying with Aidan or coming with me?" Hunter asked.

"I'm not leaving Aidan alone out here with half a body," Ryan told him.

"Ryan, I turned thirty-four last year—and I'm sad to say I've been around a ton of bodies. Go on back in with Hunter."

Ryan shook his head. He looked at Hunter. "You need me now?"

"I want to get to the hospital and question our victim and, hopefully, the man who was trying to take her. I'm hoping they got her calmed down. Not that I don't understand. Two men snatching you who want to cut your heart out must be traumatizing when you thought you were only out to take a walk and watch a few birds," Hunter said. "Everyone, keep in touch," he added.

"Of course," Aidan promised, and Ryan nodded grimly.

Hunter left them and headed toward the road, anxious to be ready when Amy got there. She must have just arrived; she was in the driver's seat with phone in hand, as if she was getting ready to call him. But she saw him and waited for him to reach the car.

He slid into the passenger's seat. She glanced at him quickly. He'd leaned back to let knots of tension he hadn't realized he'd accumulated ease away.

"I'm feeling as useless as a scared tour guide," she told him. "You've had an eventful day."

He turned to her. "Still a good thing you kept your cover. We will have to change up the location a bit, but not too far. We still need to know where they're setting up, though we have an idea. Mickey has spoken to Garza, and they're sending more teams out—FDLE and FBI—to search everywhere. As for today, the one man is dead, the other stands a chance and their intended *sacrificial* victim is alive and well. Her boyfriend isn't so well, but he was alive last time I saw him. I'm...not sure how much blood he lost or what organs were injured. With any luck, he'll make it."

"And if he lives, he might just give us what we need?"

Hunter nodded. "I don't even know the full names of either of the would-be victims yet. Sean drove in with Sandy Whoever since the ambulance couldn't take her. It was already crowded with two men on stretchers. He'll brief us on anything he's learned when we get there, though I'm willing to bet, even these hours later, the victim—Regan Whoever—is still in surgery. And as to the man who was trying to snag her with his partner—now just half a man, no pun intended—

I have no clue. The partner said two snakes bit him. I have never heard of such a thing, but I'm not from Florida."

"He might have hit a nest, I guess," Amy said. "I don't know. Where were the bites?"

"I don't even know that—I knew EMTs were close, far more experienced than I, and I made it a priority to get to them as quickly as possible. And now—"

"Hunter, we need to find every hideout they're using. We catch killers, but we aren't getting to those who are ordering the sacrifices. Okay, so, even rational people sometimes wonder if we are looking at the end of the world. Plague, war, horrible things. Maybe it isn't so strange that people cling to it when someone offers them Heaven, Nirvana, true immortality. You've been the one full of quotes—how about Joseph Goebbels and 'if you tell a lie big enough and keep repeating it, people will eventually come to believe it.'"

He managed to glance at her and give her a smile. "Well, you know, a really big solar flare could knock us right out of the galaxy."

Amy let out a deep sigh.

"Sorry! I'm just...tired."

Amy was looking straight ahead at the road. She smiled slowly. "I'm tired, too. But, Hunter, there's no choice on this. And I think we do know what's going on here. We have three people. We have Hayden Harper and Don Blake who are missing. And we suspect Hayden might be involved. And why not Don? Carey Allen was found—"

"Thanks to you," he said softly, "and you can be very proud of that."

"Thank you. So, we both suspect something not quite right with Hayden. And with Don. Then, of course, we still have the head of that advertising firm, Mr. Barrington."

"But he's in Colorado."

"Ah, but many CEOs operate from a distance."

"True. Hey, I'm heading to the closest hospital—"

"Yep. I guess we'll go through the ER and find out where our people are," Amy said.

She made a left. They had reached the hospital. As she parked, she pulled her phone out.

"If you ping Sean, it will show he's at the hospital," Hunter said.

"Right. But if I call him, he'll tell me where to go!"

"Okay, true."

He waited for her to put the call through and watched her nod.

"We should go up to the second floor and the surgical waiting room. They are letting a limited number of people wait, and this is a special circumstance."

"Regan Whoever is in surgery?" Hunter asked.

She nodded grimly. "The man who was trying to kidnap the young woman is Oscar Pitkin. He's still unconscious. Apparently, he did hit a nest of coral snakes. The venom is a neurotoxin, and they've had to put him in a medically induced coma."

"How did they find out who he was?"

"I don't know. I didn't get that far with Sean. Let's go up and talk to him."

They had to register to enter the waiting room, but apparently the woman at the desk knew they were coming.

Obviously, Sean had told them.

He was waiting in a corner of the room with Sandy. Hunter walked straight there and Amy followed. He introduced her to Amy, but didn't use her title, just her name. And he didn't call her a coworker, he called her a friend.

When Sandy saw him, she stood, tears dripping down her cheeks again. She threw herself into his arms.

"He's still in surgery! They shot him! They shot him. How can such monsters exist, how can anyone be so stupid they believe they can cure sinners by torturing them? I'm sorry, I know that man is here, too, that he's in a coma, but... It may not be a very godly attitude, but I can't help it. I don't care at all if he lives or dies, and the bad part of me wants him to die!"

"When someone has hurt you, it's just human nature to want them to hurt in turn. It's also human to rise above," Hunter said. He grimaced. "I understand. But I think I'll be happy if we can get him to trial and see he gets a nice long prison sentence."

"Life," Sandy said. "Because Regan might not have a life after this!"

Amy stepped around him, gently laying an arm around the girl's shoulders and leading her to take her seat again as she perched by her. "Regan is here, in surgery. There's a lot of hope at this point. But we do want to see justice. Can you tell us what happened, how, and where? First, what's your full name?"

"Sandra Davidson. And Regan is Regan Turnbull. And we're—we're student down here at the University of Miami. We're both in the fine arts. I'm a music major, and Regan is in photography and art. He's from Ohio and I'm from Arizona—and we met at school and...we've been together since our first year. We graduate next year. Anyway, Regan is crazy about ibises."

"Ibises—the birds?" Hunter asked.

She nodded. "Sebastian the Ibis is our official mascot at school. And they apparently don't have many in Ohio. Regan loves to come to the Everglades in both Miami-Dade and Broward Counties so that he can photograph birds—mainly the ibis—but he loves others, too. And one day—of course, we kept our distance—but we saw a Florida panther, and Regan got a great photograph. Someone told him if we came up 27 and pulled off the road, there were tons of birds because of the water coming through the different hammocks and the areas of marshy grass. So, we just came to enjoy being here, going out just like we've done dozens of times with nothing. We know how to come out here, how to be careful, how to respect nature, but…"

She broke off, huge tears forming in her eyes again.

"Sandra, it's all right, you sound like wonderful people, people who do respect the ecology and the wildlife. I'm sure Regan's photographs are wonderful—and I'm willing to bet you're a wonderful musician. Voice? An instrument?"

"I'm an okay alto, and a darned good piano player," she said. "I can manage a lead guitar, and I really love a ukulele. I want to write music, and I—I don't know if I'll ever want to do anything again if Regan doesn't make it!"

"This is a wonderful hospital. He has the best chance in the world here," Amy assured her. "And I'm grateful, we're grateful, for your help."

"I'm grateful for his help," Sandra said, indicating Hunter. "He got me away from the monsters, and if Regan does live…" She noted Sean, who had been sitting there quietly, and quickly added, "And I know you helped stop the bleeding until the EMTs came. Please, believe me, it's not that I'm ungrateful, I'm just…"

"Scared," Amy said. "And I'm so sorry. I know the feeling. But how did they get to you?"

"We—we were following a bird that was just so funny. Nothing was wrong with it—he was just a curious little thing, looking at us, hopping around. And then, suddenly, when we were on that almost nonexistent path where they shot Regan, those two men just jumped out from the brush and grabbed me. Then one of them shoved Regan, and he got mad. When the one guy grabbed me and started laughing about just needing to cut my heart out to save my soul from sin, Regan was really angry—and he went to wrench me away, telling the guy I was the kindest human being in the universe and didn't have sins. The guy laughed, and said that just looking at Regan, he knew the guy wasn't just a huge sinner, that his face was a sin in itself. They both started laughing and the guy went to grab me again, and Regan burst between us and—they shot him! He fell, and they dragged me away. I kept fighting and the one guy kept hitting me, the one who got away."

That explained the bruises forming on the girl's arms.

"He didn't get away," Hunter told her.

"You caught up with him?" Sandra asked, surprised.

"I, um, didn't have to. He apparently crossed an Everglades creature and…he's dead, Sandra. There's nothing to worry about anymore from him," Hunter said.

"He was—eaten?" Sandra asked, swallowing hard. She didn't wait for his answer; she probably didn't really want it. "He was the one who shot Regan. I know I shouldn't be glad for anyone's death, but… I'm glad. That's terrible, isn't it? To want anyone dead?"

"It's understandable under the circumstances," Amy assured her. "Okay, Sandra, did you have any idea of where they came from or where they were taking you?"

"They came out of the brush and the trees, and it was crazy. I know I was wondering if they had a hidden house really close because the one guy—that shot Regan—was wearing ridiculous sweatpants and sandals! Who wears that in the Everglades?" Sandra asked.

Hunter felt motion behind him and instinctively swung around. It was just the nurse's aide who was taking names and managing the number of those coming into the waiting room.

She smiled uneasily, knowing they were law enforcement,

and nervous just because of it. "I, um, I wanted to let you know that Mr. Turnbull is out of surgery."

"Oh, my God! And?" Sandra asked.

"He's stable."

"Can I see him?"

"I'm afraid it will still be a little while before anyone can see him. He's in recovery and he'll go to intensive care. When he's there, you may see him. But briefly. The doctors had to repair several organs, and he must be very careful in the next few days," the nurse's aide told them.

"But—but he'll...live?" Sandra asked on a whisper.

"Yes, he should eventually make a full recovery, but you'll need to speak with his doctors and they'll be in here in a few minutes."

She smiled again, nodded, and left them.

Sandra had been standing. She seemed to deflate and fell back in her chair.

"See," Amy said gently. "He will be fine."

She glanced over at Sean.

"Don't worry," he said. "I will be here, watching over them."

"Thank you," Amy murmured.

Hunter nodded to him. His phone was vibrating, and he reached quickly into his pocket for it. The call was from the hospital.

He glanced quickly at Sean, but the agent just frowned. Stepping aside, Hunter answered the phone.

"Special Agent Hunter Forrest?" a male voice queried.

"Yes. Who is speaking?" Hunter said.

"This is Dr. Clay, Lawrence Clay, and I've been told you're lead investigator on a case involving a man who was brought into the ER under arrest."

"Yes, Dr. Clay, thank you. I was told you were putting him into a medical coma."

"Yes, that was our plan. But I'm afraid he's dead."

"The toxin in his blood? Isn't it rare to die of snakebite? I understand—"

"The toxins were bad but we could fight them. No, we were working on the toxins, preparing to put him into a medically induced coma. Remember, these are neurotoxins. But… the man was in the ER, he looked up suddenly, ripped his IV needle out of his arm—and plunged it into his heart. Special Agent Forrest, we could have saved him from the snakebite. I'm afraid we couldn't save him from himself."

15

Ida Peterson, the owner, was their waitress that night. She was a friendly woman, and her restaurant had offered them a down-home place to eat—and several leads—when the "white horseman" had reigned. Located just off Route 27, the diner might not be in one of the larger cities just east on the coast, but it provided hearty homemade food to the locals in its truly rural area nonetheless.

Hunter had suggested it and Amy had agreed. She didn't think they'd find many leads this time around, but they did prepare a great pot roast and had the best mashed potatoes Amy had ever tasted.

Ida and her husband, Frank, were older, and they had help. Frank worked in the kitchen as the chef and/or burger flipper, as Ida called his job, and she managed the books and often worked on the floor with other waitstaff. There was a good feeling coming to the café—despite the reasons they had first visited. Ida greeted Hunter warmly and looked at Amy curiously, as if she should recognize her, but didn't. Ida seemed curious Hunter was here with her, and said politely, "A new partner, Special Agent Forrest?"

"In a way," Hunter said. Still curious, Ida left them.

"She thinks you're a drop-dead cheating scoundrel," Amy said.

"But she didn't recognize you with the short dark hair. And sadly, I don't think we should enlighten her right now. Just in case. People inadvertently say things."

"Right," Amy agreed. He had finally smiled.

Amy knew he was deeply disturbed by the events of the day—by a man who had been terrified of snakebites killing himself with a long needle.

Rather than face what might happen to him otherwise? That tended to be the way of things.

He was thoughtful and quiet. They had come alone. Another day was over, and when they finished eating, they'd head back to the hotel.

"They told me you two were here!"

Startled, Amy looked up. The person who had arrived was a coworker from the past as well, coworker in a loose sense.

It was Dr. Richard Carver, the medical examiner who had worked with them on the "white horseman" case.

"Dr. Carver," Hunter said.

"Wow!" he murmured, looking at Amy. "Okay, I won't stare. You're doing some kind of undercover?"

"Something like that," Amy murmured.

"So, Dr. Carver—" Hunter began.

"Rich, please, we're not at the morgue," he said, indicating the seat by Amy and asking, "May I?"

"Of course!" Amy said. "Were you just cruising diners or were you looking for us?"

"I like this place, and yes, I was looking for you," Carver said.

The man had gained respect in his field and helped to solve many a case every year. He wasn't quite forty yet, but his work was valued, and he often went on loan to different counties throughout the state and across the country.

A young waitress came by and offered him coffee and asked if he was dining as well. Carver said coffee would be great and if they had their home-baked apple pie that night, he'd love a piece.

"You've been handling Special Agent Gleason's remains?" Hunter asked.

"You mean bits and pieces and parts, right?" Carver said dryly. He nodded. "And they've gone on now to the lab in Orlando. Maybe… Well, it would be nice to give his wife a bit more to bury. But in way, that relates to the reason I'm here. Maybe nothing, maybe something."

"I'm always interested in maybes," Hunter said.

"You're still working all this together?" Rich asked, looking at Amy.

She nodded. "And it seems we're back to the beginning here."

Rich shrugged and shook his head. "From what I've heard, you two keep finding the people behind it all."

"Let's hope we keep finding them all," Hunter said. "We've had some luck on this with cult members who have seen a new light. And we have suspects. But…the power of a cult leader is truly something. We just lost another possible witness to suicide. And his partner—who raced away—has been found, too. Well, half of him has been found."

"Yes, I know. Aidan insisted I come in on it. He thinks

there's something wrong with the picture. All right, let's face it—people go into the Everglades and they disappear. Some are known to have disappeared, and then others…well, they may have disappeared in the Everglades, or they just didn't tell anybody where they were going. So I inspected the remains discovered today—one of the men who attempted to kidnap a woman and shot her boyfriend.

"And?" Amy asked.

"Aidan is right. The body definitely met with an alligator. Remember how alligators bite—bottom jaw there, top jaw doing the snapping. Well, there's more to that part of the body, but I believe the man was dead before he was even partially snacked upon by an alligator." He hesitated. "I think he might have been decapitated and the gator did what the killer was hoping—chomped down and took a large part of the body. We have no idea what specific creature might have done it. And we don't run around indiscriminately chopping up our wildlife to find which one may have a man's torso in it, but… I thought you should know."

"We're grateful for your input, anything you can give us is always tremendously helpful," Amy assured him.

Rich smiled and thanked their waitress as she delivered his coffee.

When she was gone, he said, "Well, here's another thing. I've received other body parts in the last month that were discovered in the stomachs of nuisance alligators." He glanced at over Hunter, knowing he wasn't from the area. He shrugged. "When a creature does become a menace to human life, it's first relocated, but sometimes…well. Hmm. Did you ever see the movie *Lake Placid*? Well, a little old lady was feeding alligators and they wound up with a taste for human flesh. Thing is, they aren't cute little ducks or birds you might feed in a park. And they become a menace to human beings if they become accustomed to a food source. Of course, getting an alligator to eat a victim is certainly one way to get rid of the *body of evidence.* Throughout the years, occasionally, a body part has been found in an alligator—or a crocodile, which is more aggressive, but with minuscule numbers in comparison to the alligator."

Amy looked at him, frowning. "Rich, are you trying to say someone has fed body parts to alligators many times?"

"I don't know about many. But I'd say several. We haven't found any matching body parts. And they aren't matching any known missing persons' reports. I don't know what is happening—but they were human beings. And I'm afraid—"

"Afraid this has to do with the horsemen case," Hunter finished.

Rich nodded gravely.

"Excuse me!"

Amy looked up to see that Ida Peterson had come back to the table.

"May I?" she asked.

"Of course," Amy said. Hunter moved over and Ida slid in next to him.

She frowned at Rich Carver and said, "I believe you have been here before, perhaps with Detective Mulberry or John Shultz—or even these guys," she said lightly.

Rich smiled. "I have been here. Not sure when but anyone in law enforcement or forensics has heard that this is the best place possible to eat in this area! Kudos!"

Ida laughed softly. "The only place, probably, but thank you." She grew serious. "People are being murdered again, right?" she asked them.

"I'm afraid so, Ida," Hunter told her. "We know what happened in the past, but have you seen new people hanging around, anyone acting suspiciously?"

"Not so much anything specific," Ida said. She frowned, looking at Amy, still confused she couldn't place her.

"Please, Mrs. Peterson, speak freely. She is one of us," Hunter said, his voice low, as if Ida Peterson herself was being invited into a secret realm.

"Well, of course, we're well aware body parts have been found—some of them in areas near us, just north of here."

"Yes, I'm afraid the news is true," Hunter said. "So, have you seen or heard anything suspicious?"

"Again, maybe not, maybe this is just silly. But you've heard about the Lost City, of course?"

"The Lost City of the Everglades," Amy said. She smiled. "We've talked about it lately. It was a hideout for rebels in the Civil War who stole Union gold, some claim, and were killed, they believe, by Northern forces or Native Americans. It was reported there was a moonshine still for Al Capone there. It is supposed to be haunted. Archeologists have found bones, relics, etcetera over several acres, but it's not on any maps, and is almost impossible to find."

Ida nodded. "Right—that Lost City."

"Are people in the Lost City?" Hunter asked.

"No, that's just it. Not that I've found the Lost City, but I know the general area where it's supposed to be. South of here, and far, far west. But there was a group of young people in here the other day, three couples, and they thought they had been in it, just up the road off 27. They said they were walking around, taking pictures, when one of the boys found bones, or so he said. He believed they had found an old burial ground. Then they heard sounds, strange sounds, like ghostly chanting. Well, apparently, they were all making fun of one of the girls because she heard whispering in the trees—she had an overwhelming sensation of danger and made them all leave."

Amy glanced at Hunter.

That young girl had probably had the best *sense* she'd had in her life; they might have become victims as Sandra and Regan had been when they met up with their attackers.

"Lots of people believe the Lost City is haunted. There were relics found there that might well date back to the Tequesta, and they've found Seminole relics and the remains of small groups living out there. But it isn't on any maps, and only old Gladesmen like my Frank and members of our local tribes know how to find it. But that's not it. The thing is, whatever happened out there made them all *think* they'd been in the Lost City and it *was* haunted and scary. So…"

"We'll look into it," Hunter promised her. "Thank you. And please—"

"Oh, Special Agent Hunter, of course! We know we have you out there, and Frank and I would call you immediately if we knew anything at all!" Ida promised. "You're always in with the cops and agents. Are you with the FBI or the FDLE?" she asked Rich Carver.

Rich Carver grinned. "No, I'm the—"

"He's a doctor!" Amy said.

"Nice!" Ida murmured. "All right, let me allow you to finish up your meal in peace."

She rose and left them. "What?" Rich asked Amy. "Were you afraid she might scream and run if she knows what I do?"

Amy smiled. "I think you're going to get larger pieces of apple pie if she just thinks you're a doctor."

"Hey, my profession is noble!"

"And so appreciated, respected, and needed," Amy assured him. "I just… I just think you'll get better and bigger apple pie slices." She smiled at him sweetly.

Carver studied her. "Wow. She really doesn't know you, and if I didn't know you… The look is really something. Entirely different. I take it you don't want anyone who might be involved in this to know you?"

"Right," Amy said.

They paused their conversation as Ida swung back to place a healthy serving of apple pie, looking more like a quarter of the baked good than a regular slice, on the table before moving on to another customer. Amy gave Rich a knowing look.

"You're going to entice them to snatch you, aren't you, Amy?" Carver asked. He looked at her and then stared at Hunter.

"Don't worry—she'll never be alone. Aidan is partnered with her, and I and others will be within shouting distance at all times. But they are trying to seize female victims. Mickey and my boss, Garza, have been over everything and getting an agent in there may be our only way of finding whatever hideout they're using right now. And the thing is, they lost two men and failed to find their sacrifice. Maybe they need a girl by a certain time. Things could move fast," Hunter said.

"Good luck, Amy. Good luck," Rich said. "More than luck. Be careful, extremely careful. I don't want it to be…"

"You don't want it to be my body that winds up on your table," Amy said. "I know and thank you. But they don't kill their victims right away. They hold them to be used in a ceremony. They tell their followers the victims they intend to kill are sacrifices; and by killing the victims, they're also saving their immortal souls. And because of the amount of sin the victims have in them, they won't be chosen when the Apocalypse happens. Only the chosen are taken. In other words, the heads of this cult convince their followers they are doing God's work to kill—and thus cleanse the sins of others."

Rich looked over at Hunter. "And people believe this?"

"When they begin to doubt, they wind up getting bitten by an alligator," Hunter said dryly. "People, by nature, look for companionship. When they find themselves misunderstood or not finding what they need from others in life and wind up lonely and disenfranchised, they make easy targets. It helps if you have a talent, but drones are always useful. Anyway, sometimes, someone falters at the right time—which we began to learn in Colorado. I was hoping to have a link yesterday—but both links are dead. You've seen one. I'm sure the body of the second man will find its way to you. We think we know who we're looking for, but they have something here. And whatever it is, they're well hidden."

"I take it they know and would recognize Amy and thus the new style?" Rich asked.

Amy nodded.

"Please, please…"

"We will be careful. But if they are just looking to sweep up any young woman who appears to be vulnerable, and we put her out as bait…it may be our chance," Hunter said.

"Right. The only chance to stop this," Rich said. He stood, frowned for a minute, looking at his cup and plate, and reached into his pocket.

Hunter laughed softly. "We got this," he assured Rich.

"You need me, you call me," Rich said.

"Oh, trust me, we will," Hunter told him.

He gave them a wave and left them. Amy looked over at Hunter.

"I'm proud of you," she told him.

"Oh?"

"You've accepted I should do this, and it's right. You understand I know how to play it all—and while I couldn't find the Lost City for you, I do know the environment better than most. I'm so glad you're…with me on it."

"With you? Count on it. Do I accept it? Not really. However, I can't argue the professional logic and need for what you want to do, but..."

"I know you will be right there. Hunter, something else is going on down here. I don't know how or when the last horse will arrive, but everything we do stop will save lives."

"We've lost a few along the way, too. Here's what I don't understand. We had a guy in the hospital. He was terrified about the concept of dying from his snakebites. Then, while still in the hospital when doctors are planning to induce a coma to save his life, he stabs himself in the heart with a needle. He couldn't have known his co-kidnapper or friend was dead. So..."

"I can only believe it's like you said before. Fear. Fear of what will happen to you if you don't take care of it yourself will be far worse than anything imaginable." She paused and grimaced. "Like being offered up in pieces to an alligator."

Hunter nodded. "But the thing is, he knew that. Even down here, he knew that. So, Hayden, Don, or the illustrious Mr. Barrington himself. Two of them could be here. Andy has been checking in on Barrington, and he's been going into his office. Still..."

"Still, he could be calling the shots—the person running this, we know, is acquiring charismatic leaders. Then the leaders turn their followers into murderers. And the head stays clean and neat."

"We have to get someone alive who will talk," Hunter said. He reached across the table suddenly, taking her hand. "For now, let's get back to the hotel. I'm thinking we should talk to the religious leaders in this area, as we did when it all started, and which did get us moving. But I'm also thinking—"

"That we need to head back out tomorrow and try to lure them in?" Amy asked. "I want you to be careful, too! Regan was shot trying to defend his beloved Sandra."

"Ah, but they won't even see me at first. You'll be with Aidan, and they can take Aidan, too, or he'll just moan while they take you away. He knows not to offer any resistance. Then again, you could give Aidan a speech on the history of Florida and the Everglades—or maybe he should give you, his beautiful girlfriend, a speech while you walk along hand in hand."

She smiled. "We'll give each other speeches and see how it goes. Thankfully, if nothing happens at all, we both like history!"

"Let's head out. I'm fascinated to spend the rest of what's left of the evening with this new dark-haired beauty who has walked into my life."

"Ha-ha. Maybe we could get a disguise on you, too."

"Oh? You need something new already?"

She shrugged teasingly. "No, mustaches are too...hairy. Irritating. Beards are the same. And bald men are attractive, but... No, keep your hair while you've got it!"

Hunter headed to the counter and paid the bill. She saw Ida Peterson was speaking to him earnestly.

She waved and headed to the door and Hunter joined her.

"Is everything all right? Did she think of something else?"

Hunter grinned. "No, nothing else. Everything is fine— she was worried about you."

"Me?"

"Well, of course. I used to work with that auburn-haired agent, and Ida was sure there was something special between us, and here I am today...with you."

"That's wonderful!"

"What? That she thinks I'm a louse?"

Amy laughed. "No, it's wonderful my disguise works!"

In the car, Amy watched the road as they moved along Route 27 to merge onto I-75.

There was so much land that was rich with waterways, marshes, hammocks, many different towering trees, saw grass, and so much more.

They passed areas where housing developments had become communities—stretching out into the Everglades.

The I-75 took them onto the I-595 and soon they were back at the hotel. Amy put through a call to Aidan, discussing their movement for the morning.

Hunter, Sean, Ryan, and other teams would move into the area of the Everglades, find cover in the expanse of thick grasses and trees and wait.

She and Aidan would come by airboat, stroll along and talk.

And see what happened.

When she finished her phone conversation, she looked at Hunter who was talking to someone on his own cell. She sat at the foot of the bed and waited. Eventually he hung up the phone and took a seat beside her.

"Rabbi Goldstein. And I had a brief conversation with Father Brennan. Amazing what good friends that group manages to be, trying to look for the similarities instead of all the differences in what they do. Kind of kills me—it's a small area where all this is taking place and should be a great one. Sorry, that's neither here nor there as the saying goes. But, anyway, they haven't had newcomers attend any of their services, but both told me there are members of their flocks who have talked about strange things happening. Father Brennan told me one of the sugar growers in his flock asked to come to confession—which he never does—because he was convinced he heard the song of banshees coming from the trees. Rabbi Goldstein said one of his son's friends told him he thought there were strange people running in the saw grass, but he didn't investigate because he was frightened. He thought he'd heard shots." He paused and looked at her. "I am going to be near you every second, but any of us can fall to a bullet."

"I'm more worried about Aidan than me. They prefer female sacrifices."

He nodded.

Then he stood suddenly, striding to her. He smiled, swept her up in a dramatic stance and said, "My dark-haired beauty, we've but a night...a night before the day."

"I think you usually just get one night before the day," she said, laughing.

"True! But we have this night. Hey, no chocolate or flowers for you! Where's the ridiculousness of romance in your soul?" he teased.

"I don't like flowers inside—they die. And I'm particular and don't like most of the chocolates they put in those *romantic* bundle things," she told him.

"Alas, no romance."

She shook her head. "I'm extremely romantic! All I require is a gentle touch and... Well, not always gentle, you know. Your eyes. Just your eyes. And waking up beside you, feeling your arms around me when I fall to sleep."

"I take it all back," he told her. His leaned closer, his lips covering hers, his touch a sweet and truly gentle tease at first, and then something so much more.

"But shower, shower," she murmured against his lips.

"Oh, yeah."

Discarding their clothes on the way, they headed into the bath where Hunter played with the spigot while still trying to keep his lips locked with hers. They laughed, broke apart, stepped into the spray, and felt the steam surround them. For a few moments, they held each other close. Amy leaned her head against his chest, just loving the feel of his heartbeat against her cheek and the heat and fall of the water all around them.

Then she broke away. They scrubbed and soaped gently, laughing and teasing before simultaneously deciding it was time to step out. Still laughing, they dried off, then fell back on the clean sheets and encompassing softness of the bed.

She wondered later if he had been worried about the day to come, worried this night would become the day, and the day might lead to a nightmare rather than the rest of their lives.

He was hungry, passionate, urgent. His touch was sensuous and then wild, sweeping her senses to new heights, holding her all the while, as she held him.

They lay together at last, just curled around each other.

She smoothed her fingers through his hair and said softly, "Hunter, it's going to be all right. Have faith in me."

"I do. I swear, I do. I just know…no matter how good we are, things can go south."

"We won't let them."

"Deal," he said softly.

He was on his back, staring up at the ceiling. She lay with her head on his chest, her arm around him. They slept, and when she woke, he was already showered and dressed in green and beige, ready to blend in with the elements.

"Aidan is coming for you in twenty," he told her. "I'm heading out—Ryan and Sean will be with me, and both Mickey and Garza have other teams out in various areas. But we don't want to spook anyone. We just want to make sure we're covered if there are any twists and turns getting to wherever those thugs meant to bring their victim yesterday."

She bound out of bed, knowing she needed to hurry.

"Oh, I brewed you some coffee. It's still in the pot over there," he said.

"Thank you! Coffee in the morning is much better than chocolate and flowers, I promise!" she teased.

She headed for the bathroom but he caught her. They exchanged one long kiss and an even longer look. He half smiled and half grimaced and walked out the door.

Amy hurried to get ready, trying to replicate Ryan's ability at makeup. When she was done, she was all prettied up with flattering colors and rich long lashes. She'd planned her wardrobe well, too. She wore khaki trousers with secret pockets, a knit shirt, and a khaki jacket also with a hidden pocket. She wasn't going to carry her usual service weapon—it was too large and could too easily be discovered and recognized as a law enforcement weapon. Instead, she slid a G42 Glock—less than four inches—into an inner side pocket of the shoulder bag she'd chosen to bring for the outing.

She wasn't planning on any bullets flying, but if they did, she didn't want to be defenseless.

She was ready, dressed, hopefully presentable enough to be enticing to a killer, and prepared with her handgun and a lipstick tube that wasn't lipstick at all—rather a tube that contained several shots of pepper spray.

Her nail file could double as a knife if necessary.

Her phone rang; Aidan was waiting downstairs in the car.

Amy hurried outside to meet him.

Aidan, too, had dressed for the day. Jeans and a light T-shirt that advertised a local band, a jacket to tie around his waist, and a baseball cap.

"So, am I lecturing to you, or are you lecturing to me?" she asked.

He smiled. "Special Agent Larson, I will play it any way you like." He hesitated and shrugged. "I'm just grateful they twisted the red tape they needed to twist in order to allow me out in the field. I can't help but want this to end. I know it's often a long haul. I know some criminals are never caught—but with our technology today, we are doing a hell of a lot better. I know that once you know who a criminal is, you

do everything you can to get your hands on them, but…"
He glanced her way. "You do know who this is, right? You
two figured it out in Colorado. I've been briefed, of course,
on those we're looking for."

"Of course. We have our three suspects—one of whom is
just missing. I think we're supposed to believe he was kidnapped. Another one we're definitely supposed to believe was
kidnapped. And one who was still in his office in Colorado
yesterday morning. But I'm willing to bet that one of our
suspects lived here or had family here at some point. They
also recruited someone who knew the area, but that's not a
surprise. We've had so much upheaval in the world lately, I
imagine it's even easier to cater to people's fears or hatreds
regarding society and laws now more than ever."

They reached the parking lot quickly. When they were in
the airboat, Aidan asked Jimmy to make sure he didn't come
after them.

"Stay with your airboat for three hours. If we don't return
after that, just get the hell out of here, all right? If we're both
seized, neither of us will return, but you can't panic—it's part
of the plan," Aidan told him.

"I'll do what you ask. But it's a dumb plan if you ask me,"
Jimmy said.

Amy smiled and gave him a kiss on the cheek. "We're not
asking you!"

The motor revved. They reached the point on the embankment where they wanted to be. Aidan made a point of helping
Amy from the airboat. He held her hand and laughed with
her as they walked through the grass and foliage to a point
between the water and the road—where it had been determined Aidan would act as the tour guide.

"I know I've explained this to you before," he said, grinning with an exaggerated sigh. "Along the Tamiami Trail,

you'll find the Miccosukee village, and at Big Cypress and in other areas in the state—"

"But the Seminole and the Miccosukee were both Creek, right?"

He let out another of his sighs. "Two different language groups. Okay, whatever remained of all the earlier tribes became absorbed as the people who are now the Seminole Tribe, and the Miccosukee Tribe moved south, fleeing into the Everglades. There are, even among Seminole scholars, different thoughts on the true originations. Some believe the Seminole truly absorbed the remains of the more ancient tribes. Some Seminoles—more often those above Lake Okeechobee—still speak the Creek that came before throughout the centuries, and it's complex. The Miccosukee language developed from the Lower Creek, and the Seminole developed from the Upper Creek—but they are both Muskogean languages. That's kind of like the way the German and English languages are related. Like how *and* .in English is *und* in German. *Or Spanish and Italian and Portuguese. Perfecto!* Hitchiti-Mikasuki is spoken by the—you guessed it—Miccosukee of Mikasuki. The Seminole language—sometimes here, more mainly in the north of the state—is Creek, or Muskogee. Yes, yes, yes, many of the tribes in the south *before* the Trail of Tears were close, separated sometimes by something so small as a body of water.

"Ah, like the Irish and the Scots—so similar and yet not!"

"Not so sure that would go over well with an Irishman or a Scot!"

Amy laughed and made a pretense of circling around Aidan. She thought she had sensed it or seen it—movement in the brush ahead of them.

They were far from the road.

They were far from the river.

They were in a clearing, surrounded by the voluminous

trees and brush that could grow so thickly in the hammocks that rose between waterways.

Then they appeared. Three men, rough-looking, with overgrown beards, shaggy hair, jeans, and T-shirts—and black masks that covered the majority of their faces.

"Hey!" one cried.

Aidan looked at Amy. "This is it," he whispered.

"Do not get shot!" she commanded under her breath.

"Don't intend to," Aidan said.

"Aidan! I mean it, please—"

"Amy, have faith in me!"

"I do, Aidan, I do."

He lifted a hand. "Hey!" he called back. "Why the masks? I mean, heck, we all had 'em on for COVID, but…hey! You boys in trouble? Can I give you directions or anything?"

"Yeah!" the blond one said, producing a gun he aimed at Aidan. "The girl. You can give us the girl. Well, we're taking her whether you give her to us or not, so…hand her over!"

16

Hunter saw the men come forward. He heard Aidan's casual shout.

And he saw as the three men came forward and grabbed Amy.

Aidan didn't try to stop them physically, but he announced that wherever the men were taking her, he was coming, too. That brought about laughter from the kidnappers, but they told him he could do as he pleased—except cause trouble.

"One bit of trouble and I shoot you!" one of the men warned.

"No trouble! I just go where she goes!" Aidan said.

"We'll see about that, Tonto," one of them said.

Hunter was ready to leap forward at the blatantly racist remark; Aidan showed remarkable restraint.

"Please," he said simply.

"Then come along," another of the men said. "We need to just get away from here, right? No trouble today," he said to the others.

"So, let's go," another of the men said.

Hunter noted they hadn't taken Amy's bag away from her. She was still armed. And she looked terrified as she perfectly played the part of a stunned victim.

He guessed he wasn't doing so perfectly himself.

He felt Ryan's hand on his arm. "Hunter, you could pick off those idiots in seconds flat, three shots while they were still trying to aim, but that's not the plan. Amy is good. Aidan is surprisingly good for a forensics guy! We follow. And don't forget, there are others out there. Now is the time when we're going to stop this horseman!"

And Ryan was right. Hunter lifted his hand, letting Ryan know he wasn't going to leap out of the brush and throttle the men who had taken Amy and Aidan.

"We give them another thirty feet. I'll skirt to the left. You and Sean go right."

They had already covered the ground here, and Hunter knew where they were going to reach water, low and high, and where a hammock would rise out of the muck. He also knew he'd run into a huge field of sawgrass if he didn't swing into the side of one of the hammocks.

But he did know where he was going. At one point, to avoid the saw grass, he would be close to the group ahead of him. A buzzing sounded in his ear but he didn't dare slap at the mosquito threatening to feast on his blood. He waved at the persistent creature; as he did, he saw one of the captors was swearing and swatting at an insect as well.

"I am roasting! I am being baked in this thing!" the man cried out.

He ripped off his mask and wiped at his face.

Hunter had never met Don Blake, but he had seen his picture. The man had never been missing. He hadn't been taken by the murderous group at the mud pits in the caverns in Colorado.

He was, indeed, part of the group.

But…as a leader?

That question was quickly answered. One of the other men turned, furious. "What the hell? We were told we couldn't show our faces!" he said.

"Why not? Who the hell cares? These two will be sacrifices tomorrow—who the hell are they going to tell and what would they tell if they could? They don't know me," Blake said.

Carey Allen had wasted time worrying about the man, that was certain. He had probably seen to it in some subtle manner that she had ended up in the pit.

The tallest of the men stepped back. "You're missing the point. We were given orders. We follow what the archangel tells us. I will not miss my chance for being among the chosen because you're an idiot who can't take a little heat!"

"Oh, go to hell!" Blake said.

The other man pulled out a gun—and shot Blake point-blank in the chest.

Hunter tensed, afraid that they might turn and do the same to Amy and Aidan.

Amy would never let it go so far. She was prepared, if need be, to produce her own weapon.

He had to believe that; he knew he couldn't move now. They would be no closer to the truth than they had been.

Amy didn't reach for a gun. She cried out, throwing herself in Aidan's arms. He held her as the armed gunman turned to the two of them.

"That's what happens. Step out of line once, and you die.

And when you die, you will go to Hell. We're trying to save people too stupid to know our time on earth is nothing and the war is coming. Ah, what am I trying to do? You'll never understand. You're not the kind of people with the balls to understand anything. Start moving!"

"Wait!" the third man said. He indicated Don Blake's corpse. "Can't leave this here."

"Drag it to the water over there."

"There were cops out here yesterday, I swear! They found half of Ned's body, and they'll be wondering—"

"Weight him down with some rocks. Do it now."

The masks the men wore were muffling their voices. Hunter strained to determine if he could recognize the sound of either voice.

He could not.

He held still, willing himself not to walk out, shoot both of the so-called *chosen* men and take Amy and Aidan out of the depths of this place.

He knew Ryan and Sean were not far away.

Watching. Following. And they needed to continue to do so.

The one man dragged the corpse of Don Blake to the water's edge. He searched for rocks, but there were none. Instead, he gathered broken branches and vines and tried his best to make sure the corpse would sink in the muck.

Then, they started moving again.

Hunter glanced to the water.

He remembered the event that had led to him telling his parents it was all wrong; they'd had to get out of the cult they had joined once they started believing they were the saviors of humanity.

He remembered the body of a friend. A friend who had dared to become a dissident.

Stay the course.

He was enough of a highly experienced agent to fulfill the objective.

He was also deeply involved on the human level with Amy and Aidan.

But the men were moving again, prodding Amy and Aidan ahead of them. They walked, carefully, avoiding marsh, the occasional moccasin in the road and once an alligator.

Then finally, deep back behind a field of shoulder-high saw grass, they came to a cabin. It was truly hidden from any roads, from any waterways used by fishermen or airboat guides. It appeared to be falling apart.

They were nowhere near the Lost City, Hunter knew. And yet this might have been another such area, perhaps used by an enterprising bootlegger once upon a prohibition—and now little more than a derelict shack remained with vines and trees creeping over the walls and shadowing the roof.

They knew where they were going.

He held his distance, watching, waiting.

When he was sure they were inside the cabin, he made his way to it, mindless of the rip and tear of the saw grass on his clothing and hands.

There were no windows. Time had long since rid the place of windowpanes had they ever been part of the structure.

Hunter made his way silently to the wall, knowing he didn't dare stay long, but anxious to look within.

There were a few chairs in the place around a poor excuse for a table. To one side of the room was a single bedroll, to the other, a set of children's bunks.

Amy had been ordered to the top bunk.

Aidan was on the bottom.

The man who had wielded the gun and shot his companion in cold blood was on the phone speaking with someone.

Hunter was surprised he'd managed a signal this deep in the Everglades, but a booster in the shack might have provided for better communication.

He rose just by the window and was straining to hear.

"We have not failed you, Archangel!" the man said, his voice filled with respect and maybe even awe. He clearly believed what he was being told about the Apocalypse, sinners, and sacrifice with his whole heart. "Todd and I have not failed you. We have not one but two for you, and you will be pleased. Young as the sacrifice demands, and certainly, together as sinners. They are secure here—we will guard them through the night, giving them nothing but water. Tomorrow is the day! Despite the work of the Devil, we have prevailed. We will bring them to the place of glory tomorrow for the full rise of the sun. No, Archangel! You will lead the great battle for us, and you must stay where you are in comfort and safety until tomorrow!"

The call ended and Hunter hunched down lest one of the men glance out the window.

Nothing would happen to Amy or Aidan until the next morning.

They hadn't been led to a headquarters—just to an old shack that was used to hold prisoners, the "sinners" for the "sacrifice."

Hunter needed to back away through the saw grass and communicate with Ryan and Sean.

He didn't intend to leave the area.

He'd be damned if he'd be far from the old shack until Amy and Aidan were out of it.

But there were things he needed to know as well.

If the "Archangel" was safe and secure but somewhere close enough to be able to come and inspect his prisoners, where was that place?

And just where did these people intend for their sacrifice to take place?

He started to rise. The man was talking again, talking to Amy, his head close to hers where it lay in the bunk.

"Oh, my beauty, don't be afraid! I would never hurt you. No, you're not going to be hurt. Tomorrow, they'll cut your heart out and save you from your sins, but you needn't fear me! I will guard you with my life through the night!"

"You'll guard her?" the other asked.

"We'll guard her. But you fall asleep all the time. I am the Archangel's true warrior!"

"No. I will be as great a warrior!"

"Yeah, well, we'll see. Ah, my dark-haired beauty! You are luscious! If only! But I am a man who will have immortality. If only the Apocalypse was not upon us! I could have shown you such a good time!"

Stay the course, Hunter reminded himself. Amy knew what she was doing. Tomorrow was the time when they would need to be close.

When, if nothing else, they would discover the Archangel.

Now, it was just a waiting game.

Wherever the place of sacrifice was to be at the full rise of the sun, he would be there. The law would be there, in force.

He might not know the area as Amy did, but he had learned enough to hide himself in a makeshift shelter through the night and not be seen—while still being able to see.

He would not be far from Amy. He would not be far at all.

Amy had no problem feigning terror of her captors. But she also knew that they were just as frightened as she was.

Well, they had their answers about Don Blake.

But he had just been a player! Even when she was the one who pulled the trigger—or more especially when she was the one who pulled the trigger—it was horrible to watch a man die. And maybe Don had been as much a victim as many others, believing a lie that had been told to him over and over.

Equally, she was certain her captor who had shot Don was afraid. It was clear they must follow the directive to a T—or wind up half eaten by an alligator or killing oneself with a hospital needle intended to save lives, not take them.

Eventually, her captor tired of taunting her. He moved away from Amy, almost as if he was afraid he might be burned by her. Of course, he was human. He was intrigued. He held a female victim captive, and that power alone probably stirred something in him.

Something he dared not follow.

"Hey, we have beer in that cooler around the side, right?" he asked his companion.

"Yeah. I didn't ask, but I wasn't told we weren't allowed to bring any. Maybe I was afraid to ask!" he added. "But, heck, you know, Don was right about one thing. It's hot out here, sticky—and the mosquitoes want to make blood sacrifices out of all of us!"

He wanted it to be a joke. His companion didn't laugh.

"I'm going for a beer."

He walked out, followed by the second man.

As soon as they were gone, Amy spoke softly. "Aidan?"

"I'm right down here. Can't go anywhere," he said dryly.

"Well, you can, and you must, if they drink enough beer."

"What?" Aidan demanded in a terse whisper. "Amy, I'm not a trained agent, but I have taken dozens of classes, worked at the range... I'm okay! I'm here with you. We'll get these people, I swear it. We know nothing is going to happen until tomorrow—"

"Aidan, we need to make sure the others know, and they're prepared. And here's the thing. Our best techs—FDLE, FBI, all the rest—need to find out where the hell the *Archangel* is based. He's not out here—not out here sweating and getting mosquito-bitten! Aidan, I'm barely tied. They seem to think a girl is no threat. I can get out of these ropes binding my wrists and ankles. And when I do, you disappear!"

"Amy, I can't leave you here alone—"

"You must. They want a female sacrifice. Getting to kill you, too, is just like icing on the cake. But, Aidan, I must be here—I am the cake. And please remember, I am a trained agent. You have to get out there and make sure when they take me out in the morning, our people are there following every step of the way."

"They are out there."

"Aidan—"

"Amy."

"Please!" she whispered fiercely before going silent. The door had opened; their captors were returning.

The one man, the tall one, walked over to stare down at Amy again. A mosquito buzzed by. He shook his head.

"I'll get some spray. You're not supposed to be all bitten up. You know, I'm sorry. We're not supposed to torture you. We aren't judges. That's for later. You don't know how lucky you are. We had others... Well, only one can really be the key sacrifice. I mean, we'll try to help your boyfriend, too, but there's one at each occasion. We've tried to help others, I believe, but we can't do this ceremony for just everyone."

She didn't reply.

He walked away from the cot and dug into a bag. When he returned, she caught the smell of something else before he rained bug spray around the area where she and Aidan lay.

Beer. She had a feeling he'd consumed more than one can or bottle.

A few minutes later, his companion walked in. He weaved a little as he walked.

Definitely more than one can or bottle.

As time went by, the two of them kept going out. Of course. It was boring—no television, not even a radio. It didn't seem either of them carried a tablet of any kind—or so much as a paperback novel.

They were getting bitten. Amy saw the one wince and slap his neck. And they were hot, it appeared.

Sweating.

Weren't they all?

Night finally fell. She watched the one man lie down on the bedroll across the shack from her and Aidan. She wasn't sure where the other one was. She imagined he was back out with the beer.

She waited. It wasn't that long before she heard the man snoring.

She was basically still while testing the ropes that tied her wrists together. They weren't bound behind her back, but right in front of her.

The two men really weren't expecting much trouble from a woman.

She brought the knot to her teeth, wincing at the rough feel of the rope, but working away at it. In just a matter of minutes, the knot began to give. A little more effort...

And she was free.

The knot on the ropes binding her ankles was even more poorly tied. That one took just her fingers a few seconds.

She rose carefully, watching the sleeping man and keeping her eye on the door. Crawling down carefully, she reached Aidan's side.

She clamped her hand over Aidan's mouth and shook her head.

Aidan's wrists had been bound behind his back so she

twisted him around. But even that knot had been poorly secured, and she had freed first his wrists and then his ankles.

The man on the floor kept snoring.

She shook her head as she carefully moved toward the door and sought out the second man. When she looked outside, she saw he was on a tree stump near the shack with his back and head rested against the outer wooden wall. His mouth was open.

He, too, was snoring.

"Aidan, go," she ordered.

"Amy!"

"I'm begging you. They're going to think you are an awful louse, a terrible coward," she said, managing a wry grin. "You've got to get back to Hunter and the others and make sure they know what is going on. And they need to know Don Blake *was* in on this, but he wasn't running anything, he's dead."

"You know Hunter is close. He probably knows already."

"I do know he's close, and I'm counting on it. But we don't know what he saw. We must let this get as close as possible to... Well, we have to play it out. He'll know when to... when to stop it."

"Before you die," Aidan said.

She nodded. "I will be fine! But we *must* catch this person, Aidan. Please! Go, go quick so I can retie myself!"

He stared at her a moment longer and tried one last time. "Amy, at least let me stay with you."

"Aidan, please. Make sure I'm saved tomorrow—" Amy grinned reassuringly "—and not from my sins. I'd like to keep my heart in my chest!"

At last, he looked at her, nodded, checked out the drunken man snoring open-mouthed against the wall, and agreed.

He ducked low and, despite the moonlight, disappeared into the tall saw grass surrounding the shack.

Amy quickly returned to her cot. She gathered the ropes and retied her ankles and then her wrists. Even so awkwardly, it was difficult to make the knot look as poorly tied as the one her captors had set on her.

She laid back down, closed her eyes, and even managed to doze off.

She would need all her facilities in the morning when the sun had fully risen.

Hunter quickly realized he'd startled Aidan, but to his credit, Aidan didn't let out a sound. He shook his head, studying Hunter and the array of vines and foliage he'd donned to blend in well with the night.

They were too close to the shack to take a chance on conversation so Hunter motioned the two of them needed to move back to the old hunter's shelter where the hammock rose an inch or so behind the tangled roots of several banyan trees.

"She made me leave!" Aidan told him. "She said it was important for you to know everything. A guy named Don Blake was involved—he was one of the guys who took us. But he couldn't have been a bigwig because one of the other guys shot him. Who those guys are, I don't know. They never took their masks off. The one man called whoever is the bigwig here—and Amy said you needed to get every tech department trying to figure out where he is. Apparently, the puppet master doesn't like being hot and sticky and getting bitten by mosquitoes."

"Neither Amy nor I ever met Don Blake, but we did suspect him," Hunter told Aidan. "But I saw his face and I recognized him from pictures. We are lying low in this area tonight, ready to follow in the morning."

"She said we need tech to try to find out where this top guy is. He's somewhere close, but where there's air-conditioning and creature comforts," Aidan pressed.

Hunter nodded. He had to move his phone around for a minute to get a connection, but he did. It was late at night but Mickey Hampton answered his call on the first ring.

Hunter reported what was happening.

And told Mickey he'd be there through the night and would follow the kidnappers in the morning. Ryan and Sean were still in the field as well, across from his location on the other side of the broken-down shack.

He learned other units were still out in the field. There were units from both agencies; and while they were grateful for the FBI, FDLE was going to be in on this. It was Florida, and it was the life of a Florida agent that was at risk.

"Keep an open line the minute you begin following in the morning," Mickey said.

"You got it, but I'll have you on mute. I don't want to give away my location."

"Seriously? That's a given, Hunter."

"Right, sir. We know another archangel is appearing—and hopefully that will end the reign of this horseman, and maybe even show us the true master," Hunter murmured.

"Let's get these people tomorrow," Mickey said. "Alive, if we can. We may need them to lead us onward—because a puppet master will come—but we're not sure yet from where. I have another piece of news for you. Your suspect, Malcolm Barrington, owner of the advertising agency, isn't answering his home phone or his work line. We sent plainclothes agents to his home. If he's there, he's ignoring everyone."

"Right."

They ended the call. He had barely hung up before the phone vibrated in his hands. Mickey was calling back.

"Banyan Bend," Mickey said.

"Pardon me?"

"Ask Aidan about it. My secretary said our archangel might be there. The community is actually quite old—just west of the northern Broward County cities and barely out of the Everglades. In the 1920s, there was an architect who envisioned a community created to resemble a Norse fishing village, one that was accessible by water. Anyway, the original old houses are worth a small fortune. We're going to start a discreet investigation. One of our techs grew up there, and he said he loved it when he was a kid—but the city government became wildly corrupt and used tax money for ridiculous art projects. They would fine people for putting trash out a minute before set-up time for pick-up. Imagine the worst homeowners association, and this city government makes it look like child's play. Anyway, we are FDLE, and we're going to begin some inquiries."

"If any agents see someone heading out in a cape and cowl—"

"We'll still have to follow through, Hunter. It's not illegal to wear a cape and cowl."

"I was about to say they need to make sure they don't stop him. We need to catch him just about to…"

"Slice up Amy?"

"You know, we don't have to verbalize it."

"I know. It won't happen. You're out there."

"Damned right."

"All right. I've alerted Garza, and he's using his federal power to discover what he can. You'll be out there through the night."

"With Sean, Ryan, and now Aidan," Hunter assured him.

"Like I said, keep an open line. I want to clean this up."

"Yes, sir."

He ended the call and looked at Aidan. "You can rest—we can spell one another."

Aidan grinned. "Okay, I'll try. My people might have survived by running into the Everglades and hunkering down, and I do love my culture, but I live in an air-conditioned house now without mosquitoes."

"Yeah, me, too. We'll do our best."

"Watch out for—"

"Spiders, snakes, and hmm, we're kind of far from the embankment for an alligator—or a croc. But I do know to be wary."

Aidan might live in air-conditioning, but he knew how to clear an area and make sure that, at least at the start, no other creatures would be resting with him.

Hunter watched the house, surprised he could be so alert as the hours went by.

His phone vibrated at about two in the morning. It was Ryan who wanted to assure him he and Sean were still across from them. There was no activity from their side of the shack, and they wouldn't falter.

"Close your eyes for a while," Aidan said, tapping him on the shoulder. "I slept. I really slept."

Hunter nodded and closed his eyes. He believed he did doze. They were both awake as the sun began to rise.

And they watched. And waited.

Amy kept her eyes closed long after she had woken up. She pretended she didn't hear what was going on.

Her two captors had awakened.

And discovered Aidan was no longer on his bunk. He was gone.

"Son of a bitch!" the one cried.

"He's got to be right outside."

"Why? You were awake, guarding the place?" the taller of the two demanded.

"Hey, I… What about you?"

"What kind of yellow-bellied coward runs and leaves a woman behind?"

"I wouldn't worry about it. You know how deep in we are? Even if he started out, the idiot would never be able to find this place again. But I doubt if he got out. He's probably shaking by some pond, staring at alligators. Or holding on to a tree or kicking a moccasin or something. He's probably dead—he won't cause a problem."

"That's it."

"What's it?"

"We say he's already dead. We'll tell the broad the same thing."

"Right. Okay, we can lie to the Archangel, but…"

"For now, damn it, just do it! We can't ruin the whole rite! I'm getting her ready. Don't you dare screw this up!"

The other didn't reply. Amy felt the tall one come near her, felt him shake her shoulder. He was wearing his mask as he looked down at her and said, "Up, sleeping beauty." He untied her hands and then her ankles, turned to the table and found a garment in white fabric and threw it at her. "Get that on—now. Don't make this hard."

"Where's my friend?" she asked.

"He ran. Sorry, we had to kill him."

She lowered her head, feigning sobs. The fabric was pressed to her face.

"Put this on, now!"

"I—I can't with you watching. And my friend…"

"Lady, we'll turn around! Get that on."

She'd seen a similar garment before. When Mateus had nearly killed a woman.

Today, she was to be that woman.

"I—I—"

They were both staring at her. The tall one looked at the other. "Turn around. We need to get her where she needs to be!"

To her relief, they both turned around.

Of course, even with them turned around...

She made a pretense of crying, of fumbling with buttons. And doing so, she slipped her little knife from the pocket in her jacket and, with no recourse, secured it with the elastic at the hipline of her panties.

"I'm dressed!" she whispered in tears.

They both turned to look at her.

"Too bad, she is beautiful. Like an angel."

"She's the devil!" the other snapped. "We're going to save her soul."

"Now, my lady?" he asked her politely, offering her his arm. She stared at it, confused.

"Let's go! Don't make me hurt you first!" he snarled, his tone flipping on a dime.

She took his arm and he headed outside. They walked around the shack, and she discovered there was something that resembled a path leading in a northeasterly direction.

Curious. It was deeper and deeper into nothing.

These days, with a highway that cut across the peninsula just north of where they were, civilization never felt too far away. And if someone knew something was out there...

She didn't look back. She had to believe Hunter was close. And that others weren't too far behind.

They walked at least twenty minutes at a brisk pace before coming to a clearing where the saw grass had been flattened hard against the earth. There was a waterway beyond it, and hardwood hammocks to the right and the left.

Dead center of the flattened area was a makeshift altar—a poor altar, constructed without skill from some of the cypress in the area.

But there was a flat board atop it, and she was led to the board. As they brought her there, she saw people were coming from the direction of the water. They were being brought from across it by airboat. Amy thought she could hear traffic from beyond the shoreline.

The highway ran near.

And Hunter...

Someone in a cape and cowl walked toward the altar. That person was followed by another, one who was taller but bowed in reverence.

"The Archangel!" the other cried.

"Down, now!" Amy was told, and the larger of her captors lifted her off her feet, setting her down. They made no effort to restrain her, and it was clear they thought their numbers were enough to cow her. Amy lay there silently, waiting. And it began.

"You, my chosen ones!" the caped figure cried out. "Come, that we may say the words, and save this child. We prepare ourselves for the great battle to come! For Armageddon is upon us, the Apocalypse is coming and you have listened, you have heeded the words of truth!"

Listening for a moment, Amy was stunned.

This time, the archangel was a woman! And Amy knew that it was Hayden Harper!

Amy's captors, still near the altar, knelt, as did the others who had come around.

Ordinary people, as before. Men, women, couples, even a few children. Perhaps thirty or so people in all.

The Archangel paused by the altar, speaking softly to Amy's captors.

"Where is the other? The boy?"

"We had to kill him," one of them said. "We were sorry—he won't be saved. But we had no choice."

It was a chance to change things. To shake them up.

Amy sat up on the altar/board. "They're lying! He escaped. And you're a murderer!"

"Stop!" the Archangel cried. She stared hard at the two men who might well be lying as far as she knew, but she wasn't going to be deterred. She didn't bother with any more words. Her cowled assistant stood nearby holding a pillow with a large sharp dagger upon it. Hayden Harper, the Archangel, reached for it, and raised it over Amy's head.

"I, having sworn to the great and true Power of the Apocalypse to come take the role of the Archangel himself, have sworn to fulfill the destiny of the rider of the black horse. Thus, we take the heart of the sinner, take her sins upon us, strengthen ourselves for the ultimate battle to come, and strive for this child's immortal soul!"

The knife was about to fall. Before the blade came plunging down, Amy threw herself off the board. She reached under the sacrificial robe for her own knife, ready to defend herself. But she never had to use it.

A shot rang out. A perfectly aimed shot. The bullet went straight through Hayden Harper's hand, and the "Archangel" fell to the ground, screaming.

The man beside her dropped his velvet pillow and scrambled in his coat for a weapon, but Amy jumped him and sent him crashing down to the ground.

And that was it. As others rose, screaming, confused, yet ready to fight, the clearing was suddenly filled with men and women, agents and officers. Ryan was at her side, reaching down to cuff the Archangel's assistant.

It was none other than Malcolm Barrington.

Then Hunter was there at her side. He wrenched Hayden Harper to her feet as she screamed and looked at the bloody pulp that had been her hand. He pushed her toward another agent.

Mickey. Mickey was there himself, smiling and nodding at her. But as he arrived, another shot rang out, coming from deep within the cypress.

Hayden Harper went down, shot through the back.

"Sniper! Down, everyone!" Hunter shouted.

Law enforcement and the horseman's followers dropped to the ground, but no further gunfire followed. Agents were soon tearing into the cypress, searching for the shooter.

Then confusion reigned again as people were arrested, taken away bit by bit. They were run across the water by canoes and airboats to walk the distance to cars that waited by the highway. Ryan Anders returned to the area of the sacrificial "altar." He appeared perplexed.

"I had him," he said to Mickey, Hunter, and Amy. "I had the shooter, the sniper. I yelled who I was and told him to drop his gun, and he…he didn't kill me. He put his gun in his mouth and…his head exploded. I can't begin to understand how…"

"The human mind is the most frightening weapon in the world," Hunter said quietly.

"And that puts us at a dead end," Mickey murmured. "Well, no, we have several dozen people to question—including Barrington, who must have been close to what was really going on. We can follow up on the place where Hayden had been staying. We can follow more leads, but…well, for today, the reign of the third horseman—woman—is at an end." He looked at Hunter and Amy. "Take five. After this, well, somewhere, sometime, we know one thing for sure. The fourth horseman of the Apocalypse will appear. Until then…take some time. Shake it off. I know how deeply you two are into this, but find a way to—"

"Live," Amy said, smiling.

"Exactly," Mickey said.

"Don't worry. We will," Hunter assured him.

Amy nodded. She had done her part. There were still hours to go during which they sorted through the people arrested and those killed. Forensic teams arrived, along with Dr. Richard Carver. She watched as others made the arrests and Dr. Carver began his initial investigations on the dead.

Finally, the day began to draw to an end. Barrington, his cape and cowl having fallen off as he was being led away, started screaming. "You! You people, you horrible people—"

Then he was gone, and she looked first at Hunter and then at the place where Dr. Carver knelt by Hayden's body.

"We were so close! She knew, she knew who was orchestrating everything—"

"Maybe she didn't," Hunter said. He smoothed her hair back.

"That's why she was killed—"

"Or she was killed because she failed," he said softly. He looked around. "Maybe, as Mickey pointed out, we'll learn something from someone. There were a lot of arrests made. But we're going to let others sort it out. I don't like the way it ended, but the reign of this stygian horsewoman is over. And you were brilliant, and you're alive and..." He smiled. "We're both alive, ready to fight again. We have a great team behind us. But now..."

Aidan was standing near them. "I'm going to suggest showers," he said.

Amy managed to laugh.

"We have done well, damned well," Aidan said. "But it's also that very special time between chaos. And guess what?

Hunter has a great surprise for you. I happen to know be-cause I'm in on it."

She didn't get to learn about the surprise that night.

They did shower. For a good thirty minutes.

Some serious scrubbing.

Some serious playing.

And then some more amazing time together. Because days like today, when so many innocents might live because they had stopped a charismatic murderer, were good.

And they knew to value them.

EPILOGUE

The world could be an ugly place.

And it could be almost excruciatingly beautiful.

As in now.

Amy lay by the pool on the lounge that stretched just outside the rear doors of her ground-floor room. The cascade of waterfalls could be heard, as well as the laughter of children.

She reached next to her on the white lounge for a piece of fruit from a side dish. For her main course, she had fallen in love with the tuna bowl.

There was sun, there was shade, a light breeze, and yet it was one of those days with the perfect amount of warmth to enjoy the sun and especially the water.

"How you doing there?" Hunter asked, stretched out on the second lounge in their private area, up on an elbow as he grinned at her.

"I can't believe we're here!"

"I wish I could say it was thanks to me. But Aidan is a re-markable guy. If his cousin didn't work for the casino, we'd never be here, you know. I mean, we could have sprung for a room, and I do love the lights and the fountains and the music. I love hearing rock play with our heads under the water while we're swimming. But it is thanks to Aidan and his cousin that we are exactly where we are."

"Aidan is the best."

"He's meeting us for dinner later."

"I am so glad. And still…"

She closed her eyes. It was so beautiful.

So incredible to get to relax. Swim, play, watch the light display by night and the fountain shows and even tease Hunter into trying out a few slots.

Of course, Mickey had still called to report to them. So far, they had questioned everyone they had brought in—and learned little. Except that the Apocalypse was coming, and they were idiots, they didn't understand what was happening. Occasionally, they found someone ready to change—someone who "saw the light" more or less. But no one seemed to know anything beyond the fact that Hayden hadn't just taken on the role of the Archangel, she had been the third horse-man, and she had been there to weigh the good from the bad, to sort them out, to take care that many were given a chance to redeem themselves before judgment.

In short, those in most need had been murdered.

How Barrington had run a company, Amy would never un-derstand. According to Mickey, he was the most brainwashed in the group. He had come to "salvation" through Hayden.

"Race you to the foot of the pool!" Hunter said.

"Hey, wait! We have to get around to the head of the pool!" Amy said.

Hunter was already in the water. She followed. He was a

strong swimmer, but so was she. And she had grown up in Florida, where she had truly honed her skill.

But chasing after him, she remembered what he'd said about the music beneath the water and she gave up the race to dive down and listen to Bon Jovi and "It's My Life."

Laughing, she met him on the surface, assuring him she had only let him win because she was preoccupied.

They spent a little more time in the water, a little more on the lounges, and then time just being together.

They were getting dressed to meet Aidan at the Hard Rock Cafe for dinner when Amy's phone rang.

It was Mickey.

"Hunter with you?" Mickey asked. "Put me on speakerphone."

"I'm here," Hunter said.

"So…"

"Anything new?" Amy asked anxiously. "Did Barrington know more? Or what about Banyan Bend, the community where Hayden had been staying?"

"No, we found the house she'd been renting and pulled it apart. Nothing. Oh, except for her several different passports and driver's licenses under different names. No, this is… Well, hell, no way out of saying it flatly. I don't know what is about to begin, but it's about to begin."

"Mickey, what, please!" Amy said.

"A box came to the main office addressed to the FDLE and then to you, specifically. I ordered that it be opened. And it contained one of those horses, Amy. One of those little plastic kid's horses. Stay where you are for now, please. I didn't want to call you—there's nothing to do."

"Mickey—"

"Right. I'm afraid the pale horse and his rider are on the way."

★ ★ ★ ★ ★

New York Times *bestselling author Heather Graham brings the Krewe of Hunters to Europe in the first book of her thrilling Blackbird Trilogy!*

Read on for a sneak peek of Whispers at Dusk

PROLOGUE

For Della Hamilton, it began with the old cemetery.

And Jose Garcia, her friend all through grade school, middle school and high school.

They lived on the same block. It was never romantic, just a true friendship that had been strengthened by years of shared local experiences and talks about everything: family, heartthrobs, and more. They shared everything that went into growing up.

And Jose was just a good guy. She didn't know anyone who didn't like Jose.

What killed him was a bizarre accident. Truly bizarre and tragic for all concerned. Another kid in high school would have the guilt of Jose's death on him for all the years of his life to come.

Della found out about it when she was at cheerleading practice during her senior year of high school. The blood bank called.

She gave blood with her parents' blessing several times a year. Gave. They weren't rich, but she wasn't selling her blood. Her health and the coagulating wonder of her blood was a gift from a higher power, however one chose to see God. It was an amazing thing to give the gift of her blood to others. So she did.

Della was joking with the girls when the call came, and they were all laughing and calling her a vampire. She reminded them vampires drank blood; they didn't give it to others.

It wasn't until she arrived at the hospital and saw her parents and Jose's parents that she heard what had happened. She wished she could open a vein and pour her blood straight into her friend's heart.

It had been...ridiculous. A couple of the high schools in the area had friendly rivalries going. *Usually* friendly. Occasionally something might get a little physical, but it was broken up most of the time by an authority figure, or it simply petered out with the rivals laughing.

But this time...

Jose and some friends had been at a popular South Miami restaurant. "Rivals" had been at another table. They'd been playing around, throwing napkins, then someone had picked up something heavier, a mug. It had struck Jose in the head and cracked open his skull and...

Now, they were praying for his life. If not for the mug, the day probably would have ended with laughter and with the groups picking up all the napkins together. The rivalries weren't between the junkies and the thieves and the crew of kids headed for criminal behavior. These teens were on the sports teams, the debate team, into music, movies, and theater.

But the mug had flown.

They took Della's blood.

But neither her blood nor blood from any other donor nor any help from the medical community could save Jose.

He died that night.

Her parents had taken her home. Jose's mom and dad had stayed with him to the last minute.

She heard later his mother wouldn't let the funeral home take his body.

And at the funeral, the poor woman had tried to drag him from his coffin. If she could not do so, she wanted to be buried in it with him. Her husband kept her from doing either one.

Della wished there was something she could do to help. But there wasn't. The woman had lost her only son.

It was about ten days later, and Della had just left the pool where she worked part time as a lifeguard after school until dusk. She was heading toward the cemetery where Jose was buried. She knew the area well. Her friend's father was the caretaker, and their home was on the cemetery property. They'd often had sleepovers and spent the nights trying to scare each other and outdo each other with ghost stories. The cemetery had never scared Della. She had felt *something* strange; oddly, it had been a sense of warmth and comfort. It was considered historic for their area, being over a hundred years old. There were only a few little family mausoleums in the cemetery, but there were stunning memorial statues, standing stones, and flat memorials surrounded by beautiful and lush trees. She loved the cemetery. But then, she loved old churches and cemeteries—truly old ones Winchester Cathedral in London, Westminster Abbey, Notre Dame, and so many in Rome and London. They'd visited so many. Her dad had said leaving donations was much cheaper than many things they might do on a European vacation.

Della had her radio playing as she drove home from work. Yet that day as she reached the southern end of the cemetery, she suddenly had nothing but dead air.

In the silence, she frowned and changed the station, but nothing happened.

She pulled off the road by the little coral wall that surrounded the place and looked in the cemetery. Jose wasn't buried far from the wall. She found herself tempted to jump over the two and a half feet of coral that comprised the barrier. But she didn't. She should bring flowers to Jose's grave, and do it by daylight when people were supposed to visit. Della had discovered the music stopped playing on her radio every time she passed by the little coral wall, a reminder that led to her stopping sometimes at night. The city lights from the street afforded her all the illumination she needed to reach Jose's grave.

Della decided to bring flowers that weekend. And it felt good to go and tell her friend she missed him, and to almost feel as if he were there with her.

She was back home for the summer after her first year of college when the killer they called the Canal Carnivore arrived in South Florida. The man had eluded police in the west, the northeast, and had struck in Biloxi, Mississippi, before heading farther to the southeast. Right before Della had returned home to take up her job as a lifeguard for the summer, he had attacked and killed a young woman in the Brickell area, a divorcee living alone in a condominium and working for a local bank. His signature was the removal of a patch of skin from his victims, usually a two-by-two square that contained the belly button. The one witness who discovered the victim near the old church cemetery in New York by Wall Street had seen a disappearing hooded figure chewing on something bloody as he'd hurried toward the Hudson River.

Thus, he'd been labeled the carnivore. He didn't bite the flesh out—that would leave marks for a dental impression. He didn't leave fingerprints or footprints anywhere. He didn't sexually assault his victims or torture them. He slit their throats and cut out his inches of flesh. He left no clues and had only been seen once calmly walking away from what would prove to be his victim. The "Canal" part of his moniker came from the fact that several victims had been found near water, though Biscayne Bay was hardly a canal and the Hudson River was, well, a river.

Naturally, Della's parents had been concerned. But she had assured them she went to work and came straight home. They were always there when she returned, along with her mother's giant sheepdog that looked like a mop but could be as fierce as any pit bull or rottweiler if he saw a member of the family threatened. They also lived in a friendly neighborhood and had automatic lights if she came home in the dark, along with a surprisingly modern alarm system. She was almost nineteen—an adult—and studying criminology! She knew how to be safe and smart. They had been studying serial killers just before the break. If anyone knew how to be careful, it was her.

She'd been home a week when her car suddenly started acting up. She kept a good eye on it. While it wasn't a new car, it wasn't old; the computer usually warned her if she needed maintenance or if anything was wrong.

It had given no warning. But the red light was suddenly blinking, screaming for maintenance.

She was about to drive by the cemetery. And the radio had already gone silent. The car was bucking strangely, and she quickly drove onto the grass at the side of the road only feet from the little coral wall.

No problem—other than she wouldn't have her car. She always had her phone and her AAA card.

She turned off the engine and reached to the passenger's seat for her bag. But digging inside, she couldn't find her phone. It had to be there. She had undressed and donned her swimsuit, left her bag in the women's locker room, worked her hours, gone back, and changed again. She hadn't taken her phone out. She had plans for the evening with friends and with her parents, and they were set. She hadn't needed her phone for anything, and she had just wanted to get home when her day had ended.

It had to be there.

But it wasn't.

She got out of the car. She was going to have to flag down someone driving along the street. She'd be careful. She wouldn't get in anyone's car. She'd just get someone to call for help for her.

Leaving the car's lights on, she walked over to the road. It wasn't rush hour anymore, but it wasn't that late, either. There were only a few cars. Most of them tended to be in the left lane, and one woman stared at her as if she were a crazy person.

She was about to give up when a car drove onto the grass near hers. It was oddly forming an L-shape that blocked part of the road, but she needed help, so she certainly wasn't going to comment on anyone's driving or parking.

But a shiver slid down her spine and a warning bell seemed to go off in her head as she approached the driver.

He got out of the car.

He was wearing a hoodie. Not black, dark blue, but a hoodie, and it was a warm night.

The L-shape he had created when he parked had cut Della off from the road. She never said a word. She knew.

It might have been a woman. But they'd been studying serial killers at school and, statistically, women serial killers preferred poison; they didn't seem to like the mess of knives or guns.

Small man...woman. Did it matter? Beneath the hoodie,

they were wearing a bandanna-type mask, allowing Della to see nothing of them but the eyes.

Dusk was quickly heading to darkness, but the streetlights fell on them and their cars. Looking at the person's eyes, Della knew they were smiling and loved watching the fear that filled her as she saw a streak of light catch on the blade of an enormous carving knife.

The cars would cut her off. There was no one on the road. If she ran across it, the only thing she could reach quickly would be an office complex without a single car in the parking lot.

She turned and headed for the little coral wall just a few steps from her. She leaped over it. This killer couldn't know the cemetery.

She did. She knew it so well.

If she ran hard toward the avenue that bordered the western side of the cemetery she'd get to the caretaker's house. Her friend's family had moved to the Keys a year ago. But she'd once met the new caretaker, his wife, and his child when she'd been at the cemetery. If she could just reach the house…

The killer was after her in a flash, but she weaved through headstones and around oaks, banyans, and cypress trees.

The killer remained behind.

Close behind.

She was near the backyard of the home by one of the oldest sections of the cemetery. Both Union and Confederate soldiers who had survived the Civil War to move down to South Florida were there, perhaps friends now that the fighting was over, and the cemetery had claimed them. There was a beautiful huge statue of an eagle there because one of the Union soldiers had been with the regiment that had had a mascot, Old Abe, the battle eagle. It would be a good place to slide around to get into the yard, hopping the little fence and screaming all the while for help...

But she was suddenly struck in the head. Dazed and stunned, and with her impetus, she went down on the ground.

Instinct caused her to roll. To look up into the eyes of a killer.

"That was spectacular!" the killer said. It was a "him," a small man, maybe five feet-eight inches and possibly a hundred and sixty pounds. "And you! I've been watching you the last days and the piece of skin on your midriff... Wow, kid, you're beautiful, you know."

She stared at him. She was on the ground. He was about to level his weight down on hers. She had to kick. She had to fight.

The knife... There was nothing now but moonlight, but the knife gleamed in that bit of misty light!

"Della, the rock!"

She was startled to hear the urgent whisper.

There was no one anywhere near them!

But the person who was not there kept talking. And she knew she'd been hit in the head. She was terrified. She might be going completely crazy with fear, but the person was using...

Jose's voice.

She stared at the killer and her eyes widened.

Because Jose *was* there. Something of him. She could see him, handsome in the casual suit in which he had been buried, coral shirt, gray jacket, and trousers. His dark hair was neatly combed, he looked wonderful, except...

He couldn't really be there.

"Listen to me, Della!" Jose said firmly. "He's coming down. Let him get close—despite the knife! Let him get close. Then kick him in the nuts as hard as you can and grab that rock and smash in his face. I'd do it for you, but... I can't pick anything up, I'm afraid. I'll try kicking…get it closer to you. But wait…wait…let him get down and then…"

She had to be imagining he was there, her dear friend, trying to help her, even from the grave.

She had never been so terrified in her life, watching the killer come down closer and closer to her, watching the knife gleam so strangely in the moonlight…

"Now!" Jose shouted.

She reached; she could feel the rock. Her fingers curled around it.

And she kicked. She had the leg strength of a strong swimmer, and she drew her knee up and kicked him with everything in her while slamming the rock against his head as hard as she could.

And the knife fell, dangerously close to her face, as the killer screamed in agony and clasped his bloody face and fell to her side in a fetal position.

She was up in a flash, screaming desperately for help and racing toward the caretaker's house where a door was opened for her, where the police were immediately called and then…

It seemed all hell broke loose.

They caught him that night. He still couldn't stand straight when the police arrived. He tried to say he'd just been walking down the street, and Della had attacked him. The police didn't buy it. And in the days to come, forensic science would tie him to other murders. He'd thought he'd cleaned his knife. He hadn't. Special techniques showed the knife had been used on the poor woman in the Biloxi area, and once that happened, he'd been proud to be known as the Canal Carnivore. He assured them all he was going to be immortal, one of the greatest killers ever.

An FBI agent who had been following the killer's trail of blood assured him all he had done was take some beautiful people away from those who had loved them. He wasn't famous at all. He was just Henry Worth of Los Angeles, California, and he'd be doing—at the least—life with no chance of parole.

The agent had questioned Della. A man of about forty, he was even and controlled. When they talked, Della realized just how close he'd been. He told her if it hadn't been for her, Worth might have killed again and again.

"You showed remarkable coolness in such a situation, young lady. Think about joining the Bureau. I hear you're studying criminology."

"I was thinking forensics," Della told him. "But... Well, I have three more years to go."

The agent had been kind. Her parents, of course, had been hysterical. To calm them she had reminded them she'd taken down the killer.

But in truth, Jose had done that. And when the dust had settled on it all, she returned to the cemetery just as the sun was setting in the western sky. She stood by his grave and said, "Jose! You saved my life, my friend. Please... You're here, right?"

She felt him touch her shoulders, as he had in life sometimes supporting her. She smiled and turned and he was there.

"I wasn't so sure," he told her. "I thought you might have it. Like an extra sight, the ability to see with your mind—or your heart or soul—whatever it might be. Benjamin Turner, the Yankee buried up by the house, told me about it. Some of the living have it. When I thought about the way I had seen you here at various times, I suspected you might." He grinned. "Oh, and Lieutenant Parker—he was with Lee's regiment during the Civil War, opposite side—assured me what Ben was saying was the absolute truth." He shrugged. "I enjoy the two of them. Parker is great—a man who can admit he was wrong, that a whole society was wrong... Anyway. I'm just so grateful you could see me, hear me!"

"And I'm just so grateful you saved my life," she whispered.

He smiled. "You...your folks. Always giving to others. But... I heard that FBI guy. You have what it takes, Della. I think you should consider joining the Bureau. This special thing. Whatever it is. Della, it means you have an edge. And maybe you should use that edge."

"Maybe," she whispered. "Maybe. As long as I get to keep seeing you."

Jose grinned. "We can do that! And I'll introduce you to Ben and Josiah Parker. They're great! And then... Well, talk to them, too. Then use what you've got, my dearest friend. Use what you've got!"

1

Mason Carter knew he had backup. The man now holding seventeen-year-old Melissa Wells hostage had been busy for months, and law enforcement across the country had been on his tail. Spread about in various positions outside, an FBI SWAT crew was situated along with local police who knew the area well.

Still, they were in bayou country surrounded by snake-and-alligator-infested waters and a range of high grasses, trees, and brush that might hinder any assistance.

Though he'd left a trail of carnage across the country by taking nine victims along the way, the killer's identity was unknown. He'd left behind fingerprints, but they couldn't be found in any database, and nothing else discovered by any agency across the country had given them a single clue toward discovering his identity. The truth existed somewhere; it just hadn't been found as yet.

He'd been labeled the Midnight Slasher since most of his abductions and kills had been after midnight. His note—handwritten and mailed from Las Vegas to the NYC FBI offices—had assured them he was fond of his moniker, and he'd try to make sure his murders did, indeed, occur after midnight in the future. He'd really have preferred being the Vampire, but that name had already gone to a coworker who was busy in Europe.

Coworker?

Mason knew about murders that were being called "the vampire killings" in Europe. He doubted this man and the European madman knew each other, though it appeared they were trying to outdo one another.

But then again, he didn't really know.

Maybe this killer needed the moniker because he was such an ordinary-looking man. Not exactly handsome—*cute* might be a term applied to him. He didn't appear at all insane or *creepy* as some seemed to think he must appear, not at all as people might think a maniacal killer should look.

He was about twenty-seven—the profilers had been right on his age—six feet even, perhaps a hundred and seventy pounds, with shaggy dirty blond hair, a clean-shaven face and friendly brown eyes. He smiled a lot. Mason could see how he'd managed easily enough to charm or coerce his victims out with him to a place where they might be alone.

And here they were. Mason had trailed the killer from Virginia and had suspected from the few clues he'd been told by the locals that the man would steal a boat and bring his victim far into the bayou. He'd been at the forefront of the investigation, and he called in as he made his way, seeking help from any and all law enforcement agency so they might really end the reign of the Midnight Slasher with a true force against him.

But Mason was the one who now stood alone, facing the man who held the teenaged girl, his blood-stained knife held so tightly to her throat that a trickle of blood ran down to her collarbone. Her terror-filled eyes were on Mason. She didn't want to die.

Mason didn't want her to die, either.

He was a good shot—but he'd still have to be at his fastest to hit the man before the knife could slide into the soft flesh of her throat and on to arteries and veins and…

"Okay, Midnight Slasher," he said, his Glock trained hard on the man, "do you really want to die today?"

"I've been here before, and I'm still alive!" the killer said. The girl let out a terrified whimper; the killer had jerked with his words. Another trail of blood slid down to her collarbone.

"I don't know. You're in bayou country now. With people who know it well," Mason said, shrugging.

It was truly doubtful the man would survive the day if he didn't surrender, but Mason was telling the truth. And it was true, too, that before Mason had been called in on the case, the killer had escaped a similar situation in the Shenandoah mountains.

He had killed his hostage and tossed her to his would-be captors before escaping.

Backup wasn't going to help.

Not here. Not now. While agents and officers might be all around, Mason was alone in the cabin with the man. His backup crew was holding. They all knew if the killer heard anyone trying to enter from the rear or break down any of the old wooden walls, the girl would die.

"You can do it, and there is no choice," a voice whispered to Mason.

He was alone in the cabin with the killer—and with the ghost of one Gideon Grimsby, an Englishman who had come to the new world to meet, befriend, and then serve under the legendary Jean Laffite. He had fought at the Battle of New Orleans. Gideon had survived the battle, fallen in love and changed his ways—only to be shot down in the street by a vengeful man who had once coveted the beauty who had become Gideon's wife.

Now, Gideon enjoyed the music of New Orleans, watched over his descendants and tended to haunt Frenchman Street. But having realized Mason was aware of him at a lounge one night, he'd discovered his afterlife of being a ghostly—and very helpful—investigator as well.

"Do it. Do it, Mason lad, you must!" Gideon said. "He's going to kill her. The officers and agents outside will lose patience. They'll seek entry as you know they must. And this rotten beast will die, but so will she. Dammit, man, take your shot!"

"I have to be sure!" Mason said the words aloud and cursed himself. He was accustomed to seeing the dead. And he'd learned before he was ten *not* to be seen talking to them.

But maybe this time it was good.

"Who the hell are you talking to?" the killer demanded.

Mason made a split-second decision and shrugged, saying, "I guess you can't see him. Gideon is here. You'd have liked him. He was a pirate. Well, he was, but then cleaned up his act. And sadly wound up being murdered, but he's enjoying his afterlife."

"Man, they think *I'm* crazy. You're crazy!" the killer said.

There was suddenly a gentle tap at the door to the cabin, surprising both Mason and the killer. Mason knew he frowned as the killer frowned. No one was bursting in; it was a gentle and polite tap.

The killer's young hostage let out a terrified squeak as the knife drew closer against her flesh.

"What the hell?" the killer murmured. "You—you go and see what those idiots outside want. Because I'm telling you, you can kill me today, but she will die with me." He laughed. "Maybe the two of us can haunt you, too."

"God help me," Mason murmured. "Fine. You want me to check the door?"

"Yeah. I want to see who is trying what."

His gun still trained on the killer, Mason backed to the door.

"We don't need any disruptions here," he said loudly.

"I'm not a disruption," a female voice said. "I'm unarmed. I just wanted to offer to trade myself for Melissa Wells."

"What?" Mason demanded.

"Open the door, check her out. See if she's really unarmed," the killer said. "And don't forget—if I'm going, she's going with me!"

Mason cracked the door open. There was a woman standing there, mid to late twenties, about five foot eight with long light brown hair and a striking thin face. She was wearing black knit leggings and a tunic and lifted her arms to show that she carried nothing.

"I'm really a better choice," she said, looking around Mason to see and talk to the killer. "Think of it! If you don't manage to escape and get out of this or if you do, you'll have killed a special agent or used her for your escape. I'm Della Hamilton, FBI. And I know you like your victims to have long hair. My hair is long and *I'm* the right age... Come on. This kid is a teenager. So far, you've at least chosen victims who were out of high school!" She paused, shaking her head. "You have a reputation. You're a famous killer—don't sully all that by having people think you were a pedophile."

Apparently, she'd said just the right thing.

"I am not a pedophile!" the Midnight Slasher protested. "That's disgusting. I haven't gotten it down right yet, but I'm working on it, and I will be a master! I will learn to... Well, never mind! I will achieve what is necessary!"

"Whatever," Mason said dryly. "And she has one hell of a point, I mean, you want to be a master killer, get it all right... perfect it all. But you don't want to be remembered as a pedophile. That would...well, ruin your whole legacy."

"Yeah, yeah... I never touched any of them. Except to kill them. And I was going to get it all right this time, but you found a stupid boat and followed me and... Ah, screw it! But you're right. The pretty girl at the door can get me out of here, or... Well, I will be known for having killed a special agent! Yeah! Get in here, Special Agent Whoever. You come straight to me. When I can switch the knife over, this kid can go. But you need to know—if I die today, you die, too."

"I'm willing to accept that," Special Agent Della Hamilton said.

The killer laughed. "Suicidal, eh?"

"No, I just think I can talk you down," she said. "And frankly, you fascinate me! Your mind is so amazing! And I'm older, okay, and maybe this is only in my own mind, but I think I'm...well, sexier, grown-up, and just a better choice for a victim all the way around. If you want to be famous— kill an agent!"

"Talk me down? I don't think so. But I fascinate you? And you really are pretty damned gorgeous, so...hmm. Okay, lady, come on."

"I am coming—when this guy lets me!" she said, smiling and shrugging to Mason.

"Let her by!"

"She wants you to take the shot during the exchange!"

the ghost of Gideon Grimsby said. The ghost's presence was near him. He all but whispered in Mason's ear, almost startling him.

But Mason was staring at Della Hamilton, and she nodded at the words. As if she had heard them.

Had she?

He'd heard there were others like him. He'd even heard there was a special "ghostbusters" unit in the Bureau with some nothing title like Special Circumstances Unit.

He inclined his head; she blinked, letting him know she had the message.

"I'm coming over...slowly, slowly, and I'll back up so you can free Melissa and get the knife right on me..."

She walked to him just as she had said she would do.

The killer moved the knife to push Melissa forward and reach out for Della Hamilton. And as he did, Della Hamilton dropped down, shouting, "Now!"

And Mason fired.

Melissa leaned to the side; Della was hunkered close to the floor.

The bullet hit the killer dead center in the forehead. While Melissa shrieked and cried with relief, the Midnight Slasher fell without a whimper.

The killer was dead. The reign of the Midnight Slasher had come to an end.

The wrap-up and the paperwork had just begun.

Naturally, there was chaos at first as other agents and police rushed in. The medical examiner and forensics arrived, and officers held the press at bay. Melissa's parents were called, but before she raced down to meet them, she fell hysterically into the arms of Della Hamilton and then Mason, telling them,

"Oh, my God, thank you, thank you! Thank you, both. You saved my life!"

Mason assured her he was grateful she was alive, as did Della Hamilton.

Gideon Grimsby stood by the whole time, arms crossed over his chest, a proud look on his face. Well, the ghost did like helping.

Mason saw Della Hamilton manage a wave and a nod and mouthed the words, "Thank you," To Gideon at one point. Gideon smiled and nodded in return.

Mason turned in his firearm as necessary and was surprised to hear that a counselor was waiting to see him in the city. His Glock would be returned in the morning.

Things never happened that fast. He knew something was going on.

Mason was hailed by the waiting officers and agents, and he knew everyone was relieved a serial killer's spree had come to an end. He wished he could feel celebratory, and he knew he had carried out the only feasible action. But he didn't feel celebratory, just weary.

Of course, it had been just minutes before midnight when they'd taken down the slasher. With all the aftermath, it was the next day before anyone left the bayou country. And because of where they were, the press had finally arrived, but thankfully, by then the action was over and officers arranged to maintain the crime scene. People had a right to know what was going on but keeping details of such an event within ranks might prove to be extremely important.

He was ordered back to the city and the office before Della Hamilton finished a discussion with a member of the forensic team.

He didn't see her again until they were finishing the last

of the paperwork on the case and by then everyone involved was about to keel over.

Sleep was in order. When he was finally able to return to his hotel, he had no trouble crashing down into a sound sleep—despite the fact the dawn had arrived long ago and the sun was shining brightly beyond the heavy drapes that covered his windows.

He woke in the middle of the afternoon. An evening left in NOLA, time to finish up any necessary business, and then a flight back to the DC area in the morning.

Luckily, they'd been so far back in the bayou country the media hadn't seen any of the takedown. And when asked, he assured the local powers that be he didn't want his name seen anywhere, which was the right policy as known field agents could be at risk.

A press release saying the Bureau had rescued the Slasher's latest victim and the man had been killed in the operation was just fine with Mason. He wondered if Della Hamilton was going to want more recognition.

She didn't.

Mason was out on Royal Street trying to decide on a restaurant for dinner when he looked into a shopfront and saw a TV screen showing the news.

The takedown had been perceived just as he'd hoped—a joint effort by the FBI and local authorities.

A lot of his friends at the local FBI offices and police precincts he'd come to know in NOLA had wanted to get together that night. And while he truly enjoyed a lot of the camaraderie and understood the feelings of many that a celebration was in order, he just wanted to be on his own that night.

He felt as if he needed to shake something off.

He decided then to go over to Magazine Street for dinner

and hopefully some soothing music at one of its many restaurants. He was surprised when Gideon slid into a seat beside him there; he'd been nursing a scotch and listening to some great jazz, something that helped still his mind.

"You are a strange bird," Gideon told him.

"Why?"

"That fellow stole the greatest gift from so many—the gift of life. Mason, you stopped him."

"With your help, for which I'm grateful—"

"And the help of Della Hamilton. I hung around her awhile earlier. She's something, huh? As they say in your time, that girl has balls! Wait, she can't, can she. Guts? Would that be right? She has guts!"

"She saw you in a flash," Mason said. "And by the way, I am glad I brought a killer down. I'm just tired of... I took his life. I guess I hate killing."

"But you love *saving.*"

Mason shrugged. "I will always act in the best interests of the victim. Let's listen to the music, huh?"

"Sure. There's a meeting tomorrow morning. Some bigwig with the Bureau is coming down tonight. He's coming specifically to see you—"

"Why? Wait a minute. Last I heard, I run by the NOLA office, pick up another agent to drop me and bring the car back for the next guy who needs it. How did you hear that? I'll be heading back to DC tomorrow."

"Maybe not," Gideon told him. "I heard Della talking to someone on the phone when she left the offices. She was going out, but that call changed things and she didn't. She decided she'd better get some sleep. You were busy tonight," Gideon told him, grinning. "You don't interrupt a counseling session, and then it was a long day! You were supposed to have some dinner, some downtime... You'll be informed.

Apparently, this is…big. A couple of people are heading down from Washington just to discuss this with you."

"And they informed another agent before me—about my assignment?" Mason asked.

"I'm guessing it involves her," Gideon said with a shrug. "And that would be a darned good thing. You couldn't do better, from what I saw."

"She was good, yes. But—"

Mason groaned. Strange. He'd wanted this job; he'd worked hard for this job. But after his years in the military, now he was wondering why. He was good at what he did. He was a good investigator—largely because of a lot of help from the dead. But he was also good at killing.

And it just seemed to be weighing down on him lately.

"Damn you, man!" Gideon said. His accent—which he had largely lost during the many years since his death—came back strong when he was angry. "There is a seventeen-year-old girl alive and in the arms of her family because of you."

"And Special Agent Hamilton, of course—or mainly," Mason said dryly.

Gideon nodded. "I was glad to see her. I hadn't met her, but friends saw her when she worked a case here not too long ago. The bank robbery out of Baton Rouge. They say she tricked the three—it was a woman and two men. That she got them into position by pretending to be a lost tourist, crying and desperate to find her way back to the airboat they'd been on. Anyway, she has a way that makes her excellent in this kind of case. But you! Stop it. When there is no choice, there is no choice. That teenager from today is going to need therapy for the rest of her life most probably, but she'll have a life. Do you know what that man—so called Midnight Slasher—did to some of his victims?"

"Yes, yes, I do."

"No, he wasn't a pedophile. He sliced them, Mason. Slashed and sliced them! Cut off their fingers and ears *while they were still alive.*"

"I do know," he said calmly.

Mason was glad he'd paid his tab. He stood. As he'd learned to do, he pretended he was on a phone call as he told Gideon, "I am so grateful she is alive—and our local intelligence knew where to find him before he could hurt her. Truly, I am. I just... I guess I wish I'd been a negotiator. I'd like to talk someone down for a change."

"You talk them down when you can—you save the victim when you can't," Gideon said.

Mason nodded. "Yes, I know. Guess I'm tired."

"You should be. Get some sleep."

"I'm going to."

"Finish listening to the jazz. See you in the morning," Gideon said, and then he was gone.

That was the problem sometimes befriending ghosts. Since they were excellent at slipping away through crowds and even walls, it was extremely difficult to have the last word with them.

The following morning, just as Gideon had said, Mason found himself in an office with the "bigwigs" down from Washington.

Two bigwigs.

The one was an elderly man. Mason had heard of him. His name was Adam Harrison, and he was known for both his philanthropy and the fact he'd been instrumental in forming special units of the Bureau.

He was with another man, this one in his forties, a striking fellow with Native American blood and a stature that indicated hours in the gym—and probably out in the field as well.

This man was Jackson Crow.

Mason knew who they were. Everyone in the Bureau knew about the special, separate unit that was called in for bizarre cases that included cult activity, so-called witchcraft and cases which involved "haunted" buildings, "werewolves," or any other strange manifestation. They had an amazing record for resolving cases, and while they were teasingly called "the ghostbusters," the Krewe of Hunters were also highly respected.

He had thought at times about seeking an interview with Adam Harrison or Jackson Crow. But he'd discovered he was good at working alone. He wasn't married and he didn't have children. That meant he could keep going at any time he wanted on his own—all day and into the night—when he was hot on a trail.

But now, he was intrigued.

He had been called in by them. He was sure that meant they'd been observing him from afar.

And they knew.

Just as he had known the truth about the Krewe.

That morning, the three of them were alone in the office. When the introductions were done, Jackson Crow began his speech.

"Due to recent developments, we're forming a new team, attached to our current unit. Loosely, we've been referring to our new operation as Blackbird—but officially, it will be the Euro Special Assistance Team. You'll be working with me as your immediate supervisor, and you'll still be stationed out of our Northern Virginia offices. But you'll be on the move a great deal—should you accept this, of course," Jackson Crow told him.

Mason shook his head. "Accept... I'm not sure what. I

mean... Well, truthfully, I know you run a *special* unit, and you must know that I—"

"Speak to the dead. Yes, of course. Gideon didn't fill you in?" Adam Harrison asked him.

Mason's brows shot up. Then he grimaced.

He'd assumed the people who were selected for this unit were found from across the country. Some were possibly found through the academy, and some because they stumbled into a case while working with other law enforcement or because they'd simply become involved.

Mason smiled, nodded, and leaned back. "I guess you've met Gideon."

"We started up in New Orleans," Jackson said. "We have many...friends here."

"Of course," Mason acknowledged dryly. "No, Gideon didn't tell me much. But Euro—"

"Yes, we're the Federal Bureau of Investigation, but the world has grown very small in the last several years. You are aware the Bureau has sixty legal attaché or legate offices around the world, as well as at least fifteen offices in our embassies in foreign countries?" Adam Harrison asked him.

He nodded. "Of course. I've been with the Bureau six years, ever since I got out of the service. Yes, I was aware. I admit—"

"We're federal, yes, and our focus is this country. But as Adam said, it's a small world these days, and when we have an American causing havoc abroad, conspiracies that involve Americans, felons we wish to apprehend abroad, hostage situations, and so on, we need a presence. Do we have great relationships with all countries? No. But with most of Europe and beyond, law enforcement likes to be reciprocal," Jackson said.

"Okay, so..."

"I was asked by someone as high up in the chain as you can

get to begin this project, to open support on strange cases that stretch outside of the country," Jackson told him. "Someone who doesn't want to admit we have help from strange places—yet still wants to make use of our rate in solving crimes and catching killers—wants us to get a team to Norway as quickly as possible. They've now found four bodies, stretching from France to England to Norway, completely drained of blood along with strange writing on the river embankments where the bodies have been displayed," Jackson said. "There might have been earlier victims here in the States. They are afraid the *vampire* isn't working alone, or perhaps something even more sinister is going on. You'd work with Interpol and local police over there—"

"I don't speak Norwegian."

"Neither do I. The amazing thing is most Europeans speak English or a minimum of two languages, something I wish we were better at here," Adam said.

"You said *a team*. So—"

"We'll be starting this with two agents and detectives from England, France, and Norway, as well as an Interpol liaison, a Frenchman named Bisset who seems able to get anything needed at the drop of a hat. And, you'll be working with support back here in anything tech or forensic. You'll be the first of a team with Special Agent Della Hamilton," Jackson told him, then nodded his head toward the door to the office.

It opened on cue.

And Della Hamilton walked into the room, wearing a pantsuit today, her long sweep of hair tied in a knot at the nape of her neck.

Very pro. When taking down the Midnight Slasher, she had made herself appear to be all casual and cute—and naive.

Today, the woman was all professional.

"Della, thanks. And Mason, you, too," Jackson Crow said.

"First, we'd like you both to accept this venture. As I've explained, I hope you'll still be working with me. We have Angela—my wife and one of our first Krewe members along with a few others—and an amazing team of techs and experts in our offices to help with anything at any time. We really have a great team to deal with any evidence no matter how small. They're brilliant with video and so much more. So, here we are. We want you willing to begin this new venture, ready to accept it, and move forward. If you're hesitant, that's all right. We want you, for many reasons—"

Mason was surprised to discover he was slightly amused.

"You've been stalking me?" he asked.

"Not stalking!" Adam Harrison protested. "Heaven forbid!" Grinning, he glanced at Jackson.

"Of course," Jackson continued, amused as well, "we've done our homework. If you don't choose to accept this assignment, we'd still appreciate you accepting a transfer to the Krewe."

"I'd thought about requesting an interview with you," Mason admitted.

"Why didn't you?" Jackson asked.

"I guess I got used to working alone."

"And yet, you can't imagine the amazing abilities and teamwork that exists among our people," Jackson said. "Okay, to be blunt—no recorders in here—we know you have the ability to speak with the dead. We are a small percentage of a small percentage of the world population," he added quietly. "You've never worked with anyone who was just like you."

"No, I haven't," Mason admitted.

He was silent for a minute. He turned to look at the woman who would be his partner for the enterprise, curious as to her reaction.

She was looking at Jackson, nodding. "I've been reading

about the killer they're calling the Vampire. He needs to be stopped—especially if he's gaining followers."

"We don't know that," Jackson told her. "Nor can we be certain he started this in the United States—"

"Our killer last night wasn't the Vampire killer on the move across the pond," Mason said. "He was slashing throats—not drinking blood."

"Right," Jackson said. "And he may not have known the Vampire, or wanted to emulate him."

"But...he did talk about *getting it right*," Della said.

"Most probably not associated, but...the man you brought down was William Temple of Slidell. We've investigated his background and the profilers had it just right on him. He was bullied through school. He asked a girlfriend to marry him and she turned him down and took off—he drank heavily at several of the bars along Bourbon Street. He worked for one of the bayou tour companies until he was fired for unwanted attention toward female tourists—and calling them filthy names when they spurned his advances. He was evicted from his apartment off Esplanade."

"A killer, but hardly a brilliant one." Della nodded. "And again, nothing compared to the man leaving bodies in pristine condition and beauty, just devoid of blood."

"The display of the victims has become important now. One of our Krewe members, also a medical examiner, believes the victims discovered in the Florida Everglades and the Blue Ridge in Virginia might have been this killer's beginnings for murder—practice victims, one might say. They were also exsanguinated. While the throats on the victims were slit, because of other markings, Kat believes he was perfecting his ability to pierce blood vessels perfectly—and draw blood from the neck, leaving marks that could appear to be those left by *vampire* fangs. Right now we just know he's on a cross-country killing spree in Europe, either on his own or with an accomplice. Interpol is on it—officers from three countries are now on it. But I've been asked from on high to help, so…"

"I'm in," Della said. "Of course, you knew I would be."

"Thank you, Della," Jackson said. He stared at Mason. "Special Agent Carter?"

"I… Wow. I—I admit to being intrigued. Why us?" he asked curiously.

"Well, the obvious, of course. Della had been assigned to my office already when this came up. And, yes, we have watched your work."

"Someone else knows your record for finding resolutions to cases. Remember, I told you voices on high in the government wanted this, and they were adamant you were the man for the job, Mason," Adam Harrison told him. "But you're hesitating."

Mason shrugged and grimaced. "No, not really. Maybe I'm afraid of failure. This is important to many people, naturally, and I am hoping I am capable to stop—"

"You may be afraid. We're not," Jackson told him. He leaned forward. "Should you choose to accept this assignment—not *mission*, assignment," he added dryly, "you'll be leaving this evening."

Mason lifted his hands. "I've been chasing the Midnight Slasher for months now. I guess I thought I'd be getting a few weeks of vacation."

"You get this *Vampire*," Jackson said, "And I'll see to it you get a month's vacation after, if you wish."

"I…" Mason lifted his hands again. "Honestly, it's not that I need or expect so much time off, I just…"

"You may refuse," Jackson assured him. "This isn't for everyone."

"But should you?"

He turned to see Della Hamilton had spoken quietly and was staring at him, again, as if she read something in him, as if she knew more than he did about himself.

"I..."

He didn't know what it was about the way she was looking at him. Challenging him? Or seeing something in him he really wasn't sure of himself.

He looked from her to Adam Harrison and then to Jackson Crow.

"So," he said with resolve, "we're leaving tonight. I take it we'll be briefed—"

"Every file from every country will be sent to your inboxes immediately. Along with connections here in the home office for any help you need, and bios on the members of European law enforcement you'll be involved with. We will be planning a larger team, of course, but this came up suddenly. And they need our help. Also, one of the officials in Norway has a suspicion the Vampire might well be an American."

"American?" Mason said, surprised. "I understand there were similar killings here that *might* have been this killer's start up. But now, the *display* of the killings has apparently stretched from country to county. Maybe he's gotten it all right where he wants it to be, but these killings have been in Europe—"

"I think, in the killer's mind, the killings have been perfected in Europe," Jackson said. "I believe the killer's *practices* were here in America. I have been involved in this for a long time, and I consider it an educated theory. You'll find everything you need will be sent to you, every piece of information or even supposition that we have. I've done all the reading on this and, trust me, there's plenty of reading material for a long flight."

Mason nodded.

"All right. So, tonight. When and how do we leave?"

"Private jet, Krewe jet," Adam told him. The older man shrugged. "I've been lucky in life. The plane is my gift to special agents who are...special."

"I'm packed and ready," Della said. She looked at Mason.

"I've been living out of a suitcase here in New Orleans. I'll get my things from the hotel."

"We'll meet up at Louis Armstrong International," Della said, rising. She nodded to Jackson and Adam. "I know we'll have cooperation, and I truly hope we'll do the Bureau proud."

"I know you will," Jackson said.

It took Mason less than fifteen minutes to collect his belongings from the hotel. The drive to the airport where he returned his rental car took another forty-five. He met up with Della Hamilton at the coffee bar in the terminal.

"You're here," she said.

"Of course, I'm here. I said I would be."

"But you don't seem pleased with the assignment."

"Oh, you're wrong," he said. "I'm just enthralled."

"You're just enthralled," Della murmured. "Strange choice of words."

"I was obviously being sarcastic," Mason told her dryly.

"I didn't miss your tone," she assured him. "It's just that we're headed for Norway. The word *enthralled* comes from *thrall*—which is what the Norse called the human beings they enslaved. People tend to think the Vikings were after gold and jewels—and they were, but they were also slave traders. They needed slaves to build their ships and sew their sails and work the land when it was workable, but they also found great wealth in the slave trade." She paused, shaking her head. "Humanity hasn't changed. Of course, it wasn't just the Vikings.

The Romans were big on enslaving conquered people, and so on throughout history. And still, though we try to stop it, there are still some places today that enslave others. Anyway, the conquerors could be cruel. Some of the sagas that were written in Iceland in the fourteenth century portray the invaders as great heroes—and the thralls as dull and stupid creatures who needed owners since they were fit for little more than slavery. They've found iron collars and chains in archaeological digs, proof of man's treatment of man, or in slavery, more of woman. But anyway, being *enthralled* means you're basically enslaved by someone or something."

"Woah!" Mason said. "Woah, so, I'm traveling with a walking encyclopedia! But, hmm, you are hard on those people. Are you sure *you* should be going to Norway?"

She shook her head impatiently. "I hardly blame anyone today for the Viking age. It ended a long, long time ago. We call the Dark Ages the Dark Ages because that's what they were—dark. Torture chambers abounded! Oh, and I love Norway and the Norwegian people. My maternal grandparents were born there."

"Ah, that's why they're sending you," he said. "You know the terrain?"

"Hopefully, they're sending me because I'm a competent agent, capable of rolling with whatever comes up. And yes, I know some of the terrain, of course. We traveled fairly frequently when I was a kid."

"Rich kid?"

She shook her head. "My parents just knew how to make travel with the family into both a fun and profitable event. My mother was an artist and my father was a great marketer—he found buyers for her work all over in ad campaigns and the like. So yes, I know and love Norway."

"And the Bureau?" he asked.

She shrugged. "I was majoring in criminology when an old friend suggested I use everything I have to get bad guys. I went into the academy straight from college."

"A dead friend?" he asked quietly.

"Yes, a dead friend. You?"

"College, the military, more college, the academy. Oh, and on the enthralled—maybe I said it just right. I get the feeling you're something like me."

"Oh, I doubt that! And why—"

"Because work became your life at some point. Basically, we're slaves to it."

Della shook her head. "Not true. Or I don't see it that way. I'm still dedicated. I believe in what we're doing, and the fact we can get help sometimes from those who are gone—that not everyone can—is amazing. Don't you believe in what we're doing?"

Mason hesitated. "Yes, of course. Okay, honestly? I just... I don't want to kill anymore. Maybe what I thought I needed was a breather. Not that I would have preferred to have been killed myself, I mean..." He paused. He barely knew Della Hamilton, and he wasn't really ready to pour his heart out to her. But...

"Seeing so much death," he continued, "I've gained a marked appreciation for life. I have never killed in any circumstance in which I wasn't being shot at myself or in a situation in which it was necessary to protect another—an innocent, someone stunned and terrified to suddenly find themselves the target of a killer, or in the middle of a crime, war, or violence. But I wish I was better at...negotiating! Getting people to surrender. I... No matter what, it still takes something out of you when you take a human life."

"Yes, I agree," she said, "and everyone hopes to bring a suspect in alive because our job is to uphold the law while judges and juries do the rest. I understand how you feel. I was told you were a good guy. You are. No one wants to kill, Mason. But sometimes, negotiation doesn't work, and we must care about the victim first. Negotiation is great, but when there is no choice... Well. And honestly, I guess you haven't had much chance to read about this *Vampire* yet, but... Mason, he's a truly terrifying figure. And if he has others joining his ranks... Mason, you do know there are groups of people across the world, I believe—I know of a few in the States— who call themselves vampires, right? Some just meet and drink one another's blood. Some say they are spiritual vampires, and claim it's in a good way—they can gain kindness from others and all that. But...if this guy really thinks he's a vampire, we may be looking at worse things to come. At one time, people believed in blood-sucking vampires—diseases that destroyed the blood caused that kind of theory. In the 1800s, even in the United States, people dug up their loved ones to stake them through the heart or burn their hearts, afraid they were coming back to drink their blood when in truth, the disease was just spreading. But—"

"I don't think this killer believes he's a vampire, though if he is seeking followers, he'll want to convince them he is a supernatural creature. I believe he'll be like the guy we just got—probably handsome or charming enough to lure victims. Somewhere in his twenties or thirties. Thirties, I think, old enough to have gotten clever enough to clean up a crime scene and have the finances to pull off what he's doing. He'll be making sure he gets a lot of press all over Europe. He wants the fame or the infamy."

"You spent time with profilers?"

"I did," he said. "And we all know a profile can be wrong— but most of the time, it turns out to be right on. Let's hope we have good help once we get there."

"We will. And we have tons and tons of time to study all the files on the plane. Mason, we can make this work. And I know you're a loner. This is the first time you've worked with a partner and a team in a long time. But I swear, I've got your back."

He nodded. "I've uh... I'm sorry if I'm...difficult. You're right. I've been on my own for a few years now. And—I swear—I've got your back, too."

She smiled. "Hey, I've gotten to see you do that already. And I'm so sorry. I heard. I heard your last partner was killed in the line of duty," she said.

He nodded, looking away, and not sure why he didn't want to look at her.

Yes, Stan Kier had been killed. Mason had been nearby when it happened, and seeing Stan, he had felt a burning fury. Perhaps there had been no choice, but the searing sensation of anger and hatred he'd felt when he brought down the killer had been horrible.

There were things an agent had to do. Times when he had to kill.

But the amount of hatred he'd felt then...

It had scared the hell out of him.

It was just something he didn't want to ever feel again. Though he had to admit, it didn't come close to the pain of seeing Stan die. Stan had been a great guy, a family man, a friend.

He started, feeling her hand on his knee. He looked her way. In truth, he knew nothing about her.

"Like I said. Not to worry. I've seen you in action," she said.

"Yeah, thanks. And I'm sorry. I'm not sure if I ever said anything to you after the events in the bayou. You were amazing. For what you did in that cabin. That was..."

"Unorthodox?" she asked, wincing.

"I was going to say it was very brave. Coming in unarmed."

"I had a little Beretta hidden in my waistband," she said. "I also read up on you and I knew you were a crack shot. The SWAT director there was getting edgy. And while you are such a good shot and you'd have been fine without me, I figured a little help couldn't hurt. It can be hard to get a guaranteed clean shot. I had talked to Melissa's parents and... We just couldn't let him take out another victim."

"Well, then, thanks. You threw me. I had heard things about the Krewe of Hunters, but I didn't know you were with them—"

"Newbie," she reminded him. "Not quite a year. The Krewe was formed over a decade ago. In New Orleans, as a matter of fact. There were originally just six, and now we have dozens of agents, and it's good—we're all always out, all over the country."

"So you were down in this area with the Krewe before?"

"Right before I joined the Krewe I was on assignment as a field agent down here. In fact, it was almost right after the case I was on here that I had my interview—and found out they were real. I promise you, it's like...sanity in the insane world we've chosen to work in."

"And I think I still doubted in my way—since we're taught by our parents and families not to let other people think we're crazy—that what I'd heard could be real, that the Bureau *really* had a unit in truth that was composed of..."

"Weird people like us?" she asked, grinning.

He nodded.

"As I told you, I'm still fairly new to the Krewe. Well, not that new, almost a year. I went to the academy, started in the field, and then my supervisor told me I had an interview with a special unit," she told him. "I believe sometimes, the head players at the Krewe know from our records or cases... Well, they have it themselves so they recognize it in others. They seek people from other law enforcement agencies as well. I believe Adam Harrison and Jackson Crow are pretty amazing at studying situations." She paused, smiling. "It's a wonderful place to be, with others like us, and they just have that talent for determining who the *weird* people are. And instead of hiding and feeling weird, we get to see that it is amazing, this ability we have, because it's like so many things with DNA, just a fraction of a fraction of the population has it, so..."

"Hmm."

"Hmm?" she asked.

He smiled. "I wonder if Norwegian ghosts will speak any English."

She smiled in return for a minute, and then she was dead serious. Her eyes were a true green he realized—like emerald lasers the way she was staring at him. "We're going to make this work," she told him.

"All right. We're going to make this work. Partner."

Her phone was ringing and she answered it quickly and told him, "Our plane is ready and the pilot is aboard. I understand the plane is great. So..."

"On to hours of reading in the air," he said.

"We are going to work well together," she vowed.

He forced himself to nod. He had been so uncertain; and then again, as Gideon had said, she had balls. And she was *unorthodox.*

He might even like her. He imagined she was an excellent agent, able to use her natural beauty and abilities in her investigations and takedowns.

Yeah, he liked her. But he was going to be careful.

He vowed he wasn't going to like her too much.

Because nothing changed the fact there were kill-or-be-killed situations.

It wasn't a good thing to become too involved with a partner—not in their line of business. He'd learned that the hard way. And he'd worked on his own—with plenty of backup, of course—for several years now. Working as a loner had its advantages.

He would have her back. And he'd try to be a team player. He just couldn't lose another partner.

Don't miss Whispers at Dusk
from New York Times *bestselling author Heather Graham,*
available June 2023 wherever MIRA books are sold!